A DANGEROUS
FORTUNE

KEN FOLLETT

A DANGEROUS FORTUNE

Delacorte ▰ Press

LARGE PRINT EDITION

Published by
Delacorte Press
Bantam Doubleday Dell Publishing Group, Inc.
1540 Broadway
New York, New York 10036

Library of Congress Cataloging in Publication Data

Follett, Ken
    A dangerous fortune / by Ken Follett.
        p.   cm.
    ISBN 0-385-31121-4
    ISBN 0-385-31188-5
    (large-print ed.)
    I. Title
    PR6056.045D36   1993
    823'.914—dc20   93-21912
                                                                  CIP

Manufactured in the United States of America
Published simultaneously in Canada
November 1993

10 9 8 7 6 5 4 3 2 1

**This Large Print Book carries the
Seal of Approval of N.A.V.H.**

A DANGEROUS FORTUNE

THE FAMILY TREE
OF THE
Pilasters

JOHN PILASTER (deceased)

EZEKIAL (deceased)   SETH

MADELEINE • GEORGE   "YOUNG"
HARTSHORN   WILLIAM • BEATRICE

JOSEPH • AUGUSTA   TOBIAS • LEANA   SAMUEL

EDWARD CLEMENTINE • HARRY   HUGH   DOTTY
TONKS

PROLOGUE

1866

PROLOGUE

1

ON THE DAY OF THE TRAGEDY, the boys of Windfield School had been confined to their rooms.

It was a hot Saturday in May, and they would normally have spent the afternoon on the south field, some playing cricket and others watching from the shady fringes of Bishop's Wood. But a crime had been committed. Six gold sovereigns had been stolen from the desk of Mr. Offerton, the Latin master, and the whole school was under suspicion. All the boys were to be kept in until the thief was caught.

Micky Miranda sat at a table scarred with the initials of generations of bored schoolboys. In his hand was a government publication called *Equipment of Infantry*. The engravings of swords, muskets and rifles usually fascinated him, but he was too hot to concentrate. On the other side of the table his roommate, Edward Pilaster, looked up from a Latin exercise book. He was copying out Micky's translation of a page from Plutarch, and now he pointed an inky finger and said: "I can't read this word."

Micky looked. "Decapitated," he said. "It's the same word in Latin, *decapitare.*" Micky found Latin easy, perhaps because many of the words were similar in Spanish, which was his native language.

Edward's pen scratched on. Micky got up restlessly and went to the open window. There was no breeze. He looked wistfully across the stable yard to the woods. There was a shady swimming hole in a disused quarry at the north end of Bishop's Wood. The water was cold and deep. . . .

"Let's go swimming," he said suddenly.

"We can't," Edward said.

"We could go out through the synagogue." The "synagogue" was the room next door, which was shared by three Jewish boys. Windfield School taught divinity with a light touch and was tolerant of religious differences, which was why it appealed to Jewish parents, to Edward's Methodist family, and to Micky's Catholic father. But despite the school's official attitude, Jewish boys came in for a certain amount of persecution. Micky went on: "We can go through their window and drop onto the washhouse roof, climb down the blind side of the stable and sneak into the woods."

Edward looked scared. "It's the Striper if you're caught."

The Striper was the ash cane wielded by the headmaster, Dr. Poleson. The punishment for breaking detention was twelve agonizing strokes. Micky had been flogged once by Dr. Poleson, for gambling, and he still shuddered when he thought of it. But the chance of getting caught was remote, and the idea of undressing and slipping naked into the pool was so immediate that he could almost feel the cold water on his sweaty skin.

He looked at his roommate. Edward was not well liked at school: he was too lazy to be a good student, too clumsy to do well in games and too selfish to make many friends. Micky was the only friend Edward had, and Edward hated Micky to spend time with other boys. "I'll see if Pilkington wants to go," Micky said, and he went to the door.

"No, don't do that," said Edward anxiously.

"I don't see why I shouldn't," said Micky. "You're too scared."

"I'm not scared," Edward said implausibly. "I've got to finish my Latin."

"Then finish it while I go swimming with Pilkington."

Edward looked stubborn for a moment, then caved in. "All right, I'll go," he said reluctantly.

Micky opened the door. There was a low rumble of noise from the rest of the house, but no masters to be seen in the corridor. He darted into the next room. Edward followed.

"Hello, Hebrews," Micky said.

Two of the boys were playing cards at the table. They glanced up at him then continued their game without speaking. The third, Fatty Greenbourne, was eating a cake. His mother sent him food all the time. "Hello, you two," he said amiably. "Want some cake?"

"By God, Greenbourne, you eat like a pig," Micky said.

Fatty shrugged and continued to tuck into his cake. He suffered a good deal of mockery, being fat as well as Jewish, but none of it seemed to touch him. His father was said to be the richest man in the world, and perhaps that made him impervious to name-calling, Micky thought.

Micky went to the window, opened it and looked around. The stable yard was deserted. Fatty said: "What are you fellows doing?"

"Going swimming," said Micky.

"You'll be flogged."

Edward said plaintively: "I know."

Micky sat on the windowsill, rolled over onto his stomach, wriggled backwards and then dropped the few inches onto the sloping roof of the washhouse. He thought he heard a slate crack, but the roof held his weight. He glanced up and saw Edward looking anxiously out. "Come on!" Micky said. He scrambled down the roof and used a convenient drainpipe to ease himself to the ground. A minute later Edward landed beside him.

Mickey peeked around the corner of the washhouse wall. There was no one in sight. Without further hesitation he darted across the stable yard and into the woods. He ran through the trees until he judged he was out of sight of the school buildings, then he stopped to rest. Edward came up beside him. "We did it!" Micky said. "Nobody spotted us."

"We'll probably be caught going back in," Edward said morosely.

Micky smiled at him. Edward was very English-looking, with straight fair hair and blue eyes and a nose like a broad-bladed knife. He was a big boy with wide shoulders, strong but uncoordinated. He had no sense of style, and wore his clothes awkwardly. He and Micky were the same age, sixteen, but in other ways they were very different: Micky had curly dark hair and dark eyes, and he was meticulous about his appearance, hating to be untidy or dirty. "Trust me, Pilaster," Micky said. "Don't I always take care of you?"

Edward grinned, mollified. "All right, let's go."

They followed a barely discernible path through the wood. It was a little cooler under the leaves of the beech and elm trees, and Micky began to feel better. "What will you do this summer?" he asked Edward.

"We usually go to Scotland in August."

"Do your people have a shooting-box there?" Micky had picked up the jargon of the English upper classes, and he knew that "shooting-box" was the correct term even if the house in question was a fifty-room castle.

"They rent a place," Edward replied. "But we don't shoot over it. My father's not a sportsman, you know."

Micky heard a defensive note in Edward's voice and pondered its significance. He knew that the English aristocracy liked to shoot birds in August and hunt foxes all winter. He also knew that aristocrats did not send their sons to this school. The fathers of Windfield boys were businessmen and engineers rather than earls and bishops, and such men did not have time to waste hunting and shooting. The Pilasters were bankers, and when Edward said "My father's not a sportsman" he was acknowledging that his family was not in the very highest rank of society.

It amused Micky that Englishmen respected the idle more than people who worked. In his own country, respect was given neither to aimless nobles nor to hardworking businessmen. Micky's people respected nothing but power. If a man had the power to control others—to feed or starve them, imprison or free them, kill them or let them live—what more did he need?

"What about you?" Edward said. "How will you spend the summer?"

Micky had wanted him to ask that. "Here," he said. "At school."

"You're not staying at school all through the vacation again?"

"I have to. I can't go home. It takes six weeks one way—I'd have to start back before I got there."

"By Jove, that's hard."

In fact Micky had no wish to go back. He loathed his home, and had done since his mother died. There were only men there now: his father, his older brother Paulo, some uncles and cousins, and four hundred cowboys. Papa was a hero to the men and a stranger to Micky: cold, unapproachable, impatient. But Micky's brother was the real problem. Paulo was stupid but strong. He hated Micky for being smarter, and he liked to humiliate his little brother. He never missed a chance to prove to everyone that Micky could not rope steers or break horses or shoot a snake through the head. His favorite trick was to scare Micky's horse so it would bolt, and Micky would have to shut his eyes tight and hang on, scared to death, while the horse charged madly across the pampas until it exhausted itself. No, Micky did not want to go home for the vacation. But he did not want to remain at school, either. What he really wanted was to be invited to spend the summer with the Pilaster family.

Edward did not immediately suggest this, however, and Micky let the subject drop. He felt sure it would come up again.

They clambered over a decaying picket fence and walked up a low hill. As they breasted the rise they came upon the swimming hole. The chiseled sides of the quarry were steep, but agile boys could find a way to scramble down. At the bottom was a deep pool of murky green water that contained toads, frogs and the occasional water snake.

To Micky's surprise, there were also three boys in it.

He narrowed his eyes against the sunlight glinting off the surface and peered at the naked figures. All three were in the lower fourth at Windfield.

The mop of carrot-colored hair belonged to Antonio Silva, who despite his coloring was a compatriot of Micky's. Tonio's father did not have as much land as Micky's, but the Silvas lived in the capital and had influential friends. Like Micky, Tonio could not go home in the vacations, but he was lucky enough to have friends at the Cordovan

Ministry in London, so he did not have to stay at the school all summer.

The second boy was Hugh Pilaster, a cousin of Edward's. There was no resemblance between the cousins: Hugh had black hair and small, neat features, and he usually wore an impish grin. Edward resented Hugh for being a good scholar and making Edward look like the dunce of the family.

The other was Peter Middleton, a rather timid boy who attached himself to the more confident Hugh. All three had white, hairless thirteen-year-old bodies with thin arms and legs.

Then Micky saw a fourth boy. He was swimming on his own at the far end of the pool. He was older than the other three and did not seem to be with them. Micky could not see his face well enough to identify him.

Edward was grinning evilly. He had seen an opportunity to make mischief. He put his finger to his lips in a hushing gesture then started down the side of the quarry. Micky followed.

They reached the ledge where the small boys had left their clothes. Tonio and Hugh were diving underwater, investigating something, while Peter swam quietly up and

down on his own. Peter was the first to spot
the newcomers. "Oh, no," he said.

"Well, well," said Edward. "You boys are
breaking bounds, aren't you?"

Hugh Pilaster noticed his cousin then,
and shouted back: "So are you!"

"You'd better go back, before you're
caught," Edward said. He picked up a pair
of trousers from the ground. "But don't get
your clothes wet, or everyone will know
where you've been." Then he threw the
trousers into the middle of the pool and
cackled with laughter.

"You cad!" Peter yelled as he made a
grab for the floating trousers.

Micky smiled, amused.

Edward picked up a boot and threw it in.

The small boys began to panic. Edward
picked up another pair of trousers and
threw them in. It was hilarious to see the
three victims yelling and diving for their
clothes, and Micky started to laugh.

As Edward continued to throw boots and
clothes into the water, Hugh Pilaster scrambled out of the pool. Micky expected him to
make his escape, but unexpectedly he ran
straight at Edward. Before Edward could
turn around, Hugh gave him a mighty shove.
Although Edward was much bigger, he was

caught off balance. He staggered on the ledge then toppled over and fell into the pool with a terrific splash.

It was done in a twinkling, and Hugh snatched up an armful of clothes and went up the quarry side like a monkey. Peter and Tonio shrieked with mocking laughter.

Micky chased Hugh a short way but he could not hope to catch the smaller, nimbler boy. Turning back, he looked to see whether Edward was all right. He need not have worried. Edward had surfaced. He got hold of Peter Middleton and started ducking the boy's head again and again, punishing him for that mocking laugh.

Tonio swam away and reached the edge of the pool, clutching a bundle of sodden clothing. He turned to look back. "Leave him alone, you big ape!" he yelled at Edward. Tonio had always been reckless and now Micky wondered what he would do next. Tonio went further along the side, then turned again with a stone in his hand. Micky yelled a warning to Edward, but it was too late. Tonio threw the stone with surprising accuracy and hit Edward on the head. A bright splash of blood appeared on his brow.

Edward gave a roar of pain and, leaving Peter, struck out across the pool after Tonio.

2

HUGH RACED NAKED THROUGH THE WOOD toward the school, clutching what remained of his clothes, trying to ignore the pain of his bare feet on the rough ground. Coming to a place where the path was crossed by another, he dodged to the left, ran on a little way, then dived into the bushes and hid.

He waited, trying to calm his hoarse breathing and listen. His cousin Edward and Edward's crony, Micky Miranda, were the worst beasts in the entire school: slackers, bad sports and bullies. The only thing to do was to keep out of their way. But he felt sure Edward would come after him. Edward had always hated Hugh.

Their fathers had quarreled, too. Hugh's father, Toby, had taken his capital out of the family business and started his own enterprise, trading in dyes for the textile industry. Even at thirteen Hugh knew that the worst crime in the Pilaster family was to take your capital out of the bank. Edward's father Joseph had never forgiven his brother Toby.

Hugh wondered what had happened to his friends. There had been four of them in the pool before Micky and Edward turned up: Tonio, Peter and Hugh had been splashing about on one side of the pool, and an older boy, Albert Cammel, had been swimming alone at the far end.

Tonio was normally brave to the point of recklessness, but he was terrified of Micky Miranda. They came from the same place, a South American country called Cordova, and Tonio said that Micky's family were powerful and cruel. Hugh did not really understand what that meant, but the effect was striking: Tonio might cheek the other fifthformers but he was always polite, even subservient, to Micky.

Peter would be scared out of his wits: he was frightened of his own shadow. Hugh hoped he had got away from the bullies.

Albert Cammel, nicknamed Hump, had not been with Hugh and his friends, and he had left his clothes in a different place, so he had probably escaped.

Hugh too had escaped, but he was not yet out of trouble. He had lost his underclothes, socks and boots. He would have to sneak into school in his soaking wet shirt and trousers and hope he would not be seen by a master or one of the senior boys. He groaned aloud at the thought. Why do things like this always happen to me? he asked himself miserably.

He had been in and out of trouble ever since he came to Windfield eighteen months before. He had no trouble studying: he worked hard and came top of his class in every test. But the petty rules irritated him beyond reason. Ordered to go to bed every night at a quarter to ten, he always had some compelling reason for staying up until a quarter past. He found forbidden places tantalizing, and was irresistibly drawn to explore the rectory garden, the headmaster's orchard, the coalhole and the beer cellar. He ran when he should have walked, read when he was supposed to go to sleep, and talked during prayers. And he always ended up like this, guilty and scared, wondering why he let himself in for so much grief.

The wood was silent for several minutes while he reflected gloomily on his destiny, wondering whether he would end up an outcast from society, or even a criminal, thrown in jail or transported to Australia in chains, or hanged.

At last he decided that Edward was not coming after him. He stood up and pulled on his wet trousers and shirt. Then he heard someone crying.

Cautiously, he peeped out—and saw Tonio's shock of carrot-colored hair. His friend was walking slowly along the path, naked, wet, carrying his clothes and sobbing. "What happened?" Hugh asked. "Where's Peter?"

Tonio suddenly became fierce. "I'll never tell, never!" he said. "They'll kill me."

"All right, don't tell me," Hugh said. As always, Tonio was terrified of Micky: whatever had happened, Tonio would keep quiet about it. "You'd better get dressed," Hugh said practically.

Tonio looked blankly at the bundle of sodden garments in his arms. He seemed too shocked to sort them out. Hugh took them from him. He had boots and trousers and one sock, but no shirt. Hugh helped him put on what he had, then they walked toward the school.

Tonio stopped crying, though he still looked badly shaken. Hugh hoped those bullies hadn't done something really nasty to Peter. But he had to think of saving his own skin now. "If we can get into the dormitory, we can put on fresh clothes and our spare boots," he said, planning ahead. "Then as soon as the detention is lifted we can walk into town and buy new clothes on credit at Baxted's."

Tonio nodded. "All right," he said dully.

As they wound their way through the trees, Hugh wondered again why Tonio was so disturbed. After all, bullying was nothing new at Windfield. What had happened at the pool after Hugh had escaped? But Tonio said nothing more about it all the way back.

The school was a collection of six buildings that had once been the hub of a large farm, and their dormitory was in the old dairy near the chapel. To get there they had to go over a wall and cross the fives court. They climbed the wall and peeped over. The courtyard was deserted, as Hugh had expected, but all the same he hesitated. The thought of the Striper whipping his behind made him cringe. But there was no alternative. He had to get back into school and put on dry clothes.

"All clear," he whispered. "Off we go!"

They jumped over the wall together and sprinted across the court to the cool shade of the stone-built chapel. So far, so good. Then they crept around the east end, staying close to the wall. Next there was a short dash across the drive and into their building. Hugh paused. There was no one in sight. "Now!" he said.

The two boys ran across the road. Then, as they reached the door, disaster struck. A familiar, authoritative voice rang out: "Pilaster Minor! Is that you?" And Hugh knew that the game was up.

His heart sank. He stopped and turned. Mr. Offerton had chosen that very moment to come out of the chapel, and now stood in the shadow of the porch, a tall, dyspeptic figure in a college gown and mortarboard hat. Hugh stifled a groan. Mr. Offerton, whose money had been stolen, was the least likely of all the masters to show mercy. It would be the Striper. The muscles of his bottom clenched involuntarily.

"Come here, Pilaster," Mr. Offerton said.

Hugh shuffled over to him, with Tonio following behind. Why do I take such risks? Hugh thought in despair.

"Headmaster's study, right away," said Mr. Offerton.

"Yes, sir," Hugh said miserably. It was getting worse and worse. When the head saw how he was dressed he would probably be sacked from the school. And how would he explain it to his mother?

"Off you go!" the master said impatiently.

The two boys turned away, but Mr. Offerton said: "Not you, Silva."

Hugh and Tonio exchanged a quick mystified look. Why should Hugh be punished and not Tonio? But they could not question orders, and Tonio escaped into the dormitory while Hugh made for the head's house.

He could feel the Striper already. He knew he would cry, and that was even worse than the pain, for at the age of thirteen he felt he was too old to cry.

The head's house was on the far side of the school compound, and Hugh walked very slowly, but he got there all too soon, and the maid opened the door a second after he rang.

He met Dr. Poleson in the hall. The headmaster was a bald man with a bulldog's face, but for some reason he did not look as thunderously angry as he should have. Instead of demanding to know why Hugh was out of his room *and* dripping wet, he simply opened the study door and said quietly: "In here, young Pilaster." No doubt he was saving his rage for the flogging. Hugh went in with his heart pounding.

He was astonished to see his mother sitting there.

Worse yet, she was weeping.

"I only went swimming!" Hugh blurted out.

The door closed behind him and he realized the head had not followed him in.

Then he began to understand that this had nothing to do with his breaking detention and going swimming, and losing his clothing, and being found half naked.

He had a dreadful feeling it was much worse than that.

"Mother, what is it?" he said. "Why have you come?"

"Oh, Hugh," she sobbed, "your father's dead."

3

SATURDAY WAS THE BEST DAY OF THE WEEK for Maisie Robinson. On Saturday Papa got paid. Tonight there would be meat for supper, and new bread.

She sat on the front doorstep with her brother, Danny, waiting for Papa to come home from work. Danny was thirteen, two years older than Maisie, and she thought he was wonderful, even though he was not always kind to her.

The house was one of a row of damp, airless dwellings in the dockland neighborhood of a small town on the northeast coast of England. It belonged to Mrs. MacNeil, a widow. She lived in the front room downstairs. The Robinsons lived in the back room and another family lived upstairs. When it was time for Papa to arrive home, Mrs. MacNeil would be out on the doorstep, waiting to collect the rent.

Maisie was hungry. Yesterday Maisie had begged some broken bones from the butcher and Papa had bought a turnip and made a stew, and that was the last meal she had had. But today was Saturday!

She tried not to think about supper, for it made the pain in her stomach worse. To take her mind off food she said to Danny: "Papa swore this morning."

"What did he say?"

"He said Mrs. MacNeil is a *paskudniak.*"

Danny giggled. The word meant shitbag. Both children spoke English fluently after a year in the new country, but they remembered their Yiddish.

Their name was not really Robinson, it was Rabinowicz. Mrs. MacNeil had hated them ever since she discovered they were Jews. She had never met a Jew before and when she rented them the room she thought they were French. There were no other Jews in this town. The Robinsons had never intended to come here: they had paid for passage to a place called Manchester, where there were lots of Jews, and the ship's cap-

tain had told them this was Manchester, but
he had cheated them. When they discovered
they were in the wrong place, Papa said they
would save up enough money to move to
Manchester; but then Mama had fallen ill.
She was still ill, and they were still here.

Papa worked on the waterfront, in a high
warehouse with the words "Tobias Pilaster
& Co" in big letters over the gate. Maisie
often wondered who Co was. Papa worked
as a clerk, keeping records of the barrels of
dyes that came in and out of the building.
He was a careful man, a taker of notes and a
maker of lists. Mama was the reverse. She
had always been the daring one. It was
Mama who wanted to come to England.
Mama loved to make parties, go on trips,
meet new people, dress up and play games.
That was why Papa loved her so much,
Maisie thought: because she was something
he could never be.

She was not spirited anymore. She lay all
day on the old mattress, drifting in and out
of sleep, her pale face shiny with sweat, her
breath hot and odorous. The doctor had
said she needed building up, with plenty of
fresh eggs and cream, and beef every day;
and then Papa had paid him with the money
for that night's dinner. But now Maisie felt

guilty every time she ate, knowing she was taking food that might save her mother's life.

Maisie and Danny had learned to steal. On market day they would go into the center of town and pilfer potatoes and apples from the stalls in the square. The traders were sharp-eyed but every now and again they would be distracted by something—an argument over change, a dogfight, a drunk —and the children would grab what they could. When their luck was in, they would meet a rich kid their own age; then they would set on him and rob him. Such children often had an orange or a bag of sweets in their pockets as well as a few pennies. Maisie was afraid of being caught because she knew Mama would be so ashamed, but she was hungry too.

She looked up and saw some men coming along the street in a knot. She wondered who they were. It was still a little too early for the dockworkers to be coming home. They were talking angrily, waving their arms and shaking their fists. As they came closer she recognized Mr. Ross, who lived upstairs and worked with Papa at Pilasters. Why was he not at work? Had they been sacked? He looked angry enough for that. He was red in the face and swearing, talking about stupid gits, lousy bleeders and lying bastards. When the group drew level with the house Mr. Ross left them abruptly and stomped inside, and Maisie and Danny had to dive out of the way to avoid his hobnailed boots.

When Maisie looked up again she saw Papa. A thin man with a black beard and soft brown eyes, he was following the others at a distance, walking with his head bowed; and he looked so dejected and hopeless that Maisie wanted to cry. "Papa, what's happened?" she said. "Why are you home early?"

"Come inside," he said, his voice so low that Maisie could only just hear.

The two children followed him into the back of the house. He knelt by the mattress and kissed Mama's lips. She woke up and smiled at him. He did not smile back. "The firm's bust," he said, speaking Yiddish. "Toby Pilaster went bankrupt."

Maisie was not sure what that meant but Papa's tone of voice made it sound like a disaster. She shot a look at Danny: he shrugged. He did not understand it either.

"But why?" Mama said.

"There's been a financial crash," Papa

said. "A big bank in London failed yesterday."

Mama frowned, struggling to concentrate. "But this isn't London," she said. "What's London to us?"

"The details I don't know."

"So you've got no work?"

"No work, and no pay."

"But today they've paid you."

Papa bowed his head. "No, they didn't pay us."

Maisie looked at Danny again. This they understood. No money meant no food for any of them. Danny looked scared. Maisie wanted to cry.

"They must pay you," Mama whispered. "You worked all week, they have to pay you."

"They've no money," Papa said. "That's what bankrupt means, it means you owe people money and can't pay them."

"But Mr. Pilaster is a good man, you always said."

"Toby Pilaster's dead. He hanged himself, last night, in his office in London. He had a son Danny's age."

"But how are we to feed our children?"

"I don't know," Papa said, and to Maisie's horror he began to cry. "I'm sorry, Sarah," he said as the tears rolled into his beard. "I've brought you to this awful place where there are no Jews and no one to help us. I can't pay the doctor, I can't buy medicines, I can't feed our children. I've failed you. I'm sorry, I'm sorry." He leaned forward and buried his wet face in Mama's breast. She stroked his hair with a shaky hand.

Maisie was appalled. Papa never cried. It seemed to mean the end of any hope. Perhaps they would all die now.

Danny stood up, looked at Maisie, and jerked his head toward the door. She got up and together they tiptoed out of the room. Maisie sat on the front step and began to cry. "What are we going to do?" she said.

"We'll have to run away," Danny said.

Danny's words gave her a cold feeling in her chest. "We can't," she said.

"We must. There's no food. If we stay we'll die."

Maisie didn't care if she died, but a different thought occurred to her: Mama would surely starve herself to feed the children. If they stayed, she would die. They had to leave to save her. "You're right," Maisie said to Danny. "If we go, perhaps Papa will be able to find enough food for Mama. We've got to go, for her sake." Hearing herself say the words, she was awestruck by what was happening to her family. It was worse even than the day they had left Viskis, with the village houses still burning behind them, and got on a cold train with all their belongings in two sailcloth bags; for then she had known that Papa would always look after her, no matter what else happened; and now she had to take care of herself.

"Where will we go?" she said in a whisper.

"I'm going to America."

"America! How?"

"There's a ship in the harbor that's bound for Boston on the morning tide—I'll shin up a rope tonight and hide on deck in one of the boats."

"You'll stow away," Maisie said, with fear and admiration in her voice.

"That's right."

Looking at her brother, she saw for the first time that there was the shadow of a moustache beginning to show on his upper lip. He was becoming a man, and one day he would have a full black beard like Papa's. "How long does it take to get to America?" she asked him.

He hesitated, then looked foolish and said: "I don't know."

She understood that she was not included in his plans, and she felt miserable and scared. "We're not going together, then," she said sadly.

He looked guilty, but he did not contradict her. "I'll tell you what you should do," he said. "Go to Newcastle. You can walk there in about four days. It's a huge city, bigger than Gdansk—no one will notice you there. Cut your hair, steal a pair of trousers and pretend to be a boy. Go to a big stables and help with the horses—you've always been good with horses. If they like you, you'll get tips, and after a while they might give you a proper job."

Maisie could not imagine being totally alone. "I'd rather go with you," she said.

"You can't. It's going to be hard enough anyway, to hide myself on the ship, and steal food and so on. I couldn't look after you too."

"You wouldn't have to look after me. I'd be quiet as a mouse."

"I'd feel worried about you."

"Won't you worry about leaving me all on my own?"

"We've got to take care of ourselves!" he said angrily.

She saw that his mind was made up. She

had never been able to talk him round when his mind was made up. With dread in her heart she said: "When should we go? In the morning?"

He shook his head. "Now. I'll need to get aboard the ship as soon as it's dark."

"Do you really mean it?"

"Yes." As if to prove it, he stood up.

She stood up too. "Should we take any-thing?"

"What?"

She shrugged. She had no spare clothes, no souvenirs, no possessions of any kind. There was no food or money to take. "I want to kiss Mama good-bye," she said.

"Don't," said Danny harshly. "If you do, you'll stay."

It was true. If she saw Mama now she would break down and tell everything. She swallowed hard. "All right," she said, fight-ing back the tears. "I'm ready."

They walked away side by side.

When they got to the end of the street she wanted to turn around and take a last look at the house; but she was afraid that if she did she would weaken; so she walked on, and never looked back.

4

FROM *The Times:*

*CHARACTER OF THE ENGLISH SCHOOLBOY.
—The Deputy-Coroner for Ashton,
Mr. H. S. Wasbrough, held an inquest
yesterday at the Station Hotel,
Windfield, on the body of Peter James
St John Middleton, aged 13, a schoolboy. The boy had been swimming in a
pool at a disused quarry near
Windfield School when two older boys
had seen him apparently in difficulties,
the court was told. One of the older
boys, Miguel Miranda, a native of Cordova, gave evidence that his companion, Edward Pilaster, aged 16, stripped
off his outer clothing and dived in to
try to save the younger boy, but to no
avail. The headmaster of Windfield,
Dr Herbert Poleson, testified that the
quarry was out of bounds to pupils, but
he was aware that the rule was not always obeyed. The jury returned a verdict of accidental death by drowning.
The Deputy-Coroner then called attention to the bravery of Edward Pilaster
in trying to save the life of his friend,*

and said the character of the English schoolboy, as formed by such institutions as Windfield, was a thing of which we might justifiably feel proud.

5

MICKY MIRANDA WAS CAPTIVATED by Edward's mother.

Augusta Pilaster was a tall, statuesque woman in her thirties. She had black hair and black eyebrows and a haughty, high-cheekboned face with a straight, sharp nose and a strong chin. She was not exactly beautiful, and certainly not pretty, but somehow that proud face was deeply fascinating. She wore a black coat and a black hat to the inquest, and that made her even more dramatic. And yet what was so bewitching was the unmistakable feeling she gave Micky that the formal clothes covered a voluptuous body, and the arrogant, imperious manner concealed a passionate nature. He could hardly take his eyes off her.

Beside her sat her husband Joseph, Edward's father, an ugly, sour-faced man of about forty. He had the same big blade of a nose as Edward, and the same fair coloring, but his blond hair was receding, and he had bushy Dundreary side-whiskers sprouting from his cheeks as if to compensate for his baldness. Micky wondered what had made such a splendid woman marry him. He was very rich—perhaps that was it.

They were returning to the school in a carriage hired from the Station Hotel: Mr. and Mrs. Pilaster, Edward and Micky, and the headmaster, Dr. Poleson. Micky was amused to see that the headmaster was also bowled over by Augusta Pilaster. Old Pole asked if the inquest had tired her, inquired if she was comfortable in the carriage, ordered the coachman to go slower, and leaped out at the end of the journey to have the thrill of holding her hand as she stepped down. His bulldog face had never looked so animated.

The inquest had gone well. Micky put on his most open and honest expression to tell the story he and Edward had made up, but inside he had been scared. The British could be very sanctimonious about telling the truth, and if he was found out he would be in deep trouble. But the court was so enchanted by the story of schoolboy heroism that no one questioned it. Edward was nervous, and stammered his evidence, but the coroner excused him, suggesting that he was distraught over his failure to save Peter's life, and insisting he should not blame himself.

None of the other boys was asked to the inquest. Hugh had been taken away from the school on the day of the drowning because of the death of his father. Tonio was not asked to give evidence because nobody knew he had witnessed the death: Micky had scared him into silence. The other witness, the unknown boy at the far end of the pool, had not come forward.

Peter Middleton's parents were too grief-stricken to attend. They sent their lawyer, a sleepy-eyed old man whose only object was to get the whole thing over with a minimum of fuss. Peter's older brother David was there, and became quite agitated when the lawyer declined to ask Micky or Edward any questions, but to Micky's relief the old man waved aside his whispered protests. Micky was thankful for his laziness. He was ready for cross-examination, but Edward might have crumbled.

In the head's dusty drawing room Mrs. Pilaster embraced Edward and kissed the wound on his forehead where Tonio's stone had hit him. "My poor dear child," she said. Micky and Edward had not told anyone that

Tonio had thrown a stone at Edward, for then they would have to explain why he did it. Instead they had said that Edward banged his head when he dived in to rescue Peter.

As they drank their tea, Micky saw a new side to Edward. His mother, sitting beside him on the sofa, touched him constantly and called him Teddy. Instead of being embarrassed, as most boys would, he seemed to like it, and kept giving her a winning little smile that Micky had never seen before. She's stupid about him, Micky thought, and he loves it.

After a few minutes of small talk Mrs. Pilaster stood up abruptly, startling the men, who scrambled to their feet. "I'm sure you want to smoke, Dr. Poleson," she said. Without waiting for a reply she went on: "Mr. Pilaster will take a turn around the garden with you. Teddy dear, go with your father. I should like to have a few quiet minutes in the chapel. Perhaps Micky would show me the way."

"By all means, by all means, by all means," the head stuttered, falling over himself in his eagerness to assent to this series of commands. "Off you go, Miranda."

Micky was impressed. How effortlessly

she made them all do her bidding! He held the door for her and followed her out.

In the hall he said politely: "Would you like a parasol, Mrs. Pilaster? The sun is quite strong."

"No, thank you."

They went outside. There were a lot of boys hanging around outside the head's house. Micky guessed that word had got around about Pilaster's stunning mother, and they had all come to catch a glimpse of her. Feeling pleased to be her escort, he led her through a series of courtyards and quadrangles to the school chapel. "Shall I wait outside for you?" he offered.

"Come inside. I want to talk to you."

He began to feel nervous. His pleasure in escorting a striking mature woman around the school started to fade, and he wondered why she wanted to interview him alone.

The chapel was empty. She took a back pew and invited him to sit beside her. Looking straight into his eyes, she said: "Now tell me the truth."

Augusta saw the flash of surprise and fear in the boy's expression and knew that she was right.

However, he recovered in an instant. "I've already told you the truth," he said.

She shook her head. "You have not."

He smiled.

The smile took her by surprise. She had caught him out; she knew he was on the defensive; yet he could smile at her. Few men could resist the force of her will, but it seemed he was exceptional, despite his youth. "How old are you?" she said.

"Sixteen."

She studied him. He was outrageously good-looking, with his curly dark-brown hair and smooth skin, although there was already a hint of decadence in the heavy-lidded eyes and full lips. He reminded her somewhat of the earl of Strang, with his poise and good looks. . . . She pushed that thought aside with a guilty pang. "Peter Middleton was not in difficulties when you arrived at the pool," she said. "He was swimming around quite happily."

"What makes you say this?" he said coolly.

He was scared, she sensed, but he maintained his composure. He was really quite remarkably mature. She found herself unwillingly showing more of her hand. "You're forgetting that Hugh Pilaster was there," she said. "He is my nephew. His father took his own life last week, as you probably heard, and that is why he isn't here. But he has spoken to his mother, who is my sister-in-law."

"What did he say?"

Augusta frowned. "He said that Edward threw Peter's clothes into the water," she said reluctantly. She did not really understand why Teddy would do such a thing.

"And then?"

Augusta smiled. This boy was taking control of the conversation. She was supposed to be questioning him, but instead he was interrogating her. "Just tell me what really happened," she said.

He nodded. "Very well."

When he said that, Augusta was relieved, but worried as well. She wanted to know the truth, but she feared what it might be. Poor Teddy—he had almost died, as a baby, because there had been something wrong with Augusta's breast milk, and he nearly wasted away before the doctors discovered the nature of the problem and proposed a wet nurse. Ever since then he had been vulnerable, needing her special protection. Had she had her way he would not have gone to boarding school, but his father had been intransigent about that. . . . She returned her attention to Micky.

"Edward didn't mean any harm," Micky began. "He was just ragging. He threw the other boys' clothes into the water as a joke."

Augusta nodded. That sounded normal to her: boys teasing one another. Poor Teddy must have suffered that sort of thing himself.

"Then Hugh pushed Edward in."

"That little Hugh has always been a troublemaker," Augusta said. "He's just like his wretched father was." And like his father he would probably come to a bad end, she thought to herself.

"The other boys all laughed, and Edward pushed Peter's head under, to teach him a lesson. Hugh ran off. Then Tonio threw a stone at Edward."

Augusta was horrified. "But he might have been knocked unconscious, and drowned!"

"However, he wasn't, and he went chasing after Tonio. I was watching them: no one was looking at Peter Middleton. Tonio got away from Edward eventually. That was when we noticed that Peter had gone quiet. We don't really know what happened to him: perhaps Edward's ducking exhausted

him, so that he was too tired or too breathless to get out of the pool. Anyway, he was
floating facedown. We got him out of the
water right away, but he was dead."

It was hardly Edward's fault, Augusta
thought. Boys were always rough with one
another. All the same she was deeply grateful that this story had not come out at the
inquest. Micky had covered up for Edward,
thank heavens. "What about the other
boys?" she said. "They must know what
happened."

"It was lucky that Hugh left the school
that very day."

"And the other one—did you call him
Tony?"

"Antonio Silva. Tonio for short. Don't
worry about him. He's from my country.
He'll do as I tell him."

"How can you be sure?"

"He knows that if he gets me into trouble,
his family will suffer back home."

There was something chilling in the boy's
voice as he said this, and Augusta shivered.

"May I fetch you a shawl?" Micky said
attentively.

Augusta shook her head. "No other boys
saw what happened?"

Micky frowned. "There was another boy swimming in the pool when we got there."

"Who?"

He shook his head. "I couldn't see his face, and I didn't know it was going to be important."

"Did he see what happened?"

"I don't know. I'm not sure at what point he left."

"But he had gone by the time you got the body out of the water."

"Yes."

"I wish we knew who it was," Augusta said anxiously.

"He may not even have been a school-boy," Micky pointed out. "He could be from the town. Anyway, for whatever reason, he hasn't come forward as a witness, so I suppose he's no danger to us."

No danger to us. It struck Augusta that she was involved with this boy in something dishonest, possibly illegal. She did not like the situation. She had got into it without realizing, and now she was trapped. She looked hard at him and said: "What do you want?"

She caught him off guard for the first time. Looking bewildered, he said: "What do you mean?"

"You covered up for my son. You committed perjury today." He was unbalanced by her directness, she saw. That pleased her: she was in control again. "I don't believe you took such a risk out of the goodness of your heart. I think you want something in return. Why don't you just tell me what it is?"

She saw his gaze drop momentarily to her bosom, and for a wild moment she thought he was going to make an indecent suggestion. Then he said: "I want to spend the summer with you."

She had not expected that. "Why?"

"My home is six weeks' journey away. I have to stay at school during the holidays. I hate it—it's lonely and boring. I'd like to be invited to spend the summer with Edward."

Suddenly he was a schoolboy again. She had thought he would ask for money, or perhaps a job at Pilasters Bank. But this seemed such a small, almost childish request. However, it clearly was not small to him. After all, she thought, he is only sixteen.

"You shall stay with us for the summer, and welcome," she said. The thought did not displease her. He was a rather formidable young man in some ways, but his manners were perfect and he was good-looking:

it would be no hardship to have him as a guest. And he might be a good influence on Edward. If Teddy had a fault it was that he was rather aimless. Micky was just the opposite. Perhaps some of his strength of will would rub off on her Teddy.

Micky smiled, showing white teeth. "Thank you," he said. He seemed sincerely delighted.

She felt an urge to be alone for a while and mull over what she had heard. "Leave me now," she said. "I can find my way back to the headmaster's house."

He got up from the pew. "I'm very grateful," he said, and offered his hand.

She took it. "I'm grateful to you, for protecting Teddy."

He bent down, as if he were going to kiss her hand; and then, to her astonishment, he kissed her lips. It was so quick that she had no time to turn away. She searched for words of protest as he straightened up, but she could not think what to say. A moment later he was gone.

It was outrageous! He should not have kissed her at all, let alone on the lips. Who did he think he was? Her first thought was to rescind the summer invitation. But that would never do.

Why not? she asked herself. Why could she not cancel an invitation extended to a mere schoolboy? He had acted presumptuously, so he should not come to stay.

But the thought of going back on her promise made her uncomfortable. It was not just that Micky had saved Teddy from disgrace, she realized. It was worse than that. She had entered into a criminal conspiracy with him. It made her unpleasantly vulnerable to him.

She sat in the cool chapel for a long time, staring at the bare walls and wondering, with a distinct feeling of apprehension, how that handsome, knowing boy would use his power.

PART I

1873

CHAPTER ONE

1

WHEN MICKY MIRANDA WAS TWENTY-THREE his father came to London to buy rifles.

Señor Carlos Raul Xavier Miranda, known always as Papa, was a short man with massive shoulders. His tanned face was carved in lines of aggression and brutality. In leather chaps and a broad-brimmed hat, seated on a chestnut stallion, he could make a graceful, commanding figure; but here in Hyde Park, wearing a frock coat and a top hat, he felt foolish, and that made him dangerously bad-tempered.

They were not alike. Micky was tall and slim, with regular features, and he got his way by smiling rather than frowning. He was deeply attached to the refinements of London life: beautiful clothes, polite manners, linen sheets and indoor plumbing. His great fear was that Papa would want to take him back to Cordova. He could not bear to return to days in the saddle and nights sleeping on the hard ground. Even worse was the prospect of being under the thumb of his older brother Paulo, who was a replica of Papa. Perhaps Micky would go home one day, but it would be as an important man in his own right, not as the younger son of Papa Miranda. Meanwhile he had to persuade his father that he was more useful here in London than he would be at home in Cordova.

They were walking along South Carriage Drive on a sunny Saturday afternoon. The park was thronged with well-dressed Londoners on foot, on horseback or in open carriages, enjoying the warm weather. But Papa was not enjoying himself. "I must have those rifles!" he muttered to himself in Spanish. He said it twice.

Micky spoke in the same language. "You could buy them back home," he said tentatively.

"Two thousand of them?" Papa said. "Perhaps I could. But it would be such a big purchase that everyone would know about it."

So he wanted to keep it secret. Micky had no idea what Papa was up to. Paying for two thousand guns, and the ammunition to go with them, would probably take all the family's reserves of cash. Why did Papa suddenly need so much ordnance? There had been no war in Cordova since the now legendary March of the Cowboys, when Papa had led his men across the Andes to liberate Santamaria Province from its Spanish overlords. Who were the guns for? If you added up Papa's cowboys, relatives, placemen and hangers-on it would come to fewer than a thousand men. Papa had to be planning to recruit more. Whom would they be fighting? Papa had not volunteered the information and Micky was afraid to ask.

Instead he said: "Anyway, you probably couldn't get such high-quality weapons at home."

"That's true," said Papa. "The Westley-Richards is the finest rifle I've ever seen."

Micky had been able to help Papa with his choice of rifles. Micky had always been fascinated by weapons of all kinds, and he kept up with the latest technical developments. Papa needed short-barreled rifles that would not be too cumbersome for men on horseback. Micky had taken Papa to a factory in Birmingham and shown him the Westley-Richards carbine with the breech-loading action, nicknamed the Monkeytail because of its curly lever.

"And they make them so fast," Micky said.

"I expected to wait six months for the guns to be manufactured. But they can do it in a few days!"

"It's the American machinery they use." In the old days, when guns had been made by blacksmiths who fitted the parts together by trial and error, it would indeed have taken six months to make two thousand rifles; but modern machinery was so precise that the parts of any gun would fit any other gun of the same pattern, and a well-equipped factory could turn out hundreds of identical rifles a day, like pins.

"And the machine that makes two hundred thousand cartridges a day!" Papa said, and he shook his head in wonderment. Then his mood switched again and he said grimly: "But how can they ask for the money before the rifles are delivered?"

Papa knew nothing about international trade, and he had assumed the manufac-

turer would deliver the rifles in Cordova
and accept payment there. On the contrary,
the payment was required before the weapons left the Birmingham factory.

But Papa was reluctant to ship silver coins
across the Atlantic Ocean in barrels. Worse
still, he could not hand over the entire family fortune before the arms were safely delivered.

"We'll solve this problem, Papa," Micky
said soothingly. "That's what merchant
banks are for."

"Go over it again," Papa said. "I want to
make sure I understand this."

Micky was pleased to be able to explain
something to Papa. "The bank will pay the
manufacturer in Birmingham. It will arrange for the guns to be shipped to Cordova, and insure them on the voyage. When
they arrive, the bank will accept payment
from you at their office in Cordova."

"But then they have to ship the silver to
England."

"Not necessarily. They may use it to pay
for a cargo of salt beef coming from Cordova to London."

"How do they make a living?"

"They take a cut of everything. They will
pay the rifle manufacturer a discounted

price, take a commission on the shipping and insurance, and charge you extra for the guns."

Papa nodded. He was trying not to show it but he was impressed, and that made Micky happy.

They left the park and walked along Kensington Gore to the home of Joseph and Augusta Pilaster.

In the seven years since Peter Middleton drowned, Micky had spent every vacation with the Pilasters. After school he had toured Europe with Edward for a year, and he had roomed with Edward during the three years they had spent at Oxford University, drinking and gambling and raising cain, making only the barest pretense of being students.

Micky had never again kissed Augusta. He would have liked to. He wanted to do more than just kiss her. And he sensed that she might let him. Underneath that veneer of frozen arrogance there was the hot heart of a passionate and sensual woman, he was sure. But he had held back out of prudence. He had achieved something priceless by being accepted almost as a son in one of the richest families in England, and it would be insane to jeopardize that cherished position by seducing Joseph Pilaster's wife. All the same he could not help daydreaming about it.

Edward's parents had recently moved into a new house. Kensington Gore, which not so long ago had been a country road leading from Mayfair through the fields to the village of Kensington, was now lined, along its south side, by splendid mansions. On the north side of the street were Hyde Park and the gardens of Kensington Palace. It was the perfect location for the home of a rich commercial family.

Micky was not so sure about the style of architecture.

It was certainly striking. It was of red brick and white stone, with big leaded windows on the first and second floors. Above the first floor was a huge gable, its triangular shape enclosing three rows of windows—six, then four, then two at the apex: bedrooms, presumably, for innumerable relatives, guests and servants. The sides of the gable were stepped, and on the steps were perched stone animals, lions and dragons and monkeys. At the very top was a ship in full sail. Perhaps it represented the slave ship which, according to family legend, was the foundation of the Pilasters' wealth.

"I'm sure there's not another house like this in London," Micky said as he and his father stood outside staring at it.

Papa replied in Spanish. "No doubt that is what the lady intended."

Micky nodded. Papa had not met Augusta, but he had her measure already.

The house also had a big basement. A bridge crossed the basement area and led to the entrance porch. The door was open, and they went in.

Augusta was having a drum, an afternoon tea party, to show off her house. The oak-paneled hall was jammed with people and servants. Micky and his father handed their hats to a footman then pushed through the crowd to the vast drawing room at the back of the house. The French windows were open, and the party spilled out onto a flagged terrace and a long garden.

Micky had deliberately chosen to introduce his father at a crowded occasion, for Papa's manners were not always up to London standards, and it was better that the Pilasters should get to know him gradually. Even by Cordovan standards he paid little attention to social niceties, and escorting him around London was like having a lion on a leash. He insisted on carrying his pistol beneath his coat at all times.

Papa did not need Micky to point Augusta out to him.

She stood in the center of the room, draped in a royal-blue silk dress with a low square neckline that revealed the swell of her breasts. As Papa shook her hand she gazed at him with her hypnotic dark eyes and said in a low, velvet voice: "Señor Miranda—what a pleasure to meet you at last."

Papa was immediately entranced. He bowed low over her hand. "I can never repay your kindness to Miguel," he said in halting English.

Micky studied her as she cast her spell over his father. She had changed very little since the day he had kissed her in the chapel at Windfield School. The extra line or two around her eyes only made them more fascinating; the touch of silver in her hair enhanced the blackness of the rest; and if she was a little heavier than she had been it made her body more voluptuous.

"Micky has often told me of your splendid ranch," she was saying to Papa.

Papa lowered his voice. "You must come and visit us one day."

God forbid, Micky thought. Augusta in Cordova would be as out of place as a flamingo in a coal mine.

"Perhaps I shall," Augusta said. "How far is it?"

"With the new fast ships, only a month."

He still had hold of her hand, Micky noticed. And his voice had gone furry. He had fallen for her already. Micky felt a stab of jealousy. If anyone was going to flirt with Augusta it should be Micky, not Papa.

"I hear Cordova is a beautiful country," Augusta said.

Micky prayed Papa would not do anything embarrassing. However, he could be charming when it suited him, and he was now playing the role of romantic South American grandee for Augusta's benefit. "I can promise you that we would welcome you like the queen you are," he said in a low voice; and now it was obvious that he was making up to her.

But Augusta was a match for him. "What an extraordinarily tempting prospect," she said with a shameless insincerity that went right over Papa's head. Withdrawing her hand from his without missing a beat, she looked over his shoulder and cried: "Why, Captain Tillotson, how kind of you to come!" And she turned away to greet the latest arrival.

Papa was bereft. It took him a moment to regain his composure. Then he said abruptly: "Take me to the head of the bank."

"Certainly," Micky said nervously. He looked around for old Seth. The entire Pilaster clan was here, including maiden aunts, nephews and nieces, in-laws and second cousins. He recognized a couple of members of Parliament and a sprinkling of lesser nobility. Most of the other guests were business connections, Micky judged— and rivals, too, he thought as he saw the thin, upright figure of Ben Greenbourne, head of Greenbournes Bank, said to be the richest man in the world. Ben was the father of Solomon, the boy Micky had always known as Fatty Greenbourne. They had lost touch since school: Fatty had not studied at a university or done a European tour, but had gone straight into his father's business.

The aristocracy generally thought it vulgar to talk about money, but this group had no such inhibitions, and Micky kept hearing the word "crash." In the newspapers it was sometimes spelled "Krach" because it had started in Austria. Share prices were down and the bank rate was up, according to Edward, who had recently started work at the family bank. Some people were alarmed, but the Pilasters felt confident that London would not be pulled down with Vienna.

Micky took Papa out through the French windows onto the paved terrace, where wooden benches were placed in the shade of striped awnings. There they found old Seth, sitting with a rug over his knees despite the warm spring weather. He was weak from some unspecified illness, and he looked as frail as an eggshell, but he had the Pilaster nose, a big curved blade that made him formidable still.

Another guest was gushing over the old man, saying: "What a shame you aren't well enough to go to the royal levee, Mr. Pilaster!"

Micky could have told the woman this was the wrong thing to say to a Pilaster.

"On the contrary, I'm glad of the excuse," Seth harrumphed. "I don't see why I should bow the knee to people who have never earned a penny in their lives."

"But the Prince of Wales—such an honor!"

Seth was in no mood to be argued with—indeed he rarely was—and he now said:

"Young lady, the name of Pilaster is an accepted guarantee of honest dealing in corners of the globe where they've never heard of the Prince of Wales."

"But Mr. Pilaster, you almost sound as if you disapprove of the royal family!" the woman persisted, with a strained attempt at a playful tone.

Seth had not been playful for seventy years. "I disapprove of idleness," he said. "The Bible says, 'If any would not work, neither should he eat.' Saint Paul wrote that, in Second Thessalonians, chapter three, verse ten, and he conspicuously omitted to say that royalty were an exception to the rule."

The woman retired in confusion. Suppressing a grin, Micky said: "Mr. Pilaster, may I present my father, Señor Carlos Miranda, who is over from Cordova for a visit."

Seth shook Papa's hand. "Cordova, eh? My bank has an office in your capital city, Palma."

"I go to the capital very little," Papa said. "I have a ranch in Santamaria Province."

"So you're in the beef business."

"Yes."

"Look into refrigeration."

Papa was baffled. Micky explained:

"Someone has invented a machine for keeping meat cold. If they can find a way to install it in ships, we will be able to send fresh meat all over the world without salting it."

Papa frowned. "This could be bad for us. I have a big salting plant."

"Knock it down," said Seth. "Go in for refrigeration."

Papa did not like people telling him what to do, and Micky felt a little anxious. Out of the corner of his eye he spotted Edward. "Papa, I want to introduce you to my best friend," he said. He managed to ease his father away from Seth. "Allow me to present Edward Pilaster."

Papa examined Edward with a cold, clear-eyed gaze. Edward was not good-looking—he took after his father, not his mother—but he looked like a healthy farm boy, muscular and fair-skinned. Late nights and quantities of wine had not taken their toll—not yet, anyway. Papa shook his hand and said: "You two have been friends for many years."

"Soul mates," Edward said.

Papa frowned, not understanding.

Micky said: "May we talk business for a moment?"

They stepped off the terrace and onto the newly laid lawn. The borders were freshly planted, all raw earth and tiny shrubs. "Papa has been making some large purchases here, and he needs to arrange shipping and finance," Micky went on. "It could be the first small piece of business you bring in to your family bank."

Edward looked keen. "I'll be glad to handle that for you," he said to Papa. "Would you like to come into the bank tomorrow morning, so that we can make all the necessary arrangements?"

"I will," said Papa.

Micky said: "Tell me something. What if the ship sinks? Who loses—us, or the bank?"

"Neither," Edward said smugly. "The cargo will be insured at Lloyd's. We would simply collect the insurance money and ship a new consignment to you. You don't pay until you get your goods. What is the cargo, by the way?"

"Rifles."

Edward's face fell. "Oh. Then we can't help you."

Micky was mystified. "Why?"

"Because of old Seth. He's a Methodist, you know. Well, the whole family is, but he's rather more devout than most. Anyway, he won't finance arms sales, and as he's Senior Partner, that's bank policy."

"The devil it is," Micky cursed. He shot a fearful look at his father. Fortunately, Papa had not understood the conversation. Micky had a sinking feeling in his stomach. Surely his scheme could not founder on something as stupid as Seth's religion? "The damned old hypocrite is practically dead, why should he interfere?"

"He is about to retire," Edward pointed out. "But I think Uncle Samuel will take over, and he's the same, you know."

Worse and worse. Samuel was Seth's bachelor son, fifty-three years old and in perfect health. "We'll just have to go to another merchant bank," Micky said.

Edward said: "That should be straightforward, provided you can give a couple of sound business references."

"References? Why?"

"Well, a bank always takes the risk that the buyer will renege on the deal, leaving them with a cargo of unwanted merchandise on the far side of the globe. They just need some assurance that they're dealing with a respectable businessman."

What Edward did not realize was that the concept of a respectable businessman did not yet exist in South America. Papa was a caudillo, a provincial landowner with a hundred thousand acres of pampas and a work force of cowboys that doubled as his private army. He wielded power in a way the British had not known since the Middle Ages. It was like asking William the Conqueror for references.

Micky pretended to be unperturbed. "No doubt we can provide something," he said. In fact he was stumped. But if he was going to stay in London he had to bring this deal off.

They turned and strolled back toward the crowded terrace, Micky hiding his anxiety. Papa did not yet understand that they had encountered a serious difficulty, but Micky would have to explain it later—and then there would be trouble. Papa had no patience with failure, and his anger was terrifying.

Augusta appeared on the terrace and spoke to Edward. "Find Hastead for me, Teddy darling," she said. Hastead was her obsequious Welsh butler. "There's no cordial left and the wretched man has disappeared." Edward went off. She favored Papa with a warm, intimate smile. "Are you enjoying our little gathering, Señor Miranda?"

"Very well, thank you," said Papa.

"You must have some tea, or a glass of cordial."

Papa would have preferred tequila, Micky knew, but hard alcohol was not served at Methodist tea parties.

Augusta looked at Micky. Always quick to sense other people's moods, she said: "I can see that you're not enjoying the party. What's the matter?"

He did not hesitate to confide in her. "I was hoping Papa could help Edward by bringing new business to the bank, but it involves guns and ammunition, and Edward has just explained that Uncle Seth won't finance weapons."

"Seth won't be Senior Partner much longer," Augusta said.

"Apparently Samuel feels the same as his father."

"Does he?" Augusta said, and her tone was arch. "And who says that Samuel is to be the next Senior Partner?"

2

HUGH PILASTER WAS WEARING a new sky-blue ascot-style cravat, slightly puffed at the neckline and held in place with a pin. He really should have been wearing a new coat, but he earned only 68 pounds a year, so he had to brighten up his old clothes with a new tie. The ascot was the latest fashion, and sky-blue was a daring color choice; but when he spied his reflection in the huge mirror over the mantelpiece in Aunt Augusta's drawing room he saw that the blue tie and black suit looked rather fetching with his blue eyes and black hair, and he hoped the ascot gave him an attractively rakish air. Perhaps Florence Stalworthy would think so, anyway. He had started to take an interest in clothes since he met her.

It was a bit embarrassing, living with Augusta and being so poor; but there was a tradition at Pilasters Bank that men were paid what they were worth, regardless of whether they were family members. Another tradition was that everyone started at the bottom. Hugh had been a star pupil at school, and would have been head boy if he had not got into trouble so much; but his education counted for little at the bank, and he was doing the work of an apprentice clerk—and was paid accordingly. His aunt and uncle never offered to help him out financially, so they had to put up with his looking a little shabby.

He did not much care what they thought about his appearance, of course. It was Florence Stalworthy he was worried about. She was a pale, pretty girl, the daughter of the earl of Stalworthy; but the most important thing about her was that she was interested in Hugh Pilaster. The truth was that Hugh could be fascinated by any girl who would talk to him. This bothered him, because it surely meant that his feelings were shallow; but he could not help it. If a girl touched him accidentally it was enough to make his mouth go dry. He was tormented by curiosity about what their legs looked like under all those layers of skirt and petticoat. There were times when his desire hurt like a wound. He was twenty years old, he had felt like this since he was fifteen, and in those five years he had never kissed anyone except his mother.

A party such as this drum of Augusta's was exquisite torture. Because it was a party, everyone went out of their way to be pleasant, find things to talk about, and show an interest in one another. The girls looked lovely and smiled and sometimes, discreetly, flirted. So many people were crowded into the house that inevitably some of the girls would brush up against Hugh, bump into him as they turned around, touch his arm, or even press their breasts against his back as they squeezed by. He would have a week of restless nights afterwards.

Many of the people here were his relations, inevitably. His father, Tobias, and Edward's father, Joseph, had been brothers. But Hugh's father had withdrawn his capital from the family business, started his own enterprise, gone bankrupt, and killed himself. That was why Hugh had left the expensive Windfield boarding school and become a day boy at the Folkestone Academy for the Sons of Gentlemen; it was why he started work at nineteen instead of doing a European tour and wasting a few years at a university; it was why he lived with his aunt; and it was why he did not have new clothes to wear to the party. He was a relation, but a poor one; an embarrassment to a family whose pride, confidence and social standing was based on its wealth.

It would never have occurred to any of them to solve the problem by giving him

money. Poverty was the punishment for doing business badly, and if you started to ease
the pain for failures, why, there would be no
incentive to do well. "You might as well put
feather beds in prison cells," they would say
whenever someone suggested helping life's
losers.

His father had been the victim of a financial crisis, but that made no difference. He
had failed on 11th May 1866, a date known
to bankers as Black Friday. On that day a
bill broker called Overend & Gurney Ltd
had gone bankrupt for five million pounds,
and many firms were dragged down, including the London Joint Stock Bank and Sir
Samuel Peto's building company, as well as
Tobias Pilaster & Co. But there were no excuses in business, according to the Pilaster
philosophy. Just at present there was a financial crisis, and no doubt one or two firms
would fail before it was over; but the Pilasters were vigorously protecting themselves,
shedding their weaker clients, tightening
credit, and ruthlessly turning down all but
the most unquestionably secure new business. Self-preservation was the highest duty
of the banker, they believed.

Well, I'm a Pilaster too, Hugh thought. I
may not have the Pilaster nose, but I under-

stand about self-preservation. There was a rage that boiled in his heart sometimes when he brooded about what had happened to his father, and it made him all the more determined to become the richest and most respected of the whole damn crew. His cheap day school had taught him useful arithmetic and science while his better-off cousin Edward was struggling with Latin and Greek; and not going to university had given him an early start in the business. He was never tempted to follow a different way of life, become a painter or a member of Parliament or a clergyman. Finance was in his blood. He could give the current bank rate quicker than he could say whether it was raining. He was determined he would never be as smug and hypocritical as his older relatives, but all the same he was going to be a banker.

However, he did not think about it much. Most of the time he thought about girls.

He stepped out of the drawing room onto the terrace and saw Augusta bearing down on him with a girl in tow.

"Dear Hugh," she said, "here's your friend Miss Bodwin."

Hugh groaned inwardly. Rachel Bodwin was a tall, intellectual girl of radical opinions. She was not pretty—she had dull brown hair and light eyes set rather close together—but she was lively and interesting, full of subversive ideas, and Hugh had liked her a lot when he first came to London to work at the bank. But Augusta had decided he should marry Rachel, and that had ruined the relationship. Before that they had argued fiercely and freely about divorce, religion, poverty and votes for women. Since Augusta had begun her campaign to bring them together, they just stood and exchanged awkward chitchat.

"How lovely you look, Miss Bodwin," he said automatically.

"You're very kind," she replied in a bored tone.

Augusta was turning away when she caught sight of Hugh's tie. "Heavens!" she exclaimed. "What is that? You look like an innkeeper!"

Hugh blushed crimson. If he could have thought of a sharp rejoinder he would have risked it, but nothing came to mind, and all he could do was mutter: "It's just a new tie. It's called an ascot."

"You shall give it to the bootboy tomorrow," she said, and she turned away.

Resentment flared in Hugh's breast

against the fate that forced him to live with his overbearing aunt. "Women ought not to comment on a man's clothes," he said moodily. "It's not ladylike."

Rachel said: "I think women should comment on anything that interests them, so I shall say that I like your tie, and that it matches your eyes."

Hugh smiled at her, feeling better. She was very nice, after all. However, it was not her niceness that caused Augusta to want him to marry her. Rachel was the daughter of a lawyer specializing in commercial contracts. Her family had no money other than her father's professional income, and on the social ladder they were several rungs below the Pilasters; indeed they would not be at this party at all except that Mr. Bodwin had done useful work for the bank. Rachel was a girl in a low station in life, and by marrying her Hugh would confirm his status as a lesser breed of Pilaster; and that was what Augusta wanted.

He was not completely averse to the thought of proposing to Rachel. Augusta had hinted that she would give him a generous wedding present if he married her choice. But it was not the wedding present that tempted him, it was the thought that every night he would be able to get into bed with a woman, and lift her nightdress up, past her ankles and her knees, past her thighs—

"Don't look at me that way," Rachel said shrewdly. "I only said I liked your tie."

Hugh blushed again. Surely she could not guess what had been in his mind? His thoughts about girls were so grossly physical that he felt ashamed of himself much of the time. "Sorry," he mumbled.

"What a lot of Pilasters there are," she said brightly, looking around. "How do you cope with them all?"

Hugh looked around too, and saw Florence Stalworthy come in. She was extraordinarily pretty, with her fair curls falling over her delicate shoulders, a pink dress trimmed with lace and silk ribbons, and ostrich feathers in her hat. She met Hugh's eye and smiled at him across the room.

"I can see I've lost your attention," Rachel said with characteristic bluntness.

"I'm most awfully sorry," Hugh said.

Rachel touched his arm. "Hugh, dear, listen to me for a moment. I like you. You're one of the few people in London society who aren't unspeakably dull. But I don't love you and I will never marry you, no mat-

ter how often your aunt throws us together."

Hugh was startled. "I say—" he began.

But she had not finished. "And I know
you feel much the same about me, so please
don't pretend to be heartbroken."

After a stunned moment, Hugh grinned.
This directness was what he liked about her.
But he supposed she was right: liking was
not loving. He was not sure what love was,
but she seemed to know. "Does this mean
we can go back to quarreling about women's
suffrage?" he said cheerfully.

"Yes, but not today. I'm going to talk to
your old school friend, Señor Miranda."

Hugh frowned. "Micky couldn't spell 'suffrage' let alone tell you what it means."

"All the same, half the debutantes in
London are swooning over him."

"I can't imagine why."

"He's a male Florence Stalworthy," Rachel said, and with that she left him.

Hugh frowned, thinking about that.
Micky knew Hugh was a poor relation and
he treated him accordingly, so it was difficult for Hugh to be objective about him. He
was very personable, and always beautifully
dressed. He reminded Hugh of a cat, sleek
and sensual with glossy fur. It was not quite

the thing to be so carefully groomed, and men said he was not very manly, but women did not seem to care about that.

Hugh followed Rachel with his eyes as she crossed the room to where Micky stood with his father, talking to Edward's sister Clementine, Aunt Madeleine, and young Aunt Beatrice. Now Micky turned to Rachel, giving her his full attention as he shook her hand and said something that made her laugh. Micky was always talking to three or four women.

All the same Hugh disliked the suggestion that Florence was somehow like Micky. She was attractive and popular, as he was, but Micky was something of a cad, Hugh thought.

He made his way to Florence's side, feeling thrilled but nervous. "Lady Florence, how are you?"

She smiled dazzlingly. "What an extraordinary house!"

"Do you like it?"

"I'm not sure."

"That's what most people say."

She laughed as if he had made a witty remark, and he felt inordinately pleased.

He went on: "It's very modern, you know. There are five bathrooms! And a huge boiler in the basement warms the whole place with hot-water pipes."

"Perhaps the stone ship on top of the gable is a little too much."

Hugh lowered his voice. "I think so too. It reminds me of the cow's head outside a butcher's shop."

She giggled again. Hugh was pleased that he could make her laugh. He decided it would be nice to get her away from the crowd. "Come and see the garden," he said.

"How lovely."

It was not lovely, having only just been planted, but that did not matter in the least. He led her out of the drawing room onto the terrace but there he was waylaid by Augusta, who shot him a look of reproof and said: "Lady Florence, how kind of you to come. Edward will show you the garden." She grabbed Edward, who was standing nearby, and ushered the two of them away before Hugh could say a word. He clenched his teeth in frustration and vowed he would not let her get away with this. "Hugh, dear, I know you want to talk to Rachel," she said. She took Hugh's arm and moved him back inside, and there was nothing he could do to resist her, short of snatching his arm away and making a scene. Rachel was standing with Micky Miranda and his father. "Micky, I want your father to meet my husband's cousin, Mr. Samuel Pilaster." She detached Micky and his father and took them off, leaving Hugh with Rachel again.

Rachel was laughing. "You can't argue with her."

"It would be like arguing with a dashed railway train," Hugh fumed. Through the window he could see the bustle of Florence's dress as it swayed down the garden beside Edward.

Rachel followed his eyes and said: "Go after her."

He grinned. "Thanks."

He hurried down the garden. As he caught up, a wicked idea occurred to him. Why should he not play his aunt's game and detach Edward from Florence? Augusta would be spitting mad when she found out —but it would be worth it for the sake of a few minutes alone in the garden with Florence. To hell with it, he thought. "Oh, Edward," he said. "Your mother asked me to send you to her. She's in the hall."

Edward did not question this: he was used to sudden changes of mind by his mother. He said: "Please excuse me, Lady Florence." He left them and went into the house.

Florence said: "Did she really send for him?"

"No."

"You're so bad!" she said, but she was smiling.

He looked into her eyes, basking in the sunshine of her approval. There would be hell to pay later, but he would suffer much worse for the sake of a smile like that. "Come and see the orchard," he said.

3

AUGUSTA WAS AMUSED by Papa Miranda. Such a squat peasant of a man! He was so different from his lithe, elegant son. Augusta was very fond of Micky Miranda. She always felt more of a woman when she was with him, even though he was so young. He had a way of looking at her as if she were the most desirable thing he had ever seen. There were times when she wished he would do more than just look. It was a foolish wish, of course, but all the same she felt it now and again.

She had been alarmed by their conversation about Seth. Micky assumed that when old Seth died or retired, his son Samuel would take over as Senior Partner of Pilasters Bank. Micky would not have made that assumption on his own: he must have picked it up from the family. Augusta did not want Samuel to take over. She wanted the job for her husband Joseph, who was Seth's nephew.

She glanced through the drawing room window and saw the four partners in Pilasters Bank together on the terrace. Three were Pilasters: Seth, Samuel and Joseph—the early-nineteenth-century Methodists had favored biblical names. Old Seth looked like the invalid he was, sitting with a blanket over his knees, outliving his usefulness. Beside him was his son. Samuel was not as distinguished-looking as his father. He had the same beaklike nose, but below it was a rather soft mouth with bad teeth. Tradition would favor him to succeed because he was the eldest of the partners after Seth. Joseph was speaking, making a point to his uncle and his cousin with short jabbing movements of his hand, a characteristically impatient gesture. He, too, had the Pilaster nose, but the rest of his features were rather irregular and he was losing his hair. The fourth partner was standing back, listening with his arms folded. He was Major George Harts-horn, husband of Joseph's sister Madeleine. A former army officer, he had a prominent scar on his forehead from a wound received twenty years ago in the Crimean War. He was no hero, however: his horse had been frightened by a steam-traction engine and he had fallen and banged his head on the wheel of a kitchen wagon. He had retired from the army and joined the bank when he married Madeleine. An amiable man who followed where others led, he was not clever enough to run the bank, and anyway they had never had a Senior Partner whose name was not Pilaster. The only serious candidates were Samuel and Joseph.

Technically, the decision was made by a vote of the partners. By tradition, the family generally reached a consensus. In reality, Augusta was determined to have her way. But it would not be easy.

The Senior Partner of Pilasters Bank was one of the most important people in the world. His decision to grant a loan could save a monarch; his refusal could start a revolution. Along with a handful of others— J. P. Morgan, the Rothschilds, Ben Green-bourne—he held the prosperity of nations in his hands. He was flattered by heads of state, consulted by prime ministers, and courted by diplomats; and his wife was fawned upon by them all.

Joseph wanted the job, but he had no subtlety. Augusta was terrified that he would let the opportunity slip through his fingers. Left to himself he might say bluntly that he would like to be considered then simply allow the family to decide. It might not occur to him that there were other things he should do to make sure he won the contest. For instance, he would never do anything to discredit his rival.

Augusta would have to find ways to do that for him.

She had no trouble identifying Samuel's weakness. At the age of fifty-three he was a bachelor, and lived with a young man who was blithely referred to as his "secretary." Until now the family had paid no attention to Samuel's domestic arrangements, but Augusta was wondering if she could change all that.

Samuel had to be handled carefully. He was a fussy, finicky man, the kind who would change his entire outfit of clothes because a drop of wine had fallen on the knee of his trousers; but he was not weak, and could not

be intimidated. A frontal assault was not the
way to attack him.

She would have no regrets about injuring
him. She had never liked him. He sometimes acted as if he found her amusing, and
he had a way of refusing to take her at face
value that she found deeply annoying.

As she moved among her guests, she put
out of her mind the irritating reluctance of
her nephew Hugh to pay court to a perfectly
suitable young girl. That branch of the family had always been troublesome and she
was not going to let it distract her from the
more important problem that Micky had
alerted her to, the threat of Samuel.

She spotted her sister-in-law, Madeleine
Hartshorn, in the hall. Poor Madeleine, you
could tell she was Joseph's sister, for she
had the Pilaster nose. On some of the men it
looked distinguished, but no woman could
look anything but plain with a great beak
like that.

Madeleine and Augusta had once been rivals. Years ago, when Augusta first married
Joseph, Madeleine had resented the way the
family began to center around Augusta—
even though Madeleine never had the mag-
netism or the energy to do what Augusta
did, arranging weddings and funerals,

matchmaking, patching up quarrels, and organizing support for the sick, the pregnant and the bereaved. Madeleine's attitude had come close to causing a rift within the family. Then she had delivered a weapon into Augusta's hands. One afternoon Augusta had stepped into an exclusive Bond Street silverware shop just in time to see Madeleine slipping into the back of the store. Augusta had lingered for a while, pretending to hesitate over a toast rack, until she saw a handsome young man follow the same route. She had heard that the rooms above such stores were sometimes used for romantic rendezvous, and she was now almost certain that Madeleine was having a love affair. A five-pound note had persuaded the proprietress of the shop, a Mrs. Baxter, to divulge the name of the young man, Viscount Tremain.

Augusta had been genuinely shocked, but her first thought had been that if Madeleine could do it with Viscount Tremain, Augusta could do the same with Micky Miranda. But that was out of the question, of course. Besides, if Madeleine could be found out the same could happen to Augusta.

It could have ruined Madeleine socially. A man who had a love affair was considered wicked but romantic; a woman who did the same was a whore. If her secret got out she would be shunned by society and her family would be ashamed of her. Augusta considered using the secret to control Madeleine, holding over her head the threat of exposure. But that would make Madeleine forever hostile. It was foolish to multiply enemies unnecessarily. There had to be a way she could disarm Madeleine and at the same time make an ally of her. After much thought she had evolved a strategy. Instead of intimidating Madeleine with the information, she pretended to be on her side. "A word to the wise, dear Madeleine," she had whispered. "Mrs. Baxter cannot be trusted. Tell your viscount to find a more discreet rendezvous." Madeleine had begged her to keep the secret and had been pathetically grateful when Augusta willingly promised eternal silence. Since then there had been no rivalry between them.

Now Augusta took Madeleine's arm, saying: "Come and see my room—I think you'll like it."

On the second floor of the house were her bedroom and dressing room, Joseph's bedroom and dressing room, and a study.

She led Madeleine into her bedroom, closed the door, and waited for her reaction.

She had furnished the room in the latest Japanese style, with fretwork chairs, peacock-feather wallpaper and a display of porcelain over the mantelpiece. There was an immense wardrobe painted with Japanese motifs, and the window seat in the bay was partly concealed by dragonfly curtains.

"Augusta, how daring!" said Madeleine.

"Thank you." Augusta was almost completely happy with the effect. "There was a better curtain material I wanted but Liberty's had sold out of it. Come and see Joseph's room."

She took Madeleine through the communicating door. Joseph's bedroom was furnished in a more moderate version of the same style with dark leather-paper on the walls and brocade curtains. Augusta was especially proud of a lacquered display cabinet that held his collection of jeweled snuffboxes.

"Joseph is so eccentric," said Madeleine, looking at the snuffboxes.

Augusta smiled. Her husband was not in the least eccentric, generally speaking, but it was odd for a hardheaded Methodist businessman to collect something so frivolous and exquisite, and the whole family found it amusing. "He says they're an investment," she said. A diamond necklace for her would have been an equally good investment, but he never bought her such things, for Methodists considered jewelry to be a needless extravagance.

"A man should have a hobby," Madeleine said. "It keeps him out of trouble."

Out of whorehouses was what she meant. The implied reference to men's peccadilloes reminded Augusta of her purpose. Softly, softly, she said to herself. "Madeleine, dear, what *are* we going to do about cousin Samuel and his 'secretary'?"

Madeleine looked puzzled. "Ought we to do something?"

"If Samuel is to become Senior Partner, we must."

"Why?"

"My dear, the Senior Partner of Pilasters has to meet ambassadors, heads of state, even royalty—he must be quite, *quite* irreproachable in his private life."

Comprehension dawned, and Madeleine flushed. "Surely you're not suggesting that Samuel is in some way . . . depraved?"

That was exactly what Augusta was suggesting, but she did not want to say it outright, for fear of provoking Madeleine to defend her cousin. "I trust that I shall never know," she said evasively. "The important thing is what people think."

Madeleine was unconvinced. "Do you really suppose people think . . . that?"

Augusta forced herself to have patience with Madeleine's delicacy. "My dear, we are both married women, and we know what men are like. They have animal appetites. The world assumes that a single man of fifty-three living with a pretty boy is vicious and, heaven knows, in most cases the world is probably right."

Madeleine frowned, looking worried. Before she could say anything else there was a knock at the door and Edward came in. "What is it, Mother?" he asked.

Augusta was annoyed by the interruption and she had no idea what the boy was talking about. "What do you mean?"

"You sent for me."

"I most certainly did not. I told you to show Lady Florence around the garden."

Edward looked hurt. "Hugh said you wanted to see me!"

Augusta understood. "Did he? And I suppose he is showing Lady Florence the garden now?"

Edward saw what she was getting at. "I do believe he is," he said, looking wounded. "Don't be cross with me, Mother, please."

Augusta melted instantly. "Don't worry, Teddy dear," she said. "Hugh is such a sly boy." But if he thought he could outwit his Aunt Augusta he was also foolish.

This distraction had irritated her, but on reflection she thought she had said enough to Madeleine about cousin Samuel. At this stage all she wanted was to plant the seed of doubt: anything more might be too heavy-handed. She decided to leave well enough alone. She ushered her sister-in-law and her son out of the room, saying: "Now I must return to my guests."

They went downstairs. The party was going well, to judge by the cacophony of talk, laughter, and a hundred silver teaspoons clinking in bone china saucers. Augusta briefly checked the dining room, where the servants were dispensing lobster salad, fruit-cake and iced drinks. She moved through the hall, speaking a word or two to each guest who caught her eye, but looking for a particular one—Florence's mother, Lady Stalworthy.

She was worried by the possibility that Hugh might marry Florence. Hugh was already doing far too well at the bank. He had the quick commercial brain of a barrow boy and the engaging manners of a cardsharp. Even Joseph spoke approvingly of him, oblivious of the threat to their own son. Marriage to the daughter of an earl would give Hugh social status to add to his native talents, and then he would be a dangerous rival to Edward. Dear Teddy did not have Hugh's superficial charm or his head for figures, so he needed all the help Augusta could give him.

She found Lady Stalworthy standing in the bay window of the drawing room. She was a pretty middle-aged woman in a pink dress and a little straw hat with silk flowers all over it. Augusta wondered anxiously how she would feel about Hugh and Florence. Hugh was no great catch, but from Lady Stalworthy's point of view he was not a disaster. Florence was the youngest of three daughters, and the other two had married well, so Lady Stalworthy might be indulgent. Augusta had to prevent that. But how?

She stood at Lady Stalworthy's side and saw that she was watching Hugh and Florence in the garden. Hugh was explaining something, and Florence's eyes sparkled with pleasure as she looked at him and listened. "The careless happiness of youth," said Augusta.

"Hugh seems a nice boy," Lady Stalworthy said.

Augusta looked hard at her for a moment. Lady Stalworthy had a dreamy smile on her face. She had once been as pretty as her daughter, Augusta guessed. Now she was remembering her own girlhood. She needed to be brought down to earth with a thump. "How quickly they pass, those carefree days."

"But so idyllic while they last."

It was time for the poison. "Hugh's father died, as you know," Augusta said. "And his mother lives very quietly at Folkestone, so Joseph and I feel an obligation to take a parental interest." She paused. "It is hardly necessary for me to say that an alliance with your family would be a remarkable triumph for Hugh."

"How kind of you to say that," said Lady Stalworthy, as if she had been paid a pretty compliment. "The Pilasters themselves are a family of distinction."

"Thank you. If Hugh works hard he will one day earn a comfortable living."

Lady Stalworthy looked a little taken aback. "His father left nothing at all, then?"

"No." Augusta needed to let her know that Hugh would get no money from his uncles when he married. She said: "He will have to work his way up in the bank, living on his salary."

"Ah, yes," said Lady Stalworthy, and her face showed a hint of disappointment. "Florence has a small independence, happily."

Augusta's heart sank. So Florence had money of her own. That was bad news. Augusta wondered how much it was. The Stalworthys were not as rich as the Pilasters —few people were—but they were comfortable, Augusta believed. At any rate, Hugh's poverty was not enough to turn Lady Stalworthy against him. Augusta would have to use stronger measures. "Dear Florence would be such a help to Hugh . . . a stabilizing influence, I feel sure."

"Yes," said Lady Stalworthy vaguely, and then she frowned. "Stabilizing?"

Augusta hesitated. This kind of thing was dangerous, but the risk had to be taken. "I never listen to gossip, and I'm sure you don't either," she said. "Tobias *was* quite unfortunate, of that there is no doubt, but Hugh shows *hardly* any sign of having inherited the weakness."

"Good," said Lady Stalworthy, but her face showed deep anxiety.

"All the same, Joseph and I would be very happy to see him married to such a sensible girl as Florence. One feels she would be firm with him, if . . ." Augusta trailed off.

"I . . ." Lady Stalworthy swallowed. "I don't seem to recall just what his father's weakness was."

"Well, it wasn't true, really."

"Strictly between you and me, of course."

"Perhaps I shouldn't have raised it."

"But I must know everything, for my daughter's sake. I'm sure you understand."

"Gambling," Augusta said in a lowered voice. She did not want to be overheard: there were people here who would know she was lying. "It was what led him to take his own life. The shame, you know." Pray heaven the Stalworthys don't bother to check the truth of this, she thought fervently.

"I thought his business failed."

"That, too."

"How tragic."

"Admittedly, Joseph has had to pay Hugh's debts once or twice, but he has spoken very firmly to the boy, and we feel sure it will not happen again."

"That's reassuring," said Lady Stalworthy, but her face told a different story.

Augusta felt she had probably said enough. The pretense that she was in favor of the match was wearing dangerously thin. She glanced out of the window again. Florence was laughing at something Hugh was saying, throwing her head back and showing her teeth in a way that was rather . . . unseemly. He was practically eating her up with his eyes. Everyone at the party could see they were attracted to each other. "I judge it won't be long before matters come to a head," Augusta said.

"Perhaps they have talked enough for one day," Lady Stalworthy said with a troubled look. "I had better intervene. Do excuse me."

"Of course."

Lady Stalworthy headed rapidly for the garden.

August felt relieved. She had carried off another delicate conversation. Lady Stalworthy was suspicious of Hugh now, and once a mother began to feel uneasy about a suitor she rarely came to favor him in the end.

She looked around and spotted Beatrice Pilaster, another sister-in-law. Joseph had

had two brothers: one was Tobias, Hugh's father, and the other was William, always called Young William because he was born twenty-three years after Joseph. William was now twenty-five and not yet a partner in the bank. Beatrice was his wife. She was like a large puppy, happy and clumsy and eager to be everyone's friend. Augusta decided to speak to her about Samuel and his secretary. She went over to her and said: "Beatrice, dear, would you like to see my bedroom?"

4

MICKY AND HIS FATHER left the party and set out to walk back to their lodgings. Their route lay entirely through parks—first Hyde Park, then Green Park, and St. James's Park —until they reached the river. They stopped in the middle of Westminster Bridge to rest for a spell and look at the view.

On the north shore of the river was the greatest city in the world. Upstream were the Houses of Parliament, built in a modern imitation of the neighboring thirteenth-century Westminster Abbey. Downstream they could see the gardens of Whitehall, the duke of Buccleuch's palace, and the vast brick edifice of the new Charing Cross Railway Station.

The docks were out of sight, and no big ships came this far up, but the river was busy with small boats and barges and pleasure cruisers, a pretty sight in the evening sun.

The southern shore might have been in a different country. It was the site of the Lambeth potteries, and there, in mud fields dotted with ramshackle workshops, crowds of gray-faced men and ragged women were still at work boiling bones, sorting rubbish, firing kilns and pouring paste into molds to make the drainpipes and chimney pots needed by the fast-expanding city. The smell was strong even here on the bridge, a quarter-mile away. The squat hovels in which they lived were crowded around the walls of Lambeth Palace, the London home of the Archbishop of Canterbury, like the filth left by high tide on the muddy foreshore. Despite the nearness of the archbishop's palace the neighborhood was known as the Devil's Acre, presumably because the fires and the smoke, the shuffling workers and the awful smell made people think of Hell.

Micky's lodgings were in Camberwell, a respectable suburb beyond the potteries;

but he and his father hesitated on the bridge, reluctant to plunge into the Devil's Acre. Micky was still cursing the scrupulous Methodist conscience of old Seth Pilaster for frustrating his plans. "We will solve this problem about shipping the rifles, Papa," he said. "Don't worry about it."

Papa shrugged. "Who is standing in our way?" he asked.

It was a simple question, but it had a deep meaning in the Miranda family. When they had an intractable problem, they asked *Who is standing in our way?* It really meant *Whom do we have to kill to get this done?* It brought back to Micky all the barbarism of life in Santamaria Province, all the grisly legends he preferred to forget: the story about how Papa had punished his mistress for being unfaithful to him by putting a rifle up her and pulling the trigger; the time a Jewish family opened a store next to his in the provincial capital, so he set fire to it and burned the man and his wife and children alive; the one about the dwarf who had dressed up to look like Papa during the carnival, and made everyone laugh by strutting up and down in a perfect imitation of Papa's walk—until Papa calmly went up to the dwarf, drew a pistol, and blew his head off.

Even in Cordova this was not normal, but there Papa's reckless brutality had made him a man to be feared. Here in England it would get him thrown in jail. "I don't anticipate the need for drastic action," Micky said, trying to cover his nervousness with an air of unconcern.

"For now, there is no hurry," Papa said. "Winter is beginning at home. There will be no fighting until the summer." He gave Micky a hard look. "But I *must* have the rifles by the end of October."

That look made Micky feel weak at the knees. He leaned against the stone parapet of the bridge to steady himself. "I'll see to it, Papa, don't worry," he said anxiously.

Papa nodded as if there could be no doubt about it. They were silent for a minute. Out of the blue, Papa said: "I want you to stay in London."

Micky felt his shoulders slump with relief. It was what he had been hoping for. He must have done something right, then. "I think it might be a good idea, Papa," he said, trying to hide his eagerness.

Then Papa dropped his bombshell. "But your allowance will stop."

"What?"

"The family can't keep you. You must support yourself."

Micky was appalled. Papa's meanness was as legendary as his violence, but still this was unexpected. The Mirandas were rich. Papa had thousands of head of cattle, monopolized all horse dealing over a huge territory, rented land to small farmers and owned most of the stores in Santamaria Province.

It was true that their money did not buy much in England. Back home a Cordovan silver dollar would get you a slap-up meal, a bottle of rum and a whore for the night; here it would hardly stretch to a cheap meal and a glass of weak beer. That had come as a blow to Micky when he went to Windfield School. He had managed to supplement his allowance by playing cards, but he had found it hard to make ends meet until he befriended Edward. Even now Edward paid for all the expensive entertainments they shared: the opera, visits to racecourses, hunting and whores. Still, Micky needed a basic income to pay his rent, tailor's bills, subscriptions to the gentlemen's clubs that were an essential element of London life, and tips to servants. How did Papa expect him to find that? Take a job? The idea was appalling. No member of the Miranda family worked for wages.

He was about to ask how he was expected to live on no money when Papa abruptly changed the subject and said: "I will now tell you what the rifles are for. We are going to take over the desert."

Micky did not understand. The Miranda property covered a big area of Santamaria Province. Bordering their land was a smaller property owned by the Delabarca family. To the north of both was land so arid that neither Papa nor his neighbor had ever bothered to claim it. "What do we want the desert for?" Micky said.

"Beneath the dust there is a mineral called nitrate. It's used as a fertilizer, much better than dung. It can been shipped all over the world and sold for high prices. The reason I want you to stay in London is to take charge of selling it."

"How do we know this stuff is there?"

"Delabarca has started mining it. It has made his family rich."

Micky felt excited. This could transform the family's future. Not instantly, of course; not soon enough to solve the problem of how he would live with no allowance. But in the long term . . .

"We have to act fast," Papa said. "Wealth is power, and the Delabarca family will soon be stronger than we are. Before that happens, we have to destroy them."

CHAPTER TWO

1

Whitehaven House
Kensington Gore
London, S.W.
June 2nd, 1873

My dear Florence,
 Where are you? I hoped to see you at Mrs Bridewell's ball, then at Richmond, then at the Muncasters' on Saturday . . . but you weren't at any of them! Write me a line and say you're still alive.
 Affectionately yours,
 Hugh Pilaster.

*

23, Park Lane
London, W.
June 3rd, 1873

To Hugh Pilaster, Esq.
Sir:
You will oblige me by not communicating with my daughter under any circumstances whatsoever henceforth.
Stalworthy.

*

Whitehaven House
Kensington Gore
London, S.W.
June 6th, 1873

Dearest Florence,
At last I have found a confidential messenger to smuggle a note to you. Why have you been hidden away from me? Have I offended your parents? Or —which heaven forbid—you? Your cousin Jane will bring your reply to me. Write it quickly!
With fond regards,
Hugh.

*

Stalworthy Manor
Stalworthy
Buckinghamshire
June 7th, 1873

Dear Hugh,
I am forbidden to see you because you are a gambler like your father. I am truly sorry but I must believe that my parents know what is best for me.
Sorrowfully,
Florence.

*

Whitehaven House
Kensington Gore
London, S.W.
June 8th, 1873

Dear Mother,
A young lady has just rejected me because my father was a gambler. Is it true? Please answer right away. I must know!
Your loving son,
Hugh.

*

2, Wellington Villas
Folkestone
Kent
June 9th, 1873

My dear son,
I never knew your father to gamble.
I cannot imagine who would say such
a wicked thing about him. He lost his
money in a business collapse, as you
have always been told. There was no
other cause.
I hope you are well and happy, my
dear, and that your beloved will accept
you. I continue much the same. Your sis-
ter Dorothy sends her best love, as does,
Your Mother.

*

Whitehaven House
Kensington Gore
London, S.W.
June 10th, 1873

Dear Florence,
I believe someone may have told
you a wrong thing about my father. His
business failed, it is true. It was no
fault of his own: a large firm called
Overend & Gurney went bankrupt for
five millions of pounds, and many of

their creditors were destroyed. He took his own life the same day. But he never gambled; and nor do I.

If you explain this to the noble earl your father, I believe all will be well.

Fondly yours,

Hugh.

*

Stalworthy Manor
Stalworthy
Buckinghamshire
June 11th, 1873

Hugh,

Writing falsehoods to me will do no good. I now know for sure that my parents' advice to me is right, and I must forget you.

Florence.

*

Whitehaven House
Kensington Gore
London, S.W.
June 12th, 1873

Dear Florence,

You must believe me! It is possible that I have not been told the truth about my father—although I cannot in

*all sincerity doubt my mother's word—
but in my own case I know the truth!
When I was fourteen years old I put a
shilling on the Derby and lost it, and
since then I have never seen the point
of gambling. When I see you I will
swear an oath.*

In hope—
Hugh.

*

Foljambe & Merriweather, Solicitors
Gray's Inn
London, W.C.
June 13th, 1873

To Hugh Pilaster, Esq.
Sir:
*We are instructed by our client, the
earl of Stalworthy, to require you to desist from communication with his
daughter.*

*Please be informed that the noble
earl will take any and all necessary
steps, including a High Court injunc-
tion, to enforce his will in this matter,
unless you refrain immediately.*

*For Messrs. Foljambe &
Merriwether,*
Albert C. Merriwether.

*

Hugh—

She showed your last letter to my aunt, her mother. They have taken her to Paris until the end of the London Season, and then they go to Yorkshire. It is no good—she no longer cares for you. Sorry—

Jane.

2

THE ARGYLL ROOMS were the most popular place of entertainment in London, but Hugh had never been there. It would never have occurred to Hugh to visit such a place: although not actually a brothel, it had a low reputation. However, a few days after Florence Stalworthy finally rejected him, Edward casually invited him to join him and Micky for an evening's debauchery, and he accepted.

Hugh did not spend much time with his cousin. Edward had always been spoiled rotten, a bully and a slacker who got others to do his work. Hugh had long ago been cast in the role of black sheep of the family, following in his father's footsteps. Edward and he had little in common. But despite that Hugh decided to try the pleasures of dissipation. Low dives and loose women were a way of life for thousands of upper-class Englishmen. Perhaps they knew best: perhaps this, rather than true love, was the way to happiness.

In fact he was not sure whether he had truly been in love with Florence. He was angry that her parents had turned her against him, even more so because the reason was a wicked falsehood about his father. But he found, somewhat shamefully, that he was not heartbroken. He thought about Florence often, but nevertheless he continued to sleep well, eat heartily, and concentrate on his work without difficulty. Did that mean he had never loved her? The girl he liked best in the whole world, apart from his six-year-old sister Dotty, was Rachel Bodwin, and he had toyed with the idea of marrying her. Was that love? He did not know. Perhaps he was too young to understand love. Or perhaps it simply had not happened to him yet.

The Argyll Rooms were next door to a church in Great Windmill Street, just off Piccadilly Circus. Edward paid a shilling admission for each of them and they went in-

side. They wore evening dress: black tail-
coats with silk lapels, black trousers with silk
braid, low-cut white waistcoats, white shirts
and white bow ties. Edward's suit was new
and expensive; Micky's rather cheaper, but
fashionably cut; and Hugh's had belonged
to his father.

The ballroom was an extravagantly gas-lit
arena, with huge gilt mirrors intensifying the
brilliant light. The dance floor was crowded
with couples, and behind an elaborate gold
trelliswork screen a half-concealed orchestra was playing a vigorous polka. Some of
the men wore evening dress, a sign that they
were upper-class people going slumming;
but most wore respectable black daytime
suits, identifying them as clerks and small
businessmen.

Above the ballroom was a shadowed gal-
lery. Edward pointed to it and said to Hugh:
"If you make friends with a dollymop, you
can pay another shilling and take her up
there: plush seats, dim lights, and blind wait-
ers."

Hugh felt dazzled, not just by the lights
but by the possibilities. All around him were
girls who had come here for the sole purpose of flirting! Some were with boyfriends
but others had come alone, intending to

dance with total strangers. And they were all dressed up to the nines, in evening gowns with bustles, many of them cut very low at the neckline, and the most amazing hats. But he noticed that on the dance floor they all modestly wore their cloaks. And Micky and Edward had assured him that they were not prostitutes but ordinary girls, shop assistants and parlormaids and dressmakers.

"How do you meet them?" Hugh asked. "Surely you don't just accost them like streetwalkers?"

Edward answered him by pointing to a tall, distinguished-looking man in white tie and tails, who wore some kind of badge and appeared to be supervising the dancing. "That's the master of ceremonies. He'll effect an introduction, if you tip him."

The atmosphere was a curious but exciting mixture of respectability and license, Hugh found.

The polka ended and some of the dancers returned to their tables. Edward pointed and cried: "Well, I'm damned, there's Fatty Greenbourne!"

Hugh followed his finger and saw their old schoolmate, bigger than ever, bulging out of his white waistcoat. On his arm was a stunningly beautiful girl. Fatty and the girl sat down at a table, and Micky said quietly: "Why don't we join them for a while?"

Hugh was keen for a closer look at the girl, and he assented readily. The three young men threaded their way through the tables. "Good evening, Fatty!" Edward said cheerily.

"Hullo, you lot," he replied. "People call me Solly nowadays," he added amiably.

Hugh had seen Solly now and again in the City, London's financial district. For some years Solly had been working at the head office of his family bank, just around the corner from Pilasters. Unlike Hugh, Edward had only been working in the City for a few weeks, which was why he had not previously run into Solly.

"We thought we'd join you," Edward said casually, and looked an inquiry at the girl.

Solly turned to his companion. "Miss Robinson, may I present some old school friends: Edward Pilaster, Hugh Pilaster, and Micky Miranda."

Miss Robinson's reaction was startling. She went pale beneath her rouge and said: "Pilaster? Not the same family as Tobias Pilaster?"

"My father was Tobias Pilaster," said Hugh. "How do you know the name?"

She recovered her composure quickly. "My father used to work for Tobias Pilaster and Co. As I child, I used to wonder who Co was." They laughed, and the moment of tension passed. She added: "Would you lads like to sit down?"

There was a bottle of champagne on the table. Solly poured some for Miss Robinson and called for more glasses. "Well, this is a real reunion of old Windfield chums," he said. "Guess who else is here: Tonio Silva."

"Where?" said Micky quickly. He seemed displeased to hear that Tonio was around, and Hugh wondered why. At school Tonio had always been frightened of Micky, he remembered.

"He's on the dance floor," Solly said. "He's with Miss Robinson's friend, Miss April Tilsley."

Miss Robinson said: "You could call me Maisie. I'm not a *formal* girl." And she threw a lascivious wink at Solly.

A waiter brought a plate of lobster and set it in front of Solly. He tucked a napkin into his shirt collar and started to eat.

"I thought you Jewboys weren't supposed to eat shellfish," Micky said with lazy insolence.

Solly was as impervious as ever to such

remarks. "I'm only kosher at home," he said.

Maisie Robinson gave Micky a hostile glare. "We Jewgirls eat what we like," she said, and took a morsel from Solly's plate.

Hugh was surprised that she was Jewish: he always thought of Jews as having dark coloring. He studied her. She was quite short, but added about a foot to her height by piling her tawny hair into a high chignon and topping it with a huge hat decorated with artificial leaves and fruit. Underneath the hat was a small, impudent face with a wicked twinkle in the green eyes. The cut of her chestnut-colored gown revealed an astonishing acreage of freckled bosom. Freckles were not generally thought to be attractive, but Hugh could hardly take his eyes off them. After a while Maisie felt his stare and returned it. He turned away with an apologetic smile.

He took his mind off her bosom by looking around the group and noting how his old schoolmates had changed in the last seven years. Solly Greenbourne had matured. Although he was still fat, and had the same easygoing grin, he had acquired an air of authority in his middle twenties. Perhaps it came from being so rich—but Edward was rich and he had no such aura. Solly was already respected in the City; and while it was easy to earn respect when you were the heir to Greenbournes Bank, all the same a foolish young man in that position could rapidly become a laughingstock.

Edward had grown older but unlike Solly he had not matured. For him, as for a child, play was everything. He was not stupid, but he found it difficult to concentrate on his work at the bank because he would rather be elsewhere, dancing and drinking and gambling.

Micky had become a handsome devil, with dark eyes and black eyebrows and curly hair grown a little too long. His evening dress was correct but rather dashing: his jacket had a velvet collar and cuffs, and his shirt was frilled. He had already attracted admiring glances and inviting looks from several girls seated at nearby tables, Hugh had noticed. But Maisie Robinson had taken a dislike to him, and Hugh guessed that was not just because of the remark about Jewboys. There was something sinister about Micky. He was unnervingly quiet, watchful and self-contained. He was not frank, he rarely showed hesitation, uncertainty, or vulnerability, and he never revealed anything of his soul—if he had one. Hugh did not trust him.

The next dance ended and Tonio Silva came to the table with Miss April Tilsley. Hugh had run into Tonio several times since school, but even if he had not seen him for years he would have recognized him instantly by the shock of carrot-colored hair. They had been best friends until that awful day in 1866 when Hugh's mother had come to tell him that his father was dead and to take him away from the school. They had been the bad boys of the lower fourth, always getting into scrapes, but they had enjoyed life, despite the floggings.

Hugh had often wondered, over the years, what had really happened that day at the swimming hole. He had never believed the newspaper story about Edward's trying to rescue Peter Middleton: Edward would not have had the courage. But Tonio still would not speak of it, and the only other witness, Albert "Hump" Cammel, had gone to live in the Cape Colony.

Hugh studied Tonio's face as he shook hands with Micky. Tonio still seemed somewhat in awe of Micky. "How are you, Miranda?" he said in a normal voice, but his expression showed a mixture of fear and admiration. It was the attitude a man might have toward a champion prizefighter famous for his quick temper.

Tonio's companion, April, was a little older than her friend Maisie, Hugh judged, and there was a pinched, sharp look about her that made her less attractive; but Tonio was having a great time with her, touching her arm and whispering in her ear and making her laugh.

Hugh turned back to Maisie. She was talkative and vivacious, with a lilting voice that had a trace of the accent of northeast England, where Tobias Pilaster's warehouses had been. Her expression was endlessly fascinating as she smiled, frowned, pouted, wrinkled her turned-up nose and rolled her eyes. She had fair eyelashes, he noticed, and there was a sprinkling of freckles on her nose. She was an unconventional beauty but no one would deny she was the prettiest woman in the room.

Hugh was obsessed by the thought that, since she was here at the Argyll Rooms, she was presumably willing to kiss, cuddle and perhaps even Go All The Way tonight with one of the men around the table. Hugh daydreamed about a sexual encounter with almost every girl he met—he was ashamed of how much and how often he thought about it—but normally it could only happen after courtship, engagement and marriage. Whereas Maisie might do it tonight!

She caught his eye again, and he had that embarrassing feeling that Rachel Bodwin sometimes gave him, that she knew what he was thinking. He searched around desperately for something to say, and finally blurted out: "Have you always lived in London, Miss Robinson?"

"Only for three days," she said.

It might be mundane, he thought, but at least they were talking. "So recently!" he said. "Where were you before?"

"Traveling," she said, and turned away to speak to Solly.

"Ah," Hugh said. That seemed to put an end to the conversation, and he felt disappointed. Maisie acted almost as if she had a grudge against him.

But April took pity on him and explained. "Maisie's been with a circus for four years."

"Heavens! Doing what?"

Maisie turned around again. "Bareback horse-riding," she said. "Standing on the horses, jumping from one to another, all those tricks."

April added: "In tights, of course."

The thought of Maisie in tights was unbearably tantalizing. Hugh crossed his legs
and said: "How did you get into that line of
work?"

She hesitated, then seemed to make up
her mind about something. She turned
around in her chair to face Hugh directly,
and a dangerous glint came into her eyes.
"It was like this," she said. "My father
worked for Tobias Pilaster and Co. Your father cheated my father out of a week's
wages. At that time my mother was sick.
Without that money, either I would starve
or she would die. So I ran away from home.
I was eleven years old at the time."

Hugh felt his face flush. "I don't believe
my father cheated anyone," he said. "And if
you were eleven you can't possibly have understood what happened."

"I understood hunger and cold!"

"Perhaps your father was at fault," Hugh
persisted, though he knew it was unwise.
"He shouldn't have had children if he
couldn't afford to feed them."

"He could feed them!" Maisie blazed.
"He worked like a slave—and then you stole
his money!"

"My father went bankrupt, but he never
stole."

"It's the same thing when you're the loser!"

"It's not the same, and you're foolish and insolent to pretend that it is."

The others obviously felt he had gone too far, and several people began to speak at the same time. Tonio said: "Let's not quarrel about something that happened so long ago."

Hugh knew he should stop but he was still angry. "Ever since I was thirteen years old I've had to listen to the Pilaster family running my father down but I'm not going to take it from a circus performer."

Maisie stood up, her eyes flashing like cut emeralds. For a moment Hugh thought she was going to slap him. Then she said: "Dance with me, Solly. Perhaps your rude friend will have gone when the music stops."

3

HUGH'S QUARREL WITH MAISIE broke up the party. Solly and Maisie went off on their own, and the others decided to go ratting. Ratting was against the law, but there were half a dozen regular pits within five minutes of Piccadilly Circus, and Micky Miranda knew them all.

It was dark when they emerged from the Argyll into the district of London known as Babylon. Here, out of sight of the palaces of Mayfair, but conveniently close to the gentlemen's clubs of St. James's, was a warren of narrow streets dedicated to gambling, blood sports, opium smoking, pornography, and—most of all—prostitution. It was a hot, sweaty night, and the air was heavy with the smells of cooking, beer and drains. Micky and his friends moved slowly down the middle of the crowded street. Within the first minute an old man in a battered top hat offered to sell him a book of lewd verses, a young man with rouge on his cheeks winked at him, a well-dressed woman of his own age opened her jacket quickly and gave him a glimpse of two beautiful bare breasts, and a ragged older woman offered him sex with an angel-faced girl about ten years old. The buildings, mostly pubs, dance halls, brothels and cheap lodging houses, had grimy walls and small, filthy windows through which could occasionally be glimpsed a gas-lit revel. Passing along the street were white-waistcoated swells such as Micky, bowler-hatted clerks and shopkeepers, goggle-eyed farmers, soldiers in unbuttoned uniforms, sailors with their pockets temporarily full of

money, and a surprising number of respect-
able-looking middle-class couples walking
arm-in-arm.

Micky was enjoying himself. It was the
first time in several weeks that he had managed to get away from Papa for an evening.
They were waiting for Seth Pilaster to die so
that they could close the deal for the rifles,
but the old man was clinging to life like a
limpet on a rock. Going to music halls and
brothels was no fun with your father; and
besides, Papa treated him more like a servant, sometimes even telling him to wait
outside while he went with a whore. Tonight
was a blessed relief.

He was glad to have run into Solly Greenbourne again. The Greenbournes were even
richer than the Pilasters, and Solly might
one day be useful.

He was not glad to have seen Tonio Silva.
Tonio knew too much about the death of
Peter Middleton seven years ago. In those
days Tonio had been terrified of Micky. He
was still wary, and he still looked up to
Micky, but that was not the same as being
frightened. Micky was worried about him
but at the moment he did not know what he
could do about it.

He turned off Windmill Street into a narrow alley. The eyes of cats blinked at him from piles of refuse. Checking that the others were in tow, he entered a dingy pub, walked through the bar and out of the back door, crossed a yard where a prostitute was kneeling in front of a client in the moonlight, and opened the door of a ramshackle wooden building like a stable.

A dirty-faced man in a long, greasy coat demanded fourpence as the price of admission. Edward paid and they went in.

The place was brightly lit and full of tobacco smoke, and there was a foul smell of blood and excrement. Forty or fifty men and a few women stood around a circular pit. The men were of all classes, some in the heavy wool suits and spotted neckerchiefs of well-off workers, others in frock coats or evening dress; but the women were all more or less disreputable types like April. Several of the men had dogs with them, carried in their arms or tied to chair legs.

Micky pointed out a bearded man in a tweed cap who held a muzzled dog on a heavy chain. Some of the spectators were examining the dog closely. It was a squat, muscular animal with a big head and a powerful jaw, and it looked angry and restless. "He'll be on next," Micky said.

Edward went off to buy drinks from a woman with a tray. Micky turned to Tonio and addressed him in Spanish. It was bad form to do this in front of Hugh and April, who could not understand; but Hugh was a nobody and April was even less, so it hardly mattered. "What are you doing these days?" he asked.

"I'm an attaché to the Cordovan Minister in London," Tonio replied.

"Really?" Micky was intrigued. Most South American countries saw no point in having an ambassador in London, but Cordova had had an envoy for ten years. No doubt Tonio had got the post of attaché because his family, the Silvas, were well connected in the Cordovan capital, Palma. By contrast Micky's Papa was a provincial baron and had no such strings to pull. "What do you have to do?"

"I answer letters from British firms that want to do business in Cordova. They ask about the climate, the currency, internal transport, hotels, all kinds of things."

"Do you work all day?"

"Not often." Tonio lowered his voice. "Don't tell a soul, but I have to write only two or three letters most days."

"Do they pay you?" Many diplomats were

men of independent means who worked for nothing.

"No. But I have a room at the minister's residence, and all my meals; plus an allowance for clothing. They also pay my subscriptions to clubs."

Micky was fascinated. It was just the kind of job that would have suited him, and he felt envious. Free board and lodging, and the basic expenses of a young man-about-town paid, in return for an hour's work every morning. Micky wondered if there might be some way Tonio could be eased out of the post.

Edward came back with five tots of brandy in small glasses and handed them around. Micky swallowed his at once. It was cheap and fiery.

Suddenly the dog growled and started to run around in frantic circles, pulling on its chain, the hair on its neck standing up. Micky looked around to see two men coming in carrying a cage of huge rats. The rats were even more frenzied than the dog, running over and under one another and squeaking with terror. All the dogs in the room started to bark, and for a while there was a terrific cacophony as the owners yelled at the animals to shut up.

The entrance was locked and barred from the inside, and the man in the greasy coat started to take bets. Hugh Pilaster said: "By Jove, I never saw such big rats. Where do they get them?"

Edward answered him. "They're specially bred for this," he said, and turned away to speak to one of the handlers. "How many this contest?"

"Six dozen," the man replied.

Edward explained: "That means they will put seventy-two rats into the pit."

Tonio said: "How does the betting work?"

"You can bet on the dog or the rats; and if you think the rats will win, you can bet on how many will be left when the dog dies."

The dirty man was calling out odds and taking money in exchange for scraps of paper on which he scribbled numbers with a thick pencil.

Edward put a sovereign on the dog, and Micky bet a shilling on six rats surviving, for which he got odds of five to one. Hugh declined to bet, like the dull stick he was, Micky noticed.

The pit was about four feet deep, and it was surrounded by a wood fence another four feet high. Crude candelabra set at intervals around the fence threw strong light into the hole. The dog was unmuzzled and let into the pit through a wooden gate that was shut tight behind him. He stood stiff-legged, hackles raised, staring up, waiting for the rats. The rat handlers picked up the cage. There was a quiet moment of anticipation.

Suddenly Tonio said: "Ten guineas on the dog."

Micky was surprised. Tonio had talked about his job and its perquisites as if he had to be quite careful how he spent money. Was that a sham? Or was he making bets he could not afford?

The bookmaker hesitated. It was a big bet for him, too. Nevertheless, after a moment he scribbled a slip, handed it over, and pocketed Tonio's money.

The handlers swung the cage back, then forward, as if they were going to throw the whole thing into the pit; then, at the last minute, a hinged flap at one end opened, and the rats were hurled out of the cage and through the air, squealing with terror. April screamed with shock, and Micky laughed.

The dog went to work with lethal concentration. As the rats rained down on him his jaws snapped rhythmically. He would pick one up, break its back with one hard shake of his huge head, and drop it for another.

The smell of blood became nauseating. All the dogs in the room barked madly, and the spectators added to the noise, the women shrieking to see the carnage and the men shouting encouragement to the dog or to the rats. Micky laughed and laughed.

It took a moment for the rats to discover they were trapped in the pit. Some ran around the edge, looking for a way out; others jumped up, trying without success to get a grip on the sheer sides; others formed themselves into a heap. For a few seconds the dog had it all his own way, and killed a dozen or more.

Then the rats turned, all at once, as if they had heard a signal. They began to fly at the dog, biting his legs, his haunches and his short tail. Some got on his back and bit his neck and ears, and one sank its sharp little teeth into his lower lip and clung on, swinging from his lethal jaws, until he howled with rage and slammed it against the ground, and at last it released his bleeding flesh.

The dog kept turning around in dizzying circles and caught rat after rat, killing them all; but there were always more behind him.

Half the rats were dead when he began to tire. The people who had bet on thirty-six, and got long odds, now tore up their slips; but those who had bet on lower numbers cheered louder.

The dog was bleeding from twenty or thirty bites, and the ground became slippery with his blood and the moist corpses of the dead rats. Still he swung his great head; still he cracked their brittle spines in his terrible mouth; but he moved a little less quickly, and his feet were not so sure on the slimy earth. Now, Micky thought, it starts to get interesting.

Sensing the dog's fatigue, the rats became bolder. When he had one in his jaws, another would spring for his throat. They ran between his legs and under his belly and leaped at the soft parts of his hide. One particularly big creature dug its teeth into his hind leg and refused to let go. He turned to snap at it but another rat distracted him by leaping on his snout. Then the leg seemed to give way—the rat must have severed a tendon, Micky thought—and suddenly the dog was limping.

He was much slower to turn now. As if they knew that, the dozen or so remaining rats all attacked his rear end. Wearily he snapped them up in his jaws; wearily he broke their backs; wearily he dropped them on the bloody ground. But his underside was raw flesh, and he could not hold out much longer. Micky thought he might have bet wisely, and there would be six rats left when the dog died.

Then the dog gained a sudden access of energy. Spinning around on three legs he killed another four rats in as many seconds. But it was his last gasp. He dropped a rat and then his legs buckled under him. Once more he turned his head to snap at the creatures, but this time he caught none, and his head drooped.

The rats began to feed.

Micky counted: there were six left.

He looked at his companions. Hugh looked ill. Edward said to him: "A bit strong for your stomach, eh?"

"The dog and the rats are simply behaving as nature intended," Hugh said. "It's the humans who disgust me."

Edward grunted and went to buy more drinks.

April's eyes were sparkling as she looked up at Tonio, a man—she thought—who could afford to lose ten guineas in a bet. Micky looked more closely at Tonio and saw in his face a hint of panic. I don't believe he *can* afford to lose ten guineas, Micky thought.

Micky collected his winnings from the bookmaker: five shillings. He had made a profit on the evening already. But he had a feeling that what he had learned about Tonio could in the end be worth a great deal more.

4

IT WAS MICKY who had most disgusted Hugh. Throughout the contest, Micky had been laughing hysterically. At first Hugh could not think why that laughter sounded so chillingly familiar. Then he remembered Micky's laughing just the same way when Edward threw Peter Middleton's clothes into the swimming hole. It was an unpleasant reminder of a grim memory.

Edward came back with the drinks and said: "Let's go to Nellie's."

They swallowed their tots of brandy and went out. In the street, Tonio and April took their leave and slipped into a building that looked like a cheap hotel. Hugh presumed they were going to take a room for an hour, or perhaps for the night. He wondered whether to go on with Edward and Micky. He was not having a very good time, but he was curious to know what went on at Nellie's. He had decided to try debauchery, so he probably ought to see the evening out, not quit halfway, he thought in the end.

Nellie's was in Princes Street, off Leicester Square. There were two uniformed commissionaires at the door. As the three young men arrived, the commissionaires were turning away a middle-aged man in a bowler hat. "Evening dress only," said one of the commissionaires over the man's protests.

They seemed to know Edward and Micky, for one touched his hat and the other opened the door. They went down a long passage to another door. They were inspected through a peephole, and then the door opened.

It was a bit like walking into a drawing room in a big London house. Fires blazed in two large grates, there were sofas, chairs and small tables everywhere, and the room was full of men and women in evening dress.

However, it only took another moment to see that this was no ordinary drawing room. Most of the men had their hats on. About half of them were smoking—something that was not permitted in polite drawing rooms —and some had their coats off and their ties undone. Most of the women were fully dressed but a few seemed to be in their underwear. Some of them were sitting on men's laps, others were kissing men, and one or two were permitting themselves to be fondled intimately.

For the first time in his life Hugh was in a brothel.

It was noisy, with men shouting jokes, women laughing, and a fiddler somewhere playing a waltz. Hugh followed Micky and Edward as they walked the length of the room. The walls were hung with pictures of naked women and copulating couples, and Hugh began to feel aroused. At the far end, under a huge oil painting of a complex outdoor orgy, sat the fattest person Hugh had ever seen: a vast-bosomed, heavily painted woman in a silk gown like a purple tent. She was sitting on a big regal chair and surrounded by girls. Behind her was a broad, red-carpeted staircase that presumably led up to bedrooms.

Edward and Micky approached the throne and bowed, and Hugh followed suit.

Edward said: "Nell, my pet, allow me to present my cousin, Mr. Hugh Pilaster."

"Welcome, boys," said Nell. "Come and entertain these beautiful girls."

"In a while, Nell. Is there a game to-night?"

"There's always a game at Nellie's," she said, and waved toward a door at one side of the room.

Edward bowed again and said: "We'll be back."

"Don't fail me, boys!"

They moved off. "She acts like royalty!" Hugh murmured.

Edward laughed. "This is the top stew in London. Some of the people who bow to her tonight will be bowing to the Queen in the morning."

They went into the next room, where twelve or fifteen men were sitting around two baccarat tables. Each table had a white line chalked about a foot from its edge, and the players pushed colored counters across the line to place bets. Most of them had drinks beside them, and the air was full of cigar smoke.

There were a few empty chairs at one of the tables, and Edward and Micky immediately sat down. A waiter brought them some counters, and they each signed a receipt. Hugh said quietly to Edward: "What are the stakes?"

"A pound minimum."

It occurred to Hugh that if he played and won he could afford one of the women in the next room. He did not actually have as much as a pound in his pockets, but obviously Edward's credit was good here. . . . Then he remembered Tonio's losing ten guineas at the ratting. "I shan't play," he said.

Micky said languidly: "We never imagined you would."

Hugh felt awkward. He wondered whether to ask a waiter to bring him a drink, then he reflected that it would probably cost him a week's wages. The banker dealt cards from a shoe and Micky and Edward placed bets. Hugh decided to slip away.

He returned to the main drawing room. Looking more closely at the furniture, he could see that it was quite tawdry: there were stains on the velvet upholstery and burn marks on the polished wood, and the carpets were worn and ripped. Beside him a drunk man was on his knees, singing to a whore, while two of his friends laughed uproariously. On the next couch a couple were kissing with their mouths open. Hugh had heard that people did this but he had never seen it. He watched, mesmerized, as the man unbuttoned the front of the woman's dress and started to caress her breasts. They were white and flabby, with big dark-red nipples. The whole scene aroused and revolted Hugh at the same time. Despite his distaste, his prick grew hard. The man on the couch bent his head to the woman's bosom and began to kiss her breasts. Hugh could not believe what he was seeing. The woman looked over the top of the man's head, caught Hugh's eye, and winked.

A voice in Hugh's ear said: "You could do that to me, if you like."

He spun round, feeling as guilty as if he had been caught doing something shameful. Beside him was a dark-haired girl of about his own age, heavily rouged. He could not help glancing down at her bosom. He looked away again quickly, feeling embarrassed.

"Don't be shy," she said. "Look as long as you want. They're for you to enjoy." To his horror he felt her hand on his groin. She found his stiff prick and squeezed it. "My goodness, you are excited," she said. Hugh was suffering exquisite anguish. He felt about to explode. The girl tilted her head up and kissed his lips, rubbing his prick at the same time.

It was too much. Unable to control himself, Hugh ejaculated into his underwear.

The girl felt it. For a moment she just looked surprised, then she burst out laughing. "My God, you are a green one!" she said loudly. Hugh felt humiliated. The girl looked around and said to the nearest whore: "I only touched him, and he creamed himself!" Several people laughed.

Hugh turned away and headed for the exit. The laughter seemed to follow him the length of the room. He had to restrain himself from running. At last he reached the door. A moment later he was out in the street.

The night had cooled a little, and he took a deep breath and paused to calm himself. If this was dissipation, he did not like it. The dollymop Maisie had been rude about his father; the ratting had been revolting; the whores had laughed at him. The whole lot of them could go to the devil.

A commissionaire gave him a sympathetic look. "Decided to have an early night, sir?"

"What a good idea," said Hugh, and he walked away.

*

Micky was losing money. He could cheat at baccarat if he had the bank, but tonight the bank would not come to him. He was secretly relieved when Edward said: "Let's get a couple of girls."

"You go," he said, feigning indifference. "I'll play on."

A gleam of panic showed in Edward's eyes. "It's getting late."

"I'm trying to win back my losses," Micky said stubbornly.

Edward lowered his voice. "I'll pay for your chips."

Micky pretended to hesitate, then give in. "Oh, all right."

Edward smiled.

He settled up and they went into the main room. Almost immediately, a blond girl with large breasts came up to Edward. He put his arm around her bare shoulders, and she pressed her bosom against his chest.

Micky scanned the girls. A slightly older woman with a nicely debauched look caught his eye. He smiled at her and she came over. She put her hand on his shirtfront, dug her nails into his chest, stood on tiptoe and gently bit his lower lip.

He saw Edward watching him, flushed

with excitement. Micky began to feel eager. He looked at his own woman. "What's your name?" he said.

"Alice."

"Let's go upstairs, Alice," he said.

They all went up the stairs together. On the landing was a marble statue of a centaur with a huge erect penis, which Alice rubbed as they went by. Next to it a couple were performing the sexual act standing up, oblivious of a drunk man sitting on the floor watching them.

The women headed for separate rooms, but Edward steered them into the same room. "All together tonight, boys?" said Alice.

"We're saving money," Micky said, and Edward laughed.

"At school together, were you?" she said knowingly, as she closed the door behind them. "Used to frig each other off?"

"Shut up," Micky said, embracing her.

While Micky kissed Alice, Edward came up behind her, put his arms around her, and cupped her breasts. She looked faintly surprised but made no objection. Micky felt Edward's hands moving between his body and the woman's, and he knew that Edward was rubbing himself against her rump.

After a moment the other girl said: "What shall I do? I feel a bit left out."

"Get your drawers off," Edward told her. "You're next."

CHAPTER THREE

1

AS A LITTLE BOY, Hugh had thought Pilasters bank was owned by the walkers. These personages were in fact lowly messengers, but they were all rather portly, and wore immaculate morning dress with silver watch-chains across their ample waistcoats, and they moved about the bank with such ponderous dignity that to a child they appeared the most important people there.

Hugh had been brought here at the age of ten by his grandfather, old Seth's brother. The marble-walled banking hall on the first floor had seemed like a church: huge, gracious, silent, a place where incomprehensible rites were performed by an elite priesthood in the service of a divinity called

Money. Grandfather had shown him all around: the carpeted hush of the third floor, occupied by the partners and their corre-spondence clerks, where little Hugh had been given a glass of sherry and a plate of biscuits in the Partners' Room; the senior clerks at their tables on the fourth floor, be-spectacled and anxious, surrounded by bun-dles of papers tied with ribbon like gifts; and the juniors on the top floor, sitting at their high desks in lines like Hugh's toy soldiers, scratching entries in ledgers with inky fin-gers. But best of all, for Hugh, had been the basement, where contracts even older than grandfather were kept in vaults, thousands of postage stamps waited to be licked, and there was a whole room full of ink stored in enormous glass jars. It had amazed him to reflect on the process. The ink came into the bank, it was spread over the papers by the clerks, and then the papers were re-turned to the basement to be stored forever; and somehow this made money.

The mystery had gone out of it now. He knew that the massive leather-bound led-gers were not arcane texts but simple lists of financial transactions, laboriously compiled and scrupulously updated; and his own fin-gers had become cramped and ink-stained by days of writing in them. A bill of exchange was no longer a magic spell but merely a promise to pay money at a future date, written on a piece of paper and guaranteed by a bank. Discounting, which as a child he had thought must mean counting backwards from a hundred down to one, turned out to be the practice of buying bills of exchange at a little less than their face value, keeping them until their due date, then cashing them at a small profit.

Hugh was a general assistant to Jonas Mulberry, the Principal Clerk. A bald man of about forty, Mulberry was good-hearted but a little sour. He would always take time to explain things to Hugh, but he was very quick to find fault if Hugh was in the least hasty or careless. Hugh had been working under him for the past year, and yesterday he had made a serious mistake. He had lost a bill of lading for a consignment of Bradford cloth destined for New York. The Bradford manufacturer had been downstairs in the banking hall asking for his money, but Mulberry had needed to check the bill before authorizing payment, and Hugh could not find the document. They had been obliged to ask the man to come back in the morning.

In the end Hugh had found the bill, but he had spent most of the night worrying about it, and this morning he had devised a new system of dealing with papers for Mulberry.

On the table in front of him he had two cheap wooden trays, two oblong cards, a quill pen and an inkwell. He wrote slowly and neatly on one card:

For the attention of the Principal Clerk

On the second card he wrote:

Having been dealt with by the Principal
Clerk

He carefully blotted his writing then fixed one card to each tray with tacks. He put the trays on Jonas Mulberry's table and stood back to survey his work. At that moment Mr. Mulberry came in. "Good morning, Mr. Hugh," he said. All family members were addressed this way at the bank because otherwise there would be confusion among all the different Mr. Pilasters.

"Good morning, Mr. Mulberry."

"And what the dickens is this?" Mulberry said tetchily, looking at the trays.

"Well," Hugh began. "I found that bill of lading."

"Where was it?"

"Mixed up with some letters you had signed."

Mulberry narrowed his eyes. "Are you trying to say it was my fault?"

"No," Hugh said quickly. "It's my responsibility to keep your papers in order. That's why I've instituted the tray system—to separate papers you've already dealt with from papers you haven't yet looked at."

Mulberry grunted noncommittally. He hung his bowler hat on the hook behind the door and sat down at the table. Finally he said: "We'll try it—it might be quite effective. But next time, have the courtesy to consult me before implementing your ingenious ideas. This is my room, after all, and I am the Principal Clerk."

"Certainly," Hugh said. "I'm sorry." He knew he should have asked Mulberry's permission, but he had been so keen on his new idea that he had not had the patience to wait.

"The Russian loan issue closed yesterday," Mulberry went on. "I want you to go down to the post room and organize the counting of the applications."

"Right." The bank was raising a loan of two million pounds for the government of Russia. It had issued 100-pound bonds which paid five pounds interest per year; but they were selling the bonds for 93 pounds, so the true interest rate was over five and three-eighths. Most of the bonds had been bought by other banks in London and Paris, but some had been offered to the general public, and now the applications would have to be counted.

"Let's hope we have more applications than we can fulfill," Mulberry said.

"Why?"

"That way the unlucky applicants will try to buy the bonds tomorrow on the open market, and that will drive the price up perhaps to 95 pounds—and all our customers will feel they've bought a bargain."

Hugh nodded. "And what if we have too few applications?"

"Then the bank, as underwriter, has to buy the surplus—at 93 pounds. And tomorrow the price may go down to 92 or 91 pounds, and we will have made a loss."

"I see."

"Off you go."

Hugh left Mulberry's office, which was on the fourth floor, and ran down the stairs. He was happy that Mulberry had accepted his tray idea and relieved that he was not in worse trouble over the lost bill of lading. As he reached the third floor, where the Partners' Room was, he saw Samuel Pilaster, looking dapper in a silver-gray frock coat and a navy-blue satin tie. "Good morning, Uncle Samuel," Hugh said.

"Morning, Hugh. What are you up to?" He showed more interest in Hugh than the other partners did.

"Going to count the applications for the Russian loan."

Samuel smiled, showing his crooked teeth. "I don't know how you can be so cheerful with a day of that in front of you!"

Hugh continued down the stairs. Within the family, people were beginning to talk in hushed tones about Uncle Samuel and his secretary. Hugh did not find it shocking that Samuel was what people called effeminate. Women and vicars might pretend that sex between men was perverted, but it went on all the time at schools such as Windfield and it never did anyone any harm.

He reached the first floor and entered the imposing banking hall. It was only half-past nine, and the dozens of clerks who worked at Pilasters were still streaming through the grand front door, smelling of bacon breakfasts and underground railway trains. Hugh nodded to Miss Greengrass, the only female clerk. A year ago, when she had been hired, debate had raged through the bank as to whether a woman could possibly do the work. In the event she had settled the matter by proving herself supremely competent. There would be more female clerks in the future, Hugh guessed.

He took the back stairs to the basement and made his way to the post room. Two messengers were sorting the mail, and applications for the Russian loan already filled one big sack. Hugh decided he would get two junior clerks to add up the applications, and he would check their arithmetic.

The work took most of the day. It was a few minutes before four o'clock when he double-checked the last bundle and added the last column of figures. The issue was undersubscribed: a little more than one hundred thousand pounds' worth of bonds remained unsold. It was not a big shortfall, as a proportion of a two-million-pound issue, but there was a big psychological difference between oversubscribed and undersubscribed, and the partners would be disappointed.

He wrote the tally on a clean sheet of paper and went in search of Mulberry. The banking hall was quiet now. A few customers stood at the long polished counter. Behind the counter, clerks lifted the big ledgers on and off the shelves. Pilasters did not have many private accounts. It was a merchant bank, lending money to traders to finance their ventures. As old Seth would say, the Pilasters weren't interested in counting the greasy pennies of a grocer's takings or the grubby banknotes of a tailor—there was not enough profit in it. But all the family kept accounts at the bank, and the facility was extended to a small number of very rich clients. Hugh spotted one of them now: Sir John Cammel. Hugh had known his son at Windfield. A thin man with a bald head, Sir John earned vast incomes from coal mines and docks on his lands in Yorkshire. Now he was pacing the marble floor looking impatient and bad-tempered. Hugh said: "Good afternoon, Sir John, I hope you're being attended to?"

"No, I'm not, lad. Doesn't anyone do any work in this place?"

Hugh glanced around rapidly. None of the partners or senior clerks was in sight. He decided to use his initiative. "Will you come upstairs to the Partners' Room, sir? I know they will be keen to see you."

"All right."

Hugh led him upstairs. The partners all worked together in the same room—so that they could keep an eye on one another, according to tradition. The room was furnished like the reading room in a gentlemen's club, with leather sofas, bookcases and a central table with newspapers. In framed portraits on the walls, ancestral Pilasters looked down their beaklike noses at their descendants.

The room was empty. "One of them will be back in a moment, I'm sure," Hugh said. "May I offer you a glass of Madeira?" He went to the sideboard and poured a generous measure while Sir John settled himself in a leather armchair. "I'm Hugh Pilaster, by the way."

"Oh, yes?" Sir John was somewhat mollified to find he was talking to a Pilaster, rather than an ordinary office boy. "Did you go to Windfield?"

"Yes, sir. I was there with your son Albert. We called him Hump."

"All Cammels are called Hump."

"I haven't seen him since . . . since then."

"He went to the Cape Colony, and liked it there so much that he never came back. He raises horses now."

Albert Cammel had been at the swimming hole on that fateful day in 1866. Hugh had never heard his version of how Peter Middleton drowned. "I'd like to write to him," Hugh said.

"I daresay he'll be glad of a letter from an old school friend. I'll give you his address." Sir John moved to the table, dipped a quill in the inkwell and scribbled on a sheet of paper. "There you are."

"Thank you." Sir John was mollified now, Hugh noted with satisfaction. "Is there anything else I can do for you while you're waiting?"

"Well, perhaps you can deal with this." He took a cheque out of his pocket. Hugh examined it. It was for a hundred and ten thousand pounds, the largest personal cheque Hugh had ever handled. "I've just sold a coal mine to my neighbor," Sir John explained.

"I can certainly deposit it for you."

"What interest will I get?"

"Four percent, at present."

"That'll do, I suppose."

Hugh hesitated. It occurred to him that if Sir John could be persuaded to buy Russian bonds, the loan issue could be transformed from being slightly undersubscribed to slightly oversubscribed. Should he mention it? He had already overstepped his authority by bringing a guest into the Partners' Room. He decided to take chance. "You could get five and three-eighths by buying Russian bonds."

Sir John narrowed his eyes. "Could I, now?"

"Yes. The subscription closed yesterday, but for you—"

"Are they safe?"

"As safe as the Russian government."

"I'll think about it."

Hugh's enthusiasm had been aroused now and he wanted to close the sale. "The rate may not be the same tomorrow, as you know. When the bonds come on the open market the price may go up or down." Then he decided he was sounding too eager, so he backed off. "I'll place this cheque to your account immediately, and if you wish you could talk to one of my uncles about the bonds."

"All right, young Pilaster—off you go."

Hugh went out and met Uncle Samuel in the hall. "Sir John Cammel is in there, Uncle," he said. "I found him in the banking hall looking bad-tempered, so I've given him a glass of Madeira—I hope I did the right thing."

"I'm sure you did," said Samuel. "I'll take care of him."

"He brought in this cheque for a hundred and ten thousand. I mentioned the Russian loan—it's undersubscribed by a hundred thousand."

Samuel raised his eyebrows. "That was precocious of you."

"I only said he might talk to one of the partners about it if he wanted a higher rate of interest."

"All right. It's not a bad idea."

Hugh returned to the banking hall, pulled out Sir John's ledger and entered the deposit, then took the cheque to the clearing clerk. Then he went up to the fourth floor to Mulberry's office. He handed over the tally of Russian bonds, mentioned the possibility that Sir John Cammel might buy the balance, and sat down at his own table.

A walker came in with tea and bread and butter on a tray. This light refreshment was served to all clerks who stayed at the office after four-thirty. When work was light most people left at four. Bank staff were the elite among clerks, much envied by merchants' and shippers' clerks, who often worked until late and sometimes right through the night.

A little later Samuel came in and handed some papers to Mulberry. "Sir John bought the bonds," he said to Hugh. "Good work— that was an opportunity well taken."

"Thank you."

Samuel spotted the labeled trays on Mulberry's desk. "What's this?" he said in a tone of amusement. " 'For the attention of the Principal Clerk . . . Having been dealt with by the Principal Clerk.' "

Mulberry answered him. "The purpose is to keep incoming and outgoing papers separate. It avoids confusion."

"What a good scheme. I think I might do the same."

"As a matter of fact, Mr. Samuel, it was young Mr. Hugh's idea."

Samuel turned an amused look on Hugh. "I say, you are keen, dear boy."

Hugh was sometimes told he was too cocky, so now he pretended to be humble. "I know I've got an awful lot to learn still."

"Now, now, no false modesty. Tell me something. If you were to be released from Mr. Mulberry's service, what job would you like to do next?"

Hugh did not have to think about his an-

swer. The most coveted job was that of correspondence clerk. Most clerks saw only a
part of a transaction—the part they re-
corded—but the correspondence clerk,
drafting letters to clients, saw the whole
deal. It was the best position in which to
learn, and the best from which to win promotion. And Uncle Samuel's correspondence clerk, Bill Rose, was due to retire.

Without hesitation Hugh said: "I'd like to
be your correspondence clerk."

"Would you, now? After only a year in
the bank?"

"By the time Mr. Rose goes it will be
eighteen months."

"So it will." Samuel still seemed amused,
but he had not said no. "We'll see, we'll
see," he said, and he went out.

Mulberry said to Hugh: "Did you advise
Sir John Cammel to buy the surplus Russian
bonds?"

"I just mentioned it," said Hugh.

"Well, well," said Mulberry. "Well, well."
And he sat staring at Hugh speculatively for
several minutes thereafter.

2

IT WAS A SUNNY SUNDAY AFTERNOON, and all London was out for a stroll in their best Sunday-go-to-meeting clothes. The wide avenue of Piccadilly was free from traffic, for only an invalid would drive on the Sabbath. Maisie Robinson and April Tilsley were strolling down Piccadilly, looking at the palaces of the rich and trying to pick up men.

They lived in Soho, sharing a single room in a slum house in Carnaby Street, near the St. James's Workhouse. They would get up around midday, dress carefully, and go out on the streets. By evening they had generally found a couple of men to pay for their dinner: if not, they went hungry. They had almost no money but they needed little. When the rent was due April would ask a boyfriend for a "loan." Maisie always wore the same clothes and washed her underwear every night. One of these days someone would buy her a new gown. Sooner or later, she hoped, one of the men who bought her dinner would either want to marry her or set her up as his mistress.

April was still excited about the South American she had met, Tonio Silva. "Just think, he can afford to lose ten guineas on a bet!" she said. "And I've always liked red hair."

"I didn't like the other South American, the dark one," Maisie said.

"Micky? He was gorgeous."

"Yes, but there was something sly about him, I thought."

April pointed to a huge mansion. "That's Solly's father's house."

It was set back from the road, with a semicircular drive in front. It looked like a Greek temple, with a row of pillars across the front that reached all the way up to the roof. Brass gleamed on the big front door and there were red velvet curtains at the windows.

April said: "Just think, you could be living there one day."

Maisie shook her head. "Not me."

"It's been done before," April said. "You just have to be more randy than upper-class girls, and that's not difficult. Once you're married, you can learn to imitate the accent and all that in no time. You speak nice already, except when you get cross. And Solly's a nice boy."

"A nice fat boy," Maisie said with a grimace.

"But so rich! People say his father keeps a

symphony orchestra at his country house just in case he wants to hear some music after dinner!"

Maisie sighed. She did not want to think about Solly. "Where did the rest of you go, after I shouted at that boy Hugh?"

"Ratting. Then me and Tonio went to Batt's Hotel."

"Did you do it with him?"

"Of course! Why do you think we went to Batt's?"

"To play whist?"

They giggled.

April looked suspicious. "You did it with Solly, though, didn't you?"

"I made him happy," Maisie said.

"What does that mean?"

Maisie made a gesture with her hand, and they both giggled again.

April said: "You only frigged him off? Why?"

Maisie shrugged.

"Well, perhaps you're right," April said. "Sometimes it's best not to let them have it all first time. If you lead them on a bit it can make them more keen."

Maisie changed the subject. "It brought back bad memories, meeting people called Pilaster," she said.

April nodded. "Bosses, I hate their fucking guts," she said with sudden venom.
April's language was even more earthy than
what Maisie had been used to in the circus.
"I'll never work for one. That's why I do
this. I set my own price and get paid in advance."

"My brother and me left home the day
Tobias Pilaster went bankrupt," Maisie said.
She smiled ruefully. "You could say it's be-
cause of the Pilasters that I'm here today."

"What did you do after you left? Did you
join the circus straightaway?"

"No." Maisie felt a tug at her heart as she
remembered how frightened and lonely she
had been. "My brother stowed away on a
ship going to Boston. I've not seen him or
heard from him since. I slept at a rubbish tip
for a week. Thank God the weather was
mild—it was May. It only rained one night: I
covered myself with rags and had fleas for
years afterwards. . . . I remember the funeral."

"Whose?"

"Tobias Pilaster's. The procession went
through the streets. He'd been a big man in
the town. I remember a little lad, not much
older than me, wearing a black coat and a

top hat, holding his mam's hand. It must have been Hugh."

"Fancy that," said April.

"After that I walked to Newcastle. I dressed as a lad and worked at a stables, helping out. They let me sleep in the straw at night, alongside the horses. I stayed there three years."

"Why did you leave?"

"I grew these," Maisie said, and jiggled her breasts. A middle-aged man walking by saw her, and his eyes nearly popped out. "When the head stablehand found out I was a lass he tried to rape me. I smacked him across the face with a riding crop, and that was the end of the job."

"I hope you cut him," April said.

"I certainly cooled his ardor."

"You should have whacked his thing."

"He might have liked it."

"Where did you go when you left the stable?"

"That's when I joined the circus. I started as a stablehand and eventually became one of the riders." She sighed nostalgically. "I liked the circus. The people are warm."

"Too warm, I gather."

Maisie nodded. "I never really got on with the ringmaster, and when he told me to gam him it was time to leave. I decided that if I'm going to suck cocks for a living I want a better wage. And here I am." She always picked up speech mannerisms and she had adopted April's unrestrained vocabulary.

April gave her a shrewd look. "Just how many cocks have you sucked since then?"

"None, to tell the truth." Maisie felt embarrassed. "I can't lie to you, April—I'm not sure I'm cut out for this trade."

"You're perfect for it!" April protested. "You've got that twinkle in your eye that men can't resist. Listen. Persist with Solly Greenbourne. Give him a bit more each time. Let him feel your pussy one day, let him see you naked the next. . . . In about three weeks he'll be panting for it. One night when you've got his trousers down and his tool in your mouth, say: 'If you bought me a little house in Chelsea, we could do this any time you wanted to.' I swear to you, Maisie, if Solly says no to that, I'll become a nun."

Maisie knew she was right, but her soul revolted against it. She was not sure why. It was partly because she was not attracted to Solly. Paradoxically, another reason was that he was so nice. She could not bring herself to manipulate him heartlessly. But worst of all, she felt she would be giving up all hope of real love—a real marriage with a man she really burned for. On the other hand, she had to live somehow, and she was determined not to live like her parents, waiting all week for a pittance on payday and forever at risk of unemployment because of some financial crisis hundreds of miles away.

April said: "What about one of the others? You could have had your pick of them."

"I liked Hugh, but I offended him."

"He's got no money, anyway."

"Edward's a pig, Micky frightens me, and Tonio is yours."

"Solly's your man, then."

"I don't know."

"I do. If you let him slip through your fingers, you'll spend the rest of your life walking down Piccadilly and thinking 'I could be living in that house now.'"

"Yes, I probably will."

"And if not Solly, who? You could end up with a nasty little middle-aged grocer who keeps you short of money and expects you to launder your own sheets."

Maisie brooded on that prospect as they came to the western end of Piccadilly and turned north into Mayfair. She probably could make Solly marry her if she put her mind to it. And she would be able to play the part of a grand lady without too much difficulty. Speech was half the battle and she had always been a good mimic. But the thought of trapping kind Solly into a loveless marriage sickened her.

Cutting through a mews, they passed a big livery stable. Maisie felt nostalgic for the circus, and stopped to pet a tall chestnut stallion. The horse immediately nuzzled her hand. A man's voice said: "Redboy don't generally allow strangers to touch him."

Maisie turned around to see a middle-aged man in a black morning coat with a yellow waistcoat. His formal clothes clashed with his weatherbeaten face and uneducated speech, and she guessed he was a former stablehand who had started his own business and done well. She smiled and said: "He's doesn't mind me, do you, Redboy?"

"I don't suppose you could ride him, now, could you?"

"Ride him? Yes, I could ride him, without a saddle, and stand upright on his back, too. Is he yours?"

The man made a small bow and said: "George Sammles, at your service, ladies;

proprietor, as it says there." He pointed to where his name was painted over the door.

Maisie said: "I shouldn't boast, Mr. Sammles, but I've spent the last four years in a circus, so I can probably ride anything you have in your stables."

"Is that a fact?" he said thoughtfully. "Well, well."

April put in: "What's on your mind, Mr. Sammles?"

He hesitated. "This may seem a mite sudden, but I was asking myself whether this lady might be interested in a business proposition."

Maisie wondered what was coming next. Until this moment she had thought the conversation was no more than idle banter. "Go on."

April said suggestively: "We're always interested in business propositions." But Maisie had a feeling Sammles was not after what April had in mind.

"You see, Redboy's for sale," the man began. "But you don't sell horses by keeping them indoors. Whereas, if you was to ride him around the park for an hour or so, a lady such as yourself, looking, if I may be so bold, as pretty as a pitcher, you'd attract a deal of attention, and chances are that sooner or later someone would ask you how much you wanted for the horse."

Was there money in this, Maisie wondered? Did it offer her a way of paying the rent without selling her body or her soul? But she did not ask the question that was on her mind. Instead she said: "And then I'd tell the person: 'Away and see Mr. Sammles in the Curzon Mews, for the nag's his.' Is that what you mean?"

"Exackly so, except that, rather than call Redboy a nag, you might term him 'this magnificent creature,' or 'this fine specimen of horseflesh,' or such."

"Maybe," said Maisie, thinking to herself that she would use her own words, not Sammles's. "Now then, to business." She could no longer pretend to be casual about the money. "How much would you pay?"

"What do you think it's worth?"

Maisie picked a ridiculous sum. "A pound a day."

"Too much," he said promptly. "I'll give you half that."

She could hardly believe her luck. Ten shillings a day was an enormous wage: girls of her age who worked as housemaids were lucky to get a shilling a day. Her heart beat faster. "Done," she said quickly, afraid he might change his mind. "When do I start?"

"Come tomorrow at half-past ten."

"I'll be here."

They shook hands and the girls moved off. Sammles called after her: "Mind you wear the dress you've got on today—it's fetching."

"Have no fear," Maisie said. It was the only one she had. But she did not tell Sammles that.

3

TRAFFIC IN THE PARK

TO THE EDITOR OF *THE TIMES*

Sir,—There has been noted in Hyde Park, in recent days, at about half-past eleven o'clock each morning, a jamb of carriages, so large, that there has been no getting forward for up to an hour. Numerous explanations have been suggested; as, that too many Country residents come up to Town for the Season; or, that the prosperity of London is now such that even trades-men's wives keep carriages and drive in the Park; but the real truth has no-where been mentioned. The fault lies with a lady, whose name is unknown, but whom men term "The Lioness," doubtless on account of the tawny colour of her hair; a charming creature, beautifully dressed, who rides, with ease and spirit, horses that would daunt many males; and drives, with equal facility, a carriage, drawn by perfectly matched pairs. The fame of her beauty and equestrian daring is such that all London migrates to the Park at the hour when she is expected; and, once there, finds it cannot move. Could not you, sir, whose business it is to know everything and everyone, and who possibly, therefore, may know the true identity of The Lioness, prevail upon her to desist, so that the Park may return to its normal state of quiet decorum and ease of passage?

I am, Sir, your obedient servant,

AN OBSERVER.

The letter had to be a joke, Hugh thought as he put down the newspaper. The Lioness was real enough—he had heard the clerks at the bank talking about her—but she was not the cause of carriage congestion. All the same he was intrigued. He gazed through

the leaded windows of Whitehaven House
to the park. Today was a holiday. The sun
was shining and there were already lots of
people walking, riding and driving carriages.
Hugh thought he might just go to the park
in the hope of seeing what the fuss was all
about.

Aunt Augusta was also planning to go
into the park. Her barouche was drawn up
in front of the house. The coachman was
wearing his wig and the liveried footman
was ready to ride behind. She drove in the
park at this time most mornings, as did all
upper-class women and idle men. They said
they did it for fresh air and exercise, but
more importantly it was a place to see and
be seen. The real cause of congestion was
people stopping their carriages to gossip,
and blocking the road.

Hugh heard his aunt's voice. He got up
from the breakfast table and went into the
hall. As usual, Aunt Augusta was beautifully
dressed. Today she wore a purple day gown
with a tight jacket bodice and yards of ruf-
fles below. The hat was a mistake, though: it
was a miniature straw boater, no more than
three inches across, perched on top of her
coiffure at the front. It was the latest fashion, and on pretty girls it was sweet; but Au-

gusta was anything but sweet, and on her it
was ludicrous. She did not often make such
errors, but when she did it was usually because she was following fashion too faith-
fully.

She was talking to Uncle Joseph. He had
the harassed air he often wore when Augusta was talking to him. He stood in front
of her, half turning away, stroking his bushy
side-whiskers impatiently. Hugh wondered
whether there was any affection between
them. There must have been at one time, he
supposed, for they had conceived Edward
and Clementine. They rarely showed fond-
ness, but every now and again, Hugh reflected, Augusta would do something
thoughtful for Joseph. Yes, he thought they
probably still loved each other.

Augusta carried on speaking as if Hugh
were not there, which was her usual way.
"The whole family is worried," she was saying insistently, as if Uncle Joseph had suggested the opposite. "There could be a scandal."

"But the situation—whatever it may be—
has been going on for years, and no one has
ever thought it scandalous."

"Because Samuel is not the Senior Partner. An ordinary person can do many things

without attracting notice. But the Senior Partner of Pilasters Bank is a public figure."

"Well, the matter may not be urgent. Uncle Seth is still alive and shows every sign of hanging on indefinitely."

"I know," Augusta said, and there was a telling note of frustration in her voice. "I sometimes wish. . . ." She stopped before revealing herself too much. "Sooner or later he will hand over the reins. It could happen tomorrow. Cousin Samuel cannot pretend there is nothing to worry about."

"Perhaps," said Joseph. "But if he does so pretend, I'm not sure what can be done."

"Seth may have to be told about the problem."

Hugh wondered how much old Seth knew about his son's life. In his heart he probably knew the truth, but perhaps he never admitted it, even to himself.

Joseph looked uneasy. "Heaven forbid."

"It would certainly be unfortunate," Augusta said with brisk hypocrisy. "But you must make Samuel understand that unless he gives way his father will have to be brought in, and if that happens Seth must have all the facts."

Hugh could not help admiring her cunning and ruthlessness. She was sending

Samuel a message: Give up your secretary or we'll force your father to confront the reality that his son is more or less married to a man.

In truth she did not care a straw about Samuel and his secretary. She just wanted to make it impossible for him to become Senior Partner—so that the mantle would fall on her husband. It was pretty low, and Hugh wondered whether Joseph fully understood what Augusta was doing.

Now Joseph said uneasily: "I should like to resolve matters without such drastic action."

Augusta lowered her voice to an intimate murmur. When she did this, Hugh always thought, she was transparently insincere, like a dragon trying to purr. "I'm quite sure you'll find a way to do just that," she said. She smiled beseechingly. "Will you drive with me today? I should so like your company."

He shook his head. "I must go to the bank."

"What a shame, to be shut up in a dusty office on a beautiful day like this."

"There has been a panic in Bologna."

Hugh was intrigued. Since the Vienna "Krach" there had been several bank failures and company liquidations in different parts of Europe, but this was the first "panic." London had escaped damage, so far. In June the bank rate, the thermometer of the financial world, had risen to seven percent—not quite fever level—and it had already dropped back to six percent. However, there might be some excitement today

Augusta said: "I trust the panic won't affect us."

"So long as we take care, no," said Joseph.

"But it's a holiday today—there will be no one at the bank to make your tea!"

"I daresay I shall survive half a day without tea."

"I'll send Sara to you in an hour. She's made a cherry cake, your favorite—she shall bring you some, and make your tea."

Hugh saw an opportunity. "Shall I come with you, Uncle? You may want a clerk."

Joseph shook his head. "I shan't need you."

Augusta said: "You may want him to run errands, my dear."

Hugh said with a grin: "Or he may want to ask my advice."

Joseph did not appreciate the joke. "I shall just read the telegraph messages and decide what is to be done when the markets open again tomorrow morning."

Foolishly, Hugh persisted. "I should like to come, all the same—just out of interest."

It was always a mistake to badger Joseph. "I tell you I don't need you," he said irritably. "Drive in the park with your aunt, she needs an escort." He put his hat on his head and went out.

Augusta said: "You have a talent for needlessly annoying people, Hugh. Get your hat, I'm ready to go."

Hugh did not really want to drive with Augusta, but his uncle had commanded him to do so, and he was curious to see the Lioness, so he did not argue.

Augusta's daughter Clementine appeared, dressed to go out. Hugh had played with his cousin when they were children, and she had always been a telltale. At the age of seven she had asked Hugh to show her his doodle, and then told her mother what he had done, and Hugh had been thrashed. Now twenty years old, Clementine looked like her mother, but where Augusta was overbearing, Clementine was sly.

They all went out. The footman handed them up into the carriage. It was a new vehicle, painted bright blue and drawn by a superb pair of gray geldings—an equipage fit for the wife of a great banker. Augusta and Clementine sat facing forward, and Hugh settled himself opposite them. The top was down because of the brilliant sunshine, but the ladies opened their parasols. The coachman flicked his whip and they set off.

A few moments later they were on South Carriage Drive. It was as crowded as the writer of the letter to *The Times* had claimed. There were hundreds of horses ridden by top-hatted men and sidesaddle women; dozens of carriages of every type— open and closed, two-wheel and four-wheel; plus children on ponies, couples on foot, nurses with baby carriages and people with dogs. The carriages gleamed with new paint, the horses were brushed and combed, the men wore full morning dress and the women sported all the bright colors that the new chemical dyes could produce. Everyone moved slowly, the better to scrutinize horses and carriages, dresses and hats. Augusta talked to her daughter, and the conversation required no contribution from Hugh other than the occasional indication of agreement.

"There's Lady St. Ann in a Dolly Varden hat!" Clementine exclaimed.

"They went out of fashion a year ago," said Augusta.

"Well, well," said Hugh.

Another carriage pulled alongside, and Hugh saw his aunt Madeleine Hartshorn. If she had whiskers she'd look just like her brother Joseph, he thought. She was Augusta's closest crony within the family. Together they controlled the social life of the family. Augusta was the driving force, but Madeleine was her faithful acolyte.

Both carriages stopped, and the ladies exchanged greetings. They were obstructing the road, and two or three carriages pulled up behind them. Augusta said: "Take a turn with us, Madeleine, I want to talk to you." Madeleine's footman helped her down from her own carriage and into Augusta's and they drove off again.

"They're threatening to tell old Seth about Samuel's secretary," Augusta said.

"Oh, no!" said Madeleine. "They mustn't!"

"I've spoken to Joseph, but they won't be stopped," Augusta went on. Her tone of sincere concern took Hugh's breath away. How did she manage it? Perhaps she convinced herself that the truth was whatever it suited her to say at any moment.

"I shall speak to George," said Madeleine. "The shock could kill dear Uncle Seth."

Hugh toyed with the idea of reporting this conversation to his uncle Joseph. Surely, he thought, Joseph would be appalled to know how he and the other partners were being manipulated by their wives? But they would not believe Hugh. He was a nobody—and that was why Augusta did not care what she said in front of him.

Their carriage slowed almost to a halt. There was a knot of horses and vehicles up ahead. Augusta said irritably: "What's the cause of this?"

"It must be the Lioness," Clementine said excitedly.

Hugh scanned the crowd eagerly but could not see what was causing the holdup. There were several carriages of different kinds, nine or ten horses and some pedestrians.

Augusta said: "What's this about a lioness?"

"Oh, Mother, she's notorious!"

As Augusta's carriage drew nearer, a smart little victoria emerged from the ruck, pulled by a pair of high-stepping ponies and driven by a woman.

"It *is* the Lioness!" Clementine squealed.

Hugh looked at the woman driving the victoria and was astonished to recognize her.

It was Maisie Robinson.

She cracked a whip and the ponies picked up speed. She was wearing a brown merino costume with flounces of silk, and a mushroom-colored tie with a bow at her throat. On her head was a perky little top hat with a curly brim.

Hugh felt angry with her all over again for what she had said about his father. She knew nothing about finance and she had no right to accuse people of dishonesty in that casual way. But all the same he could not help thinking that she looked absolutely ravishing. There was something irresistibly charming about the set of that small, neat body in the driving seat, the tilt of the hat, even the way she held the whip and shook the reins.

So the Lioness was Maisie Robinson! But how come she suddenly had horses and carriages? Had she come into money? What was she up to?

While Hugh was still marveling, there was an accident.

A nervous thoroughbred trotted past Augusta's carriage and was startled by a small, noisy terrier. It reared up and the rider fell off into the road—right in front of Maisie's victoria.

Quickly she changed direction, showing impressive control of her vehicle, and pulled across the road. Her evasive action took her right in front of Augusta's horses, causing the coachman to haul on his reins and let out an oath.

She brought her carriage to an abrupt stop alongside. Everyone looked at the thrown rider. He appeared unhurt. He got to his feet unaided, dusted himself down, and walked off, cursing, to catch his horse.

Maisie recognized Hugh. "Hugh Pilaster, I do declare!" she cried.

Hugh blushed. "Good morning," he said, and had no idea what to do next.

He had made a serious error of etiquette. He ought not to have acknowledged Maisie while he was with his aunts, for he could not possibly introduce such a person to them. He should have snubbed her.

However, Maisie made no attempt to address the ladies. "How do you like these ponies?" she said. She seemed to have forgotten their quarrel.

Hugh was completely thrown by this

beautiful, surprising woman, her skillful driving and her careless manners. "They're very fine," he said without looking at them.

"They're for sale."

Aunt Augusta said icily: "Hugh, kindly tell this *person* to let us pass!"

Maisie looked at Augusta for the first time. "Shut your gob, you old bitch," she said casually.

Clementine gasped and Aunt Madeleine gave a small scream of horror. Hugh's mouth dropped open. Maisie's gorgeous clothes and expensive equipage had made it easy to forget that she was an urchin from the slums. Her words were so splendidly vulgar that for a moment Augusta was too stunned to reply. Nobody ever dared to speak to her this way.

Maisie did not give her time to recover. Turning back to Hugh, she said: "Tell your cousin Edward he should buy my ponies!" Then she cracked her whip and drove away.

Augusta erupted. "How dare you expose me to such a person!" She boiled. "How dare you take off your hat to her!"

Hugh was staring after Maisie, watching her neat back and jaunty hat recede along the drive.

Aunt Madeleine joined in. "How can you

possibly know her, Hugh?" she said. "No well-bred young man would be acquainted with that type! And it seems you have even introduced her to Edward!"

It was Edward who had introduced Maisie to Hugh, but Hugh was not going to try to put the blame on Edward. They would not have believed him anyway. "I don't actually know her very well," he said.

Clementine was intrigued. "Where on earth did you meet her?"

"A place called the Argyll Rooms."

Augusta frowned at Clementine and said: "I don't wish to know such things. Hugh, tell Baxter to drive home."

Hugh said: "I'm going to walk for a while." He opened the door of the carriage.

"You're going after that woman!" Augusta said. "I forbid it!"

"Drive on, Baxter," said Hugh as he stepped down. The coachman shook the reins, the wheels turned, and Hugh politely doffed his hat as his angry aunts were driven away.

He had not heard the last of this. There would be more trouble later. Uncle Joseph would be told, and soon all the partners would know that Hugh consorted with low women.

But it was a holiday, the sun was shining, and the park was full of people enjoying themselves, and Hugh could not get worried about his aunt's rage today.

He felt lighthearted as he strode along the path. He headed in the direction opposite to that Maisie had taken. People drove around in circles, so he might run into her again.

He was keen to talk to her more. He wanted to set her straight about his father. Oddly enough he no longer felt angry with her about what she had said. She was simply mistaken, he thought, and she would understand if it was explained to her. Anyway, just talking to her was exciting.

He reached Hyde Park Corner and turned north along Park Lane. He doffed his hat to numerous relations and acquaintances: Young William and Beatrice in a brougham, Uncle Samuel on a chestnut mare, Mr. Mulberry with his wife and children. Maisie might have stopped on the far side, or she might have left by now. He began to feel that he would not see her again.

But he did.

She was just leaving, crossing Park Lane. It was undoubtedly her, with that mush-

room-colored silk tie at her throat. She did
not see him.

On impulse he followed her across the
road, into Mayfair, and down a mews, running to keep up with her. She pulled the
victoria up to a stable and jumped down. A
groom came out and began to help her with
the horses.

Hugh came up beside her, breathing
hard. He wondered why he had done this.
"Hello, Miss Robinson," he said.

"Hello again!"

"I followed you," he said superfluously.

She gave him a frank look. "Why?"

Without thinking he blurted out: "I was
wondering if you would go out with me one
night."

She put her head to one side and frowned
slightly, considering his proposal. Her expression was friendly, as if she liked the
idea, and he thought she would accept. But
it seemed some practical consideration was
at war with her inclinations. She looked
away from him, and a little frown appeared
on her brow; then she appeared to make up
her mind. "You can't afford me," she said
decisively; and she turned her back on him
and walked into the stable.

4

Cammel Farm
Cape Colony
South Africa
14th July 1873

Dear Hugh,

Jolly nice to hear from you! One is rather isolated out here, and you can't imagine the pleasure we get out of a long, newsy letter from home. Mrs. Cammel, who used to be the Hon. Amelia Clapham until she married me, was especially amused by your account of the Lioness. . . .

It's a bit late to say this, I know, but I was dreadfully shocked by the death of your father. Schoolboys don't write condolence notes. And your own tragedy was somewhat eclipsed by the drowning of Peter Middleton on the very same day. But believe me, many of us thought of you and talked about you after you were so abruptly taken away from school. . . .

I'm glad you asked me about Peter. I have felt guilty ever since that day. I didn't actually see the poor chap die, but I saw enough to guess the rest.

Your cousin Edward was, as you so colourfully put it, more rotten than a dead cat. You managed to get most of your clothes out of the water and scarper, but Peter and Tonio weren't so quick.

I was over the other side, and I don't think Edward and Micky even noticed me. Or perhaps they didn't recognise me. At any rate they never spoke to me about the incident.

Anyway, after you had gone Edward proceeded to torment Peter even more, pushing his head under the water and splashing his face while the poor boy struggled to retrieve his clothes.

I could see it was getting out of hand but I was a complete coward, I'm afraid. I should have gone to Peter's aid but I was not much bigger myself, certainly no match for Edward and Micky Miranda, and I didn't want my clothes soaked as well. Do you remember the punishment for breaking bounds? It was twelve strokes of the Striper, and I don't mind admitting I was more frightened of that than anything else. Anyway, I grabbed my clothes and sneaked away without attracting any attention.

I looked back once, from the lip of the quarry. I don't know what had happened in the meantime, but Tonio was scrambling up the side, naked and clutching a bundle of wet clothes, and Edward was swimming across the pool after him, leaving Peter gasping and spluttering in the middle.

I thought Peter would be all right, but obviously I was wrong. He must have been at the end of his tether. While Edward was chasing Tonio, and Micky was watching, Peter drowned without anyone's noticing.

I didn't know that until later, of course. I got back to school and slipped into my dorm. When the masters started asking questions, I swore I had been there all afternoon. As the ghastly story began to emerge I never had the guts to admit that I had seen what happened.

Not a tale to be proud of, Hugh. But telling the truth at last has made me feel a bit better, at any rate. . . .

Hugh put down Albert Cammel's letter and stared out of his bedroom window. The letter explained both more and less than Cammel imagined.

It explained how Micky Miranda had insinuated himself into the Pilaster family to such an extent that he spent every vacation with Edward and had all his expenses paid by Edward's parents. No doubt Micky had told Augusta that Edward had virtually killed Peter. But in court Micky said Edward had tried to rescue the drowning boy. And in telling that lie Micky had saved the Pilasters from public disgrace. Augusta would have been powerfully grateful—and perhaps, also, fearful that Micky might one day turn against them and reveal the truth. It gave Hugh a cold, rather scared feeling in the pit of his stomach. Albert Cammel, all unknowing, had revealed that Augusta's relationship with Micky was deep, dark and corrupt.

But another puzzle remained. For Hugh knew something about Peter Middleton that almost no one else was aware of. Peter had been something of a weakling, and all the boys treated him as a weed. Embarrassed about his weakness, he had embarked on a training program—and his main exercise was swimming. He stroked across that pool hour after hour, trying to build his physique. It had not worked: a thirteen-year-old boy could not become broad-shouldered and deep-chested except by growing into a man, and that was a process that could not be hurried.

The only effect of all his efforts was to make him like a fish in the water. He could dive to the bottom, hold his breath for several minutes, float on his back, and keep his eyes open underwater. It would have taken more than Edward Pilaster to drown him.

So why had he died?

Albert Cammel had told the truth, as far as he knew it, Hugh was sure. But there had to be more. Something else had happened on that hot afternoon in Bishop's Wood. A poor swimmer might have been killed accidentally, drowned because Edward's rough-housing was too much for him to take. But casual horseplay could not have killed Peter. And if his death was not accidental, it was deliberate.

And that was murder.

Hugh shuddered.

There had been only three people there:

Edward, Micky and Peter. Peter must have been murdered by Edward or Micky.

Or both.

5

AUGUSTA WAS ALREADY DISSATISFIED with her Japanese decor. The drawing room was full of oriental screens, angular furniture on spindly legs, and Japanese fans and vases in black lacquered cabinets. It was all very expensive, but cheap copies were already appearing in the Oxford Street stores, and the look was no longer exclusive to the very best houses. Unfortunately, Joseph would not permit redecoration so soon, and Augusta would have to live with increasingly common furniture for several years.

The drawing room was where Augusta held court at teatime every weekday. The women usually came first: her sisters-in-law Madeleine and Beatrice, and her daughter Clementine. The partners would arrive from the bank at about five: Joseph, old Seth, Madeleine's husband George Hartshorn, and occasionally Samuel. If business was quiet the boys would come too: Edward, Hugh and Young William. The only non-member of the family who was a regular teatime guest was Micky Miranda, but occasionally there would be a visiting Methodist clergyman, perhaps a missionary seeking funds to convert the heathens in the South Seas, Malaya, or the newly opened-up Japan.

Augusta worked hard to keep people coming. All the Pilasters liked sweet things, and she provided delicious buns and cakes as well as the very best tea from Assam and Ceylon. Big events such as family holidays and weddings would be planned during these sessions, so anyone who stopped coming would soon lose touch with what was going on.

Despite all that, every now and again one of them would go through a phase of wanting to be independent. The most recent example had been Young William's wife Beatrice, a year or so before, after Augusta had been rather insistent about a dress fabric Beatrice had chosen that did not suit her. When this happened Augusta would leave them for a while, then win them back with some extravagantly generous gesture. In Beatrice's case Augusta had thrown an expensive birthday party for Beatrice's old mother, who was virtually senile and only barely presentable in public. Beatrice had been so grateful that she had forgotten all about the dress fabric—just as Augusta had intended.

Here at these teatime gatherings Augusta found out what was going on in the family and at the bank. Right now she was anxious about old Seth. She was carefully working the family around to the idea that Samuel could not be the next Senior Partner, but Seth showed no inclination to retire, despite his failing health. She found it maddening to have her careful plans held up by the stubborn tenacity of an old man.

It was the end of July, and London was becoming quieter. The aristocracy moved out of town at this time of year, on their way to yachts at Cowes or shooting-boxes in Scotland. They would stay in the country, slaughtering birds, hunting foxes and stalking deer, until after Christmas. Between February and Easter they would start to drift back, and by May the London "season" would be in full swing.

The Pilaster family did not follow this routine. Although richer by far than most of the aristocracy, they were businesspeople, and had no thought of spending half the year idly persecuting dumb animals in the countryside. However, the partners could generally be persuaded to holiday for most of the month of August, provided there was no undue excitement in the banking world.

This year the holiday had been in doubt all summer, as a distant storm had rumbled threateningly across the financial capitals of Europe; but the worst seemed to be over, the bank rate was down to three percent, and Augusta had rented a small castle in Scotland. She and Madeleine planned to leave in a week or so, and the men would follow a day or two later.

A few minutes before four o'clock, as she was standing in the drawing room feeling discontented with her furniture and old Seth's obstinacy, Samuel walked in.

All the Pilasters were ugly, but Samuel was the worst, she thought. He had the big nose, but he also had a weak, womanish mouth and irregular teeth. He was a fussy man, immaculately dressed, fastidious about his food, a lover of cats and a hater of dogs.

But what made Augusta dislike him was that of all the men in the family he was the most difficult to persuade. She could charm old Seth, who was susceptible to an attractive woman even at his advanced age; she could generally get around Joseph by wearing down his patience; George Hartshorn was under Madeleine's thumb and so could be manipulated indirectly; and the others were young enough to be intimidated, although Hugh sometimes gave her trouble.

Nothing worked on Samuel—least of all her feminine charms. He had an infuriating way of laughing at her when she thought she was being subtle and clever. He gave the impression that she was not to be taken seriously—and that offended her mortally. She was much more wounded by Samuel's quiet mockery than she was at being called an old bitch by a trollop in the park.

Today, however, Samuel did not wear that amused, skeptical smile. He looked angry, so angry that for a moment Augusta was alarmed. He had obviously come early in order to find her alone. It struck her that for two months she had been conspiring to ruin him and that people had been murdered for less than that. He did not shake her hand, but stood in front of her, wearing a pearl-gray morning coat and a deep wine-red tie, smelling faintly of cologne. Augusta held up her hands in a defensive gesture.

Samuel gave a humorless laugh and moved away. "I'm not going to strike you, Augusta," he said. "Though heaven knows you deserve a whipping."

Of course he would not touch her. He was a gentle soul who refused to finance the export of rifles. Augusta's confidence came back in a rush, and she said disdainfully: "How dare you criticize me!"

"Criticize?" he said, and the rage flashed again in his eyes. "I don't stoop to criticize you." He paused, then spoke again in a voice of controlled anger. "I despise you."

Augusta could not be intimidated a second time. "Have you come here to tell me that you are willing to give up your vicious ways?" she said in a ringing voice.

"My vicious ways," he repeated. "You're willing to destroy my father's happiness and make my own life miserable, all for the sake of your ambition, and yet you can talk about *my* vicious ways! I believe you're so steeped in evil that you've forgotten what it is."

He was so convinced and passionate that Augusta wondered if perhaps it really was wicked of her to threaten him. Then she realized he was trying to weaken her resolve by playing on her sympathy. "I'm only concerned for the bank," she said coldly.

"Is that your excuse? Is that what you'll tell the Almighty, on the Day of Judgment, when he asks you why you blackmailed me?"

"I'm doing my duty." Now that she felt in control again she began to wonder why he had come here. Was it to concede defeat—or to defy her? If he gave in she could rest assured that soon she would be the wife of the Senior Partner. But the alternative made her want to bite her nails. If he defied her there was a long, difficult struggle ahead, with no certainty of the outcome.

Samuel went to the window and looked out at the garden. "I remember you as a pretty little girl," he said meditatively. Augusta grunted impatiently. "You used to come to church in a white dress with white ribbons in your hair," he went on. "The ribbons didn't fool anyone. You were a tyrant even then. Everyone used to walk in the park after the service, and the other children were scared of you, but they played with you because you organized the games. You even terrorized your parents. If you didn't get what you wanted you could throw a tantrum so noisy that people would stop their carriages to see what was going on. Your father, God rest his soul, had the haunted look of a man who cannot understand how he has brought such a monster into the world."

What he was saying was close to the truth

and it made her uncomfortable. "That all happened years ago," she said, looking away.

He went on as if she had not spoken. "It's not for myself that I'm worried. I'd like to be Senior Partner, but I can live without it. I'd be a good one—not as dynamic as my father, perhaps; more of a teamworker. But Joseph isn't up to the job. He's bad-tempered and impulsive, and he makes poor decisions; and you make it worse, by inflaming his ambition and clouding his vision. He's all right in a group, where others can guide him and restrain him. But he can't be the leader, his judgment isn't good enough. He'll harm the bank, in the long run. Don't you care about that?"

For a moment Augusta wondered if he was right. Was she in danger of killing the goose that laid the golden eggs? But there was so much money in the bank that they could never spend it all even if none of them ever did another day's work. Anyway, it was ridiculous to say that Joseph would be bad for the bank. There was nothing very difficult about what the partners did: they went into the bank, read the financial pages of the newspapers, loaned people money and collected the interest. Joseph could do that as well as any of them. "You men always pretend that banking is complex and mysterious," she said. "But you don't fool me." She realized that she was being defensive. "I'll justify myself to God, not to you," she said.

"Would you really go to my father, as you have threatened?" Samuel said. "You know it could kill him."

She hesitated only for an instant. "There is no alternative," she said firmly.

He stared at her for a long time. "You devil, I believe you," he said.

Augusta held her breath. Would he give in? She felt that victory was almost in her grasp, and in her imagination she heard someone say respectfully, *Allow me to present Mrs. Joseph Pilaster—the wife of the Senior Partner of Pilasters Bank. . . .*

He hesitated, then spoke with obvious distaste. "Very well. I shall tell the others that I don't wish to become Senior Partner when my father retires."

Augusta repressed a smile of triumph. She had won. She turned away to conceal her elation.

"Enjoy your victory," Samuel said bitterly. "But remember, Augusta, that we all have secrets—even you. One day someone will use your secrets against you this way, and you'll remember what you did to me."

Augusta was mystified. What was he referring to? For no reason at all the thought of Micky Miranda came into her mind, but she pushed it aside. "I have no secrets to be ashamed of," she said.

"Don't you?"

"No!" she said, but his confidence worried her.

He gave her a peculiar look. "A young lawyer called David Middleton came to see me yesterday."

For a moment she did not understand. "Should I know him?" The name was disturbingly familiar.

"You met him once, seven years ago, at an inquest."

Suddenly Augusta felt cold. Middleton: that had been the name of the boy who drowned.

Samuel said: "David Middleton believes that his brother Peter was killed—by Edward."

Augusta wanted desperately to sit down, but she refused to give Samuel the satisfaction of seeing her rattled. "Why on earth is he trying to make trouble now, after seven years?"

"He told me he was never satisfied with the inquest, but he remained silent for fear of causing his parents even more distress. However, his mother died soon after Peter, and his father died this year."

"Why did he approach you—not me?"

"He belongs to my club. Anyway, he has re-read the inquest records and he says that there were several eyewitnesses who were never called to give evidence."

There certainly were, Augusta thought anxiously. There was mischievous Hugh Pilaster; a South American boy called Tony or something; and a third person who had never been identified. If David Middleton got hold of one of them the whole story might come out.

Samuel was looking thoughtful. "From your point of view it was a pity the coroner made those remarks about Edward's heroism. That made people suspicious. They would have believed that Edward stood on the edge dithering while a boy drowned. But everyone who's ever met him knows he wouldn't cross the street to help someone, let alone dive into a pool to rescue a drowning boy."

This sort of talk was complete rubbish, and insulting too. "How dare you," Augusta said, but she could not muster her usual tone of authority.

Samuel ignored her. "The schoolboys never believed it. David had been to the same school not many years earlier and he knew many of the older boys. Talking to them increased his suspicions."

"The whole idea is absurd."

"Middleton is a quarrelsome individual, like all lawyers," Samuel said, heedless of her protests. "He's not going to let this rest."

"He doesn't frighten me in the least."

"That's good, because I'm sure you'll be receiving a visit from him soon." He went to the door. "I won't stay for tea. Good afternoon, Augusta."

Augusta sat down heavily on a sofa. She had not foreseen this—how could she? Her triumph over Samuel was blighted. That old business had come up again, seven years later, when it ought to have been completely forgotten! She was dreadfully frightened for Edward. She could not bear anything bad to happen to him. She held her head to stop it throbbing. What could she do?

Hastead, her butler, came in, followed by two parlormaids with trays of tea and cakes. "With your permission, madam?" he said in his Welsh accent. Hastead's eyes seemed to look in different directions and people were never quite sure which one to concentrate on. At first this was disconcerting, but Augusta was used to him. She nodded. "Thank you, madam," he said, and they began to set out the china. Augusta could sometimes be soothed by Hastead's obsequious manner and the sight of servants doing her bidding; but today it did not work. She got up and went to the open French doors. The sunny garden did nothing for her either. How was she going to stop David Middleton?

She was still agonizing over the problem when Micky Miranda arrived.

She was glad to see him. He looked as fetching as always, in his black morning coat and striped trousers, a spotless white collar around his neck, a black satin tie knotted at his throat. He saw that she was distressed and he was instantly sympathetic. He came across the room with the grace and speed of a jungle cat, and his voice was like a caress: "Mrs. Pilaster, what on earth has upset you?"

She was grateful that he was the first to come. She grabbed him by the arms. "Something frightful has happened."

His hands rested on her waist, as if they

were dancing, and she felt a shiver of plea-
sure as his fingertips pressed her hips.
"Don't be distressed," he said soothingly.
"Tell me about it."

She began to feel calmer. At moments
like these she was very fond of Micky. It
reminded her of how she had felt about the
young earl of Strang, when she was a girl.
Micky reminded her powerfully of Strang:
his graceful manners, his beautiful clothes,
and most of all the way he moved, the sup-
pleness of his limbs and the oiled machinery
of his body. Strang had been fair and English, where Micky was dark and Latin, but
they both had that ability to make her feel
so feminine. She wanted to draw his body to
hers and rest her cheek on his shoulder. . . .

She saw the maids staring at her, and realized that it was mildly indecent for Micky
to stand there with both hands on her hips.
She detached herself from him, took his arm
and led him through the French windows
into the garden, where they would be out of
earshot of the servants. The air was warm
and balmy. They sat close together on a
wooden bench in the shade, and Augusta
turned sideways to look at him. She longed

to hold his hand but that would have been improper.

He said: "I saw Samuel leaving—has he got something to do with this?"

Augusta spoke quietly, and Micky leaned close to hear her, so close she could have kissed him almost without moving. "He came to tell me he will not seek the position of Senior Partner."

"Good news!"

"Yes. It means that the post will certainly go to my husband."

"And Papa can have his rifles."

"As soon as Seth retires."

"It's maddening the way old Seth hangs on!" Micky exclaimed. "Papa keeps asking me when it will happen."

Augusta knew why Micky was so worried: he was afraid his father would send him back to Cordova. "I can't imagine Seth will last much longer," she said to comfort him.

He looked into her eyes. "But that's not what has upset you."

"No. It's that wretched boy who drowned at your school—Peter Middleton. Samuel told me that Peter's brother, a lawyer, has started asking questions."

Micky's fine face darkened. "After all these years?"

"Apparently he kept quiet for his parents' sake, but now they're dead."

Micky frowned. "How much of a problem is this?"

"You may know better than I." Augusta hesitated. There was a question she had to ask, but she was afraid of the answer. She screwed up her nerve. "Micky . . . do you think it was Edward's fault the boy died?"

"Well. . . ."

"Say yes or no!" she commanded.

Micky paused, then at last said: "Yes."

Augusta closed her eyes. Darling Teddy, she thought, why did you do it?

Micky said quietly: "Peter was a poor swimmer. Edward didn't drown him, but he did exhaust him. Peter was alive when Edward left him to chase after Tonio. But I believe he was too weak to swim to the side, and he drowned while no one was watching."

"Teddy didn't want to kill him."

"Of course not."

"It was just schoolboy horseplay."

"Edward meant no real harm."

"So it's not murder."

"I'm afraid it is," Micky said gravely, and Augusta's heart missed a beat. "If a thief throws a man to the ground, intending only to rob him, but the man suffers a heart attack and dies, the thief is guilty of murder, even though he did not intend to kill."

"How do you know this?"

"I checked with a lawyer, years ago."

"Why?"

"I wanted to know Edward's position."

Augusta buried her face in her hands. It was worse than she had imagined.

Micky prised her hands away from her face and kissed each hand in turn. The gesture was so tender that it made her want to cry. He continued to hold her hands as he said: "No sensible person would persecute Edward over something that happened when he was a child."

"But is David Middleton a sensible person?" Augusta cried.

"Perhaps not. He appears to have nursed his obsession through the years. God forbid that his persistence should lead him to the truth."

Augusta shuddered as she imagined the consequences. There would be a scandal; the gutter press would say SHAMEFUL SECRET OF BANKING HEIR; the police would be brought in; poor dear Teddy might have to go on trial; and if he should be found guilty—

"Micky, it's too awful to contemplate!" she whispered.

"Then we must do something."

Augusta squeezed his hands, then released them and took stock. She had faced the magnitude of the problem. She had seen the shadow of the gallows fall on her only son. It was time to stop agonizing and take action. Thank God, Edward had a true friend in Micky. "We must make sure David Middleton's inquiries lead nowhere. How many people know the truth?"

"Six," Micky said immediately. "Edward, you and me make three, but we aren't going to tell him anything. Then there is Hugh."

"He wasn't there when the boy died."

"No, but he saw enough to know that the story we told the coroner was false. And the fact that we lied makes us look guilty."

"Hugh is a problem, then. The others?"

"Tonio Silva saw it all."

"He never said anything at the time."

"He was too frightened of me then. But I'm not sure he is now."

"And the sixth?"

"We never found out who that was. I didn't see his face at the time, and he has never come forward. I'm afraid there's nothing we can do about him. However, if nobody knows who he is I don't suppose he's any danger to us."

Augusta felt a fresh tremor of fear: she was not sure about that. There was always a danger the unknown witness might reveal himself. But Micky was right to say there was nothing they could do. "Two people we can deal with, then: Hugh and Tonio."

There was a thoughtful silence.

Hugh could no longer be regarded as a minor nuisance, Augusta reflected. His pushy ways were gaining him credit at the bank, and Teddy looked plodding by comparison. Augusta had managed to sabotage the romance between Hugh and Lady Florence Stalworthy. But now Hugh was threatening Teddy in a much more dangerous way. Something had to be done about him. But what? He was a Pilaster, albeit a bad one. She racked her brains and came up with nothing.

Micky said thoughtfully: "Tonio has a weakness."

"Ah, yes?"

"He's a bad gambler. Bets more than he can afford, and loses."

"Perhaps you could arrange a game?"

"Perhaps."

The thought crossed Augusta's mind that

Micky might know how to cheat at cards. However, she could not possibly ask him: the suggestion would be mortally insulting to any gentleman.

Micky said: "It might be expensive. Would you stake me?"

"How much would you need?"

"A hundred pounds, I fear."

Augusta did not hesitate: Teddy's life was at stake. "Very well," she said. She heard voices in the house: other teatime guests were beginning to arrive. She stood up. "I'm not sure how to deal with Hugh," she went on worriedly. "I'll have to think about it. We must go inside."

Her sister-in-law Madeleine was there, and began talking as soon as they stepped through the door. "That dressmaker will drive me to drink, two hours to pin a hem, I can't wait for a cup of tea, oh, and you've got more of that heavenly almond cake, but my goodness, isn't the weather hot?"

Augusta gave Micky's hand a conspiratorial squeeze and sat down to pour the tea.

CHAPTER FOUR

1

LONDON WAS HOT AND STICKY, and the popula-
tion longed for fresh air and open fields. On
the first day of August everyone went to the
races at Goodwood.

They traveled by special trains from Victoria Station in south London. The divisions
of British society were carefully mirrored in
the transport arrangements—high society in
the upholstered luxury of the first-class
coaches, shopkeepers and schoolteachers
crowded but comfortable in second class,
factory workers and domestic servants
crammed together on hard wooden benches
in third. When they got off the train the aristocracy took carriages, the middle class
boarded horse buses, and the workers

walked. The picnics of the rich had been
sent by earlier trains: scores of hampers,
carried on the shoulders of strapping young
footmen, packed with china and linen,
cooked chickens and cucumbers, champagne and hothouse peaches. For the less
wealthy there were stalls selling sausages,
shellfish and beer. The poor brought bread
and cheese wrapped in handkerchiefs.

Maisie Robinson and April Tilsley went
with Solly Greenbourne and Tonio Silva.
Their position in the social hierarchy was
dubious. Solly and Tonio clearly belonged in
first class, but Maisie and April should have
gone third. Solly compromised by buying
second-class tickets, and they took the horse
bus from the station across the downs to the
racecourse.

However, Solly was too fond of his food
to settle for a lunch bought off a stall, and
he had sent four servants ahead with a vast
picnic of cold salmon and white wine
packed in ice. They spread a snow-white ta-
blecloth on the ground and sat around it on
the springy turf. Maisie fed Solly titbits. She
was growing more and more fond of him.
He was kind to everyone, full of fun, and
interesting to talk to. Gluttony was his only
real vice. She still had not let him have his

way with her, but it seemed that the more she refused him, the more devoted to her he became.

The racing began after lunch. There was a bookmaker nearby, standing on a box and shouting odds. He wore a loud checked suit, a flowing silk tie, a huge spray of flowers in his buttonhole, and a white hat. He carried a leather satchel full of money slung over his shoulder and stood under a banner which read: "Wm. Tucker, the King's Head, Chichester."

Tonio and Solly bet on every race. Maisie got bored: one horse race was the same as another if you didn't gamble. April would not leave Tonio's side, but Maisie decided to leave the others for a while and look around.

The horses were not the only attraction. The downs around the racecourse were crowded with tents, stalls and carts. There were gambling booths, freak shows, and dark-skinned gypsies in bright head scarves telling fortunes. People were selling gin, cider, meat pies, oranges and Bibles. Barrel organs and bands competed with one another, and through the crowds wandered conjurers and jugglers and acrobats, all asking for pennies. There were dancing dogs, dwarfs and giants and men on stilts. The boisterous carnival atmosphere reminded Maisie powerfully of the circus, and she suffered a nostalgic twinge of regret for the life she had left behind. The entertainers were here to take money from the public any way they could and it warmed her heart to see them succeed.

She knew she should be taking more from Solly. It was crazy to be walking out with one of the richest men in the world and living in one room in Soho. By now she ought to be wearing diamonds and furs and have her eye on a little suburban house in St. John's Wood or Clapham. Her job riding Sammles's horses would not last much longer: the London season was coming to an end and the people who could afford to buy horses were leaving for the country. But she would not let Solly give her anything but flowers. It drove April mad.

She passed a big marquee. Outside were two girls dressed as bookmakers and a man in a black suit shouting: "The only racing certainty at Goodwood today is the coming Day of Judgment! Stake your faith on Jesus, and the payout is eternal life." The interior of the tent looked cool and shady, and on impulse she went in. Most of the people sitting on the benches looked as if they were already converted. Maisie sat near the exit and picked up a hymnbook.

She could understand why people joined chapels and went preaching at race meetings. It made them feel they belonged to something. The feeling of belonging was the real temptation Solly offered her: not so much the diamonds and furs, but the prospect of being Solly Greenbourne's mistress, with somewhere to live and a regular income and a position in the scheme of things. It was not a respectable position, nor permanent—the arrangement would end the moment Solly got bored with her—but it was a lot more than she had now.

The congregation stood up to sing a hymn. It was all about being washed in the blood of the Lamb, and it made Maisie feel ill. She went out.

She passed a puppet show as it was reaching its climax, with the irascible Mr. Punch being knocked from one side of the little stage to the other by his club-wielding wife. She studied the crowd with a knowledgeable eye. There was not much money in a Punch-and-Judy show if it was operated honestly: most of the audience would slip away without paying anything and the rest would give halfpennies. But there were other ways to fleece the customers. After a few moments she spotted a boy at the back robbing a man in a top hat. Everyone but Maisie was watching the show, and no one else saw the small grubby hand sliding into the man's waistcoat pocket.

Maisie had no intention of doing anything about it. Wealthy and careless young men deserved to lose their pocket watches, and bold thieves earned their loot, in her opinion. But when she looked more closely at the victim she recognized the black hair and blue eyes of Hugh Pilaster. She recalled April's telling her that Hugh had no money. He could not afford to lose his watch. She decided on impulse to save him from his own carelessness.

She made her way quickly around to the back of the crowd. The pickpocket was a ragged sandy-haired boy of about eleven years, just the age Maisie had been when she ran away from home. He was delicately drawing Hugh's watch chain out of his waistcoat. There was a burst of uproarious laughter from the audience watching the show, and at that moment the pickpocket edged away with the watch in his hand.

Maisie grabbed him by the wrist.

He gave a small cry of fear and tried to wriggle free, but she was too strong for him. "Give it to me and I'll say nothing," she hissed.

He hesitated for a moment. Maisie saw fear and greed at war on his dirty face. Then a kind of weary resignation took over, and he dropped the watch on the ground.

"Away and steal someone else's watch," she said. She released his hand and he was gone in a twinkling.

She picked up the watch. It was a gold hunter. She opened the front and checked the time: ten past three. On the back of the watch was inscribed:

> *Tobias Pilaster*
> *from your loving wife*
> *Lydia*
> *23rd May 1851*

The watch had been a gift from Hugh's mother to his father. Maisie was glad she had rescued it. She closed the face and tapped Hugh on the shoulder.

He turned around, annoyed at being distracted from the entertainment; then his bright blue eyes widened in surprise. "Miss Robinson!"

"What's the time?" she said.

He reached automatically for his watch and found his pocket empty. "That's funny . . ." He looked around as if he might have dropped it. "I do hope I haven't—"

She held it up.

"By Jove!" he said. "How on earth did you find it?"

"I saw you being robbed, and rescued it."

"Where's the thief?"

"I let him go. He was only a wee lad."

"But . . ." He was nonplussed.

"I'd have let him take the watch, only I know you can't afford to buy another."

"You don't really mean that."

"I do. I used to steal, when I was a child, any time I could get away with it."

"How dreadful."

Maisie found herself once again becoming annoyed by him. To her way of thinking there was something sanctimonious in his attitude. She said: "I remember your father's funeral. It was a cold day, and raining. Your father died owing my father money— yet you had a coat that day, and I had none. Was that honest?"

"I don't know," he said with sudden anger. "I was thirteen years old when my father went bankrupt—does that mean I have to turn a blind eye to villainy all my life?"

Maisie was taken aback. It was not often that men snapped at her, and this was the second time Hugh had done it. But she did not want to quarrel with him again. She touched his arm. "I'm sorry," she said. "I didn't mean to criticize your father. I just wanted you to understand why a child might steal."

He softened immediately. "And I haven't thanked you for saving my watch. It was my mother's wedding gift to my father, so it's more precious than its price."

"And the child will find another fool to rob."

He laughed. "I've never met anyone like you!" he said. "Would you like to have a glass of beer? It's so hot."

It was just what she felt like. "Yes, please."

A few yards off there was a heavy four-wheeled cart loaded with huge barrels. Hugh bought two pottery tankards of warm, malty ale. Maisie took a long draught: she had been thirsty. It tasted better than Solly's French wine. Fixed to the cart was a sign chalked in rough capital letters saying WALK

OFF WITH A POT AND IT WILL BE BROKE OVER YOUR HED.

A meditative look came over Hugh's usually lively face, and after a while he said: "Do you realize we were both victims of the same catastrophe?"

She did not. "What do you mean?"

"There was a financial crisis in 1866. When that happens, perfectly honest companies fail . . . like when one horse in a team falls and drags the others down with it. My father's business collapsed because people owed him money and didn't pay; and he was so distraught that he took his own life, and left my mother a widow and me fatherless at the age of thirteen. Your father couldn't feed you because people owed him money and couldn't pay, and you ran away at the age of eleven."

Maisie saw the logic of what he was saying, but her heart would not let her agree: she had hated Tobias Pilaster for too long. "It's not the same," she protested. "Workingmen have no control over these things— they just do what they're told. Bosses have the power. It's their fault if things go wrong."

Hugh looked thoughtful. "I don't know, perhaps you're right. Bosses certainly take the lion's share of the rewards. But I'm sure of one thing, at least: bosses or workers, their children aren't to blame."

Maisie smiled. "It's hard to believe we've found something to agree about."

They finished their drinks, returned the pots and walked a few yards to a merry-go-round with wooden horses. "Do you want a ride?" said Hugh.

Maisie smiled. "No."

"Are you here on your own?"

"No, I'm with . . . friends." For some reason she did not want him to know she had been brought here by Solly. "And you? Are you with your awful aunt?"

He grimaced. "No. Methodists don't approve of race meetings—she'd be horrified if she knew I was here."

"Is she fond of you?"

"Not in the least."

"Then why does she let you live with her?"

"She likes to keep people in sight, so she can control them."

"Does she control you?"

"She tries." He grinned. "Sometimes I escape."

"It must be hard, living with her."

"I can't afford to live on my own. I have

to be patient and work hard at the bank. Eventually I'll get promoted and then I'll be independent." He grinned again. "And then I'll tell her to shut her gob like you did."

"I hope you didn't get into trouble."

"I did, but it was worth it to see the expression on her face. That was when I started to like you."

"Is that why you asked me to dine with you?"

"Yes. Why did you refuse?"

"Because April told me you haven't a penny to your name."

"I've enough for a couple of chops and a plum pudding."

"How could a girl resist that?" she said mockingly.

He laughed. "Come out with me tonight. We'll go to Cremorne Gardens and dance."

She was tempted, but she thought of Solly and felt guilty. "No, thank you."

"Why not?"

She asked herself the same question. She was not in love with Solly and she was taking no money from him: why was she saving herself for him? I'm eighteen years old, she thought, and if I can't go out dancing with a boy I like, what's the point in living? "All right, then."

"You'll come?"

"Aye."

He grinned. She had made him happy. "Shall I fetch you?"

She did not want him to see the Soho slum where she shared a room with April. "No, let's meet somewhere."

"All right—we'll go to Westminster Pier and take the steamer to Chelsea."

"Yes!" She felt more excited than she had for months. "What time?"

"Eight o'clock?"

She made a rapid calculation. Solly and Tonio would want to stay until the last race. Then they had to get the train back to London. She would say good-bye to Solly at Victoria Station and walk to Westminster. She thought she could make it. "But if I'm late, you'll wait?"

"All night, if necessary."

Thinking of Solly made her feel guilty. "I'd better get back to my friends now."

"I'll walk with you," he said eagerly.

She did not want that. "Best you don't."

"As you wish."

She put out her hand and they shook. It seemed oddly formal. "Until tonight," she said.

"I'll be there."

She turned and walked away, feeling that he was watching her. Now why did I do that? she thought. Do I want to go out with him? Do I really like him? The first time we met we had a quarrel that broke up the party, and today he was ready to squabble again if I hadn't smoothed it over. We really don't get on. We'll never be able to dance together. Perhaps I won't go.

But he's got lovely blue eyes.

She made up her mind not to think about it anymore. She had agreed to meet him and she would. She might enjoy it or she might not, but fretting beforehand would not help.

She would have to invent a reason for leaving Solly. He was expecting to take her out to dinner. However, he never questioned her—he would accept any excuse, no matter how implausible. All the same she would try to think of something convincing, for it made her feel bad to abuse his easygoing nature.

She found the others where she had left them. They had spent the whole afternoon between the rail and the bookmaker in the checked suit. April and Tonio were looking bright-eyed and triumphant. As soon as April saw Maisie she said: "We've won a hundred and ten pounds—isn't it wonderful?"

Maisie was happy for April. It was such a lot of money to get for nothing. As she was congratulating them, Micky Miranda appeared, strolling along with his thumbs in the pockets of his dove-gray waistcoat. She was not surprised to see him: everyone went to Goodwood.

Although Micky was startlingly good-looking, Maisie disliked him. He reminded her of the circus ringmaster, who had thought all women should be thrilled to be propositioned by him, and was highly affronted when one turned him down. Micky had Edward Pilaster in tow, as always. Maisie was curious about their relationship. They were so different: Micky slim, immaculate, confident; Edward big, clumsy, hoggish. Why were they so inseparable? But most people were enchanted by Micky. Tonio regarded him with a kind of nervous veneration, like a puppy with a cruel master.

Behind them were an older man and a young woman. Micky introduced the man as his father. Maisie studied him with interest. He did not resemble Micky at all. He was a short man with bowed legs, very broad shoulders and a weatherbeaten face. Unlike his son he did not look comfortable in a stiff collar and a top hat. The woman was clinging to him like a lover but she had to be younger than him by thirty years. Micky introduced her as Miss Cox.

They all talked about their winnings. Both Edward and Tonio had made a lot on a horse called Prince Charlie. Solly had won money then lost it again, and seemed to enjoy both equally. Micky did not say how he had fared, and Maisie guessed he had not bet as much as the others: he seemed too careful a person, too calculating, to be a heavy gambler.

However, with his next breath he surprised her. He said to Solly: "We're going to have a heavyweight game tonight, Greenbourne—a pound minimum. Will you join in?"

She was struck by the thought that Micky's languid posture was covering up considerable tension. He was a deep one.

Solly would go along with anything. "I'll join in," he said.

Micky turned to Tonio. "Would you care to join us?" His take-it-or-leave-it tone sounded false to Maisie.

"Count on me," Tonio said excitedly. "I'll be there!"

April looked troubled and said: "Tonio, not tonight—you promised me." Maisie suspected that Tonio could not afford to play when the minimum stake was a pound.

"What did I promise?" he said with a wink at his friends.

She whispered something in his ear, and the men all laughed.

Micky said: "It's be the last big game of the season, Silva. You'll be sorry if you miss it."

That surprised Maisie. At the Argyll Rooms she had got the impression that Micky disliked Tonio. Why was he now trying to talk Tonio into joining the card game?

Tonio said: "I'm lucky today—look how much I've won on the horses! I shall play cards tonight."

Micky glanced at Edward, and Maisie caught a look of relief in their eyes. Edward said: "Shall we all dine together at the club?"

Solly looked at Maisie, and she realized she had been provided with a ready-made excuse for not spending the evening with him. "Dine with the boys, Solly," she said. "I don't mind."

"Are you sure?"

"Yes. I've had a lovely day. You spend the evening at your club."

"That's settled, then," said Micky.

He and his father, Miss Cox and Edward took their leave.

Tonio and April went to place a bet on the next race. Solly offered Maisie his arm and said: "Shall we walk for a while?"

They strolled along the white-painted rail that bounded the track. The sun was warm and the country air smelled good. After a while Solly said: "Do you like me, Maisie?"

She stopped, stood on tiptoe, and kissed his cheek. "I like you a lot."

He looked into her eyes, and she was mystified to see tears behind his spectacles. "Solly, dear, what is it?" she said.

"I like you, too," he said. "More than anyone I've ever met."

"Thank you." She was touched. It was unusual for Solly to show any emotion stronger than mild enthusiasm.

Then he said: "Will you marry me?"

She was flabbergasted. This was the last thing in the world she had expected. Men of Solly's class did not propose to girls like her. They seduced them, gave them money, kept them as mistresses, and had children by them, but they did not marry them. She was too astounded to speak.

Solly went on: "I'd give you anything you want. Please say yes."

Marriage to Solly! Maisie would be unbelievably rich for ever and ever. A soft bed every night, a blazing fire in every room of the house, and as much butter as she could eat. She would get up when she pleased, not when she had to. She would never be cold again, never hungry, never shabbily dressed, never weary.

The word "yes" trembled on the tip of her tongue.

She thought of April's tiny room in Soho, with its nest of mice in the wall; she thought of how the privy stank on warm days; she thought of the nights they went without dinner; she thought of how her feet ached after a day of walking the streets.

She looked at Solly. How hard could it be, to marry this man?

He said: "I love you so much, I'm just desperate for you."

He really did love her, she could tell.

And that was the trouble.

She did not love him.

He deserved better. He deserved a wife who really loved him, not a hard-hearted guttersnipe on the make. If she married him she would be cheating him. And he was too good for that.

She felt close to tears. She said: "You're the kindest, most gentle man I've ever met—"

"Don't say no, please?" he interrupted. "If you can't say yes, say nothing. Think about it, at least for a day, perhaps longer."

Maisie sighed. She knew she should turn him down, and it would have been easier to do so right away. But he was begging her. "I'll think about it," she said.

He beamed. "Thank you."

She shook her head ruefully. "Whatever happens, Solly, I believe I'll never be proposed to by a better man."

2

HUGH AND MAISIE TOOK THE PENNY RIDE on the pleasure steamer from Westminster Pier to Chelsea. It was a warm, light evening, and the muddy river was busy with cockle-boats, barges and ferries. They steamed upstream, under the new railway bridge for Victoria Station, passing Christopher Wren's Chelsea Hospital on the north shore and, on the south, the flowers of Battersea Fields, London's traditional dueling ground. Battersea Bridge was a ramshackle wooden structure that looked ready to fall down. At its south end were chemical factories, but on the opposite side pretty cottages clustered around Chelsea Old Church, and naked children splashed in the shallows.

Less than a mile beyond the bridge they disembarked and walked up the wharf to the magnificent gilded gateway of Cremorne Gardens. The Gardens consisted of twelve acres of groves and grottoes, flower beds and lawns, ferneries and copses between the river and the King's Road. It was dusk when they arrived, and there were Chinese lanterns in the trees and gaslight along the winding paths. The place was packed: many of the younger people who had been at the races had decided to finish the day here. Everyone was dressed up to the nines, and they sauntered carefree through the gardens, laughing and flirting, the girls in pairs, the young men in larger groups, the couples arm-in-arm.

The weather had been fine all day, sunny and warm, but now it was becoming a hot, thundery night that threatened a storm. Hugh felt at once elated and nervous. He was thrilled to have Maisie on his arm, but

he had the insecure sense that he did not
know the rules of the game he was playing.
What did she expect? Would she let him kiss
her? Would she let him do anything he
wanted? He longed to touch her body, but
he did not know where to begin. Would she
expect him to go all the way? He wanted to,
but he had never done it before and he was
afraid of making a fool of himself. The
other clerks at Pilasters talked a lot about
dollymops, and what they would and would
not do, but Hugh suspected that much of
what they said was boasting. Anyway, Maisie
could not be treated as a dollymop. She was
more complex than that.

He was also a little worried that he might
be seen by someone he knew. His family
would disapprove powerfully of what he was
doing. Cremorne Gardens was not only a
lower-class place, it was thought by Methodists to encourage immorality. If he were
found out, Augusta would be sure to use it
against him. It was one thing for Edward to
take loose women to disreputable places: he
was the son and heir. It was different for
Hugh, penniless and poorly educated and
expected to be a failure like his father: they
would say that licentious pleasure gardens
were his natural habitat, and he belonged

with clerks and artisans and girls like Maisie.

Hugh was at a critical point in his career. He was on the point of getting promoted to correspondence clerk—at a salary of 150 pounds a year, more than double what he was getting now—and that could be jeopardized by a report of dissolute behavior.

He looked anxiously at the other men walking along the winding paths between the flower beds, fearful of recognizing someone. There was a sprinkling of upper-class men, some with girls on their arms; but they all carefully avoided Hugh's eye, and he realized they too were apprehensive about being seen there. He decided that if he saw people he knew they would probably be as keen as he to keep it quiet; and he felt reassured.

He was proud of Maisie. She was wearing a blue-green gown with a low neckline and a bustle behind, and a sailor hat poised jauntily on her piled-up hair. She attracted a lot of admiring glances.

They passed a ballet theatre, an oriental circus, an American bowling green and several shooting galleries, then went into a restaurant to dine. This was a new experience for Hugh. Although restaurants were becoming more common, they were mostly used by the middle classes: upper-class people still did not like the idea of eating in public. Young men such as Edward and Micky ate out quite often, but they thought of themselves as slumming, and they only did it when they were either looking for or had already found dollymops to keep them company.

All through dinner Hugh tried not to think about Maisie's breasts. The tops of them showed lusciously above the neckline of her gown, and they were very pale, with freckles. He had seen bare breasts, just once —at Nellie's brothel a few weeks ago. But he had never touched one. Were they firm, like muscles, or limp? When a woman took off her corset, did her breasts move as she walked, or remain rigid? If you touched them, would they yield to pressure, or were they hard, like kneecaps? Would she let him touch them? He sometimes even thought about kissing them, the way the man in the brothel had kissed the whore's breasts, but this was a secret desire that he felt ashamed of. In fact he was vaguely ashamed of all these feelings. It seemed brutish to sit with a woman and think all the time of her naked body, as if he cared nothing for her, but just wanted to use her. However, he could not help it, especially with Maisie, who was so alluring.

While they were eating there was a fireworks display in another part of the gardens. The bangs and flashes upset the lions and tigers in the menagerie, and they roared their disapproval. Hugh recalled that Maisie had worked in a circus, and he asked her what it was like.

"You get to know people very well when you live so close together," she said thoughtfully. "It's good in some ways, bad in others. People help each other all the time. There are love affairs, lots of quarrels, sometimes fights—there were two murders in the four years I was with the circus."

"Good heavens."

"And the money is unreliable."

"Why?"

"When people need to economize, entertainment is the first thing they cut out."

"I'd never thought of that. I must remember not to invest the bank's money in any form of entertainment business."

She smiled. "Do you think about finance all the time?"

No, Hugh thought, I think about your breasts all the time. He said: "You have to understand that I'm the son of the black sheep of the family. I know more about banking than the other young Pilasters, but I have to work doubly hard to prove my worth."

"Why is it so important to prove yourself?"

Good question, Hugh thought. He considered. After a minute he said: "I've always been that way, I suppose. At school I just had to be top of the class. And my father's failure made it worse: everyone thinks I'm going to go the same way, and I have to show them they're wrong."

"In a way I feel the same, you know. I'm never going to live the way my Mam did, always on the edge of destitution. I'm going to have money, I don't care what I have to do."

As gently as he could, Hugh said: "Is that why you go around with Solly?"

She frowned, and for a moment he thought she was going to be angry, but that passed and she smiled ironically. "I suppose that's a fair question. If you want to know the truth, I'm not proud of my connection with Solly. I misled him with certain . . . expectations."

Hugh was surprised. Did that mean she

had not gone all the way with Solly? "He seems to like you."

"And I like him. But comradeship isn't what he wants, and it never was, and I always knew that."

"I see what you mean." Hugh decided she had not gone all the way with Solly, and that meant she might not be willing to do it with him. He felt both disappointed and relieved: disappointed because he was so hungry for her, relieved because he was so nervous about it.

"You seem pleased about something," said Maisie.

"I suppose I'm glad to hear that you and Solly are only comrades."

She looked a little sad, and he wondered if he had said the wrong thing.

He paid for their dinner. It was quite expensive but he had brought the money he had been saving for his next suit of clothes, nineteen shillings, so he had plenty of cash. When they left the restaurant the people in the gardens seemed more boisterous than they had earlier, no doubt because they had consumed a good deal of beer and gin in the interim.

They came upon a dance floor. Dancing was something Hugh felt confident about: it was the only subject that had been well taught at the Folkestone Academy for the Sons of Gentlemen.

He led Maisie onto the floor and took her in his arms for the first time. His fingertips tingled as he rested his right hand in the small of her back, just above her bustle. He could feel the warmth of her body through her clothing. With his left hand he held hers, and she gave it a squeeze: the sensation thrilled him.

At the end of the first dance he smiled at her, feeling pleased, and to his surprise she reached up and touched his mouth with a fingertip. "I like it when you grin," she said. "You look boyish."

"Boyish" was not exactly the impression he was trying to give, but at this point anything that pleased her was all right with him.

They danced again. They were good partners: although Maisie was short, Hugh was only a little taller, and they were both light on their feet. He had danced with dozens of girls, if not hundreds, but he had never enjoyed it this much. He felt as if he was only now discovering the delightful sensation of holding a woman close, moving and swaying with the music, and executing complicated steps in unison.

"Are you tired?" he asked her at the end of the dance.

"Certainly not!"

They danced again.

At society balls it was bad manners to dance with the same girl more than twice. You had to lead her off the floor and offer to fetch her some champagne or a sorbet. Hugh had always chafed at such regulations, and now he felt joyfully liberated to be an anonymous reveler at this public dance.

They stayed on the floor until midnight, when the music stopped.

All the couples left the dance floor and moved on to the garden paths. Hugh noticed that many of the men kept their arms around their partners, even though they were no longer dancing; so, with some trepidation, he did the same. Maisie did not seem to mind.

The festivities were becoming unruly. Beside the paths there were occasional small cabins, like boxes at the opera, where people could sit and dine and watch the crowds walk by. Some of the cabins had been rented by groups of undergraduates who were now drunk. A man walking in front of Hugh had his top hat playfully knocked off his head, and Hugh himself had to duck to avoid a flying loaf of bread. He held Maisie closer to him, protectively, and to his delight she wound her arm around his waist and gave him a squeeze.

There were numerous shadowy groves and bowers off the main footpath, and Hugh could dimly perceive couples on the wooden seats, although he could not be sure whether they were embracing or just sitting together. He was surprised when the couple walking in front of them stopped and kissed passionately in the middle of the path. He led Maisie around them, feeling awkward. But after a while he got over his embarrassment and began to feel excited. A few minutes later they passed another embracing couple. Hugh caught Maisie's eye, and she smiled at him in a way that he felt sure was meant to be encouraging. But somehow he could not summon up the nerve to just go ahead and kiss her.

The gardens were becoming more rowdy. They had to detour around a scuffle involving six or seven young men, all shouting drunkenly, punching and knocking one another down. Hugh began to notice a number of unaccompanied women, and wondered if they were prostitutes. The atmosphere was turning threatening, and he felt the need to protect Maisie.

Then a group of thirty or forty young men came charging along, tipping people's hats off, pushing women aside and throwing men to the ground. There was no escaping them: they spread out across the lawns on either side of the path. Hugh acted quickly. He stood in front of Maisie with his back to the onslaught, then took off his hat and put both arms around her, holding her tight. The mob swept by. A heavy shoulder hit Hugh in the back, and he staggered, still holding Maisie; but he managed to remain upright. On one side of him a girl was knocked over, and on the other a man was punched in the face. Then the hooligans were gone.

Hugh relaxed his grip and looked down at Maisie. She looked back at him expectantly. Hesitantly, he leaned down and kissed her lips. They were deliciously soft and mobile. He closed his eyes. He had waited years for this: it was his first kiss. And it was as delightful as he had dreamed. He breathed in the scent of her. Her lips moved delicately against his. He wanted never to stop.

She broke the kiss. She looked hard at him, then hugged him tight, pulling his body against hers. "You could spoil all my plans," she said quietly.

He was not sure what she meant.

He looked to one side. There was a bower with an empty seat. Screwing up his courage, he said: "Shall we sit down?"

"All right."

They made their way into the darkness and sat on the wooden seat. Hugh kissed her again.

This time he felt a little less tentative. He put his arm around her shoulders and pulled her to him, and with his other hand he tilted her chin; and he kissed her more passionately than before, pressing his lips to hers hard. She responded enthusiastically, arching her back so that he could feel her bosom crushed against his chest. It surprised him that she should be so keen, though he knew of no reason why girls should not like kissing as much as men did. Her eagerness made it doubly exciting.

He stroked her cheek and her neck, and his hand fell to her shoulder. He wanted to touch her breasts, but he was afraid she would be offended, so he hesitated. She put her lips to his ear, and in a whisper that was also a kiss, she said: "You can touch them."

It startled him that she had been able to

read his mind, but the invitation excited him almost beyond endurance—not just because she was willing, but that she should actually speak of it. *You can touch them.* His fingertips traced a line from her shoulder, across her collarbone, down to her bosom, and he touched the swell of her breast above the neckline of her gown. Her skin was soft and warm. He was not sure what he should do next. Should he try to put his hand inside?

Maisie answered his unspoken question by taking his hand and pressing it to her dress below the neckline. "Squeeze them, but gently," she whispered.

He did so. They were not like muscles or kneecaps, he found, but more yielding, except for the hard nipples. His hand went from one to the other, stroking and squeezing alternately. Maisie's breath was hot against his neck. He felt as if he could do this all night, but he paused to kiss her lips again. This time she kissed him briefly then pulled away, kissed then pulled away, again and again, and that was even more thrilling. There were lots of ways to kiss, he realized.

Suddenly she froze. "Listen," she said.

Hugh had been vaguely aware that the gardens were getting very noisy, and now he was hearing shouting and crashing. Looking toward the footpath he saw that everyone was running in different directions. "There must be a fight," he said.

Then he heard a police whistle.

"Damn," he said. "Now there'll be trouble."

"We'd better leave," Maisie said.

"Let's find our way to the King's Road entrance and see if we can pick up a hansom cab."

"All right."

He hesitated, reluctant to leave. "One more kiss."

"Yes."

He kissed her and she hugged him hard.

"Hugh," she said, "I'm glad I met you."

He thought it was the nicest thing anyone had ever said to him.

They regained the footpath and headed north, hurrying. A moment later two young men came hurtling along, one chasing the other; and the first crashed into Hugh, sending him flying. When he scrambled to his feet they had gone.

Maisie was concerned. "Are you all right?"

He brushed himself off and picked up his hat. "No damage," he said. "But I don't want it to happen to you. Let's cut across the lawns—it might be safer."

As they stepped off the path, the gaslights went out.

They pressed forward in the dark. Now there was a continuous clamor of men shouting and women screaming, punctuated by police whistles. It suddenly occurred to Hugh that he might be arrested. Then everyone would find out what he had been up to. Augusta would say he was too dissolute to be given a responsible post at the bank. He groaned. Then he recalled how it had felt to touch Maisie's breasts, and he decided he did not care what Augusta said.

They kept away from paths and open spaces, and picked their way through trees and shrubbery. The ground rose slightly from the riverbank, so Hugh knew they were headed the right way as long as they were going uphill.

In the distance he saw lanterns twinkling, and steered toward the lights. They began to meet up with other couples going the same way. Hugh hoped there would be less chance of trouble with the police if they were in a group of obviously respectable and sober people.

As they approached the gate a troop of

thirty or forty policemen entered. Fighting to get into the park against the flow of the crowd, the police started indiscriminately clubbing men and women. The crowd turned and began to run in the opposite direction.

Hugh thought fast. "Let me carry you," he said to Maisie.

She looked puzzled but said: "All right."

He stooped and picked her up, with one arm under her knees and the other around her shoulders. "Pretend you've fainted," he said, and she closed her eyes and went limp. He walked forward, against the press of the crowd, shouting: "Make way, there! Make way!" in his most authoritative voice. Seeing an apparently sick woman, even the fleeing people tried to get out of the way. He came up against the advancing policemen, who were as panicky as the public. "Stand aside, constable! Let the lady through!" he shouted at one of them. The man looked hostile and for a moment he thought his bluff would be called. Then a sergeant shouted: "Let the gentleman pass!" He advanced through the line of police and suddenly found himself in the clear.

Maisie opened her eyes and he smiled at her. He liked holding her this way and he was in no hurry to lay down his burden. "Are you all right?"

She nodded. She seemed tearful. "Put me down."

He put her down gently and hugged her. "I say, don't cry," he said. "It's all over now."

She shook her head. "It's not the riot," she said. "I've seen fights before. But this is the first time anyone ever took care of me. All my life I've had to look after myself. It's a new experience."

He did not know what to say. All the girls he had ever met assumed that men would take care of them automatically. Being with Maisie was a constant revelation.

Hugh looked about for a cab. There were none to be seen. "I'm afraid we may have to walk."

"When I was eleven years old I walked for four days to get to Newcastle," she said. "I think I can make it from Chelsea to Soho."

3

MICKY MIRANDA HAD BEGUN to cheat at cards while he was at Windfield School, to supplement the inadequate allowance he received from home. The methods he invented for himself had been crude, but good enough to fool schoolboys. Then, on the long transatlantic voyage home which he had taken between school and university, he had tried to fleece a fellow passenger who turned out to be a professional cardsharp. The older man had been amused, and had taken Micky under his wing, teaching him all the basic principles of the craft.

Cheating was most dangerous when the stakes were high. If people were playing for pennies it never occurred to them that someone would cheat. Suspicion mounted with the size of the bets.

If he were caught tonight it would not just mean the failure of his scheme to ruin Tonio. Cheating at cards was the worst crime a gentleman could commit in England. He would be asked to resign from his clubs, his friends would be "not at home" any time he called at their houses, and no one would speak to him in the street. The rare stories he had heard about Englishmen cheating always ended with the culprit's leaving the country to make a fresh start in some untamed territory such as Malaya or Hudson Bay. Micky's fate would be to go back to Cordova, endure the taunts of his older brother, and spend the rest of his life raising cattle. The thought made him feel ill.

But the rewards tonight were as dramatic as the risks.

He was not doing this just to please Augusta. That was important enough: she was his passport into the society of London's wealthy and powerful people. But he also wanted Tonio's job.

Papa had said Micky would have to earn his keep in London—there would be no more money from home. Tonio's job was ideal. It would enable Micky to live like a gentleman while doing hardly any work. And it would also be a step on the ladder to a higher position. One day Micky might become the minister. And then he would be able to hold his head high in any company. Even his brother would not be able to sneer at that.

Micky, Edward, Solly and Tonio dined early at the Cowes, the club they all favored. By ten o'clock they were in the card room. They were joined at the baccarat table by two other club gamblers who had heard of the high stakes: Captain Carter and Viscount Montagne. Montagne was a fool, but Carter was a hard-headed type, and Micky would have to be wary of him.

There was a white line drawn around the table ten or twelve inches from the edge. Each of the players had a pile of gold sovereigns in front of him, outside the white square. Once money crossed the line into the square it was staked.

Micky had spent the day pretending to drink. At lunch he had wet his lips with champagne and surreptitiously poured it out on the grass. On the train back to London he had accepted the offer of Edward's flask several times, but had always blocked the neck with his tongue while appearing to toss off a swig. At dinner he had poured himself a small glass of claret then added to it twice without ever drinking any. Now he quietly ordered ginger beer, which looked like brandy and soda. He had to be stone-cold sober to perform the delicate sleight-of-hand operations that would enable him to ruin Tonio Silva.

He licked his lips nervously, caught himself, and tried to relax.

Of all games the cardsharp's favorite was baccarat. It might have been invented, Micky thought, to enable the smart to steal from the rich.

In the first place, it was a game purely of chance, with no skill or strategy. The player received two cards and added up their values: a three and a four would make seven, a two and a six would make eight. If the total came to more than nine, only the last digit counted; so fifteen was five, twenty was zero, and the highest possible score was nine.

A player with a low score could draw a third card, which would be dealt faceup, so everyone could see it.

The banker dealt just three hands: one to his left, one to his right, and one to himself. Players bet on either the left or the right hand. The banker paid out to any hand higher than his own.

The second great advantage of baccarat, from the cheat's point of view, was that it was played with a pack of at least three decks of cards. This meant the cheat could use a fourth deck and confidently deal a card out of his sleeve without worrying whether another player already had the same card in his hand.

While the others were still making themselves comfortable and lighting their cigars he asked a waiter for three new decks of cards. When the man came back he naturally handed the cards to Micky.

In order to control the game Micky had to deal, so his first challenge was to make sure he was banker. This involved two tricks: neutralizing the cut, and second-card dealing. They were both relatively simple, but he was stiff with tension, and that could make a man bungle the easiest maneuvers.

He broke the seals. The cards were always packed the same way, with the jokers on top and the ace of spades at the bottom. Micky took out the jokers and shuffled, enjoying the clean slippery feel of the new cards. It was the simplest of operations to move an ace from the bottom to the top of the pack; but then he had to let one of the other players cut the cards without moving the ace from the top.

He passed the pack to Solly, sitting on his right. As he put it down he contracted his hand a fraction, so that the top card—the ace of spades—stayed in his palm, concealed by the breadth of his hand. Solly cut. Keeping his hand palm-downward all the time to conceal the ace, Micky picked up the pack, replacing the hidden card on top as he did so. He had successfully neutralized the cut.

"High card gets the bank?" he said, forcing himself to sound indifferent as to whether they said yes or no.

There was a murmur of assent.

Holding the pack firmly, he slid the top card back a fraction of an inch and began to deal fast, keeping the top card back and always dealing the second until he came to himself, when at last he dealt the ace. They all turned over their cards. Micky's was the only ace, so he was banker.

He managed a casual smile. "I think I'm going to be lucky tonight," he said.

No one commented.

He relaxed a little.

Concealing his relief, he dealt the first hand.

Tonio was playing on his left, with Edward and Viscount Montagne. On his right were Solly and Captain Carter. Micky did not want to win: that was not his purpose tonight. He just wanted Tonio to lose.

He played fair for a while, losing a little of Augusta's money. The others relaxed and ordered another round of drinks. When the time was right, Micky lit a cigar.

In the inside pocket of his dress coat, next to his cigar case, was another deck of cards —bought at the stationer's in St. James's Street where the club's playing cards came from, so that they would match.

He had arranged the extra deck in winning pairs, all giving a total of nine, the highest score: four and five, nine and ten, nine and jack, and so on. The surplus cards, all tens and court cards, he had left at home.

Returning his cigar case to his pocket, he palmed the extra deck; then, picking up the pack from the table with his other hand, he slid the new cards to the bottom of the old pack. While the others mixed their brandy and water he shuffled, carefully bringing to the top of the pack, in order, one card from the bottom, two cards at random, another from the bottom, and another two at random. Then, dealing first to his left, then to his right, then to himself, he gave himself the winning pair.

Next time around he gave Solly's side a winning hand. For a while he continued the same way, making Tonio lose and Solly win. The money he won from Tonio's side was thus paid out to Solly's side, and no suspicion attached to Micky, for the pile of sovereigns in front of him remained about the same.

Tonio had started by putting on the table most of the money he had won at the races —about a hundred pounds. When it was down to about fifty, he stood up and said: "This side is unlucky—I'm going to sit by

Solly." He moved to the other side of the table.

That won't help you, Micky thought. It was no more difficult to make the left side win and the right side lose from now on. But it made him nervous to hear Tonio talk about bad luck. He wanted Tonio to go on thinking he was lucky today, even while he was losing money.

Occasionally Tonio would vary his style by betting five or ten sovereigns on a hand instead of two or three. When this happened, Micky dealt him a winning hand. Tonio would rake in his winnings and say gleefully: "I'm lucky today, I'm sure of it!" even though his pile of coins was steadily getting smaller.

Micky was feeling more relaxed now. He studied his victim's mental state while he smoothly manipulated the cards. It was not enough that Tonio should be cleaned out. Micky wanted him to play with money he didn't have, to gamble on borrowed money and be unable to repay his debts. Only then would he be thoroughly disgraced.

Micky waited with trepidation while Tonio lost more and more. Tonio was awestruck by Micky and would generally do whatever Micky suggested, but he was not a complete fool and there was still a chance he might have the sense to draw back from the brink of ruin.

When Tonio's money was almost gone Micky made his next move. He took out his cigar case again. "These are from home, Tonio," he said. "Try one." To his relief, Tonio accepted. The cigars were long and would take a good half-hour to smoke. Tonio would not want to leave before finishing his cigar.

When they had lit up Micky moved in for the kill.

A couple of hands later Tonio was broke. "Well, that's everything I won at Goodwood this afternoon," he said despondently.

"We ought to give you a chance to win it back," Micky said. "Pilaster will lend you a hundred pounds, I'm sure."

Edward looked a little startled, but it would have seemed ungenerous to refuse when he had such a big pile of winnings in front of him, and he said: "By all means."

Solly intervened. "Perhaps you should retire, Silva, and be grateful that you've had a great day's gambling at no cost."

Micky silently cursed Solly for being a good-natured nuisance. If Tonio did the sensible thing now the whole scheme was ruined.

Tonio hesitated.

Micky held his breath.

But it was not in Tonio's nature to gamble prudently, and as Micky had calculated, he could not resist the temptation to carry on. "All right," he said. "I might as well play on until I finish my cigar."

Micky let out a discreet sigh of relief.

Tonio beckoned to a waiter and ordered pen, paper and ink. Edward counted out a hundred sovereigns and Tonio scribbled an IOU. Micky knew that if Tonio lost all that he could never repay the debt.

The game went on. Micky found himself sweating a little as he held the delicate balance, ensuring that Tonio lost steadily, with the occasional big win to keep him optimistic. But this time when he was down to fifty pounds he said: "I only win when I gamble high. I'm putting the lot on this next hand."

It was a big bet even for the Cowes Club. If Tonio lost he was finished. One or two club members saw the size of the stake and stood near the table to watch the play.

Micky dealt the cards.

He looked at Edward, on the left, who

shook his head to indicate that he did not want another card.

On the right, Solly did the same.

Micky turned over his own cards. He had given himself an eight and an ace, making nine.

Edward turned over the hand on the left. Micky did not know what the cards were: he knew in advance what he himself was going to get, but he dealt the others at random. Edward had a five and a two, making seven. He and Captain Carter had lost their money.

Solly turned over his hand, the cards on which Tonio had staked his future.

He had a nine and a ten. That made nineteen, which counted as nine. This equaled the bank's score, so there was no winner or loser, and Tonio got to keep his fifty pounds.

Micky cursed under his breath.

He wanted Tonio to leave those fifty sovereigns on the table now. He gathered up the cards quickly. With a mocking note into his voice he said: "Going to reduce your stake, Silva?"

"Certainly not," said Tonio. "Deal the cards."

Micky thanked his stars and dealt, giving himself another winning hand.

This time Edward tapped his cards, indicating that he wanted a third. Micky dealt him a four of clubs and turned to Solly. Solly passed.

Micky turned over his cards and showed a five and a four. Edward had a four showing, and turned over a worthless king and another four, making eight. His side had lost.

Solly turned up a two and a four, making six. The right side had also lost to the banker.

And Tonio was ruined.

He turned pale and looked ill, and muttered something that Micky recognized as a Spanish curse.

Micky suppressed a smile of triumph and raked in his winnings—then he saw something that took his breath away and stopped his heart with dread.

There were four fours of clubs on the table.

They were supposed to be playing with three decks of cards. Anyone who noticed the four identical fours would immediately know that extra cards had somehow been added to the pack.

It was a hazard of this particular method of cheating, and the chances of its happening were roughly one in a hundred thousand.

If the anomaly were seen, it would be Micky, not Tonio, who was ruined.

So far no one had spotted it. Suits had no significance in this game, so the irregularity was not glaring. Micky picked up the cards swiftly, his heart beating hard. He was just thanking his stars that he had got away with it when Edward said: "Hang on—there were four fours of clubs on the table."

Micky cursed him for a blundering elephant. Edward was just thinking aloud. Of course he had no idea of Micky's scheme.

"Couldn't be," said Viscount Montagne. "We're playing with three decks of cards, so there are only three fours of clubs."

"Exactly," said Edward.

Micky puffed on his cigar. "You're drunk, Pilaster. One of them was a four of spades."

"Oh, sorry."

Viscount Montagne said: "At this time of night, who can tell the difference between spades and clubs?"

Once again Micky thought he had got away with it—and once again his elation was premature.

Tonio said belligerently: "Let's look at the cards."

Micky's heart seemed to stop. The cards from the last hand were placed on a pile which was shuffled and reused when the pack ran out. If the discards were turned over, the four identical fours would be seen, and Micky would be finished.

Desperately he said: "I hope you're not questioning my word."

This was a dramatic challenge to make in a gentlemen's club: it was not very many years since such words would have led to a duel. People at the neighboring tables began to watch what was happening. Everyone looked at Tonio for his response.

Micky was thinking fast. He had said that one of the fours had been a four of spades, not clubs. If he could produce the four of spades from the top of the discard pile he would have proved his point—and with luck no one would look at the rest of the discards.

But first he had to find a four of spades. There were three. Some might be in the discard pile on the table, but the odds were that at least one was in the pack they had been playing with, which was in his hand.

It was his only chance.

While all eyes were on Tonio, he turned the pack so that the cards faced him. With infinitesimal movements of his thumb he exposed a corner of each card in turn. He kept his eyes firmly fixed on Tonio, but held the cards within his vision so that he could still read the letters and symbols in the corners.

Tonio said stubbornly: "Let's look at the discards."

The others turned to Micky. Steeling his nerve, he carried on fiddling with the pack, praying for a four of spades. In the midst of such drama no one remarked on what he was doing. The cards in contention were in the pile on the table, so it would seem to make no difference what he did with those in his hand. They would have to look quite hard to see that behind his hands he was sorting through the pack, but even if they did so they would not immediately realize he was up to no good.

But he could stand on his dignity indefinitely. Sooner or later one of them would lose patience, abandon courtesy, and pick up the discards. To gain a few precious moments he said: "If you can't lose like a man, perhaps you oughtn't to play." He felt a slight sweat break out on his forehead. He wondered whether he had missed a four of spades in his haste.

Solly said mildly: "It can't hurt to look, can it?"

Damn Solly, always so sickeningly reasonable, Micky thought desperately.

Then at last he found a four of spades.

He palmed it.

"Oh, very well," he said with a feigned nonchalance that was the polar opposite of what he was feeling.

Everyone became very still and quiet.

Micky put down the pack he had been furtively sorting through, keeping the four of spades in his palm. He reached out and picked up the discard pile, dropping the four on top. He placed the pile in front of Solly and said: "There will be a four of spades in there, I guarantee."

Solly turned over the top card, and they all saw that it was the four of spades.

A hum of conversation broke out around the room as they all relaxed.

Micky was still terrified that someone might turn over more cards and see that there were four fours of clubs underneath.

Viscount Montagne said: "I think that settles it, and speaking for myself, Miranda, I can only apologize if any doubt has been cast upon your word."

"Good of you to say so," Micky said.

They all looked at Tonio. He stood up, his face working. "Damn the lot of you, then," he said, and he walked out.

Micky swept up all the cards on the table. Now no one would ever know the truth.

His palms were wet with perspiration. He wiped them surreptitiously on his trousers. "I'm sorry about my compatriot's behavior," he said. "If there's one thing I hate it's a fellow who can't play cards like a gentleman."

4

IN THE EARLY HOURS OF THE MORNING Maisie and Hugh walked north through the raw new suburbs of Fulham and South Kensington. The night became hotter and the stars disappeared. They held hands, even though their palms were sweaty in the heat. Maisie felt bewildered but happy.

Something odd had happened tonight. She did not understand it but she liked it. In the past, when men had kissed her and touched her breasts, she had felt it was part of a transaction, something she gave in return for whatever she needed from them. Tonight had been different. She had *wanted*

him to touch her—and he had been too polite to do anything without being asked!

It had started while they were dancing.
Until then she had not been aware that this
was going to be radically different from any
previous evening spent with an upper-class
young man. Hugh was more charming than
most, and he looked good in his white waistcoat and silk tie, but still he was just a nice
boy. Then, on the dance floor, she had begun to think how pleasant it would be to kiss
him. The feeling had got stronger as they
walked around the gardens after the dancing and saw all the other courting couples.
His hesitation had been engaging. Other
men saw dinner and conversation as a tedious preliminary to the important business
of the evening, and could hardly wait to get
her in a dark place and start groping, but
Hugh had been shy.

In other respects he was the opposite of
shy. In the riot he had been completely fear-
less. After he was knocked to the ground his
only concern had been to make sure the
same thing did not happen to her. There
was a lot more to Hugh than the average
young man-about-town.

When finally she had made him understand that she wanted to be kissed, it had

been delicious, quite unlike any kiss she had had before. Yet he was not skillful or experienced. Quite the reverse: he was naive and uncertain. So why had she enjoyed it so much? And why had she suddenly longed to feel his hands on her breasts?

She was not tormented by these questions, just intrigued. She was contented, walking through London in the darkness with Hugh. Now and again she felt a few drops of rain, but the threatened cloudburst did not materialize. She began to think it would be nice to be kissed again soon.

They reached Kensington Gore and turned right, along the south side of the park, heading for the city center where she lived. Hugh stopped opposite a huge house whose front was illuminated by two gaslights. He put his arm around her shoulders. "That's my aunt Augusta's house," he said. "That's where I live."

She put her arm around his waist and stared at the house, wondering what it was like to live in such a vast mansion. She found it hard to imagine what you would do with all the rooms. After all, if you had somewhere to sleep and somewhere to cook, and perhaps the luxury of another room in which to entertain guests, what else did you need? There was no point in having two kitchens or two sitting-rooms: you could only be in one at a time. It reminded her that she and Hugh lived on separate islands in society, divided by an ocean of money and privilege. The thought troubled her. "I was born in a one-room hut," she said.

"In the northeast?"

"No, in Russia."

"Really? 'Maisie Robinson' doesn't sound like a Russian name."

"I was born Miriam Rabinowicz. We all changed our names when we came here."

"Miriam," he said softly. "I like it." He drew her to him and kissed her. Her anxiety evaporated and she gave herself up to the sensation. He was less hesitant now: he knew what he liked. She drank his kisses thirstily, like a glass of cold water on a hot day. She hoped he would touch her breasts again.

He did not disappoint her. A moment later she felt his hand close gently over her left breast. Almost immediately her nipple grew taut, and his fingertips touched it through the silk of her dress. She felt embarrassed that her desire should be so obvious, but it only inflamed him more.

After a while she wanted to feel his body.

She reached inside his dress coat and ran her hands up and down his back, feeling the hot skin through the thin cotton of his shirt. She was behaving like a man, she thought. She wondered if he minded. But she was enjoying it too much to stop.

Then it started to rain.

It happened not gradually but all at once. There was a flash of lightning, a clap of thunder right afterwards, and an instant downpour. By the time they broke the kiss their faces were wet.

Hugh seized her hand and pulled. "Let's take shelter in the house!" he said.

They ran across the road. Hugh led her down the steps, past a sign saying "Tradesmen's Entrance," to the basement area. By the time they reached the doorway she was soaked to the skin. Hugh unlocked the door. Putting a finger to his lips to indicate silence, he ushered her inside.

She hesitated for a fraction of a second, wondering whether she should ask exactly what he had in mind; but the thought slipped away and she stepped through the door.

They tiptoed through a kitchen the size of a small church to a narrow staircase. Hugh put his mouth to her ear and said: "There'll be clean towels upstairs. We'll take the back staircase."

She followed him up three long flights, then they passed through another door and emerged on a landing. He glanced through an open doorway into a bedroom where a night-light burned. In a normal voice he said: "Edward's still out. There's no one else on this floor. Aunt and Uncle's rooms are on the floor below us and the servants above. Come."

He led her into his bedroom and turned up the gaslight. "I'll fetch towels," he said, and he went out again.

She took off her hat and looked around the room. It was surprisingly small, and furnished simply, with a single bed, a dresser, a plain wardrobe, and a small desk. She had expected something much more luxurious—but Hugh was a poor relation, and his room reflected that.

She looked with interest at his things. He had a pair of silver-backed hair brushes engraved with the initials *T.P.*—another heirloom from his father. He was reading a book called *The Handbook of Good Commercial Practice.* On the desk was a framed photograph of a woman and a girl about six years old. She slid open the drawer of his

bedside table. There was a Bible and another book underneath it. She moved the
Bible aside and read the title of the concealed book: it was called *The Duchess of
Sodom.* She realized she was prying. Feeling
guilty, she closed the drawer quickly.

Hugh came back with a pile of towels.
Maisie took one. It was warm from an airing
cupboard, and she buried her wet face in it
gratefully. This is what it's like to be rich,
she thought; great piles of warm towels
whenever you need them. She dried her
bare arms and her bosom. "Who's the picture of?" she asked him.

"My mother and my sister. My sister was
born after my father died."

"What's her name?"

"Dorothy. I call her Dotty. I'm very fond
of her."

"Where do they live?"

"In Folkestone, by the sea."

Maisie wondered if she would ever meet
them.

Hugh drew up the chair from the desk
and made her sit down. He knelt in front of
her, took off her shoes, and dried her wet
feet with a fresh towel. She closed her eyes:
the sensation of the warm, soft towel on the
soles of her feet was exquisite.

Her dress was wet through, and she shivered. Hugh removed his coat and boots. Maisie knew she could not get dry without taking off her dress. Underneath she was quite decent. She was not wearing knickers —only rich women did—but she had on a full-length petticoat and a chemise. Impulsively she stood up, turned her back to Hugh and said: "Will you undo me?"

She could feel his hands shaking as his fingers fumbled with the hooks-and-eyes that fastened her dress. She was nervous too, but she could not back out now. When he was done she thanked him and stepped out of the dress.

She turned to face him.

His expression was a touching mixture of embarrassment and desire. He stood like Ali Baba staring at the thieves' treasure. She had thought vaguely that she would simply dry herself with a towel and put her dress back on later, when it had dried, but now she knew it was not going to be like that. And she was glad.

She put her hands on his cheeks, pulled his head down and kissed him. This time she opened her mouth, expecting him to do the same, but he did not. He had never kissed that way, she guessed. She teased his lips

with the tip of her tongue. She sensed that
he was shocked but excited too, and after a
moment he opened his mouth a fraction and
responded shyly with his tongue. He began
to breathe harder.

After a while he broke the kiss, reached
for the top of her chemise and tried to undo
the button. He fumbled for a moment then
grasped the garment with both hands and
tore it open, sending buttons flying. His
hands closed over her bare breasts and he
shut his eyes and groaned. She felt as if she
were melting inside. She wanted more of
this, now and always.

"Maisie," he said.

She looked at him.

"I want to . . ."

She smiled. "So do I."

When the words were out she wondered
where they came from. She had spoken
without thinking. But she had no doubts.
She wanted him more than she had ever
wanted anything.

He stroked her hair. "I've never done it
before," he said.

"Nor have I."

He stared at her. "But I thought—" He
stopped.

She felt a spasm of anger, then controlled

herself. It was her own fault if he had thought she was promiscuous. "Let's lie down," she said.

He sighed happily, then said: "Are you sure?"

"Am I sure?" she repeated. She could hardly believe he had said that. She had never known a man who would ask that question. They never thought about how she felt. She took his hand in hers and kissed the palm. "If I wasn't sure before, I am now."

She lay down on the narrow bed. The mattress was hard but the sheet was cool. He lay beside her and said: "What now?"

They were approaching the limits of her experience, but she knew the next step. "Feel me," she said. He touched her tentatively through her clothing. Suddenly she was impatient. She pulled up her petticoat —she had nothing on underneath—and pressed his hand to her mound.

He stroked her, kissing her face, his breath hot and fast. She knew she should be afraid of getting pregnant, but she could not focus on the danger. She was out of control: the pleasure was too intense for her to think. This was as far as she had ever gone with a man, but all the same she knew ex-

actly what she wanted next. She put her lips
to his ear and murmured: "Push your finger
in."

He did so. "It's all wet," he said wonderingly.

"That's to help you."

His fingers explored her delicately. "It
seems so small."

"You'll have to be gentle," she said, although a part of her wanted to be taken furiously.

"Shall we do it now?"

She was suddenly impatient. "Yes, please,
quickly."

She sensed him fumbling with his trousers, then he lay between her legs. She was
frightened—she had heard stories about
how much it hurt the first time—but she was
also consumed by longing for him.

She felt him ease into her. After a moment he encountered resistance. He pushed
gently, and it hurt. "Stop!" she said.

He looked at her worriedly. "I'm sorry—"

"It will be all right. Kiss me."

He lowered his face to hers and kissed
her lips, gently at first and then passionately.
She put her hands on his waist, lifted her
hips off the bed a little, then pulled him to
her. There was a pain, sharp enough to

make her cry out, then something gave way inside her and she felt a tremendous release of tension. She broke the kiss and looked at him.

"Are you all right?" he said.

She nodded. "Did I make a noise?"

"Yes, but I don't think anyone heard."

"Don't stop," she said.

He hesitated a moment longer. "Maisie," he murmured, "is this a dream?"

"If it is, let's not wake up yet." She moved against him, guiding him with her hands on his hips. He followed her lead. It reminded her of how they had danced together just a few hours earlier. She gave herself up to the sensation. He began to pant.

Distantly, above the noise of his breathing and hers, she heard a door open.

She was so absorbed in her feelings and Hugh's body that the sound failed to alarm her.

Suddenly a harsh voice shattered the mood like a stone through a window. "Well, well, Hugh—what's all this?"

Maisie froze.

Hugh gave a despairing groan, and she felt his seed spurt warm inside her.

She wanted to cry.

The sneering voice came again. "What do you think this house is, a brothel?"

Maisie whispered: "Hugh—get off me."

He withdrew from her and rolled off the bed. She saw his cousin Edward standing in the doorway, smoking a cigar and staring at them intently. Hugh quickly covered her with a big towel. She sat upright and pulled it up to her neck.

Edward grinned nastily. "Well, if you've finished I might give her a go."

Hugh wrapped a towel around his waist. Controlling his anger with a visible effort, he said: "You're drunk, Edward—go to your room before you say something completely unforgivable."

Edward ignored him and approached the bed. "Why, it's Solly Greenbourne's dollymop! But I won't tell him—so long as you're nice to me."

Maisie saw that he was in earnest, and she shuddered with loathing. She knew that some men were inflamed by a woman who had just been with another man—April had told her the slang term for a woman in that state, a buttered bun—and she knew intuitively that Edward was such a man.

Hugh was enraged. "Get out of here, you damn fool," he said.

"Be a sport," Edward persisted. "After all, she's only a damn whore." With that he reached down and snatched away Maisie's towel.

She jumped off the bed from the other side, covering herself with her arms; but there was no need. Hugh took two strides across the little room and hit Edward a mighty punch on the nose. Blood spurted and Edward let out a roar of agony.

Edward was rendered harmless instantly, but Hugh was still angry, and he hit him again.

Edward screamed in fear and pain and blundered to the door. Hugh went after him, throwing punches at the back of his head. Edward began to yell: "Leave me alone, stop it, please!" He fell through the doorway.

Maisie followed them out. Edward was stretched out on the floor and Hugh was sitting on top of him, still hitting him. She cried: "Hugh, stop, you'll kill him!" She tried to grab Hugh's arms, but he was in a fury and it was hard to restrain him.

A moment later she glimpsed a movement out of the corner of her eye. She looked up and saw Hugh's aunt Augusta standing at the top of the stairs in a black silk peignoir, staring at her. In the flickering gaslight she looked like a voluptuous ghost.

There was a strange look in Augusta's eyes. At first Maisie could not read her expression; then, after a moment, she understood, and she was frightened.

It was a look of triumph.

5

AS SOON AS AUGUSTA SAW THE NAKED GIRL she sensed that this was her chance to get rid of Hugh once and for all.

She recognized her immediately. This was the trollop who had insulted her in the park, the one they called the Lioness. The thought had crossed her mind even then that this little minx might one day get Hugh into serious trouble: there was something arrogant and uncompromising in the set of her head and the light in her eyes. Even now, when she ought to be mortified by shame, she stood there, stark naked, and stared back at Augusta coolly. She had a magnificent body, small but shapely, with plump white breasts and a riot of sand-colored hair at her groin. Her look was so haughty that she almost made Augusta feel like the intruder. But she would be the downfall of Hugh.

The outlines of a plan were forming in Augusta's mind when suddenly she saw Edward lying on the floor with blood all over his face.

All her old fears rose up in force, and she was taken back twenty-three years, to when he had nearly died as a baby. Blind panic swamped her. "Teddy!" she screamed. "What's happened to Teddy!" She fell to her knees beside him. "Speak to me, speak to me!" she yelled. She was possessed by an unbearable dread, just as she had been when her baby kept getting thinner and thinner every day and the doctors could not understand why.

Edward sat up and groaned.

"Say something!" she pleaded.

"Don't call me Teddy," he said.

Her terror eased a fraction. He was conscious and could speak. But his voice was thick and his nose looked out of shape. "What happened?" she said.

"I caught Hugh with his whore, and he just went mad!" Edward said.

Forcing down her rage and fear, she reached out gently and touched Edward's nose. He gave a loud yelp, but permitted her to press delicately. There was nothing broken, she thought; it was just swelling up.

She heard her husband's voice say: "What the deuce is going on?"

She stood up. "Hugh has attacked Edward," she said.

"Is the boy all right?"

"I think so."

Joseph turned to Hugh. "Damnation, sir, what do you mean by it?"

"The silly fool asked for it," Hugh said defiantly.

That's right, Hugh, make it worse, Augusta thought. Whatever you do, don't apologize. I want your uncle to stay angry with you.

However, Joseph's attention was torn between the boys and the woman, and his eyes kept switching to her naked body. Augusta felt a stab of jealousy.

That made her calmer. There was nothing much wrong with Edward. She began to think rapidly. How could she best exploit this situation? Hugh was totally vulnerable now: she could do anything to him. She thought immediately of her conversation with Micky Miranda. Hugh had to be silenced, for he knew too much about the death of Peter Middleton. Now was the moment to strike.

First she had to separate him from the girl.

Some servants had appeared in their nightclothes and were hovering in the doorway that led to the back stairs, looking aghast but fascinated by the scene on the landing. Augusta saw her butler, Hastead, in a yellow silk dressing gown that Joseph had discarded some years ago, and Williams, a footman, in a striped nightshirt. "Hastead and Williams, help Mr. Edward to his bed, will you?" The two men bustled forward and got Teddy to his feet.

Next Augusta spoke to her housekeeper. "Mrs. Merton, cover this girl with a sheet, or something, and take her to my room and get her dressed." Mrs. Merton took off her own dressing gown and draped it around the girl's shoulders. She pulled it closed over her nakedness but made no move to leave.

Augusta said: "Hugh, run to Dr. Humbold's house in Church Street: he'd better have a look at poor Edward's nose."

"I'm not leaving Maisie," Hugh said.

Augusta said sharply: "Since you've done the damage, it's the least you can do to fetch a doctor!"

Maisie said: "I'll be all right, Hugh. Fetch the doctor. I'll be here when you get back."

Still Hugh stood his ground.

Mrs. Merton said: "This way, please," and indicated the back stairs.

Maisie said: "Oh, I think we'll use the main staircase." Then, walking like a queen, she crossed the landing and went down the stairs. Mrs. Merton followed.

Augusta said: "Hugh?"

He was still reluctant to go, she could see, but on the other hand he could think of no good reason to refuse. After a moment he said: "I'll put my boots on."

Augusta concealed her relief. She had separated them. Now, if her luck held, she would be able to seal Hugh's fate. She turned to her husband. "Come. Let's go to your room and discuss this."

They went down the stairs and entered his bedroom. As soon as the door was closed Joseph took her in his arms and kissed her. She realized he wanted to make love.

That was unusual. They made love once or twice a week, but she was always the initiator: she would go to his room and get into his bed. She saw it as part of her wifely duty to keep him satisfied, but she liked to be in control, so she discouraged him from coming to her room. When they were first married he had been harder to restrain. He had insisted on taking her whenever he wanted, and for a while she had been obliged to let him have his way; but eventually he had come round to her way of thinking. Then, for a while, he had bothered her with unseemly suggestions, such as that they should make love with the light on, that she should lie on top of him, and even that she should do unspeakable things to him with her mouth. But she had firmly resisted and he had long ago ceased to express such ideas.

Now, however, he was breaking the pattern. She knew why. He had been inflamed by the sight of Maisie's naked body, those firm young breasts and that bush of sandy hair. The thought left a bad taste in her mouth, and she pushed him away.

He looked resentful. She wanted him angry with Hugh, not with her, so she touched his arm in a conciliatory gesture. "Later," she said. "I'll come to you later."

He accepted that. "There's bad blood in Hugh," he said. "He gets it from my brother."

"He can't continue to live here after this,"

Augusta said in a tone that did not invite discussion.

Joseph was not disposed to argue that point. "Indeed not."

"You must discharge him from the bank," she went on.

Joseph looked mulish. "I beg you not to make announcements about what should happen at the bank."

"Joseph, he has just insulted you by bringing into the house an unfortunate woman," she said, using the euphemism for prostitute.

Joseph went and sat at his writing table. "I know what he's done. I merely ask that you keep what happens in the house separate from what happens at the bank."

She decided to retreat for a moment. "Very well. I'm sure you know best."

It always deflated him when she gave in unexpectedly. "I suppose I had better discharge him," he said after a moment. "I imagine he will go back to his mother in Folkestone."

Augusta was not sure about that. She had not yet worked out her strategy: she was thinking on her feet. "What would he do for work?"

"I don't know."

Augusta saw she had made a mistake. Hugh would be even more dangerous if he were unemployed, resentful and knocking around with nothing to do. David Middleton had not yet approached him—possibly Middleton had not yet learned that Hugh had been at the swimming hole on the fateful day—but sooner or later he would. She became flustered, wishing she had thought more before insisting Hugh should be dismissed. She felt exasperated with herself.

Could she to make Joseph change his mind back again?

She had to try. "Perhaps we're being harsh," she said.

He raised his eyebrows, surprised at this sudden display of mercy.

Augusta went on: "Well, you keep saying that he has a great deal of potential as a banker. Perhaps it's unwise to throw that away."

Joseph became annoyed. "Augusta, do make up your mind what you want!"

She sat down on a low chair near his desk. She let her nightdress ride up and stretched out her legs. She still had good legs. He looked at them and his expression softened.

While he was distracted she racked her

brains. Suddenly she was inspired. "Send him abroad," she said.

"Eh?"

The more she thought of the idea, the better she liked it. He would be out of reach of David Middleton, but still within her sphere of influence. "The Far East, or South America," she went on, warming to her theme. "Someplace where his bad behavior will not reflect directly on my house."

Joseph forgot his irritation with her. "It's not a bad idea," he said reflectively. "There's an opening in the United States. The old boy who runs our Boston office needs an assistant."

America would be perfect, Augusta thought. She was pleased with her own brilliance.

But at the moment Joseph was only toying with the idea. She wanted him to commit himself to it. "Let Hugh go as soon as possible," she said. "I don't want him in the house another day."

"He can book his passage in the morning," Joseph said. "After that there is no reason for him to stay in London. He can go down to Folkestone to say good-bye to his mother, and stay there until his ship sails."

And he won't see David Middleton for

years, Augusta thought with satisfaction.
"Splendid. It's settled, then." Were there
any other snags? She remembered Maisie.
Did Hugh care for her? It seemed unlikely,
but anything was possible. He might refuse
to be parted from her. It was a loose end,
and it worried Augusta. Hugh could not
possibly take a trollop to Boston with him,
but on the other hand he might refuse to
leave London without her. Augusta wondered if she could nip the romance in the
bud, just as a precaution.

She stood up and moved to the door that
communicated with her bedroom. Joseph
looked disappointed. "I must get rid of that
girl," she said.

"Anything I can do?"

The question surprised her. It was not
like him to make generalized offers of help.
He wanted another look at the whore, she
thought sourly. She shook her head. "I'll
come back. Get into bed."

"Very well," he said reluctantly.

She went into her own room and closed
the door firmly behind her.

Maisie was clothed again and pinning her
hat to her hair. Mrs. Merton was folding up
a rather flashy blue-green gown and cram-
ming it into a cheap bag. "I've loaned her a

dress of mine, as hers is soaked, mum," said the housekeeper.

That answered a little question that had been nagging Augusta. She had thought it was unlike Hugh to do something as blatantly stupid as to bring home a whore. Now she saw how it had come about. They had been caught in the sudden storm, and Hugh had brought the woman inside to get dry, then one thing had led to another.

"What is your name?" she said to the girl.

"Maisie Robinson. I know yours."

Augusta found that she loathed Maisie Robinson. She was not sure why: the girl was hardly worthy of such strong feelings. It had something to do with the way she had looked when naked: so proud, so voluptuous, so independent. "I suppose you want money," Augusta said disdainfully.

"You hypocritical cow," Maisie said. "You didn't marry that rich, ugly husband of yours for love."

It was the truth, and the words took Augusta's breath away. She had underestimated this young woman. She had made a bad beginning, and now she had to dig herself out of the hole. From now on she must handle Maisie carefully. This was a providential opportunity, and she must not waste it.

She swallowed hard and forced herself to sound neutral. "Will you sit down for a moment?" She indicated a chair.

Maisie looked surprised, but after a moment's hesitation she took a seat.

Augusta sat opposite her.

The girl had to be made to give Hugh up. She had been scornful when Augusta had hinted at a bribe, and Augusta was reluctant to repeat the offer: she sensed that money would not work with this girl. But she was clearly not the type to be bullied either.

Augusta would have to make her believe that separation would be the best thing for both Maisie and Hugh. It would work best if Maisie thought that giving Hugh up was her own idea. And that might be best achieved by Augusta arguing the opposite. Now, there was a good notion. . . .

Augusta said: "If you want to marry him, I can't stop you." The girl looked surprised, and Augusta congratulated herself on having caught her off guard.

"What makes you think I want to marry him?" Maisie said.

Augusta almost laughed. She wanted to say *The fact that you're a scheming little gold digger,* but instead she said: "What girl wouldn't want to marry him? He's personable and good-looking and he comes from a great family. He has no money, but his prospects are excellent."

Maisie narrowed her eyes and said: "It almost sounds as if you want me to marry him."

Augusta intended to give exactly that impression, but she had to tread delicately. Maisie was suspicious and seemed too bright to be easily hoodwinked. "Let's not be fanciful, Maisie," she said. "Forgive me for saying so, but no woman of my class would wish a man of her family to marry quite so far below him."

Maisie showed no resentment. "She might if she hated him enough."

Feeling encouraged, Augusta continued to lead her on. "But I don't hate Hugh," she said. "Whatever gave you that idea?"

"He did. He told me you treat him as a poor relation and make sure everyone else does the same."

"How ungrateful people can be. But why would I wish to ruin his career?"

"Because he shows up that ass of a son of yours, Edward."

A wave of anger engulfed Augusta. Once

again Maisie had come uncomfortably close to the truth. It was true that Edward lacked Hugh's low cunning, but Edward was a fine, sweet young man and Hugh was ill-bred. "I think you had better not mention the name of my son," Augusta said in a low voice.

Maisie grinned. "I seem to have touched a sore place." She immediately became grave again. "So that's your game. Well, I won't play it."

"What do you mean?" said Augusta.

Suddenly there were tears in Maisie's eyes. "I like Hugh too much to ruin him."

Augusta was surprised and pleased by the strength of Maisie's passion. This was working out perfectly, despite the bad beginning. "What are you going to do?" Augusta asked.

Maisie struggled not to cry. "I shan't see him anymore. You may yet destroy him, but you won't have my help."

"He might come after you."

"I shall disappear. He doesn't know where I live. I'll stay away from the places where he might look for me."

A good plan, Augusta thought; you'll only need to keep it up for a short while, then he will go abroad and be away for years, perhaps forever. But she said nothing. She had led Maisie to the obvious conclusion and now the girl needed no further help.

Maisie wiped her face on her sleeve. "I'd better go now, before he comes back with the doctor." She stood up. "Thank you for lending me your dress, Mrs. Merton."

The housekeeper opened the door for her. "I'll show you out."

"We'll take the back stairs this time, please," Maisie said. "I don't want—" She stopped, swallowed hard, and said in a near-whisper: "I don't want to see Hugh again."

Then she went out.

Mrs. Merton followed and closed the door.

Augusta let out a long breath. She had done it. She had stunted Hugh's career, neutralized Maisie Robinson, and averted the danger from David Middleton, all in one night. Maisie had been a formidable opponent, but in the end she had proved too emotional.

Augusta savored her triumph for a few moments then went to Edward's room.

He was sitting up in bed, sipping brandy from a goblet. His nose was bruised and there was dried blood around it, and he looked somewhat sorry for himself. "My poor boy," Augusta said. She went to his nightstand and damped a corner of a towel, then sat on the edge of the bed and wiped the blood from his upper lip. He winced. "Sorry!" she said.

He gave her a smile. "That's all right, Mother," he said. "Do carry on. It's very soothing."

While she was washing him Dr. Humbold came in, closely followed by Hugh. "Have you been fighting, young man?" the doctor said cheerily.

Augusta took exception to that suggestion. "He certainly has not," she said crossly. "He has been attacked."

Humbold was crushed. "Quite so, quite so," he muttered.

Hugh said: "Where's Maisie?"

Augusta did not want to talk about Maisie in front of the doctor. She stood up and took Hugh outside. "She left."

"Did you send her away?" he demanded.

Augusta was inclined to tell him not to speak to her in that tone of voice, but she decided there was nothing to be gained by angering him: her victory over him was already total, though he did not know it. She said in a conciliatory tone: "If I had thrown her out, do you not think she would have been waiting in the street to tell you so? No, she left of her own accord, and she said she would write to you tomorrow."

"But she said she would still be here when I got back with the doctor."

"Then she changed her mind. Have you never known a girl of her age to do that?"

Hugh looked bewildered, but he did not know what to say next.

Augusta added: "No doubt she wished to extricate herself as quickly as possible from the embarrassing position in which you had put her."

That seemed to make sense to him. "I suppose you made her feel so uncomfortable that she couldn't bear to remain in the house."

"That will do," she said severely. "I don't wish to hear your opinions. Your uncle Joseph will see you first thing in the morning, before you leave for the bank. Now good night."

For a moment it seemed as if he would argue. However, there was really nothing for him to say. "Very well," he muttered at last. He turned into his room.

Augusta went back into Edward's room. The doctor was closing his bag. "No real damage," he said. "His nose will feel tender for a few days, and he may have a black eye tomorrow; but he's young, and he'll soon heal."

"Thank you, Doctor. Hastead will see you out."

"Good night."

Augusta bent over the bed and kissed Edward. "Good night, dear Teddy. Go to sleep, now."

"Very well, Mother dear. Good night."

She had one more task to perform.

She went down the stairs and entered Joseph's room. She was hoping he would have gone to sleep waiting for her, but he was sitting up in bed, reading the *Pall Mall Gazette.* He put it aside immediately and lifted the covers to let her in.

He embraced her immediately. It was quite light in the room: dawn had broken without her noticing it. She closed her eyes.

He entered her quickly. She put her arms around him and responded to his movements. She thought of herself when she was sixteen, lying on a riverbank in a raspberry-pink dress and a straw hat, being kissed by the young earl of Strang; only in her mind he did not stop at kissing her, but lifted her skirts and made love to her in the hot sunshine, with the river lapping at their feet. . . .

When it was over she lay beside Joseph for a while, reflecting on her victory.

"Extraordinary night," he murmured sleepily.

"Yes," she said. "That awful girl."

"Mmm," he grunted. "Very striking-looking . . . arrogant and willful . . . thinks she's as good as anyone . . . lovely figure . . . just like you at that age."

Augusta was mortally offended. "Joseph!" she said. "How could you say such an awful thing?"

He made no reply, and she saw that he was asleep.

Enraged, she threw back the covers, got out of bed and stamped out of the room.

She did not go back to sleep that night.

6

MICKY MIRANDA'S LODGINGS IN CAMBERWELL consisted of two rooms in the house of a widow with a grown son. None of his high-class friends had ever visited him there, not even Edward Pilaster. Micky played the role of a young man-about-town on a very tight budget, and elegant accommodation was one of the things he could manage without.

At nine o'clock each morning the landlady brought coffee and hot rolls for him and Papa. Over breakfast, Micky explained how he had caused Tonio Silva to lose a hundred pounds he did not have. He did not expect his father to sing his praises, but he did hope for a grudging acknowledgment of his ingenuity. However, Papa was not impressed. He blew on his coffee and slurped it noisily. "So, has he gone back to Cordova?"

"Not yet, but he will."

"You hope. So much trouble, and still you only *hope* he will go."

Micky felt wounded. "I'll seal his fate today," he protested.

"When I was your age . . ."

"You would have slit his throat, I know. But this is London, not Santamaria Province, and if I go around cutting people's throats they'll hang me."

"There are times when you have no choice."

"But there are other times when it's better to tread softly, Papa. Think of Samuel Pilaster, and his milk-and-water objections to dealing in guns. I got him out of the way without bloodshed, didn't I?" In fact Augusta had done it, but Micky had not told Papa that.

"I don't know," Papa said stubbornly. "When do I get the rifles?"

It was a sore point. Old Seth was still alive, still Senior Partner of Pilasters Bank. It was August. In September the winter snow would start to melt on the mountains of Santamaria. Papa wanted to go home—with his weapons. As soon as Joseph became Senior Partner, Edward would put the deal through and the guns would be shipped. But old Seth clung on with infuriating stubbornness to his post and his life.

"You'll get them soon, Papa," said Micky. "Seth can't last much longer."

"Good," said Papa, with the smug expression of one who has won an argument.

Micky buttered a roll. It had always been like this. He could never please his father no matter how he tried.

He turned his mind to the day ahead. Tonio now owed money he could never pay. The next step was to turn a problem into a crisis. He wanted Edward and Tonio to quarrel publicly. If he could arrange that, Tonio's disgrace would become general knowledge and he would be obliged to resign from his job and go home to Cordova. That would put him comfortably out of the reach of David Middleton.

Micky wanted to do all this without making an enemy of Tonio. For he had another purpose: he wanted Tonio's job. Tonio could make matters difficult, if he felt so inclined, by maligning Micky to the minister. Micky wanted to persuade him to smooth the path.

The whole situation was complicated by the history of his relationship with Tonio. At school Tonio had hated and feared Micky; more recently Tonio had been admiring of him. Now Micky needed to become Tonio's best friend—at the same time as he ruined his life.

While Micky was brooding over the tricky day ahead of him, there was a knock at the door to the room and the landlady announced a visitor. A moment later Tonio came in.

Micky had been planning to call on him after breakfast. This would save him the trouble.

"Sit down, have some coffee," he said cheerfully. "Bad luck last night! Still, winning and losing, that's what cards are all about."

Tonio bowed to Papa and sat down. He looked as if he had not slept. "I lost more than I can afford," he said.

Papa grunted impatiently. He had no patience with people feeling sorry for themselves, and anyway he despised the Silva family as lily-livered city dwellers who lived by patronage and corruption.

Micky pretended sympathy and said solemnly: "I'm sorry to hear that."

"You know what it means. In this country, a man who doesn't pay his gambling debts isn't a gentleman. And a man who isn't a gentleman can't be a diplomat. I might have to resign and go home."

Exactly, thought Micky; but he said in a sorrowful voice: "I do see the problem."

Tonio went on: "You know what fellows are like about these things—if you don't pay up the next day you're already under suspicion. But it would take me years to pay back a hundred pounds. That's why I've come to you."

"I don't understand," said Micky, though he understood perfectly.

"Will you give me the money?" Tonio pleaded. "You're Cordovan, not like these English; you don't condemn a man for one mistake. And I would pay you back, eventually."

"If I had the money I'd give it to you," said Micky. "I wish I were that well off."

Tonio looked at Papa, who stared at him coldly and said simply: "No."

Tonio hung his head. "I'm such a fool about gambling," he said in a hollow voice. "I don't know what I'm going to do. If I go home in disgrace I won't be able to face my family."

Micky said thoughtfully: "Perhaps there is something else I can do to help."

Tonio brightened. "Oh, please, anything!"

"Edward and I are good friends, as you know. I could speak to him on your behalf, explain the circumstances, and ask him to be lenient—as a personal favor to me."

"Would you?" Tonio's face was suffused with hope.

"I'll ask him to wait for his money, and not to tell anyone. I don't say he'll agree to it, mind you. The Pilasters have money by the bucketful but they're a hard-headed bunch. I'll try, anyway."

Tonio clasped Micky's hand. "I don't know how to thank you," he said fervently. "I'll never forget this."

"Don't raise your hopes too high—"

"I can't help it. I've been in despair, and you've given me a reason to go on." Tonio looked shamefaced and added: "I thought of killing myself this morning. I walked across London Bridge and I was going to throw myself into the river."

There was a soft grunt from Papa, who clearly thought that would have been the best thing all round.

Micky said hastily: "Thank God you changed your mind. Now, I'd better go along to Pilasters Bank and talk to Edward."

"When will I see you?"

"Will you be at the club at lunchtime?"

"Of course, if you want me to."

"Meet me there, then."

"Right." Tonio stood up. "I'll leave you to finish your breakfast. And—"

"Don't thank me," Micky said, holding up his hand in a silencing gesture. "It's unlucky. Wait and hope."

"Yes. All right." Tonio bowed again to Papa. "Good-bye, Señor Miranda." He went out.

"Stupid boy," Papa muttered.

"A complete fool," Micky agreed.

Micky went into the next room and dressed in his morning clothes: a white shirt with a stiff upright collar and starched cuffs, buff-colored trousers, a black satin stock which he took the trouble to tie perfectly, and a black double-breasted frock coat. His shoes gleamed with wax and his hair shone with macassar oil. He always dressed elegantly but conservatively: he would never wear one of the fashionable new turndown collars, or carry a monocle like a dandy. The English were ever ready to believe that a foreigner was a cad, and he took care to give them no excuse.

Leaving Papa to his own devices for the day, he went out and walked across the bridge into the financial district, which was called the City because it covered the square mile of the original Roman city of London. Traffic was at a complete standstill around St. Paul's Cathedral as carriages, horse buses, brewers' drays, hansom cabs and costermongers' barrows competed for space with a huge flock of sheep being driven to Smithfield meat market.

Pilasters Bank was a big new building with a long classical frontage and an imposing entrance flanked by massive fluted pillars. It was a few minutes past noon when Micky went through the double doors into the banking hall. Although Edward rarely got to work before ten, he could generally be persuaded to leave for lunch any time after twelve.

Micky approached one of the "walkers"

and said: "Be good enough to tell Mr. Edward Pilaster that Mr. Miranda has called."

"Very good, sir."

Here more than anywhere Micky envied the Pilasters. Their wealth and power was proclaimed by every detail: the polished marble floor, the rich paneling, the hushed voices, the scratch of pens in ledgers, and perhaps most of all by the overfed, overdressed messengers. All this space and all these people were basically employed in counting the Pilaster family's money. No one here raised cattle, mined nitrate or built railroads: the work was done by others far away. The Pilasters just watched the money multiply. To Micky it seemed the best possible way to live now that slavery had been abolished.

There was also something false about the atmosphere here. It was solemn and dignified, like a church, or the court of a president, or a museum. They were moneylenders, but they acted as if charging interest were a noble calling, like the priesthood.

After a few minutes Edward appeared—with a bruised nose and a black eye. Micky raised his eyebrows. "My dear fellow, what happened to you?"

"I had a fight with Hugh."

"What about?"

"I told him off for bringing a whore into the house and he lost his temper."

It occurred to Micky that this might have given Augusta the opportunity she had been seeking to get rid of Hugh. "What happened to Hugh?"

"You won't see him again for a long time. He's been sent to Boston."

Well done, Augusta, thought Micky. It would be neat if both Hugh and Tonio could be dealt with on the same day. He said: "You look as if you might benefit from a bottle of champagne and some lunch."

"Splendid idea."

They left the bank and headed west. There was no point in getting into a hansom here because the streets were blocked by the sheep and the cabs were all held up in the traffic. They passed the meat market which was the destination of the sheep. The stench from the slaughterhouses was unbearably disgusting. The sheep were thrown from the street through a trapdoor down into the underground abattoir. The fall was sufficient to break their legs, which rendered them motionless until the slaughterer was ready to cut their throats. "It's enough to put you off mutton for life," Edward said as they covered their faces with handkerchiefs. Micky thought it would take a lot more than that to put Edward off his lunch.

Once out of the City they hailed a hansom and directed it to Pall Mall. As soon as they were on their way, Micky began his prepared speech. He started by saying: "I hate a chap who spreads reports about another chap's bad behavior."

"Yes," Edward said vaguely.

"But when it affects a chap's friends, a chap is more or less obliged to say something."

"Mmm." Edward clearly had no idea what Micky was talking about.

"And I'd hate you to think I kept quiet about it just because he was a countryman of mine."

There was a moment's silence, then Edward said: "I'm not quite sure I follow you."

"I'm talking about Tonio Silva."

"Ah, yes. I suppose he can't afford to pay what he owes me."

"Utter nonsense. I know his family. They're almost as rich as yours." Micky was not afraid to tell this outrageous lie: people in London had no idea how wealthy South American families might be.

Edward was surprised. "Good Lord. I thought the opposite."

"Not at all. He can afford it easily. That makes it worse."

"What? Makes what worse?"

Micky gave a heavy sigh. "I'm afraid he has no intention of paying you. And he's been going around boasting about it, saying you aren't man enough to make him pay."

Edward reddened. "Has he, by the devil! Not man enough! We'll see about that."

"I warned him not to underestimate you. I told him I was afraid you might not stand to be made a fool of. But he chose to ignore my advice."

"The scoundrel. Well, if he won't listen to wise counsel he may have to find out the truth the hard way."

"It's a shame," said Micky.

Edward fumed in silence.

Micky fretted impatiently while the hansom crawled along the Strand. Tonio should be at the club by now. Edward was in just the right mood to quarrel. Everything was working out.

At last the cab pulled up outside the club. Micky waited while Edward paid the driver. They went inside. In the cloakroom, in a knot of people hanging up their hats, they met Tonio.

Micky tensed. He had put everything in place: now he could only cross his fingers and hope that the drama he had envisioned would play itself out as planned.

Tonio caught Edward's eye, looked awkward, and said: "By Jove . . . Good morning, you two."

Micky looked at Edward. His face turned pink and his eyes bulged, and he said: "See here, Silva."

Tonio stared at him fearfully. "What is it, Pilaster?"

Edward said loudly: "About that hundred pounds."

The room went suddenly quiet. Several people looked around and two men on their way out stopped in the doorway and turned to see. It was bad behavior to talk about money, and a gentleman would do so only in extreme circumstances. Everyone knew that Edward Pilaster had more money than he knew what to do with, so it was obvious he had some other motive for publicly mentioning Tonio's debt. Bystanders sensed a scandal.

Tonio went white. "Yes?"

Edward said brutally: "You can let me

have it today, if it would suit your convenience."

A challenge had been issued. Plenty of people knew the debt was real, so there was no point in arguing about it. As a gentleman, Tonio had only one option. He had to say *By all means. If it's important, you shall have your money right away. Let's go upstairs, and I'll write you a cheque—or shall we step around the corner to my bank?* If he did not do that, everyone would know he could not pay, and he would be ostracized.

Micky watched with horrid fascination. At first a look of panic came over Tonio's face, and for a moment Micky wondered whether he would do something crazy. Then fear gave way to anger, and he opened his mouth to protest, but no words came out. Instead he spread his hands in a pleading gesture; but he quickly abandoned that, too. Finally his face crumpled like the face of a child about to cry. At that point he turned and ran. The two men in the doorway dodged out of his way, and he dashed through the lobby and out into the street without his hat.

Micky was elated: it had all gone perfectly.

The men in the cloakroom all coughed and fidgeted to disguise their embarrassment. An older member muttered: "That was a bit hard, Pilaster."

Micky said quickly: "He deserved it."

"No doubt, no doubt," said the older man.

Edward said: "I need a drink."

Micky said: "Order a brandy for me, would you? I'd better go after Silva and make sure he doesn't throw himself under the wheels of a horse bus." He dashed out.

This was the most subtle part of his plan: he now had to convince the man he had ruined that he was his best friend.

Tonio was hurrying along in the direction of St. James's, not looking where he was going, bumping into people. Micky ran and caught up with him. "I say, Silva, I'm dreadfully sorry," he said.

Tonio stopped. There were tears on his cheeks. "I'm finished," he said. "It's all over."

"Pilaster turned me down flat," Micky said. "I did my best. . . ."

"I know. Thank you."

"Don't thank me. I failed."

"But you tried. I wish there was something I could do to show my appreciation."

Micky hesitated, thinking: *Do I dare to ask him for his job, right now?* He decided to be bold. "As a matter of fact there is—but we should talk about it another time."

"No, tell me now."

"I'd feel bad. Let's leave it until another day."

"I don't know how many more days I'll be here. What is it?"

"Well . . ." Micky feigned embarrassment. "I suppose the Cordovan Minister will eventually be looking for someone to replace you."

"He'll need someone right away." Comprehension showed on Tonio's tear-stained face. "Of course—you should have the job! You'd be perfect!"

"If you could put in a word. . . ."

"I'll do more than that. I'll tell him what a help you've been, and how you tried to get me out of the mess I got myself into. I'm sure he'll want to appoint you."

"I wish I weren't benefiting from your troubles," Micky said. "I feel I'm behaving like a rat."

"Not at all." Tonio took Micky's hand in both of his. "You're a true friend."

CHAPTER FIVE

SEPTEMBER

1

HUGH'S SIX-YEAR-OLD SISTER Dorothy was folding his shirts and packing them into his trunk. He knew that as soon as she went to bed he would have to take them all out and do them again, because her folding was hopelessly untidy; but he pretended she was very good at it, and encouraged her.

"Tell me about America again," she said.

"America is so far away that in the morning the sun takes four hours to get there."

"Do they stay in bed all morning?"

"Yes—then they get up at lunchtime and have breakfast!"

She giggled. "They're lazy."

"Not really. You see, it doesn't get dark

until midnight, so they have to work all evening."

"And they go to bed late! I like going to bed late. I'd like America. Why can't we go with you?"

"I wish you could, Dotty." Hugh felt rather wistful: he would not see his baby sister again for years. She would be changed when he returned. She would understand time zones.

September rain drummed on the windows, and down in the bay the wind lashed the waves, but here there was a coal fire and a soft hearth-rug. Hugh packed a handful of books: *Modern Business Methods, The Successful Commercial Clerk, The Wealth of Nations, Robinson Crusoe.* The older clerks at Pilasters Bank were contemptuous of what they called "book-learning," and were fond of saying that experience was the best teacher, but they were wrong: Hugh had been able to understand the workings of the different departments much more quickly because he had studied the theory beforehand.

He was going to America at a time of crisis. In the early 1870s several of the banks had made large loans on the security of speculative railway stocks, and when railway construction ran into trouble in the middle of 1873 the banks started to look shaky. A few days ago Jay Cooke & Co., the agents of the American government, had gone bust, dragging the First National Bank of Washington down with them; and the news had reached London the same day via the transatlantic telegraph cable. Now five New York banks had suspended business, including the Union Trust Company—a major bank—and the old-established Mechanics' Banking Association. The Stock Exchange had closed its doors. Businesses would fall, thousands of people would be thrown out of work, trade would suffer, and Pilasters' American operation would get smaller and more cautious—so that it would be harder for Hugh to make his mark.

So far the crisis had had little impact in London. The bank rate had gone up a point, to four percent, and a small London bank with close American links had failed, but there was no panic. All the same, old Seth insisted there was trouble ahead. He was quite weak now. He had moved into Augusta's house and spent most days in bed. But he stubbornly refused to resign until he had steered Pilasters through the storm.

Hugh began to fold his clothes. The bank

had paid for two new suits: he had a suspicion his mother had persuaded his grandfather to authorize that. Old Seth was as tight-fisted as the rest of the Pilasters but he had a soft spot for Hugh's mother; in fact it was the small allowance Seth gave her that she had been living on all these years.

Mother had also insisted Hugh be allowed a few weeks off before leaving, to give him more time to get ready and say his good-byes. She had not seen much of him since he had gone to work at the bank—he could not afford the train fare to Folkestone very often—and she wanted to have some time with him before he left the country. They had spent most of August here, at the seaside, while Augusta and her family had been on holiday in Scotland. Now the holidays were over and it was time to leave, and Hugh was saying good-bye to his mother.

While he was thinking about her she came into the room. She was in her eighth year of widowhood but she still wore black. She did not seem to want to marry again, although she easily could have—she was still beautiful, with serene gray eyes and thick blond hair.

He knew she was sad that she would not see him for years. But she had not spoken of her sadness: rather, she shared his excitement and trepidation at the challenge of a new country.

"It's almost bedtime, Dorothy," she said. "Go and put on your nightdress." As soon as Dotty was out of the room, Mother began to refold Hugh's shirts.

He wanted to talk to her about Maisie, but he felt shy. Augusta had written to her, he knew. She might also have heard from other family members, or even seen them on one of her rare shopping trips to London. The story she had heard might be a long way from the truth. After a moment he said: "Mother . . ."

"What is it, dear?"

"Aunt Augusta doesn't always say quite what is true."

"No need to be so polite," she said with a bitter smile. "Augusta has been telling lies about your father for years."

Hugh was startled by her frankness. "Do you think it was she who told Florence Stalworthy's parents that he was a gambler?"

"I'm quite sure of it, unfortunately."

"Why is she this way?"

His mother put down the shirt she was folding and thought for a minute. "Augusta was a very beautiful girl," she said. "Her family worshiped at Kensington Methodist Hall, which is how we knew them. She was an only child, willful and spoiled. Her parents were nothing special: her father was a shop assistant who had started his own business and ended up with three little grocery stores in the west London suburbs. But Augusta was clearly destined for higher things."

She went to the rainy window and looked out, seeing not the stormy English Channel but the past. "When she was seventeen the earl of Strang fell for her. He was a lovely boy—comely, kind, high-born and rich. Naturally his parents were horrified at the prospect that he should marry a grocer's daughter. However, she was very beautiful, and even then, though she was young, she had a dignified air that could carry her through most social situations."

"Did they become engaged?" Hugh asked.

"Not formally. But everyone assumed it was a foregone conclusion. Then there was a dreadful scandal. Her father was accused of systematically giving short weight in his shops. An employee he had sacked reported him to the Board of Trade. It was said that he had even cheated the church, which bought tea from him for the Tuesday evening Bible study groups and so on. There was a chance he would go to jail. He denied everything vehemently, and in the end nothing came of it. But Strang dropped Augusta."

"She must have been heartbroken."

"No," Mother said. "Not heartbroken. She was wild with rage. All her life she had been able to have her own way. Now she wanted Strang more than she had ever wanted anything—and she couldn't have him."

"And she married Uncle Joseph on the rebound, as they say."

"I'd say she married him in a fit of temper. He was older than she by seven years, which is a lot when you're seventeen; and he wasn't much better-looking then than he is now; but he was very rich, even richer than Strang. To give her credit, she has done all she can to be a good wife to him. But he will never be Strang, and she is still angry about that."

"What happened to Strang?"

"He married a French countess and died in a hunting accident."

"I almost feel sorry for Augusta."

"No matter what she has, she always wants more: more money, a more important job for her husband, a higher social position for herself. The reason she is so ambitious— for herself, for Joseph and for Edward—is that she still yearns for what Strang could have given her: the title, the ancestral home, the life of endless leisure, wealth without work. But that isn't what Strang offered her, in truth. He offered her love. That's what she's really lost. And nothing will ever make up for it."

Hugh had never had such an intimate conversation with his mother. He felt encouraged to open his heart to her. "Mother," he began. "About Maisie . . ."

She looked puzzled. "Maisie?"

"The girl . . . all the trouble is about. Maisie Robinson."

Her face cleared. "Augusta never told anyone her name."

He hesitated, then blurted out: "She's not an 'unfortunate' woman."

Mother was embarrassed: men never mentioned such things as prostitution to their mothers. "I see," she said, looking away.

Hugh plowed on. "She is lower class, that much is right. And Jewish." He looked at her face and saw that she was startled, but not horrified. "She's nothing worse than that. In fact . . ." He hesitated.

Mother looked at him. "Go on."

"In fact, she was a maiden."

Mother blushed.

"I'm sorry to speak of such things, Mother," he said. "But if I don't you'll only know Aunt Augusta's version of the story."

Mother swallowed. "Were you fond of her, Hugh?"

"Rather." He felt tears come to his eyes. "I don't understand why she disappeared. I've no idea where she went. I never knew her address. I've inquired at the livery stables she worked for, and at the Argyll Rooms where I met her. Solly Greenbourne was fond of her too, and he's as baffled as I am. Tonio Silva knew her friend April, but Tonio has gone back to South America and I can't find April."

"How mysterious."

"I'm sure Aunt Augusta arranged this somehow."

"I have no doubt of it. I can't imagine how, but she is appallingly devious. However, you must look to the future now, Hugh. Boston will be such an opportunity for you. You must work hard and conscientiously."

"She really is an extraordinary girl, Mother."

Mother did not believe him, he could tell. She said: "But you'll forget her."

"I wonder if I ever shall."

Mother kissed his forehead. "You will. I promise."

2

THERE WAS ONLY ONE PICTURE ON THE WALL in the attic room Maisie shared with April. It was a garish circus poster showing Maisie, in spangled tights, standing on the back of a galloping horse. Underneath, in red letters, were the words "The Amazing Maisie." The picture was not very true to life, for the circus had not actually had any white horses, and Maisie's legs had never been that long. All the same she cherished the poster. It was her only souvenir of those days.

Otherwise the room contained only a narrow bed, a washstand, one chair and a three-legged stool. The girls' clothes hung from nails banged into the wall. The dirt on the window served instead of curtains. They tried to keep the place clean but it was impossible. Soot fell down the chimney, mice came up through the cracks in the floor-boards, and dirt and insects crept in through the gaps between the window frame and the surrounding brickwork. Today it was raining, and water dripped from the windowsill and from a crack in the ceiling.

Maisie was getting dressed. It was Rosh Hashanah, when the Book of Life was open, and at this time of year she always wondered what was being written for her. She never actually prayed, but she did sort of hope, in a solemn kind of way, that something good was going on her page of the Book.

April had gone to make tea in the communal kitchen, but now she came back, bursting into the room with a newspaper in her hand. "It's you, Maisie, it's you!" she said.

"What?"

"In the *Lloyd's Weekly News*. Listen to this. 'Miss Maisie Robinson, formerly Miriam Rabinowicz. If Miss Robinson will contact Messrs. Goldman and Jay, Solicitors, at Gray's Inn, she will learn something to her advantage.' It must be you!"

Maisie's heart beat faster, but she made

her expression stern and her voice cold. "It's Hugh," she said. "I'll not go."

April looked disappointed. "You might have inherited money from a long-lost relation."

"I might be the Queen of Mongolia, but I'll not walk all the way to Gray's Inn on the off-chance." She was managing to sound flippant, but her heart ached. She thought about Hugh every day and every night, and she was miserable. She hardly knew him, but it was impossible to forget him.

Nevertheless she was determined to try. She knew he had been searching for her. He had been at the Argyll Rooms every night, he had badgered Sammles the stable owner, and he had inquired for her at half the cheap lodging houses in London. Then the inquiries had ceased, and Maisie assumed he had given up. Now it seemed he had merely changed his tactics, and was trying to reach her with newspaper advertisements. It was very hard to continue to avoid him when he was searching so persistently for her and she wanted so badly to see him again. But she had made her decision. She loved him too much to ruin him.

She put her arms into her corset. "Help me with my stays," she said to April.

April began pulling the laces. "I've never had my name in the paper," she said enviously. "You have twice, now, if you count 'The Lioness' as a name."

"And how much good has it done me? By God, I'm getting fat."

April tied the laces and helped her into her gown. They were going out tonight. April had a new lover, a middle-aged magazine editor with a wife and six children in Clapham. This evening he and a friend were taking April and Maisie to a music hall.

Between now and then they would walk along Bond Street and stare into the windows of fashionable shops. They would not buy anything. In order to hide from Hugh, Maisie had been obliged to give up working for Sammles—much to Sammles's regret, for she had sold five horses and a pony-and-trap—and the money she had saved was rapidly running out. But they had to go out, regardless of the weather: it was too depressing to stay in the room.

Maisie's gown was tight across her breasts and she winced as April did it up. April gave her a curious look and said: "Are your nipples sore?"

"Yes, they are—I wonder why?"

"Maisie," said April in a worried tone, "when did you last have the curse?"

"I never keep count." Maisie thought for a moment, and a chill descended on her. "Oh, dear God," she said.

"When?"

"I think it was before we went to the races at Goodwood. Do you think I'm pregnant?"

"Your waist is bigger and your nipples hurt and you haven't had the curse for two months—yes, you're pregnant," April said in an exasperated voice. "I can't believe you've been so stupid. Who was it?"

"Hugh, of course. But we only did it once. How can you get pregnant from one fuck?"

"You *always* get pregnant from one fuck."

"Oh, my God." Maisie felt as if she had been hit by a train. Shocked, bewildered and frightened, she sat down on the bed and began to cry. "What am I going to do?" she said helplessly.

"We could go to that lawyer's office, for a start."

Suddenly everything was different.

At first Maisie was scared and angry. Then she realized that she was now obliged to get in touch with Hugh, for the sake of the child inside her. And when she admitted this to herself she felt more glad than frightened. She was longing to see him again. She had convinced herself that it would be wrong to. But the baby made everything different. Now it was her duty to contact Hugh, and the prospect made her weak with relief.

All the same she was nervous as she and April climbed the steep staircase to the lawyer's rooms at Gray's Inn. The advertisement might not have been placed by Hugh. It would hardly be surprising if he had given up the search for her. She had been as discouraging as a girl could, and no man would carry the torch forever. The advertisement might be something to do with her parents, if they were still alive. Perhaps things had begun to go well for them at last, and they had the money to search for her. She was not sure how she felt about that. There had been many times when she had longed to see Mama and Papa again, but she was afraid they would be ashamed of her way of life.

They reached the top of the stairs and entered the outer office. The lawyer's clerk was a young man wearing a mustard-colored waistcoat and a condescending smile. The girls were wet and bedraggled, but all the same he was disposed to flirt. "Ladies!" he said. "How could two such goddesses have need of the services of Messrs. Goldman and Jay? What could I possibly do for you?"

April rose to the occasion. "You could take off that waistcoat, it's hurting my eyes," she said.

Maisie had no patience with gallantry today. "My name is Maisie Robinson," she said.

"Aha! The advertisement. By a happy chance, the gentleman in question is with Mr. Jay at this very minute."

Maisie felt faint with trepidation. "Tell me something," she said hesitantly. "The gentleman in question . . . Is he by any chance Mr. Hugh Pilaster?" She looked pleadingly at the clerk.

He failed to notice her look and replied in his ebullient tone: "Good Lord, no!"

Maisie's hopes collapsed again. She sat down on a hard wooden bench by the door, fighting back tears. "Not him," she said.

"No," said the clerk. "As a matter of fact, I know Hugh Pilaster—we were at school together in Folkestone. He's gone to America."

Maisie rocked back as if she had been punched. "America?" she whispered.

"Boston, Massachusetts. Took ship a couple of weeks ago. You know him, then?"

Maisie ignored the question. Her heart felt like a stone, heavy and cold. Gone to America. And she had his child inside her. She was too horrified to cry.

April said aggressively: "Who is it, then?"

The clerk began to feel out of his depth. He lost his superior air and said nervously: "I'd better let him tell you himself. Excuse me for a moment." He disappeared through an inner door.

Maisie stared blankly at the boxes of papers stacked against the wall, reading the titles marked on the sides: *Blenkinsop Estate, Regina versus Wiltshire Flour Millers, Great Southern Railway, Mrs. Stanley Evans (deceased).* Everything that happened in this office was a tragedy for someone, she reflected: death, bankruptcy, divorce, prosecution.

When the door opened again, a different man came out, a man of striking appearance. Not much older than Maisie, he had the face of a biblical prophet, with dark eyes staring out from under black eyebrows, a big nose with flaring nostrils, and a bushy beard. He looked familiar, and after a moment she decided he reminded her a little of her father, although Papa had never looked so fierce.

"Maisie?" he said. "Maisie Robinson?"

His clothes were a little odd, as if they had been bought in a foreign country, and his accent was American. "Yes, I'm Maisie Robinson," she said. "Who the devil are you?"

"Don't you recognize me?"

Suddenly she remembered a wire-thin boy, ragged and barefoot, with the first shadow of a moustache on his lip and a do-or-die look in his eye. "Oh, my God!" she yelped. "Danny!" For a moment she forgot her troubles as she ran to his arms. "Danny, is it really you?"

He hugged her so hard it hurt. "Sure it's me," he said.

"Who?" April was saying. "Who is he?"

"My brother!" Maisie said. "The one that ran away to America! He came back!"

Danny broke their embrace to stare at her. "How did you get to be beautiful?" he said. "You used to be a skinny little runt!"

She touched his beard. "I might have known you without all this fur round your gob."

There was a discreet cough from behind Danny, and Maisie looked up to see an elderly man standing in the doorway looking faintly disdainful. "Apparently we have been successful," he said.

Danny said: "Mr. Jay, may I present my sister, Miss Robinson."

"Your servant, Miss Robinson. If I may make a suggestion . . . ?"

"Why not?" said Danny.

"There is a coffeehouse in Theobald's Road, just a few steps away. You must have a lot to talk about."

He obviously wanted them out of his office, but Danny did not seem to care what Mr. Jay wanted. Whatever else might have happened he had not learned to be deferential. "What do you say, girls? Would you like to talk here, or shall we go and drink coffee?"

"Let's go," Maisie said.

Mr. Jay added: "And perhaps you might come back to settle your account a little later, Mr. Robinson?"

"I won't forget. Come on, girls."

They left the office and went down the stairs. Maisie was bursting with questions, but controlled her curiosity with an effort while they found the coffeehouse and settled themselves at a table. At last she said:

"What have you been doing for the last seven years?"

"Building railways," he said. "It so happened that I arrived at a good time. The war between the states had just ended and the railway boom was beginning. They were so desperate for workers that they were shipping them over from Europe. Even a skinny thirteen-year-old could get a job. I worked on the first-ever steel bridge, over the Mississippi at St Louis; then I got a job building the Union Pacific Railroad in Utah. I was a ganger by the time I was nineteen—it's young men's work. And I joined the trade union and led a strike."

"Why did you come back?"

"There's been a stock market crash. The railroads have run out of money, and the banks that were financing them have gone bust. There are thousands of men, hundreds of thousands, looking for work. I decided to come home and make a new start."

"What will you do—build railroads here?"

He shook his head. "I've got a new idea. You see, it's happened to me twice, that my life has been wrecked by a financial crash. The men who own banks are the stupidest people in the world. They never learn, so they make the same mistakes again and again. And it's the workingmen who suffer. Nobody ever helps them—nobody ever will. They have to help each other."

April said: "People never help each other. It's everyone for himself in this world. You've got to be selfish."

April often said that, Maisie recalled, even though in practice she was a generous person and would do anything for a friend.

Danny said: "I'm going to start a kind of club for workingmen. They'll pay sixpence a week, and if they're thrown out of work through no fault of their own the club will pay them a pound a week while they look for a new job."

Maisie stared at her brother in admiration. The plan was formidably ambitious—but she had thought the same when at the age of thirteen he had said *There's a ship in the harbor that's bound for Boston on the morning tide—I'll shin up a rope tonight and hide on deck in one of the boats.* He had done what he said then and he probably would now. He said he had led a strike. He seemed to have grown into the kind of person other men would follow.

"But what about Papa and Mama?" he said. "Have you been in touch with them?"

Maisie shook her head and then, surprising herself, she began to cry. Suddenly she felt the pain of losing her family, a pain she had refused to acknowledge all these years.

Danny put a hand on her shoulder. "I'll go back up north and see if I can trace them."

"I hope you find them," Maisie said. "I miss them so much." She caught the eye of April, who was staring at her in astonishment. "I'm so afraid they'll be ashamed of me."

"And why should they?" he said.

"I'm pregnant."

His face reddened. "And not married?"

"No."

"Going to get married?"

"No."

Danny was angry. "Who is the swine?"

Maisie raised her voice. "Spare me the outraged-brother act, will you?"

"I'd like to break his neck—"

"Shut up, Danny!" Maisie said angrily. "You left me alone seven years ago and you've no business to come back and act as if you own me." He looked abashed, and she went on in a quieter voice: "It doesn't matter. He would have married me, I expect, but I didn't want him to, so forget about him. Anyway, he's gone to America."

Danny calmed down. "If I wasn't your brother I'd marry you myself. You're pretty enough! Anyway, you can have what little money I've got left."

"I don't want it." She was sounding ungracious, but she could not help it. "There's no need for you to take care of me, Danny. Use your money for your workingmen's club. I'll look after myself. I managed when I was eleven years old, so I suppose I can now."

3

MICKY MIRANDA AND PAPA were in a small eating house in Soho, lunching off oyster stew —the cheapest dish on the menu—and strong beer. The restaurant was a few minutes from the Cordovan Ministry in Portland Place, where Micky now sat at a writing table every morning for an hour or two, dealing with the minister's mail. He was finished for the day and had met Papa for lunch. They sat opposite each other on hard wooden high-backed benches. There was sawdust on the floor and years of grease on the low ceiling. Micky hated eating in such places, but all the same he did it often, to save money. He ate at the Cowes Club only when Edward was paying. Besides, taking Papa to the club was a strain: Micky was constantly afraid the old man would start a fight, or pull a gun, or spit on the rug.

Papa wiped his bowl with a chunk of bread and pushed it aside. "I must explain something to you," he said.

Micky put down his spoon.

Papa said: "I need rifles to fight the Delabarca family. When I have destroyed them I will take over their nitrate mines. The mines will make our family rich."

Micky nodded silently. He had heard all this before but he would not dare to say so.

"The nitrate mines are only the beginning, the first step," Papa went on. "When we have more money, we will buy more rifles. Different family members will become important people in the province."

Micky's ears pricked up. This was a new line.

"Your cousin Jorge will be a colonel in the army. Your brother Paulo will become chief of police in Santamaria Province."

So that he can be a professional bully instead of an amateur, Micky thought.

Papa said: "Then I will become governor of the province."

Governor! Micky had not realized that Papa's aspirations were so high.

But he had not finished. "When we control the province, we will look to the nation. We will become fervent supporters of President Garcia. You will be his envoy in London. Your brother will become his minister of justice, perhaps. Your uncles will be generals. Your half-brother Dominic, the priest, will become archbishop of Palma."

Micky was astonished: he never knew he had a half-brother. But he said nothing, for he did not want to interrupt.

"And then," Papa said, "when the time is right, we will move the Garcia family aside and we will step in."

"You mean we will take over the government?" Micky said, wide-eyed. He was bowled over by Papa's audacity and confidence.

"Yes. In twenty years time, my son, either I will be president of Cordova . . . or you will."

Micky tried to take it in. Cordova had a constitution which provided for democratic elections, but none had ever been held. President Garcia had taken power in a coup

ten years ago; previously he had been commander-in-chief of the armed forces under
President Lopez, who had led the rebellion
against the Spanish rule in which Papa and
his cowboys had fought.

Papa surprised Micky by the subtlety of
his strategy: to become a fervent supporter
of the current ruler and then betray him.
But what was Micky's role? He should become the Cordovan Minister in London. He
had already taken the first step by elbowing
Tonio Silva aside and getting his job. He
would have to find a way to do the same to
the minister.

And then what? If his father were president, Micky might be foreign minister, and
travel the world as the representative of his
country. But Papa had said Micky himself
might be president—not Paulo, not Uncle
Rico, but Micky. Was it really possible?

Why not? Micky was clever, ruthless and
well connected: what more did he need?
The prospect of ruling a whole country was
intoxicating. Everyone would bow to him;
the most beautiful women in the land would
be his to take, whether they wished it or not;
he would be as rich as the Pilasters.

"President," he said dreamily. "I like it."

Papa reached out casually and slapped his face.

The old man had a powerful arm and a horny hand, and the slap rocked Micky. He cried out, shocked and hurt, and leaped to his feet. He tasted blood in his mouth. The place went quiet and everyone looked.

"Sit down," Papa said.

Slowly and reluctantly, Micky obeyed.

Papa reached across the table with both hands and grabbed him by the lapels. In a voice full of scorn he said: "This entire plan has been put at risk because you have completely failed in the simple, small task allotted to you!"

Micky was terrified of him in this mood. "Papa, you'll get your rifles!" he said.

"In one more month it will be spring in Cordova. We have to take the Delabarca mines this season—next year will be too late. I have booked passage on a freighter bound for Panama. The captain has been bribed to put me and the weapons ashore on the Atlantic coast of Santamaria." Papa stood up, dragging Micky upright, tearing his shirt by the force of his grip. His face was suffused with anger. "The ship sails in five days time," he said in a voice that filled

Micky with fear. "Now get out of here and buy me those guns!"

Augusta Pilaster's servile butler, Hastead, took Micky's wet coat and hung it near the fire that blazed in the hall. Micky did not thank him. They disliked each other. Hastead was jealous of anyone Augusta favored, and Micky despised the man for fawning. Besides, Micky never knew which way Hastead's eyes were looking, and that unnerved him.

Micky went into the drawing room and found Augusta alone. She looked pleased to see him. She held his hand in both of hers and said: "You're so cold."

"I walked across the park."

"Foolish boy, you should have taken a hansom." Micky could not afford hansom cabs, but Augusta did not know that. She pressed his hand to her bosom and smiled. It was like a sexual invitation, but she acted as if she were innocently warming his cold fingers.

She did this kind of thing a lot when they were alone together, and normally Micky enjoyed it. She would hold his hand and touch his thigh, and he would touch her arm or her shoulder, and look into her eyes, and they would talk in low voices, like lovers, without ever acknowledging that they were flirting. He found it exciting, and so did she. But today he was too desperately worried to dally with her. "How is old Seth?" he asked, hoping to hear of a sudden relapse.

She sensed his mood and let go of his hand without protest, although she looked disappointed. "Come close to the fire," she said. She sat on a sofa and patted the seat beside her. "Seth is much better."

Micky's heart sank.

She went on: "He may be with us for years yet." She could not keep the irritation out of her voice. She was impatient for her husband to take over. "You know he is living here now. You shall visit him when you have had some tea."

"He must retire soon, surely?" said Micky.

"There is no sign of it, regrettably. Just this morning he forbade another issue of Russian railway stock." She patted his knee. "Be patient. Your papa shall have his rifles eventually."

"He can't wait much longer," Micky said worriedly. "He has to leave next week."

"So that's why you're looking so tense,"

she said. "Poor boy. I wish I could do something to help.

"You don't know my father," Micky said, and he could not keep the note of despair out of his voice. "He pretends to be civilized when he sees you, but in reality he's a barbarian. God knows what he'll do to me if I let him down."

There were voices in the hall. "There's something I must tell you before the others come in," Augusta said hastily. "I finally met Mr. David Middleton."

Micky nodded. "What did he say?"

"He was polite, but frank. Said he did not believe that the entire truth about his brother's death had been told, and asked if I could put him in touch with either Hugh Pilaster or Antonio Silva. I told him they were both abroad, and he was wasting his time."

"I wish we could solve the problem of old Seth as neatly as we solved that one," Micky said as the door opened.

Edward came in, then his sister Clementine. Clementine looked like Augusta but did not have the same force of personality, and she had none of her mother's sexual allure. Augusta poured tea. Micky talked to Edward in a desultory way about their plans for the evening. There were no parties or balls in September: the aristocracy stayed away from London until after Christmas, and only the politicians and their wives were in town. But there was no shortage of middle-class entertainment, and Edward had tickets for a play. Micky pretended to be looking forward to it, but his mind was on Papa.

Hastead brought in hot buttered muffins. Edward ate several but Micky had no appetite. More family members arrived: Joseph's brother Young William; Joseph's ugly sister Madeleine; and Madeleine's husband Major Hartshorn, with the scar on his forehead. They all talked of the financial crisis, but Micky could tell they were not afraid: old Seth had seen it coming and had made sure that Pilasters Bank was not exposed. High-risk securities had lost value—Egyptian, Peruvian and Turkish bonds had crashed—but English government securities and English railway shares had suffered only modest falls.

One by one they all went up to visit Seth; one by one they came down and said how marvelous he was. Micky waited until last. He finally went up at half-past five.

Seth was in what used to be Hugh's room. A nurse sat outside with the door ajar in case he should call her. Micky went in and closed the door.

Seth was sitting up in bed reading *The Economist.* Micky said: "Good afternoon, Mr. Pilaster. How are you feeling?"

The old man put his journal aside with obvious reluctance. "I'm feeling well, I thank you. How is your father?"

"Impatient to be home." Micky stared at the frail old man on the white sheets. The skin of his face was translucent, and the curved knife of the Pilaster nose seemed sharper than ever, but there was lively intelligence in the eyes. He looked as if he could live and run the bank for another decade.

Micky seemed to hear his father's voice in his ear, saying *Who is standing in our way?*

The old man was weak and helpless, and there was only Micky in the room and the nurse outside.

Micky realized he had to kill Seth.

His father's voice said *Do it now.*

He could suffocate the old man with a pillow and leave no evidence. Everyone would think he had died a natural death.

Micky's heart filled with loathing and he felt ill.

"What's the matter?" Seth said. "You look sicker than I."

"Are you quite comfortable, sir?" Micky said. "Let me adjust your pillows."

"Please don't trouble, they're all right," said Seth, but Micky reached behind him and pulled out a big feather pillow.

Micky looked at the old man and hesitated.

Fear flashed in Seth's eyes and he opened his mouth to call out.

Before he could make a sound Micky smothered his face with the pillow and pushed his head back down.

Unfortunately, Seth's arms were outside the bedclothes, and now his hands grasped Micky's forearms with surprising strength. Micky stared in horror at the aged talons clamped to his coat sleeves, but he held on with all his might. Seth clawed desperately at Micky's arms but the younger man was stronger.

When that failed Seth began to kick his legs and squirm. He could not escape from Micky's grasp, but Hugh's old bed squeaked, and Micky was terrified that the nurse might hear and come in to investigate. The only way he could think of to keep the old man still was to lie on top of him. Still holding the pillow over Seth's face, Micky got on the bed and lay on the writhing body.

It was grotesquely reminiscent of sex with an unwilling woman, Micky thought crazily, and he suppressed the hysterical laughter that bubbled to his lips. Seth continued to struggle but his movements were restrained by Micky's weight and the bed ceased to squeak. Micky held on grimly.

At last all movement ceased. Micky remained in place as long as he dared, to make sure; then he cautiously removed the pillow and stared at the white, still face. The eyes were closed but the features were still. The old man looked dead. Micky had to check for a heartbeat. Slowly and fearfully, he lowered his head to Seth's chest.

Suddenly the old man's eyes opened wide and he took a huge, dragging breath.

Micky almost cried aloud with horror. A moment later he regained his wits and shoved the pillow over Seth's face again. He felt himself shaking weakly with fear and disgust as he held it down; but there was no more resistance.

He knew he should keep it there for several minutes, to be sure the old man really was dead this time; but he was worried about the nurse. She might notice the silence. He had to speak, for a pretense of normality. But he could not think what to say to a dead man. Say anything, he told himself, it doesn't matter so long as she hears the murmur of conversation. "I'm pretty well," he mumbled desperately. "Pretty well, pretty well. And how are you? Well, well. I'm glad to hear you're feeling better. Splendid, Mr. Pilaster. I'm very glad to see you looking so well, so splendid, so much better, oh dear God I can't keep this up, very well, splendid, splendid . . ."

He could stand it no longer. He took his weight off the pillow. Grimacing with distaste, he put his hand on Seth's chest where he imagined the heart would be. There were sparse white hairs on the old man's pale skin. The body was warm beneath the nightshirt, but there was no heartbeat. *Are you really dead this time?* he thought. And then he seemed to hear Papa's voice, angry and impatient, saying *Yes, you fool, he's dead, now get out of there!* Leaving the pillow over the face, he rolled off the corpse and stood up.

A wave of nausea engulfed him. He felt weak and faint, and he grabbed the bedpost to steady himself. I killed him, he thought. I killed him.

There was a voice on the landing.

Micky looked at the body on the bed. The

pillow was still over Seth's face. He snatched it up. Seth's dead eyes were open and staring.

The door opened.

Augusta walked in.

She stood in the doorway, looking at the rumpled bed, the still face of Seth with its staring eyes, and the pillow in Micky's hands. The blood drained from her cheeks.

Micky stared at her, silent and helpless, waiting for her to speak.

She stood there, looking from Seth to Micky and back again, for a long moment.

Then, slowly and quietly, she closed the door.

She took the pillow from Micky. She lifted Seth's lifeless head and replaced the pillow, then she straightened the sheets. She picked up *The Economist* from the floor, placed it on his chest, and folded his hands over it, so that he looked as if he had fallen asleep reading it.

Then she closed his eyes.

She came to Micky. "You're shaking," she said. She took his face in her hands and kissed his mouth.

For a moment he was too stunned to react. Then he went from terror to desire in a flash. He put his arms around her and embraced her, feeling her bosom against his chest. She opened her mouth and their tongues met. Micky grasped her breasts in both hands and squeezed them hard. She gasped. His erection came immediately. Augusta began to grind her pelvis against his, rubbing herself on his stiff penis. They were both breathing hard. Augusta took his hand, put it in her mouth, and bit down, to stop herself crying out. Her eyes closed tight and she shuddered. He realized she was having an orgasm and he was so inflamed that he, too, reached a climax.

It had taken only a few moments. Afterwards they clung together, panting, for a little longer. Micky was too bewildered to think.

When Augusta had caught her breath she broke the embrace. "I'm going to my room," she said quietly. "You should leave the house immediately."

"Augusta—"

"Call me Mrs. Pilaster!"

"All right—"

"This never happened," she said in a fierce whisper. "Do you understand me? *None of it ever happened!*"

"All right," he said again.

She smoothed the front of her dress and

patted her hair. He watched helplessly, im-mobilized by the force of her will. She turned and went to the door. Automatically, he opened it for her. He followed her out.

The nurse looked an inquiry at them. Augusta put her finger to her lips in a hushing gesture. "He's just dropped off to sleep," she said quietly.

Micky was amazed and appalled by her coolness.

"Best thing for him," said the nurse. "I'll leave him in peace for an hour or so."

Augusta nodded agreement. "I should, if I were you. Believe me, he's quite comfortable now."

PART II

1879

PART II

CHAPTER ONE

1

HUGH RETURNED TO LONDON after six years.

In that period the Pilasters had doubled their wealth—and Hugh was partly responsible.

He had done extraordinarily well in Boston, better than he could have dreamed. Transatlantic trade was booming as the United States recovered from the Civil War, and Hugh had made sure Pilasters Bank was financing a healthy chunk of that business.

Then he had guided the partners into a series of lucrative issues of North American stocks and bonds. After the war, government and business needed cash, and Pilasters Bank raised the money.

Finally, he had developed an expertise in

the chaotic market for railway stocks, learning to tell which railroads would make fortunes and which would never get past the
first mountain range. Uncle Joseph had
been wary at first, remembering the New
York crash of 1873; but Hugh had inherited
the anxious conservatism of the Pilasters,
and he had recommended only the good-
quality shares, scrupulously avoiding anything that smacked of flashy speculation;
and his judgment had proved sound. Now
Pilasters was the world leader in the business of raising capital for the industrial development of North America. Hugh was being paid a thousand pounds a year, and he
knew he was worth more.

When he docked at Liverpool he was met
off the ship by the chief clerk of Pilasters'
local branch, a man with whom he had exchanged telegrams at least once a week ever
since he went to Boston. They had never
met, and when they identified each other
the clerk said: "Goodness me, I didn't know
you were so young, sir!" This pleased Hugh,
as he had found a silver hair in his otherwise
jet-black head that very morning. He was
twenty-six.

He went by train to Folkestone, not paus-
ing in London. The partners of Pilasters

Bank might have felt he should call on them before going to see his mother but he thought otherwise: he had given them the last six years of his life and he owed his mother at least a day.

He found her more serenely beautiful than ever but still wearing black in memory of his father. His sister Dotty, now twelve, hardly remembered him and was shy until he sat her on his knee and reminded her how badly she had folded his shirts.

He begged his mother to move to a bigger house: he could easily afford to pay the rent. She refused, and told him to save his money and build up his capital. However, he persuaded her to take on another servant to help Mrs. Builth, her aging housekeeper.

Next day he took the London, Chatham and Dover Railway and arrived in London at Holborn Viaduct Station. A vast new hotel had been built at the station by people who thought Holborn was going to become a busy stopover for Englishmen on their way to Nice or St. Petersburg. Hugh would not have put money into it: he guessed the station would be used mostly by City workers who lived in the expanding suburbs of southeast London.

It was a bright spring morning. He walked

to Pilasters Bank. He had forgotten the smoky taste of London's air, much worse than Boston or New York. He paused for a moment outside the bank, looking at its grandiose facade.

He had told the partners that he wanted to come home on furlough, to see his mother and sister and the old country. But he had another reason for returning to London.

He was about to drop a bombshell.

He had arrived with a proposal to merge Pilasters' North American operation with the New York bank of Madler and Bell, forming a new partnership that would be called Madler, Bell and Pilaster. It would make a lot of money for the bank; it would crown his achievements in the United States; and it would allow him to return to London and graduate from scout to decision maker. It would mean the end of his period of exile.

He straightened his tie nervously and went in.

The banking hall, which years ago had so impressed him with its marble floors and ponderous walkers, now seemed merely staid. As he started up the stairs he met Jonas Mulberry, his former supervisor. Mulberry was startled and pleased to see him. "Mr. Hugh!" he said, shaking hands vigorously. "Are you back permanently?"

"I hope so. How is Mrs. Mulberry?"

"Very well, thank you."

"Give her my regards. And the three little ones?"

"Five, now. All in fine health, God be thanked."

It occurred to Hugh that the Principal Clerk might know the answer to a question on Hugh's mind. "Mulberry, were you here when Mr. Joseph was made a partner?"

"I was a new junior. That was twenty-five years ago come June."

"So Mr. Joseph would have been . . ."

"Twenty-nine."

"Thank you."

Hugh went on up to the Partners' Room, knocked on the door and went in. The four partners were there: Uncle Joseph, sitting at the Senior Partner's desk, looking older and balder and more like old Seth; Aunt Madeleine's husband, Major Hartshorn, his nose turning red to match the scar on his forehead, reading *The Times* beside the fire; Uncle Samuel, beautifully dressed as ever in a charcoal-gray double-breasted cutaway jacket with a pearl-gray waistcoat, frowning over a contract; and the newest partner, Young William, now thirty-one, sitting at his desk and writing in a notebook.

Samuel was the first to greet Hugh. "My dear boy!" he said, getting up and shaking hands. "How well you look!"

Hugh shook hands with all of them and accepted a glass of sherry. He looked around at the portraits of previous Senior Partners on the walls. "Six years ago in this room I sold Sir John Cammel a hundred thousand pounds' worth of Russian government bonds," he remembered.

"So you did," said Samuel.

"Pilasters' commission on that sale, at five percent, still amounts to more than I've been paid in the entire eight years I've worked for the bank," he said with a smile.

Joseph said tetchily: "I hope you're not asking for a rise in salary. You're already the highest-paid employee in the entire firm."

"Except the partners," said Hugh.

"Naturally," Joseph snapped.

Hugh perceived that he had got off to a bad start. Too eager, as always, he told himself. Slow down. "I'm not asking for a rise," he said. "However, I do have a proposition to put to the partners."

Samuel said: "You'd better sit down and tell us about it."

Hugh put his drink down untasted and gathered his thoughts. He desperately wanted them to agree to his proposition. It was both the culmination and the proof of his triumph over adversity. It would bring more business to the bank at one stroke than most partners could attract in a year. And if they agreed they would be more or less obliged to make him a partner.

"Boston is no longer the financial center of the United States," he began. "New York's the place now. We really ought to move our office. But there's a snag. A good deal of the business I've done in the last six years has been undertaken jointly with the New York house of Madler and Bell. Sidney Madler rather took me under his wing when I was green. If we moved to New York we'd be in competition with them."

"Nothing wrong with competition, where appropriate," Major Hartshorn asserted. He rarely had anything of value to contribute to a discussion, but rather than stay silent he would state the obvious in a dogmatic way.

"Perhaps. But I've got a better idea. Why not merge our North American operation with Madler and Bell?"

"Merge?" said Hartshorn. "What do you mean?"

"Set up a joint venture. Call it Madler, Bell and Pilaster. It would have an office in New York and one in Boston."

"How would it work?"

"The new house would deal with all the import-export financing currently done by both separate houses, and the profits would be shared. Pilasters would have the chance to participate in all new issues of bonds and stocks marketed by Madler and Bell. I would handle that business from London."

"I don't like it," said Joseph. "It's just handing over our business to someone else's control."

"But you haven't heard the best part," Hugh said. "All of Madler and Bell's European business, currently distributed among several agents in London, would be handed over to Pilasters."

Joseph grunted in surprise. "That must amount to . . ."

"More than fifty thousand pounds a year in commissions."

Hartshorn said: "Good Lord!"

They were all startled. They had never set up a joint venture before and they did not expect such an innovative proposition from someone who was not even a partner. But the prospect of fifty thousand a year in commissions was irresistible.

Samuel said: "You've obviously talked this over with them."

"Yes. Madler is very keen, and so is his partner, John James Bell."

Young William said: "And you would supervise the joint venture from London."

Hugh saw that William regarded him as a rival who was much less dangerous three thousand miles away. "Why not?" he said. "After all, London is where the money is raised."

"And what would your status be?"

It was a question Hugh would have preferred not to answer so soon. William had shrewdly raised it to embarrass him. Now he had to bite the bullet. "I think Mr. Madler and Mr. Bell would expect to deal with a partner."

"You're too young to be a partner," Joseph said immediately.

"I'm twenty-six, Uncle," Hugh said. "You were made a partner when you were twenty-nine."

"Three years is a long time."

"And fifty thousand pounds is a lot of money." Hugh realized he was sounding cocky—a fault he was prone to—and he backed off quickly. He knew that if he pushed them into a corner they would turn him down just out of conservatism. "But there is much to be weighed up. I know you'll want to talk it over. Perhaps I should leave you?" Samuel nodded discreetly and Hugh went to the door.

Samuel said: "Whether this works out or not, Hugh, you're to be congratulated on a jolly enterprising proposition—I'm sure we all agree on that."

He looked inquiringly at his partners and they all nodded assent. Uncle Joseph murmured: "Quite so, quite so."

Hugh did not know whether to be frustrated, because they had not agreed to his plan, or pleased that they had not turned it down flat. He had a dispiriting sense of anticlimax. But there was no more he could do. "Thank you," he said, and he went out.

At four o'clock that afternoon he stood outside Augusta's enormous, elaborate house in Kensington Gore.

Six years of London soot had darkened the red brick and smudged the white stone, but it still had the statues of birds and beasts on the stepped gable, with the ship in full sail at the apex of the roof. And they say Americans are ostentatious! thought Hugh.

He knew from his mother's letters that Joseph and Augusta had spent some of their ever-growing wealth on two other homes, a castle in Scotland and a country mansion in Buckinghamshire. Augusta had wanted to sell the Kensington house and buy a mansion in Mayfair, but Joseph had put his foot down: he liked it here.

The place had been relatively new when Hugh left, but still it was a house full of memories for him. Here he had suffered Augusta's persecution, courted Florence Stalworthy, punched Edward's nose, and made love to Maisie Robinson. The recollection of Maisie was the most poignant. It was not the humiliation and disgrace he recalled so much as the passion and the thrill. He had not seen or heard anything of Maisie since that night but he still thought about her every day of his life.

The family would remember the scandal as retailed by Augusta: how Tobias Pilaster's depraved son had brought a whore into the house and then, on being caught, had viciously attacked poor blameless Edward. So be it. They could think what they liked, but they had to acknowledge him as a Pilaster and a banker, and soon, with luck, they would have to make him a partner.

He wondered how much the family had changed in six years. Hugh's mother had kept him abreast of domestic events in monthly letters. His cousin Clementine was engaged to be married; Edward was not, despite Augusta's efforts; Young William and Beatrice had a baby girl. But Mother had not told him the underlying changes. Did Uncle Samuel still live with his "secretary"? Was Augusta as ruthless as ever, or had she mellowed with age? Had Edward sobered up and settled down? Had Micky Miranda finally married one of the flock of girls who fell in love with him every season?

It was time to face them all. He crossed the street and knocked on the door.

It was opened by Hastead, Augusta's oily butler. He did not appear to have changed: his eyes still looked in different directions. "Good afternoon, Mr. Hugh," he said, but his Welsh voice was frosty, which indicated that Hugh was still out of favor in this house. Hastead's welcome could always be relied upon to reflect what Augusta was feeling.

He passed through the entrance lobby and into the hall. There like a reception committee stood the three harridans of the Pilaster family: Augusta, her sister-in-law Madeleine, and her daughter Clementine. Augusta at forty-seven was as striking-looking as ever: she still had a classic face with dark eyebrows and a proud look, and if she was a little heavier than six years ago she had the height to carry it. Clementine was a slimmer edition of the same book, but she did not have the indomitable air of her mother and she missed being beautiful. Aunt Madeleine was every inch a Pilaster, from the curved nose down the thin, angular figure to the expensive lace trim around the hem of her ice-blue dress.

Hugh gritted his teeth and kissed them all.

Augusta said: "Well, Hugh, I trust your foreign experiences have made you a wiser young man than you were?"

She was not going to let anyone forget that he had left under a cloud. Hugh replied: "I trust we all grow wiser as we age, dear Aunt," and he had the satisfaction of seeing her face darken with anger.

"Indeed!" she said frostily.

Clementine said: "Hugh, allow me to present my fiancé, Sir Harry Tonks."

Hugh shook hands. Harry was too young

to have a knighthood, so the "sir" must mean he was a baronet, a kind of second-class aristocrat. Hugh did not envy him marriage to Clementine. She was not as bad as her mother, but she had always had a mean streak.

Harry asked Hugh: "How was your crossing?"

"Very quick," said Hugh. "I came in one of the new screw steamers. It only took seven days."

"By Jove! Marvelous, marvelous."

"What part of England are you from, Sir Harry?" Hugh asked, probing into the man's background.

"I've a place in Dorsetshire. Most of my tenants grow hops."

Landed gentry, Hugh concluded; if he has any sense he will sell his farms and put the money into Pilasters Bank. In fact Harry did not seem very bright, but he might be biddable. The Pilaster women liked to marry men who would do as they were told, and Harry was a younger version of Madeleine's husband George. As they grew older they became grumpy and resentful but they rarely rebelled.

"Come into the drawing room," Augusta

commanded. "Everyone's waiting to see you."

He followed her in, but stopped short in the doorway. The familiar wide room, with its big fireplaces at either end and the French windows leading to the long garden, had been quite transformed. All the Japanese furniture and fabrics had gone, and the room had been redecorated in a profusion of bold, richly colored patterns. Looking more closely, Hugh saw that they were all flowers: big yellow daisies in the carpet, red roses climbing a trellis in the wallpaper, poppies in the curtains, and pink chrysanthemums in the silk that draped chair legs, mirrors, occasional tables and the piano. "You've changed this room, Aunt," he said superfluously.

Clementine said: "It all comes from William Morris's new shop in Oxford Street—it's the latest thing."

Augusta said: "The carpet has to be changed, though. It's not the right color."

She was never satisfied, Hugh recalled.

Most of the Pilaster family were here. They were all curious about Hugh, naturally. He had gone away in disgrace and they may have thought they would never see him again—but they had underestimated him, and he had returned a conquering hero. Now they were all keen to take a second look.

The first person he shook hands with was his cousin Edward. He was twenty-nine but he looked older: he was already becoming stout and his face had the flushed look of a glutton. "So, you're back," he said. He tried a smile but it turned into a resentful sneer. Hugh could hardly blame him. The two cousins had always been compared to each other. Now Hugh's success drew attention to Edward's lack of achievement at the bank.

Micky Miranda stood next to Edward. Still handsome and immaculately dressed, Micky seemed even more sleek and self-assured. Hugh said: "Hullo, Miranda, are you still working for the Cordovan Minister?"

"I *am* the Cordovan Minister," Micky replied.

Somehow Hugh was not surprised.

He was pleased to see his old friend Rachel Bodwin. "Hullo, Rachel, how are you?" he said. She had never been a pretty girl but she was turning into a handsome woman, he realized. The angular features and close-set eyes that he thought plain six years ago were now oddly intriguing. "What are you doing with yourself these days?"

"Campaigning to reform the law on women's property," she said. Then she grinned and added: "Much to the embarrassment of my parents, who would prefer me to campaign for a husband."

She had always been alarmingly candid, Hugh recalled. He found her interesting on that account, but he could imagine that many eligible bachelors would be intimidated by her. Men liked women to be a little shy and not too clever.

As he exchanged small talk with her, he wondered whether Augusta still wanted to make a match between the two of them. It hardly mattered: the only man Rachel had ever shown any real interest in was Micky Miranda. Even now she was taking care to include Micky in the conversation with Hugh. He had never understood why girls found Micky irresistible, and Rachel surprised him more than most, for she was intelligent enough to realize that Micky was a rotter; yet it was almost as if he fascinated them more on that account.

He moved on and shook hands with Young William and his wife. Beatrice greeted Hugh warmly, and he concluded that she was not as much under Augusta's influence as the other Pilaster women.

Hastead interrupted them to give Hugh an envelope. "This just arrived by messenger," he said.

It contained a note in what looked to Hugh like a secretary's handwriting:

> *123, Piccadilly*
> *London, W.*
>
> *Tuesday*
> *Mrs Solomon Greenbourne requests the pleasure of your company at dinner tonight.*

Below, in a familiar scrawl, was written:

> *Welcome home!—Solly.*

He was pleased. Solly was always amiable and easygoing. Why could the Pilasters not be as relaxed, he wondered? Were Methodists naturally more tense than Jews? But perhaps there were tensions he did not know about in the Greenbourne family.

Hastead said: "The messenger is waiting for a reply, Mr. Hugh."

Hugh said: "My compliments to Mrs.

Greenbourne, and I shall be delighted to join them for dinner."

Hastead bowed and withdrew. Beatrice said: "My goodness, are you dining with the Solomon Greenbournes? How marvelous!"

Hugh was surprised. "I don't expect it to be marvelous," he said. "I was at school with Solly and I've always like him, but an invitation to dine with him was never a coveted privilege."

"It is now," said Beatrice.

"Solly married a fireball," William explained. "Mrs. Greenbourne loves to entertain, and her parties are the best in London."

"They're part of the Marlborough Set," Beatrice said reverently. "They're friends with the Prince of Wales."

Clementine's fiancé, Harry, overheard this and said in a resentful tone: "I don't know what English society is coming to, when the heir to throne prefers Jews to Christians."

"Really?" said Hugh. "I must say I've never understood why people dislike Jews."

"Can't stand 'em, myself," Harry said.

"Well, you're marrying into a banking

family, so you're going to meet an awful lot more of them in the future."

Harry looked mildly offended.

William said: "Augusta disapproves of the entire Marlborough Set, Jews and others. Apparently their morals aren't what they should be."

Hugh said: "And I bet they don't invite Augusta to their parties."

Beatrice giggled at the thought and William said: "Certainly not!"

"Well," said Hugh, "I can't wait to meet Mrs. Greenbourne."

Piccadilly was a street of palaces. At eight o'clock on a chilly January evening it was busy, the wide road hectic with carriages and cabs, the gas-lit pavements thronged by men dressed like Hugh in white tie and tails, women in velvet cloaks and fur collars, and painted prostitutes of both sexes.

Hugh walked along deep in thought. Augusta was as implacably hostile to him as ever. He had cherished a secret faint hope that she might have mellowed, but she had not. And she was still the matriarch, so to have her as enemy was to be at odds with the family.

The situation at the bank was better. The

business obliged the men to be more objective. Inevitably Augusta would try to block his advancement there, but he had more chance to defend himself on that territory. She knew how to manipulate people but she was hopelessly ignorant about banking.

On balance the day had not gone badly and now he looked forward to a relaxing evening with friends.

When Hugh left for America, Solly Greenbourne had been living with his father, Ben, in a vast house overlooking Green Park. Now Solly had a house of his own, just down the street from his father's place and not much smaller. Hugh passed through an imposing doorway into a vast hall lined with green marble, and stopped to stare at the extravagant sweep of a black-and-orange marble staircase. Mrs. Greenbourne had something in common with Augusta Pilaster: neither woman believed in understatement.

A butler and two footmen were in the hall. The butler took Hugh's hat, only to hand it to a footman; then the second footman led him up the staircase. On the landing he glanced through an open door and saw the bare polished floor of a ballroom with a long sweep of curtained windows, then he was led into a drawing room.

Hugh was no expert on decoration but he immediately recognized the gorgeous, extravagant style of Louis XVI. The ceiling was a riot of plaster molding, the walls had inset panels of flock wallpaper, and all the tables and chairs were perched on thin gilded legs that looked as if they might snap. The colors were yellow, orange-red, gold and green. Hugh could easily imagine prim people saying it was vulgar, concealing their envy beneath a pretence of distaste. In fact it was sensual. It was a room in which impossibly wealthy people did anything they pleased.

Several other guests had arrived already and stood around drinking champagne and smoking cigarettes. This was new to Hugh: he had never seen people smoking in a drawing room. Solly caught his eye and detached himself from a group of laughing people to come over. "Pilaster, how nice of you to come! How are you, for goodness' sake?"

Hugh perceived that Solly had become a little more extrovert. He was still fat and bespectacled, and there was already a stain of some kind on his white waistcoat, but he was jollier than ever and, Hugh immediately sensed, happier too.

"I'm very well, thanks, Greenbourne," Hugh said.

"I know it! I've been watching your progress. I wish our bank had someone like you in America. I hope the Pilasters are paying you a fortune—you deserve it."

"And you've become a socialite, they say."

"None of my doing. I got married, you know." He turned and tapped the bare white shoulder of a short woman in an eggshell-green dress. She was facing the other way but her back was oddly familiar, and a feeling of déjà vu came over Hugh, making him unaccountably sad. Solly said to her: "My dear, do you remember my old friend Hugh Pilaster?"

She paused a moment longer, finishing what she was saying to her companions, and Hugh thought: Why do I feel breathless at the sight of her? Then she turned very slowly, like a door opening into the past, and Hugh's heart stopped as he saw her face.

"Of course I remember him," she said. "How are you, Mr. Pilaster?"

Hugh stared, speechless, at the woman

who had become Mrs. Solomon Greenbourne.

It was Maisie.

2

AUGUSTA SAT AT HER DRESSING TABLE and put
on the single row of pearls that she always
wore at dinner parties. It was her most expensive piece of jewelery. Methodists did
not believe in costly ornament, and her par-
simonious husband Joseph used that as an
excuse not to buy her jewelery. He would
have liked to stop her redecorating the
house so often, but she did it without asking
him: if he had his way they might live no
better than his clerks. He accepted the redecoration grumpily, insisting only that she
leave his bedroom alone.

She took from her open jewelry box the
ring Strang had given her thirty years ago. It
was in the form of a gold serpent with a
diamond head and ruby eyes. She put it on
her finger and, as she had done a thousand
times before, brushed the raised head
against her lips, remembering.

Her mother had said: "Send back his ring,
and try to forget him."

The seventeen-year-old Augusta had said:

"I have sent it back already, and I will forget him," but it was a lie. She kept the ring concealed in the spine of her Bible, and she had never forgotten Strang. If she could not have his love, she vowed, all the other things he could have given her would be hers somehow, one day.

She would never be the countess of Strang, she had accepted that years ago. But she was determined to have a title. And since Joseph did not have one she would have to get him one.

She had brooded over the problem for years, studying the mechanisms by which men gained titles, and many sleepless nights of planning and longing had gone into her strategy. Now she was ready and the time was right.

She would begin her campaign tonight, over dinner. Among her guests were three people who would play a crucial part in having Joseph made an earl.

He might take the title earl of Whitehaven, she thought. Whitehaven was the port where the Pilaster family had begun in business, four generations ago. Joseph's great-grandfather Amos Pilaster had made his fortune with a legendary gamble, putting all his money in a slave ship. But then he had gone into a less chancy business, buying serge cloth and printed calico from Lancashire textile mills and shipping it to the Americas. Their London home was already called Whitehaven House in acknowledgment of the birthplace of the business. Augusta would be countess of Whitehaven if her plans worked out.

She imagined herself and Joseph entering a grand drawing room as a butler announced: "The earl and countess of Whitehaven," and the thought made her smile. She saw Joseph making his maiden speech in the House of Lords, on a topic connected with high finance, and the other peers listening with respectful attention. Shopkeepers would call her "Lady Whitehaven" in loud tones and people would look around to see who it was.

However, she wanted this for Edward as much as anything else, she told herself. One day he would inherit his father's title, and meanwhile he would be able to put "The Hon. Edward Pilaster" on his visiting card.

She knew exactly what she had to do, but all the same she felt uneasy. Getting a peerage was not like buying a carpet—you could not go to the supplier and say: "I want that one, how much is it?" Everything had to be done with hints. She would need to be very surefooted tonight. If she made a wrong move, her careful plans could go wrong very quickly. If she had misjudged her people she was doomed.

A parlormaid knocked and said: "Mr. Hobbes has arrived, madam."

She'll have to call me "my lady" soon, Augusta thought.

She put Strang's ring away, got up from her dressing table, and went through the communicating door into Joseph's room. He was dressed for dinner, sitting at the cabinet where he kept his collection of jeweled snuffboxes, looking at one of them in the gaslight. Augusta wondered whether to mention Hugh to him now.

Hugh continued to be a nuisance. Six years ago she thought she had dealt with him once and for all, but he was once again threatening to overshadow Edward. There was talk of his becoming a partner: Augusta could not tolerate that. She was determined that Edward would be Senior Partner one day, and she could not let Hugh get ahead.

Was she right to worry so much? Perhaps it would be as well to let Hugh run the business. Edward could do something else, go into politics perhaps. But the bank was the heart of this family. People who left, like Hugh's father Tobias, always came to nothing in the end. The bank was where the money was made and the power exercised. Pilasters could bring down a monarch by refusing him a loan: few politicians had that ability. It was dreadful to think of Hugh's being Senior Partner, entertaining ambassadors, drinking coffee with the chancellor of the Exchequer, and taking first place at family gatherings, lording it over Augusta and her side of the family.

But it would be difficult to get rid of Hugh this time. He was older and wiser and he had an established position at the bank. The wretched boy had worked hard and patiently for six years to rehabilitate his reputation. Could she undo all that?

However, this was not the moment to confront Joseph about Hugh. She wanted him in a good mood for the dinner party. "Stay up here a few more minutes, if you like," she said to him. "Only Arnold Hobbes has arrived."

"Very well, if you don't mind," he said.

It would suit her to have Hobbes alone for a while.

Hobbes was the editor of a political journal called *The Forum.* It generally sided with the Conservatives, who stood for the aristocracy and the established church, and against the Liberals, the party of businessmen and Methodists. The Pilasters were both businessmen and Methodists, but the Conservatives were in power.

She had met Hobbes only once or twice before, and she guessed he might have been surprised to receive her invitation. However, she had been confident he would accept. He would not get many invitations to homes as wealthy as Augusta's.

Hobbes was in a curious position. He was powerful, because his journal was widely read and respected; yet he was poor, for he did not make much money out of it. The combination was awkward for him—and perfectly suited to Augusta's purpose. He had the power to help her and he might be bought.

There was just one possible snag. She hoped he did not have high principles: that would destroy his usefulness. But if she had judged him aright he was corruptible.

She felt nervous and jittery. She stood outside the drawing room door for a moment, saying to herself *Relax, Mrs. Pilaster, you're good at this*. After a moment she felt calmer, and she went in.

He stood up eagerly to greet her. He was a nervous, quick-witted man, birdlike in his movements. His dress suit was at least ten years old, Augusta thought. She led him to the window seat, to give their conversation a feeling of intimacy even though they were not old friends. "Tell me what mischief you have been at today," she said playfully. "Trouncing Mr. Gladstone? Undermining our India policy? Persecuting Catholics?"

He peered at her through smeared spectacles. "I've been writing about the City of Glasgow Bank," he said.

Augusta frowned. "This is the bank that failed a little while ago."

"Exactly. Many of the Scottish trade unions have been ruined, you know."

"I seem to remember hearing talk of it," she said. "My husband said the City of Glasgow had been known for years to be unsound."

"I don't understand this," he said excitedly. "People know a bank is no good, yet it is allowed to continue in business until it crashes, and thousands of people lose their life savings!"

Augusta did not understand it either. She knew next to nothing about business. But she now saw a chance to lead the conversation in the direction she wanted. "Perhaps the worlds of commerce and government are too widely separated," she said.

"It must be so. Better communication between businessmen and statesmen might prevent such catastrophes."

"I wonder. . . ." Augusta hesitated as if considering an idea that had just struck her. "I wonder whether someone such as yourself would consider becoming a director of one or two companies."

He was surprised. "Indeed, I might."

"You see . . . some firsthand experience of participating in the direction of a business enterprise might help you when you comment, in your journal, on the world of commerce."

"I've no doubt it would."

"The rewards are not great—a hundred or two a year, at best." She saw his eyes light up: that was a lot of money to him. "But the obligations are small."

"A most interesting thought," he said. He was working hard to conceal his excitement, she could tell.

"My husband could arrange it, if you were interested. He has constantly to recommend directors for the boards of enterprises in which he has some interest. Do think it over and tell me if you would like me to mention it."

"Very well, I shall."

So far, so good, Augusta thought. But showing him the bait was the easy part. Now she had to get him on the hook. She said thoughtfully: "And the world of commerce should reciprocate, of course. More businessmen should serve their country in the House of Lords, I feel."

His eyes narrowed slightly, and she guessed that his quick mind was beginning to understand the bargain he was being offered. "No doubt," he said noncommitally.

Augusta developed her theme. "Both Houses of Parliament would benefit from the knowledge and wisdom of senior businessmen, especially when debating the nation's finances. Yet there is a curious prejudice against a businessman's being elevated to the peerage."

"There is, and it is quite irrational," Hobbes admitted. "Our merchants, manufacturers and bankers are responsible for the nation's prosperity, much more so than landowners and clergymen; yet it is the latter who are ennobled for their services to the nation, while the men who really make and do things are overlooked."

"You should write an article about the question. It is the kind of cause for which your journal has campaigned in the past— the modernization of our ancient institutions." She gave him her warmest smile. Her cards were on the table now. He could hardly fail to see that this campaign was the price he had to pay for the company directorships she was offering. Would he stiffen, look offended, and beg to differ? Would he walk out in a huff? Would he smile and turn her down gracefully? If he did any of those things she would have to start all over again with someone else.

There was a long pause, then he said: "Perhaps you're right."

Augusta relaxed.

"Perhaps we should take this up," he went on. "Closer links between commerce and government."

"Peerages for businessmen," Augusta said.

"And company directorships for journalists," he added.

Augusta sensed that they had gone as far as they could in the direction of frankness, and it was time to pull back. If it were admitted that she was bribing him he might be humiliated and refuse. She was well satisfied with what she had achieved, and she was about to change the subject when more guests arrived and she was saved the trouble.

The rest of the party arrived in a bunch, and Joseph appeared at the same time. A few moments later Hastead came in and said: "Dinner is served, sir," and Augusta longed to hear him say *my lord* instead of *sir.*

They walked from the drawing room through the hall to the dining room. The rather short procession bothered Augusta. In aristocratic houses there was often a long and very elegant walk to the dining room, and it was a high point of the dinner-party ritual. The Pilasters traditionally scorned to copy upper-class manners, but Augusta felt differently. To her this house seemed irredeemably suburban. But she had failed to persuade Joseph to move.

Tonight she had arranged for Edward to walk in to dinner with Emily Maple, a shy, pretty girl of nineteen who was with her father, a Methodist minister, and her mother. They were plainly overwhelmed by the house and the company, and hardly fitted in, but Augusta was getting desperate in her search for a suitable bride for Edward. The boy was now twenty-nine years old and he had never shown a spark of interest in any eligible girl, to his mother's frustration. He could hardly fail to find Emily attractive: she had big blue eyes and a sweet smile. The parents would be thrilled by such a match. As for the girl, she would have to do as she was told. But Edward might need to be pushed. The trouble was, he saw no reason to marry. He enjoyed his life with his male friends, going to his club and so on, and settling down to married life had little appeal. For a while she had blithely assumed this was just a normal phase in a young man's life, but it had gone on too long, and lately she had begun to worry whether he would ever come out of it. She would have to put pressure on him.

On her left at the table Augusta placed Michael Fortescue, a personable young man with political aspirations. He was said to be close to the prime minister, Benjamin Disraeli, who had been ennobled and was now Lord Beaconsfield. Fortescue was the second of the three people Augusta needed to help her get Joseph a peerage. He was not as clever as Hobbes but he was more sophisticated and self-assured. Augusta had been able to overawe Hobbes, but she would have to seduce Fortescue.

Deacon Maple said grace and Hastead poured wine. Neither Joseph nor Augusta would drink wine, but they offered it to their guests. As the consommé was served Augusta smiled warmly at Fortescue and said in a low, intimate voice: "When are we going to see you in Parliament?"

"I wish I knew," he said.

"Everyone speaks of you as a brilliant young man, as you must know."

He was pleased but embarrassed by her flattery. "I'm not sure I do know."

"And you're so good-looking, too—that never hurts."

He looked rather startled. He had not expected her to flirt—but he was not averse to it.

"You shouldn't wait for a general election," she went on. "Why don't you stand in a by-election? It should be easy enough to arrange—people say you have the ear of the prime minister."

"You're very kind—but by-elections are expensive, Mrs. Pilaster."

It was the response she had been hoping for, but she did not let him know that. "Are they?" she said.

"And I am not a wealthy man."

"I didn't know that," she lied. "You should find a sponsor, then."

"A banker, perhaps?" he said in a tone that was half playful, half wistful.

"It's not impossible. Mr. Pilaster is keen to take a more active part in the government of the nation." He would be, if a peerage were offered. "And he doesn't see why commercial men should feel obliged to be Liberals. Between you and me, he often finds himself more in agreement with the younger Conservatives."

Her confidential tone encouraged him to be frank—as she intended—and now he said directly: "In what way would Mr. Pilaster like to serve the nation—other than by sponsoring a by-election candidate?"

This was a challenge. Should she answer his question, or continue to be indirect? Augusta decided to match his frankness. "Perhaps in the House of Lords. Do you think it is possible?" She was enjoying this—and so was he.

"Possible? Certainly. Whether it is likely, is another question. Shall I inquire?"

This was more straightforward than Augusta had anticipated. "Could you do so discreetly?"

He hesitated. "I believe I could."

"It would be most kind," she said with satisfaction. She had turned him into a co-conspirator.

"I shall let you know what I find out."

"And if a suitable by-election should be called . . ."

"You're very good."

She touched his arm. He was a very attractive young man, she thought. She enjoyed plotting with him. "I believe we understand one another perfectly," she murmured. She noticed that he had unusually big hands. She held his arm a moment longer, looking into his eyes; then she turned away.

She was feeling good. She had dealt with two of the three key people and she had not yet slipped. Throughout the next course she talked to Lord Morte, who was sitting on her right. With him she made polite, pointless conversation: it was his wife she wanted to influence and for that she had to wait until after dinner.

The men stayed in the dining room to smoke and Augusta took the ladies upstairs to her bedroom. There she got Lady Morte alone for a few minutes. Fifteen years older than Augusta, Harriet Morte was a lady-in-waiting to Queen Victoria. She had iron-gray hair and a superior manner. Like Arnold Hobbes and Michael Fortescue, she had influence; and Augusta hoped that, like them, she would be corruptible. Hobbes and Fortescue were vulnerable because they were poor. Lord and Lady Morte were not so much poor as improvident: they had plenty of money, but they spent more than they had. Lady Morte's gowns were splendid and her jewelery was magnificent, and Lord Morte believed, against the evidence of forty years, that he had a good eye for a racehorse.

Augusta was more nervous about Lady Morte than she had been about the men. Women were more difficult. They would not take anything at face value and they knew when they were being manipulated. Thirty years as a courtier would have refined Lady Morte's sensibility to the point where nothing could slip by her.

Augusta began by saying: "Mr. Pilaster and I are such admirers of the dear queen."

Lady Morte nodded, as if to say *Of course.* However, there was no *of course* about it: Queen Victoria was disliked by much of the nation for being withdrawn, staid, remote and inflexible.

Augusta went on: "If there were ever anything we could do to help you with your noble duties, we would be thrilled."

"How very kind." Lady Morte looked a little puzzled. She hesitated, then decided to ask. "But what could you possibly do?"

"What do bankers do? They lend." Augusta lowered her voice. "Court life must be cripplingly expensive, I imagine."

Lady Morte stiffened. There was a taboo on talking about money in her class and Augusta was breaking it flagrantly.

But Augusta plowed on. "If you were to open an account with Pilasters, there would never be any problems in that area. . . ."

Lady Morte was offended, but on the other hand she was being offered the remarkable privilege of unlimited credit at one of the largest banks in the world. Her instincts told her to snub Augusta, but greed held her back: Augusta could read the conflict in her face.

Augusta did not give her time to think about it. "Please forgive my being so frightfully candid," she went on. "It comes only from a wish to be of service." Lady Morte would not believe that, but she would assume Augusta simply wanted to curry favor with royalty. She would not look for a more specific motive, and Augusta would give her no more clues tonight.

Lady Morte hesitated a moment longer, then said: "You're very kind."

Mrs. Maple, the mother of Emily, returned from the bathroom, and Lady Morte took her turn. She went out with an expression of mild embarrassment frozen to her face. Augusta knew that she and Lord Morte would agree, in the carriage going home, that commercial people were impossibly vulgar and ill-mannered; but one day soon he would lose a thousand guineas on a horse, and on the same day her dressmaker would demand payment of a six-month-old bill for three hundred pounds, and the two of them would remember Augusta's offer, and they would decide that vulgar commercial people did after all have their uses.

Augusta had cleared the third hurdle. If she had assessed the woman correctly, Lady Morte would be hopelessly in debt to Pilasters Bank within six months. Then she would find out what Augusta wanted from her.

The ladies reconvened in the drawing room on the first floor and took coffee. Lady Morte was still distant, but stopped short of being rude. The men joined them a few minutes later. Joseph took Deacon Maple upstairs to show him his collection of snuffboxes. Augusta was pleased: Joseph only did that when he liked someone. Emily played the piano. Mrs. Maple asked her to sing, but she said she had a cold, and stuck to her refusal with remarkable obstinacy despite her mother's pleas, making Augusta think anxiously that she might not be as submissive as she looked.

She had done her work for the night: she wanted them all to go home now so that she could run over the evening in her mind and assess how much she had achieved. She did not actually like any of them except for Michael Fortescue. However, she forced herself to be polite and make conversation for another hour. Hobbes was hooked, she thought; Fortescue had made a bargain and would keep it; Lady Morte had been shown the slippery slope that led to perdition and it was only a matter of time before she started down it. Augusta was relieved and satisfied.

When at last they departed, Edward was ready to go to his club, but Augusta stopped him. "Sit down and listen for a moment," she said. "I want to talk to you and your father." Joseph, who was heading for bed, sat down again. She addressed him. "When are you going to make Edward a partner in the bank?"

Joseph immediately looked cross. "When he is older."

"But I hear that Hugh may be made a partner, and he is three years younger than Edward." Although Augusta had no idea how money was made she always knew what was happening at the bank in terms of the personal advancement or otherwise of family members. Men did not normally talk business in front of ladies, but Augusta got it all out of them at her teatime gatherings.

"Seniority is only one of the ways in which a man may qualify as a partner," Joseph said irritably. "Another is the ability to bring in business, which Hugh has to a degree I have never seen in so young a man. Other qualifications would be a large capital investment in the bank, high social position, or political influence. I am afraid that as yet Edward has none of these."

"But he is your son."

"A bank is a business, not a dinner party!" Joseph said, getting angrier. He hated her to challenge him. "Position is not merely a question of rank or precedence. Ability to make money is the test."

Augusta suffered a moment of doubt. Ought she to push for Edward's advancement if he was not really able? But that was nonsense. He was perfectly all right. He might not be able to add up a column of figures as fast as Hugh, but breeding would tell in the end. She said: "Edward could have a large capital investment in the bank, if you so wished. You can settle money on him anytime you please."

Joseph's face took on the stubborn look that Augusta knew well, the look he wore when he refused to move house or forbade her to redecorate his bedroom. "Not before the boy marries!" he said, and with that he left the room.

Edward said: "You've made him angry."

"It's only for your sake, Teddy darling."

"But you've made matters worse!"

"No, I haven't." Augusta sighed. "Sometimes your generous outlook prevents you from seeing what is going on. Your papa may believe that he has taken a firm stand, but if you think about what he said you'll realize that he has promised to settle a large sum on you *and* make you a partner as soon as you get married."

"Goodness, I suppose he has," Edward

said in surprise. "I didn't look at it that way."

"That's your trouble, dear. You're not sly, like Hugh."

"Hugh was very lucky in America."

"Of course he was. You would like to get married, wouldn't you?"

He sat beside her and took her hand. "Why should I, when I have you to take care of me?"

"But who will you have when I'm gone? Did you like that little Emily Maple? I thought she was charming."

"She told me that hunting is cruel to the fox," Edward said in a tone of disdain.

"Your father will settle at least a hundred thousand on you—perhaps more, perhaps a quarter of a million."

Edward was not impressed. "I have everything I want, and I like living with you," he said.

"And I like having you near me. But I want to see you happily married, with a lovely wife and your own fortune and a partnership at the bank. Say you'll think about it."

"I'll think about it." He kissed her cheek. "And now I really must go, Mama. I promised to meet some fellows half an hour ago."

"Go on, then."

He got up and went to the door. "Good night, Mama."

"Good night," she said. "Think about Emily!"

3

KINGSBRIDGE MANOR was one of the largest houses in England. Maisie had stayed there three or four times and she still had not seen half of it. The house had twenty principal bedrooms, not counting the rooms of the fifty or so servants. It was heated by coal fires and lit by candles, and it had only one bathroom, but what it lacked in modern conveniences it made up for in old-fashioned luxury: four-poster beds curtained with heavy silk, delicious old wines from the vast underground cellars, horses and guns and books and games without end.

The young duke of Kingsbridge had once owned a hundred thousand acres of best Wiltshire farmland, but on Solly's advice he had sold half of it and bought a big chunk of South Kensington with the proceeds. Consequently the agricultural depression that had impoverished many great families had left

"Kingo" untouched, and he was still able to entertain his friends in the grand style.

The Prince of Wales had been with them for the first week. Solly and Kingo and the prince shared a taste for boisterous fun, and Maisie had helped to provide it. She had substituted soapsuds for whipped cream on Kingo's dessert; she had unbuttoned Solly's braces while he dozed in the library, so that his trousers fell down when he stood up; and she had glued together the pages of *The Times* so that it could not be opened. By hazard the prince himself had been the first to pick up the newspaper, and as he fumbled with the pages there had been a moment of suspense when everyone wondered how he would take it—for though the heir to the throne loved practical jokes, he was never the victim—but then he began to chuckle as he realized what had happened, and the others all laughed uproariously, from relief as much as amusement.

The prince had left, and Hugh Pilaster had arrived; and then the trouble had started.

It was Solly's idea to get Hugh invited here. Solly liked Hugh. Maisie could not think of a plausible reason to object. It had been Solly who asked Hugh to dinner in London, too.

He had recovered his composure quickly enough, that evening, and had proved himself a perfectly eligible dinner guest. Perhaps his manners were not quite as refined as they might have been if he had spent the last six years in London drawing rooms instead of Boston warehouses, but his natural charm made up for any shortcomings. In the two days he had been at Kingsbridge he had entertained them all with tales of life in America, a place none of them had visited.

It was ironic that she should find Hugh's manners a little rough. Six years ago it had been the other way around. But she was a quick learner. She had acquired the accent of the upper classes with no trouble. The grammar had taken her a little longer. Hardest of all had been the little subtleties of behavior, the grace notes of social superiority: the way they walked through a door, spoke to a pet dog, changed the subject of a conversation, ignored a drunk. But she had studied hard, and now it all came naturally to her.

Hugh had recovered from the shock of their meeting, but Maisie had not. She would never forget his expression when he first saw her. She had been prepared, but for Hugh it had been a complete surprise. Because of his surprise he had shown his feelings quite nakedly, and Maisie had been dismayed to see the hurt in his eyes. She had wounded him deeply, six years ago, and he had not got over it.

The look on his face had haunted her ever since. She had been upset when she learned he was coming here. She did not want to see him. She did not want the past brought back. She was married to Solly, who was a good husband, and she could not bear the thought of hurting him. And there was Bertie, her reason for living.

Their child was named Hubert, but they called him Bertie, which was also the name of the Prince of Wales. Bertie Greenbourne would be five years old on May 1st, but that was a secret: his birthday was celebrated in September, to hide the fact that he had been born only six months after the wedding. Solly's family knew the truth, but no one else did: Bertie had been born in Switzerland, during the world tour that had been their honeymoon. Since then Maisie had been happy.

Solly's parents had not welcomed Maisie. They were stiff-necked snobbish German

Jews who had been living in England for generations, and they looked down on Yiddish-speaking Russian Jews just off the boat. The fact that she was carrying another man's child confirmed their prejudice and gave them an excuse for rejecting her. However, Solly's sister Kate, who was about Maisie's age and had a seven-year-old daughter, was nice to Maisie when her parents were not around.

Solly loved her, and he loved Bertie too, although he did not know whose child he was; and that was enough for Maisie—until Hugh came back.

She got up early, as always, and went along to the nursery wing of the great house. Bertie was having breakfast in the nursery dining room with Kingo's children Anne and Alfred, supervised by three nursery maids. She kissed his sticky face and said: "What are you having?"

"Porridge with honey." He spoke with the drawling accent of the upper classes, the accent Maisie had been at pains to learn, and from which she still occasionally slipped.

"Is it nice?"

"The honey's nice."

"I think I'll have some," said Maisie, sitting down. It would be more digestible than the kippers and deviled kidneys the adults had for breakfast.

Bertie did not take after Hugh. As a baby he had resembled Solly, for all babies looked like Solly; and now he was like Maisie's father, with dark hair and brown eyes. Maisie could see something of Hugh in him now and again, especially when he gave a mischievous grin; but there was no obvious resemblance, fortunately.

A nursery maid brought Maisie a dish of porridge with honey and she tasted it.

"Do you like it, Mama?" said Bertie.

Anne said: "Don't speak with your mouth full, Bertie." Anne Kingsbridge was a superior seven-year-old and she lorded it over Bertie and her five-year-old brother Freddy.

"It's delicious," said Maisie.

Another maid said: "Would you like some buttered toast, children?" and they all said yes in a chorus.

Maisie had at first felt it was unnatural for a child to grow up surrounded by servants, and she feared that Bertie would be overprotected; but she had learned that rich children played in the dirt and climbed walls and got into fights just as much as the poor, and the main difference was that the people who cleaned up after them got paid.

She would have liked to have more children—Solly's children—but something had gone wrong inside her when Bertie was born and the Swiss doctors had said she would not conceive again. They had been proved right, for she had been sleeping with Solly for five years without once missing the monthly curse. Bertie was the only child she would ever have. She was bitterly sorry for Solly, who would never have children of his own; although he said he already had more happiness than any man deserved.

Kingo's wife the duchess, known to her friends as Liz, joined the nursery breakfast party soon after Maisie. As they were washing their children's hands and faces, Liz said: "You know, my mother would never have done this. She only saw us when we were scrubbed clean and dressed up. So unnatural." Maisie smiled. Liz thought herself very down-to-earth because she washed her own children's faces.

They stayed in the nursery until ten o'clock, when the governess arrived and set the children to work drawing and painting. Maisie and Liz returned to their rooms. Today was a quiet day, with no hunting. Some of the men were going fishing and others would stroll in the woods with a dog or two, shooting rabbits. The ladies, and the men who liked ladies better than dogs, would walk around the park before lunch.

Solly had eaten breakfast and was getting ready to go out. He was dressed in a brown tweed lounge suit with a short jacket. Maisie kissed him and helped him put on his ankle boots: if she had not been there he would have called his valet, for he could not bend down far enough to tie the laces himself. She put on a fur coat and hat and Solly donned a heavy plaid Inverness coat with a cape and matching bowler hat, then they went down to the hall to meet the others.

It was a bright, frosty morning, delightful if you had a fur coat, torture if you lived in a drafty slum and had to walk barefoot. Maisie liked to remember the privations of her childhood: it intensified the pleasure she took in being married to one of the richest men in the world.

She walked with Kingo on one side of her and Solly on the other. Hugh was behind with Liz. Although Maisie could not see him she could feel his presence, hear him chatting with Liz and making her giggle, and imagine the twinkle in his blue eyes. After about half a mile they came to the main gate. As they were turning to stroll through the orchard Maisie saw a familiar tall, black-bearded figure approaching from the village. For a moment she imagined it was her papa; then she recognized her brother Danny.

Danny had returned to their hometown six years ago to find that their parents no longer lived in the old house, and had left no other address. Disappointed, he traveled further north, to Glasgow, and founded the Working Men's Welfare Association, which not only insured workingmen against unemployment but also campaigned for safety rules in factories, the right to join trade unions, and financial regulation of corporations. His name started appearing in the newspapers—Dan Robinson, not Danny, for he was too formidable to be a Danny now. Papa read about him and came to his office, and there was a joyful reunion.

It turned out that Papa and Mama had at last met other Jews soon after Maisie and Danny ran away. They borrowed the money to move to Manchester, where Papa found another job, and they never sank so low again. Mama survived her illness and was now quite healthy.

Maisie was married to Solly by the time the family was reunited. Solly would cheerfully have given Papa a house and an income for life, but Papa did not want to retire, and instead asked Solly to lend him the money to open a shop. Now Mama and Papa sold caviar and other delicacies to the wealthy citizens of Manchester. When Maisie went to visit she took off her diamonds, put on a pinafore and served behind the counter, confident that none of the Marlborough Set were likely to go to Manchester and if they did they would not do their own shopping.

Seeing Danny here at Kingsbridge, Maisie immediately feared something had happened to their parents, and she ran to him, her heart in her mouth, saying, "Danny! What's wrong? Is it Mama?"

"Papa and Mama are just fine, so are all the rest," he said in his American accent.

"Thank God. How did you know I was here?"

"You wrote to me."

"Oh, yes."

Danny looked like a Turkish warrior with his curly beard and flashing eyes, but he was dressed like a clerk, in a well-worn black suit and a bowler hat, and he appeared to have walked a long way, for he had muddy boots and a weary expression. Kingo looked at him askance, but Solly rose to the occasion with his usual social grace. He shook Danny's hand and said: "How are you, Robinson? This is my friend the duke of Kingsbridge. Kingo, allow me to present my brother-in-law Dan Robinson, general secretary of the Working Men's Welfare Association."

Many men would have been dumbstruck to be introduced to a duke, but not Danny. "How do you do, Duke?" he said with easy courtesy.

Kingo shook hands warily. Maisie guessed he was thinking that being polite to the lower classes was all very well up to a point, but it should not be taken too far.

Then Solly said: "And this is our friend Hugh Pilaster."

Maisie tensed. In her anxiety about Mama and Papa she had forgotten that Hugh was behind her. Danny knew secrets about Hugh, secrets Maisie had never told her husband. He knew that Hugh was the father of Bertie. Danny had once wanted to break Hugh's neck. They had never met, but Danny had not forgotten. What would he do?

However, he was six years older now. He

gave Hugh a cold look, but shook hands civilly.

Hugh, who did not know he was a father and had no inkling of these undertones, spoke to Danny in a friendly way. "Are you the brother who ran away from home and went to Boston?"

"I sure am."

Solly said: "Fancy Hugh knowing that!"

Solly had no idea how much Hugh and Maisie knew about one another: he did not know that they had spent a night together telling one another their life stories.

Maisie felt bewildered by the conversation: it was skating over the surface of too many secrets, and the ice was thin. She hastened to get back onto firm ground. "Danny, why are you here?"

His weary face took on an expression of bitterness. "I'm no longer the secretary of the Working Men's Welfare Association," he said. "I'm ruined, for the third time in my life, by incompetent bankers."

"Danny, please!" Maisie protested. He knew perfectly well that both Solly and Hugh were bankers.

But Hugh said: "Don't worry! We hate incompetent bankers too. They're a menace to everyone. But what exactly has happened, Mr. Robinson?"

"I spent five years building up the Welfare Association," Danny said. "It was a mighty big success. We paid out hundreds of pounds every week in benefits and took in thousands in subscriptions. But what were we to do with the surplus?"

Solly said: "I assume you put it aside against the possibility of a bad year."

"And where do you think we put it?"

"In a bank, I trust."

"In the City of Glasgow Bank, to be exact."

"Oh, dear," said Solly.

Maisie said: "I don't understand."

Solly explained: "The City of Glasgow Bank went bankrupt."

"Oh, no!" Maisie cried. It made her want to weep.

Danny nodded. "All those shillings paid in by hardworking men—lost by fools in top hats. And you wonder why they talk about revolution." He sighed. "I've been trying to rescue the Association since it happened, but the task was hopeless, and I've given up."

Kingo said abruptly: "Mr. Robinson, I am sorry for you and your members. Will you take some refreshment? You must have walked seven miles if you came from the railway station."

"I will, and thank you."

Maisie said: "I'll take Danny indoors, and leave you to finish your walk." She felt her brother was wounded, and she wanted to get him alone and do what she could to ease his pain.

The others obviously felt the tragedy too. Kingo said: "Will you stop for the night, Mr. Robinson?"

Maisie winced. Kingo was being too generous. It was easy enough to be civil to Danny for a few minutes out here in the park, but if he stayed overnight Kingo and his lotus-eating friends would soon get fed up with Danny's coarse clothes and working-class concerns, then they would snub him and he would be hurt.

But Danny said: "I have to be back in London tonight. I just came to spend a few hours with my sister."

Kingo said: "In that case allow me to have you driven to the station in my carriage, whenever you're ready."

"That's real kind of you."

Maisie took her brother's arm. "Come with me and I'll get you some lunch."

*

After Danny left for London, Maisie joined Solly for an afternoon nap.

Solly lay on the bed in a red silk bathrobe and watched her undress. "I can't rescue Dan's Welfare Association," he said. "Even if it made financial sense to me—which it doesn't—I couldn't persuade the other partners."

Maisie felt a sudden surge of affection for him. She had not asked him to help Danny. "You're such a good man," she said. She opened his bathrobe and kissed his vast belly. "You've already done so much for my family, you never have to apologize. Besides, Danny won't take anything from you, you know that; he's too proud."

"But what will he do?"

She stepped out of her petticoats and rolled down her stockings. "Tomorrow he's meeting with the Amalgamated Society of Engineers. He wants to be a member of Parliament and he hopes they will sponsor him."

"And I suppose he'll campaign for stricter government regulation of banks."

"Would you be against that?"

"We never like the government to tell us what to do. True, there are too many crashes; but there might be even more if the politicians ran the banks." He rolled on his side and propped his head up on his elbow to get a better view of her taking off her underwear. "I wish I weren't leaving you tonight."

Maisie wished the same. A part of her was excited at the prospect of being with Hugh when Solly was away, but that made her feel more guilty still. "I don't mind," she said.

"I feel so ashamed of my family."

"You shouldn't." It was Passover, and Solly was going to celebrate the ritual of seder with his parents. Maisie was not invited. She understood Ben Greenbourne's dislike of her, and half felt she deserved the way he treated her, but Solly was deeply upset by it. Indeed, he would have quarreled with his father if Maisie had let him, but she did not want that on her conscience too, and she insisted he continue to see his parents in a normal way.

"Are you sure you don't mind?" he said anxiously.

"I'm sure. Listen, if I felt strongly about it I could go to Manchester and spend Passover with my own parents." She became thoughtful. "The fact is that I've never felt part of all that Jewish stuff, not since we left Russia. When we came to England there were no Jews in the town. The people I lived with in the circus had no religion at all, mostly. Even when I married a Jew, your family made me feel unwelcome. I'm fated to be an outsider, and to tell you the truth I don't mind. God never did anything for me." She smiled. "Mama says God gave you to me, but that's rubbish: I got you all by myself."

He was reassured. "I'll miss you tonight."

She sat on the edge of the bed and leaned over him so that he could nuzzle her breasts. "I'll miss you too."

"Mmm."

After a while they lay side by side, head to tail, and he caressed her between her legs while she kissed and licked and then sucked his penis. He loved to do this in the afternoon, and he cried out softly as he came in her mouth.

She changed her position and nestled in the crook of his arm.

"What does it taste like?" he said sleepily.

She smacked her lips. "Caviar."

He giggled and closed his eyes.

She began to stroke herself. Soon he was snoring. When she came he did not stir.

*

"The men who ran the City of Glasgow Bank should go to jail," Maisie said shortly before dinner.

"That's a bit hard," Hugh responded.

The remark struck her as smug. "Hard?" she said irritably. "Not as hard as what happened to the workingmen whose money was lost!"

"Still, no one is perfect, not even those workingmen," Hugh persisted. "If a carpenter makes a mistake, and a house falls down, should he go to jail?"

"It's not the same!"

"And why not?"

"Because the carpenter is paid thirty shillings a week and obliged to follow a foreman's orders, whereas a banker gets thousands, and justifies it by saying he carries a weight of responsibility."

"All true. But the banker is human, and has a wife and children to support."

"You might say the same of murderers, yet we hang them regardless of the fate of their orphaned children."

"But if a man kills another accidentally, for example by shooting at a rabbit and hitting a man behind a bush, we don't even send him to jail. So why should we jail bankers who lose other people's money?"

"To make other bankers more careful!"

"And by the same logic we might hang the man who shot at the rabbit, to make other shooters more careful."

"Hugh, you're just being perverse."

"No, I'm not. Why treat careless bankers more harshly than careless rabbit-shooters?"

"The difference is that careless shots do not throw thousands of working people into destitution every few years, whereas careless bankers do."

At this point Kingo interjected languidly: "The directors of the City of Glasgow Bank probably *will* go to jail, I hear; and the manager too."

Hugh said: "So I believe."

Maisie felt like screaming with frustration. "Then why have you been contradicting me?"

He grinned. "To see whether you could justify your attitude."

Maisie remembered that Hugh had always had the power to do this to her, and she bit her tongue. Her spitfire personality was part of her appeal to the Marlborough Set, one of the reasons they accepted her despite her background; but they would get bored if she let her tantrums go on too long. Her mood changed in a flash. "Sir, you have insulted me!" she cried theatrically. "I challenge you to a duel!"

"What weapons do ladies duel with?" Hugh laughed.

"Crochet hooks at dawn!"

They all laughed at that, then a servant came in and announced dinner.

They were always eighteen or twenty around the long table. Maisie loved to see the crisp linen and fine china, the hundreds of candles reflected in the shining glassware, the immaculate black-and-white evening dress of the men and the gorgeous colors and priceless jewelry of the women. There was champagne every night, but it went straight to Maisie's waist, so she allowed herself only a sip or two.

She found herself seated next to Hugh. The duchess normally put her next to Kingo, for Kingo liked pretty women and the duchess was tolerant; but tonight she had apparently decided to vary the formula. No one said grace, for in this set religion was kept for Sundays only. The soup was served and Maisie chatted brightly to the men on either side of her. However, her mind was on her brother. Poor Danny! So clever, so dedicated, such a great leader—and so unlucky. She wondered if he would succeed in his new ambition of becoming a member of Parliament. She hoped so. Papa would be so proud.

Today, unusually, her background had intruded visibly into her new life. It was surprising how little difference it made. Like her, Danny did not appear to belong to any particular class of society. He represented workingmen; his dress was middle class; yet he had the same confident, slightly arrogant manners as Kingo and his friends. They could not easily tell whether he was an upper-class boy who chose martyrdom among the workers or a working-class boy who had risen in life.

Something similar was true of Maisie. Anyone with the least instinct for class differences could tell she was not a born lady. However, she played the part so well, and she was so pretty and charming, that they could not quite bring themselves to believe the persistent rumor that Solly had picked her up in a dance parlor. If there had been any question of her acceptance by London society, it had been answered when the Prince of Wales, son of Queen Victoria—

and future king—had confessed himself "captivated" by her and sent her a gold cigarette box with a diamond clasp.

As the meal progressed she felt the presence of Hugh by her side more and more. She made an effort to keep the conversation light, and took care to talk at least as much to the man on her other side; but the past seemed to stand at her shoulder, waiting to be acknowledged, like a weary, patient supplicant.

She and Hugh had met three or four times since his return to London, and now they had spent forty-eight hours in the same house, but they had never spoken of what had happened six years ago. All Hugh knew was that she had disappeared without a trace, only to surface as Mrs. Solomon Greenbourne. Sooner or later she was going to have to give him some explanation. She was afraid that talking about it would bring back all the old feelings, in him as well as her. But it had to be done, and perhaps this was a good time, when Solly was away.

A moment came when several people around them were talking noisily. Maisie decided she should speak now. She turned to Hugh, and suddenly she was overcome with emotion. She began speaking three or

four times and could not go on. Finally she
managed to get a few words out. "I would
have ruined your career, you know." Then
she had to make such an effort not to cry
that she could say no more.

He understood right away what she was
talking about. "Who told you that you
would have ruined my career?"

If he had been sympathetic she might
have broken down, but luckily he was aggressive, and that enabled her to reply.
"Your aunt Augusta."

"I suspected she was involved somehow."

"But she was right."

"I don't believe that," he said, getting angry very quickly. "You didn't ruin Solly's career."

"Calm down. Solly wasn't already the
black sheep of the family. Even so, it was
difficult enough. His family hates me still."

"Even though you're Jewish?"

"Yes. Jews can be as snobbish as anyone
else." He would never know the real reason
—that Bertie was not Solly's child.

"Why didn't you simply tell me what you
were doing, and why?"

"I couldn't." Remembering those awful
days, she felt choked up again and had to
take a deep breath to calm herself. "I found

it very hard to cut myself off like that; it broke my heart. I couldn't have done it at all if I'd had to justify myself to you as well."

Still he would not let her off the hook. "You could have sent me a note."

Maisie's voice dropped almost to a whisper. "I couldn't bring myself to write it."

At last he seemed to relent. He took a gulp of his wine and averted his eyes from her. "It was awful, not understanding, not knowing if you were even alive." He was speaking harshly, but now she could see the remembered pain in his eyes.

"I'm sorry," she said feebly. "I'm so sorry I hurt you. I didn't want to. I wanted to save you from unhappiness. I did it for love." As soon as she heard herself say the word "love" she regretted it.

He picked up on it. "Do you love Solly now?" he said abruptly.

"Yes."

"The two of you seem very settled."

"The way we live . . . it isn't difficult to be contented."

He had not finished being angry with her. "You've got what you always wanted."

That was a bit hard, but she felt that perhaps she deserved it, so she just nodded.

"What happened to April?"

Maisie hesitated. This was going a bit too far. "You class me with April, then, do you?" she said, feeling hurt.

Somehow that deflated his anger. He smiled ruefully and said: "No, you were never like April. I know that. All the same I'd like to know what became of her. Do you still see her?"

"Yes—discreetly." April was a neutral topic: talking about her would get them off this dangerously emotional ground. Maisie decided to satisfy his curiosity. "Do you know a place called Nellie's?"

He lowered his voice. "It's a brothel."

She could not restrain herself from asking: "Did you ever go there?"

He looked embarrassed. "Yes, once. It was a fiasco."

That did not surprise her: she remembered how naive and inexperienced the twenty-year-old Hugh had been. "Well, April now owns the place."

"Goodness! How did that happen?"

"First she became the mistress of a famous novelist and lived in the prettiest little cottage in Clapham. He tired of her at about the time Nell was thinking about retirement. So April sold the cottage and bought Nell out."

"Fancy that," said Hugh. "I'll never forget Nell. She was the fattest woman I've ever seen."

The table had suddenly gone quiet, and his last sentence was heard by several people nearby. There was general laughter, and someone said: "Who was this fat lady?" Hugh just grinned and made no reply.

After that they stayed off dangerous topics, but Maisie felt subdued and somewhat fragile, as if she had suffered a fall and bruised herself.

When dinner was over and the men had smoked their cigars Kingo announced that he wanted to dance. The drawing room carpet was rolled up and a footman who could play polkas on the piano was summoned and set to work.

Maisie danced with everyone except Hugh, then it was obvious she was avoiding him, so she danced with him; and it was as if six years had rolled back and they were in Cremorne Gardens again. He hardly led her: they seemed instinctively to do the same thing. Maisie could not suppress the disloyal thought that Solly was a clumsy dancer.

After Hugh she took another partner; but then the other men stopped asking her. As ten o'clock turned to eleven and the brandy appeared, convention was abandoned: white ties were loosened, some of the women kicked off their shoes, and Maisie danced every dance with Hugh. She knew she ought to feel guilty, but she had never been much good at guilt: she was enjoying herself and she was not going to stop.

When the piano-playing footman was exhausted, the duchess demanded a breath of air, and maids were sent scurrying for coats so they could all take a turn around the garden. Out in the darkness, Maisie took Hugh's arm. "The whole world knows what I've been doing for the last six years, but what about you?"

"I like America," he said. "There's no class system. There are rich and poor, but no aristocracy, no nonsense about rank and protocol. What you've done, in marrying Solly and becoming a friend of the highest in the land, is pretty unusual here, and even now I bet you never actually tell the truth about your origins—"

"They have their suspicions, I think—but you're right, I don't own up."

"In America you'd boast about your humble beginnings the way Kingo boasts about his ancestors fighting at the battle of Agincourt."

She was interested in Hugh, not America. "You haven't married."

"No."

"In Boston . . . was there a girl you liked?"

"I tried, Maisie," he said.

Suddenly she wished she had not asked him about this, for she had a premonition that his answer would destroy her happiness; but it was too late, the question had been raised and he was already speaking.

"There were pretty girls in Boston, and pleasant girls, and intelligent girls, and girls who would make wonderful wives and mothers. I paid attention to some of them, and they seemed to like me. But when it came to the point where I had to make a proposal or back off I realized, each time, that what I felt was not enough. It was not what I felt for you. It wasn't love."

Now he had said it. "Stop," Maisie whispered.

"Two or three mothers got rather cross with me, then my reputation spread around, and the girls became wary. They were nice enough to me, but they knew there was something wrong with me, I wasn't serious, not the marrying kind. Hugh Pilaster, the English banker and breaker of hearts. And if a girl did seem to fall for me, despite my record, I would discourage her. I don't like to break people's hearts. I know too well what it feels like."

Her face was wet with tears, and she was glad of the tactful dark. "I'm sorry," she said, but she whispered so softly that she could hardly hear her own voice.

"Anyway, I know what's wrong with me now. I guess I always knew, but the last two days have removed any doubts."

They had fallen behind the others, and now he stopped and faced her.

She said: "Don't say it, Hugh, please."

"I still love you. That's all."

It was out, and everything was ruined.

"I think you love me too," he went on mercilessly. "Don't you?"

She looked up at him. She could see, reflected in his eyes, the lights of the house across the lawn, but his face was in shadow. He inclined his head and kissed her lips, and she did not turn away. "Salt tears," he said after a minute. "You do love me. I knew it." He took a folded handkerchief from his pocket and touched her face gently, mopping the teardrops from her cheeks.

She had to put a stop to this. "We must catch up with the others," she said. "People will talk." She turned and began to walk, so that he had to either release her arm or go with her. He went with her.

"I'm surprised that you worry about people talking," he said. "Your set is famous for not minding anything of that sort."

She was not really concerned about the others. It was herself she was worried about. She made him walk faster until they rejoined the rest of the party, then she let go of his arm and talked to the duchess.

She was obscurely bothered by Hugh's saying that the Marlborough Set was famous for its tolerance. It was true, but she wished he hadn't used the phrase *anything of that sort;* she was not sure why.

When they reentered the house the tall clock in the hall was striking midnight. Maisie suddenly felt drained by the tensions of the day. "I'm going to bed," she announced.

She saw the duchess look reflexively at Hugh, then back at her, and suppress a little smile; and she realized that they all thought Hugh would sleep with her tonight.

The ladies went upstairs together, leaving the men to play billiards and drink a night-cap. As the women kissed her good night Maisie saw the same look in the eyes of each one, a gleam of excitement tinged with envy.

She went into her bedroom and closed the door. A coal fire burned merrily in the grate, and there were candles on the mantelpiece and the dressing table. On the bed-side table, as usual, there was a plate of sandwiches and a bottle of sherry in case she got peckish in the night: she never touched them, but the well-trained staff of Kingsbridge Manor put a tray beside every bed without fail.

She began to take off her clothes. They might all be wrong: perhaps Hugh would not come to her tonight. The thought stabbed her like a pain, and she longed for him to come through the door so that she could take him in her arms and kiss him, really kiss him, not guiltily as she had in the garden, but hungrily and shamelessly. The feeling brought back an overwhelming memory of the night of the Goodwood races six years ago, the narrow bed in his aunt's house, and the expression on his face when she took off her dress.

She looked at her body in the long mirror. Hugh would notice how it had changed. Six years ago she had had tiny turned-in pink nipples like dimples, but now, after nursing Bertie, they were enlarged and strawberry-colored, and stuck out. As a girl she had not needed to wear a corset—she had been naturally wasp-shaped—but her waist had never quite returned to normal after pregnancy.

She heard the men coming up the stairs, heavy-footed and laughing at some joke. Hugh had been right: not one of them would be shocked by a little adultery at a country-house party. Did they not feel disloyal to their friend Solly, she thought derisively? And then it hit her like a slap in the face that she was the one who ought to feel disloyal.

She had put Solly out of her mind all evening, but now he came back to her in spirit: harmless, amiable Solly; kind, generous Solly; the man who loved her to distraction, the man who cared for Bertie, knowing he was another man's child. Within hours of his leaving the house Maisie was about to let another man come into her bed. What kind of woman am I? she thought.

On impulse she went to the door and locked it.

She understood now why she had disliked Hugh's saying *Your set is famous for not minding anything of that sort.* It made her feeling for Hugh seem commonplace, just another one of the many flirtations, romances and infidelities that gave society ladies something to gossip about. Solly deserved better than to be betrayed by a commonplace affair.

But I want Hugh, she thought.

The idea of forgoing this night with him made her want to weep. She thought of his boyish grin and his bony chest, his blue eyes and smooth white skin; and she remembered the expression on his face when he looked at her body, the expression of wonder and happiness, desire and delight; and it seemed so hard to give that up.

There was a soft tap at the door.

She stood naked in the middle of the room, paralyzed and dumb.

The handle turned and the door was pushed, but of course it would not open.

She heard her name spoken in a low voice.

She went to the door and put her hand to the key.

"Maisie!" he called softly. "It's me, Hugh."

She longed for him so much that the sound of his voice made her moist inside. She put her finger in her mouth and bit herself hard, but the pain did not mask the desire.

He tapped on the door again. "Maisie! Let me in?"

She leaned her back against the wall, and the tears streamed down her face, dripping off her chin onto her breasts.

"At least let us talk!"

She knew that if she opened the door there would be no talking—she would take him in her arms and they would fall to the floor in a frenzy of desire.

"Say *something*. Are you there? I know you're there."

She stood still, crying silently.

"Please?" he said. "Please?"

After a while he went away.

Maisie slept badly and woke early, but as the new day dawned her spirits lifted a little. Before the other guests were up she went along to the nursery wing as usual. Outside the door of the nursery dining room she stopped suddenly. She was not the first guest to rise, after all. She could hear a man's voice inside. She paused and listened. It was Hugh.

He was saying: "And just at that moment, the giant woke up."

There was a childish squeal of delighted terror that Maisie recognized as coming from Bertie.

Hugh went on: "Jack went down the beanstalk as fast as his legs could carry him —but the giant came after him!"

Kingo's daughter Anne said in the superior voice of a knowing seven-year-old: "Bertie's hiding behind his chair because he's scared. I'm not scared."

Maisie wanted to hide like Bertie, and she turned and began to walk back to her room, but she stopped again. She had to face Hugh sometime today, and here in the nursery might be the easiest place. She composed herself and went in.

Hugh had the three children enraptured. Bertie hardly saw his mother come in. Hugh looked up at Maisie with hurt in his eyes. "Don't stop," Maisie said, and she sat down by Bertie and hugged him.

Hugh returned his attention to the children. "And what do you think Jack did next?"

"I know," said Anne. "He got an ax."

"That's right."

Maisie sat there hugging Bertie, while Bertie stared big-eyed at the man who was his real father. If I can stand this, I can do anything, Maisie thought.

Hugh said: "And while the giant was still halfway up the beanstalk, Jack chopped it down! And the giant fell all the way to the earth . . . and died. And Jack and his mother lived happily ever after."

Bertie said: "Tell it again."

4

THE CORDOVAN MINISTRY was busy. Tomorrow was Cordovan Independence Day and there would be a big afternoon reception for members of Parliament, Foreign Office officials, diplomats and journalists. This morning, to add to his worries, Micky Miranda had received a stiff note from the British Foreign Secretary about two English tourists who had been murdered while exploring the Andes. But when Edward Pilaster called, Micky Miranda dropped everything, for what he had to say to Edward was much more important than either the reception or the note. He needed half a million pounds, and he was hoping to get the money from Edward.

Micky had been the Cordovan Minister for a year. Getting the job had required all his cunning, but it had also cost his family a fortune in bribes back home. He had promised Papa that all that money would return to the family, and now he had to make good his promise. He would rather die than let his father down.

He brought Edward into the minister's chamber, a grand room dominated by a full-size Cordovan flag. He went to the big table and spread out a map of Cordova, weighing down the corners with his cigar case, the sherry decanter, a glass, and Edward's gray top hat. He hesitated. It was the first time he had ever asked someone for half a million pounds.

"Here is Santamaria Province, in the north of the country," he began.

"I do know the geography of Cordova," Edward said peevishly.

"Of course you do," said Micky in a soothing voice. It was true. Pilasters Bank did a healthy volume of business with Cordova, financing its exports of nitrate, salt beef and silver and its imports of mining equipment, guns and luxury goods. Edward handled all that business, thanks to Micky, who as attaché and then minister had made life difficult for anyone who did not want to use Pilasters Bank to finance their trade with his country. In consequence Edward was now seen as the leading London expert on Cordova. "Of course you do," Micky repeated. "And you know that all the nitrate mined by my father has to be transported by mule train from Santamaria to Palma. But what you may not know is that it is perfectly possible to build a railroad along that route."

"How can you be sure? A railroad is a complicated thing."

Micky took a bound volume from his desk. "Because my father commissioned a survey by a Scottish engineer, Gordon Halfpenny. All the details are in here—including the costs. Take a look."

"How much?" Edward said.

"Five hundred thousand pounds."

Edward riffled through the pages of the report. "What about politics?"

Micky glanced up at the big portrait of President Garcia in the uniform of commander-in-chief. Every time Micky looked at the picture he vowed that one day his own portrait would occupy that spot on the

wall. "The president favors the idea. He believes it will strengthen his military grip on
the countryside." Garcia trusted Papa. Ever
since Papa had become governor of
Santamaria Province—with the help of two
thousand Westley-Richards short-barreled
rifles made in Birmingham—the Miranda
family had been the president's fervent supporters and close allies. Garcia did not suspect Papa's motive for wanting a railway to
Palma: it would enable the Miranda family
to attack the capital within two days instead
of two weeks.

"How will it be paid for?" said Edward.

"We'll raise the money on the London
market," Micky said airily. "In fact I
thought Pilasters Bank might like to have
the business." He tried to breathe slowly
and normally. This was the climax of his
long and painstaking cultivation of the Pilaster family: this was to be his reward for
years of preparation.

But Edward shook his head and said: "I
don't think so."

Micky was astonished and dismayed. At
worst he had thought Edward would agree
to think about it. "But you raise money for
railroads all the time—I thought you'd be
pleased to have the opportunity!"

"Cordova isn't the same as Canada or Russia," Edward said. "Investors don't like your political setup, with every provincial caudillo having his own personal army. It's medieval."

Micky had not thought of that. "You floated Papa's silver mine." That had happened three years ago, and had brought Papa a useful hundred thousand pounds.

"Exactly! It turned out to be the only silver mine in South America that struggles to make a profit."

In truth the mine was very rich, but Papa was skimming the profits off the top and leaving nothing for the shareholders. If only he had left a little margin for the sake of respectability! But Papa never listened to such counsel.

Micky fought down a panicky feeling, but his emotions must have shown on his face, for Edward said worriedly: "I say, old boy, is it terribly important? You look upset."

"To tell you the truth, it would mean quite a lot to my family," Micky admitted. He felt that Edward must be able to raise this money if he really wanted to; it could not be impossible. "Surely, if a bank with the prestige of Pilasters were to back the project, people would conclude that Cordova must be a good place to invest."

"There's something in that," Edward said. "If one of the partners put the idea up, and really wanted to push it through, it could probably be done. But I'm not a partner."

Micky had underestimated the difficulty of raising half a million pounds. But he was not beaten. He would find a way. "I'll have to think again," he said with forced cheerfulness.

Edward drained his sherry glass and stood up. "Shall we go to lunch?"

That night Micky and the Pilasters went to see *H.M.S. Pinafore* at the Opera Comique. Micky got there a few minutes early. While he was waiting in the foyer he ran into the Bodwin family, who were Pilaster hangers-on: Albert Bodwin was a lawyer who did a lot of work for the bank, and Augusta had once tried quite hard to get the daughter, Rachel Bodwin, to marry Hugh.

Micky's mind was on the problem of raising the money for the railroad, but he flirted with Rachel Bodwin automatically, as he did with all girls and many married women.

"And how is the movement for female emancipation, Miss Bodwin?"

Her mother blushed and said: "I wish you wouldn't speak of it, Señor Miranda."

"Then I shan't, Mrs. Bodwin, for your wishes are to me as Acts of Parliament, legally binding." He turned back to Rachel. She was not exactly pretty—her eyes were a little too close together—but she had a good figure: long legs, a narrow waist and a deep bust. In a sudden flash of fantasy he imagined her with her hands tied to the head of a bed and her naked legs spread, and he enjoyed the picture. Glancing up from her bosom he caught her eye. Most girls would have blushed and turned away, but she gave him a look of remarkable frankness and smiled, and it was he who felt embarrassed. Looking for something to talk about he said: "Did you know that our old friend Hugh Pilaster has returned from the colonies?"

"Yes, I saw him at Whitehaven House. You were there."

"Ah yes, I forgot."

"I always liked Hugh."

But you didn't want to marry him, Micky thought. Rachel had now been on offer in the marriage market for many years, and she was beginning to look like stale goods, he thought unkindly. Yet his instincts told him she was a deeply sexual person. Her problem was undoubtedly that she was too formidable. She frightened men off. But she must be getting desperate. Approaching thirty and still single, she would surely be wondering if she were doomed to the life of a spinster. Some women might contemplate that with equanimity, but not Rachel, Micky felt.

She was attracted to him, but then so was almost everyone, old and young, male and female. Micky liked it when rich and influential people fell for him, for it gave him power; but Rachel was nobody and her interest in him was valueless.

The Pilasters arrived and Micky turned his attention to Augusta. She was wearing a striking evening gown in deep raspberry-pink. "You look . . . delicious, Mrs. Pilaster," he said in a low voice, and she smiled with pleasure. The two families chatted for a few minutes, then it was time to take their seats.

The Bodwins were in the stalls but the Pilasters had a box. As they separated, Rachel gave Micky a warm smile and said quietly: "Perhaps we will see you later, Señor

Miranda." Her father overheard and looked disapproving as he took her arm and hurried her away, but Mrs. Bodwin smiled at Micky as they left. Mr. Bodwin doesn't want his daughter to fall for a foreigner, Micky thought, but Mrs. Bodwin is not so choosy anymore.

He worried over his railroad loan throughout the first act. It had not occurred to him that Cordova's primitive political setup, which had allowed the Miranda family to fight their way to wealth and power, might be seen by investors as risky. That probably meant he could not get the railroad project financed by any other bank. The only way to raise the money would be to use his inside influence with Pilasters. And the only people he might be able to influence were Edward and Augusta.

During the first interval he found himself alone in the box with Augusta for a few moments, and he tackled her immediately, knowing that she appreciated the direct approach. "When will Edward be made a partner in the bank?"

"That's a sore point," she said sourly. "Why do you ask?"

He told her briefly about the railroad, leaving out Papa's long-term aim of attacking the capital. "I can't get the money from another bank—none of them knows anything about Cordova, because I've kept them all away for Edward's sake." It was not the real reason but Augusta would not know that: she did not understand the business. "But it would be a success if Edward could push it through."

Augusta nodded. "My husband has promised to make Edward a partner as soon as he marries," she said.

Micky was surprised. Edward marry! The idea was startling—and yet why should it be?

Augusta went on: "We have even agreed on a bride: Emily Maple, the daughter of Deacon Maple."

"What's she like?"

"Pretty, young—she's only nineteen—and sensible. Her parents approve of the match."

She sounded about right for Edward, Micky thought: he liked pretty girls but he needed one he could dominate. "So what obstacle is there?"

Augusta frowned. "I simply don't know. But somehow Edward never quite gets around to asking her."

This did not surprise Micky. He could not

imagine Edward's marrying, no matter how suitable the girl. What did he have to gain from marriage? He had no desire for children. But now there was an incentive: the partnership. Even if Edward did not care about that, Micky did. "What can we do to encourage him?"

Augusta gave Micky a sharp look and said: "I have a funny feeling that he might go ahead if you were married."

Micky looked away. That was perceptive of her. She had no idea what went on in the private rooms of Nellie's brothel—but she had a mother's intuition. He, too, felt that if he married first, Edward might be more willing. "Me, marry?" he said with a little laugh. Naturally he would marry, sooner or later—everyone did—but he saw no reason to do so yet.

However, if it was the price of financing the railroad . . .

It was not just the railroad, he reflected. One successful loan would lead to another. Countries such as Russia and Canada raised fresh loans every year on the London market—for railroads, harbors, water supply companies and general government finance. There was no reason why Cordova should not do the same. Micky would take a commission, official or unofficial, on every penny raised; but more importantly, the money would be channeled to his family's interests back home, making them ever richer and more powerful.

And the alternative was unthinkable. If he let his father down over this he would be never be forgiven. To avert his father's wrath he would marry three times over.

He looked back at Augusta. They never spoke of what had happened in old Seth's bedroom back in the September of 1873, but she could not possibly have forgotten it. It had been sex without intercourse, infidelity without adultery, something and nothing. They had both been fully clothed, it had lasted only seconds, yet it had been more passionate and moving and searingly unforgettable than anything Micky had ever done with the whores at Nellie's brothel, and he felt sure it had been a momentous passage for Augusta too. How did she really feel about the prospect of Micky's getting married? Half the women in London would be jealous, but it was so hard to know what Augusta felt in her heart. He decided to ask her directly. He looked into her eyes and said: "Do you want me to marry?"

She hesitated. He saw regret in her face

for a moment. Then her expression hardened and she said firmly: "Yes."

He stared at her. She held his look. He saw that she meant what she said, and he was oddly disappointed.

Augusta said: "It must be settled soon. Emily Maple and her parents won't be kept in suspense indefinitely."

In other words I'd better get married quickly, Micky thought.

I will, then. So be it.

Joseph and Edward returned to the box and the conversation turned to other matters.

Throughout the next act Micky thought about Edward. They had been friends now for fifteen years. Edward was weak and insecure, eager to please but without initiative or drive. His life's project was to get people to encourage and support him, and Micky had been supplying that need ever since he started doing Edward's Latin prep at school. Now Edward needed to be pushed into the marriage that was necessary for his career—and for Micky's.

During the second interval Micky said to Augusta: "Edward needs someone to help him at the bank—a clever clerk who will be loyal to him and look after his interests."

Augusta thought for a moment. "That's a very good notion indeed," she said. "Someone you and I know and trust."

"Exactly."

Augusta said: "Do you have someone in mind?"

"I have a cousin working for me at the ministry. His name is Simon Oliver. It was Olivera but he anglicized it. He's a smart boy and completely trustworthy."

"Bring him to tea," Augusta said. "If I like the looks of him I'll speak to Joseph."

"Very well."

The last act began. He and Augusta often thought alike, Micky mused. It was Augusta he should be married to: together they could conquer the world. He pushed that fantastic notion out of his head. Who was he going to marry? She should not be an heiress, for he had nothing to offer such a girl. There were several heiresses he could easily captivate, but winning their hearts was only the start: there would be a prolonged battle with the parents and no guarantee of the right result. No, he needed a girl of modest background, one who liked him already and would accept him with alacrity. His eye roamed idly around the stalls of the theatre —and lit on Rachel Bodwin.

She fit the bill perfectly. She was already half in love with him. She was getting desperate for a husband. Her father did not like Micky much but her mother did, and the mother and daughter together would soon overcome the father's opposition.

But most importantly, she aroused him.

She would be a virgin, innocent and apprehensive. He would do things to her that would bewilder and disgust her. She might resist, which would make it even better. In the end a wife had to give in to her husband's sexual demands, regardless of how bizarre or distasteful they might be, for she had no one to complain to. Once again he pictured her tied to the bed, only this time she was writhing, either in pain or desire or both. . . .

The show came to an end. As they left the theatre Micky looked out for the Bodwins. They met on the pavement, as the Pilasters were waiting for their carriage and Albert Bodwin was hailing a hansom. Micky gave Mrs. Bodwin a winning smile and said: "May I do myself the honor of calling on you tomorrow afternoon?"

She was obviously startled. "The honor would be all mine, Señor Miranda."

"You're too kind." He shook hands with

Rachel, looked her in the eye, and said: "Until tomorrow, then."

"I look forward to it," she said.

Augusta's carriage arrived and Micky opened the door. "What do you think of her?" he murmured.

"Her eyes are too close together," Augusta said as she climbed in. She settled in her seat then spoke to him through the open door. "Other than that, she looks like me." She slammed the door and the carriage drove off.

An hour later Micky and Edward were eating supper in a private room at Nellie's. Apart from the table, the room contained a sofa, a wardrobe, a washstand and a big bed. April Tilsley had redecorated the whole place, and this room had fashionable William Morris fabrics and a set of framed drawings of people performing sexual acts with a variety of fruits and vegetables. But it was in the nature of the business that people got drunk and misbehaved, and already the wallpaper was torn, the curtains stained and the carpet ripped. However, low candlelight hid the tawdriness of the room as well as taking years off the ages of the women.

The men were being waited on by two of

their favorite girls, Muriel and Lily, who were wearing red silk shoes and huge, elaborate hats but were otherwise naked. From outside the room came the sounds of raucous singing and some kind of heated quarrel, but in here it was peaceful, with the crackling of the coal fire and the murmured words of the two girls as they served supper. The atmosphere relaxed Micky, and he began to feel less anxious about the railroad loan. He had a plan, at least. He could only try it out. He looked across the table at Edward. Theirs had been a fruitful friendship, he mused. There were times when he felt almost fond of Edward. Edward's dependency was tiresome, but it was what gave Micky power over him. He had helped Edward, Edward had helped him, and together they had enjoyed all the vices of the most sophisticated city in the world.

When they finished eating Micky poured another glass of wine and said: "I'm going to marry Rachel Bodwin."

Muriel and Lily giggled.

Edward stared at him for a long moment then said: "I don't believe it."

Micky shrugged. "Believe what you wish. It's true, all the same."

"Do you really mean it?"

"Yes."

"You swine!"

Micky stared at his friend in surprise. "What? Why shouldn't I marry?"

Edward stood up and leaned over the table aggressively. "You're a damned swine, Miranda, and that's all there is to say."

Micky had not anticipated such a reaction. "What the devil has got into you?" he said. "Aren't you going to marry Emily Maple?"

"Who told you that?"

"Your mother."

"Well, I'm not marrying anyone."

"Why not? You're twenty-nine years old. So am I. It's time for a man to equip himself with the semblance of a respectable household."

"To the devil with a respectable household!" Edward roared, and he overturned the table. Micky sprang back as crockery smashed and wine spilled. The two naked women cringed away fearfully.

"Calm down!" Micky cried.

"After all these years!" Edward raged. "After all I've done for you!"

Micky was baffled by Edward's fury. He had to calm the man down. A scene like this could prejudice him against marriage, and that was the opposite of what Micky wanted. "It's not a disaster," he said in a reasonable tone. "It's not going to make any difference to us."

"It's bound to!"

"No, it's not. We'll still come here."

Edward looked suspicious. In a quieter voice he said: "Will we?"

"Yes. And we'll still go to the club. That's what clubs are for. Men go to clubs to get away from their wives."

"I suppose they do."

The door opened and April swept in. "What's the noise about?" she said. "Edward, have you been breaking my china?"

"I'm sorry, April. I'll pay for it."

Micky said to April: "I was just explaining to Edward that he can still come here after he's married."

"Good God, I should hope so," April said. "If no married men came here I'd have to close the place." She turned toward the doorway and called out: "Sid! Fetch a broom."

Edward was calming down rapidly, to Micky's relief. Micky said: "When we're first married, we should probably spend a few evenings at home, and give the occasional dinner party. But after a while we'll go right back to normal."

Edward frowned. "Don't wives mind that?"

Micky shrugged. "Who cares whether they mind? What can a wife do?"

"If she's discontented I suppose she can bother her husband."

Micky realized that Edward was taking his mother as a typical wife. Fortunately few women were as strong-willed or as clever as Augusta. "The trick is not to be too good to them," Micky said, speaking from observation of married cronies at the Cowes Club. "If you're good to a wife she'll want you to stay with her. Treat her roughly and she'll be only too glad to see you go off to your club in the evening and leave her in peace."

Muriel put her arms around Edward's neck. "It'll be just the same when you're married, Edward, I promise," she said. "I'll suck your cock while you watch Micky fuck Lily, just the way you like."

"Will you?" he said with a foolish grin.

"Course I will."

"So nothing will change, really," he said, looking at Micky.

"Oh, yes," said Micky. "One thing will change. You'll be a partner in the bank."

CHAPTER TWO

1

THE MUSIC HALL was as hot as a Turkish bath. The air smelled of beer, shellfish and un-washed people. Onstage a young woman dressed in elaborate rags stood in front of a painted backdrop of a pub. She was holding a doll, to represent a newborn baby, and singing about how she had been seduced and abandoned. The audience, sitting on benches at long trestle-tables, linked arms and joined in the chorus:

And all it took was a little drop of gin!

Hugh sang at the top of his voice. He was feeling good. He had eaten a pint of winkles and drunk several glasses of warm, malty beer, and he was pressed up against Nora Dempster, a pleasant person to be squashed by. She had a soft, plump body and a beguiling smile, and she had probably saved his life.

After his visit to Kingsbridge Manor he had fallen into the pit of a black depression. Seeing Maisie had raised old ghosts, and since she rejected him again the ghosts had haunted him without respite.

He had been able to live through the daytime, for at work there were challenges and problems to take his mind off his grief: he was busy organizing the joint enterprise with Madler and Bell, which the Pilasters partners had finally approved. And he was soon to become a partner himself, something he had dreamed of. But in the evenings he had no enthusiasm for anything. He was invited to a great many parties, balls and dinners, for he was a member of the Marlborough Set by virtue of his friendship with Solly, and he often went, but if Maisie was not there he was bored and if she was he was miserable. So most evenings he sat in his rooms thinking about her, or walked the streets hoping against all likelihood to bump into her.

It was on the street that he had met Nora.

He had gone to Peter Robinson's in Oxford Street—a shop that had once been a linen draper's but was now called a "department store"—to get a present for his sister Dotty: he planned to take the train to Folkestone immediately afterwards. But he was so miserable that he did not know how he was going to face his family, and a kind of paralysis of choice made him incapable of selecting a gift. He came out empty-handed as it was getting dark, and Nora literally bumped into him. She stumbled and he caught her in his arms.

He would never forget how it had felt to hold her. Even though she was wrapped up, her body was soft and yielding, and she smelled warm and scented. For a moment the cold, dark London street vanished and he was in a closed world of sudden delight. Then she dropped her purchase, a pottery vase, and it smashed on the pavement. She gave a cry of dismay and looked as if she might burst into tears. Hugh naturally insisted on buying a replacement.

She was a year or two younger than he, twenty-four or twenty-five. She had a pretty round face with sandy-blond curls poking out from a bonnet, and her clothes were cheap but pleasing: a pink wool dress embroidered with flowers and worn over a bustle, and a tight-fitting French-navy velvet jacket trimmed with rabbit fur. She spoke with a broad cockney drawl.

While they were buying the replacement vase he told her, by way of conversation, that he could not decide what to give his sister. Nora suggested a colorful umbrella, and then she insisted on helping him choose it.

Finally he took her home in a hansom. She told him she lived with her father, a traveling salesman of patent medicines. Her mother was dead. The neighborhood where she lived was rather less respectable than he had guessed, poor working class rather than middle class.

He assumed he would never see her again, and all day Sunday at Folkestone he brooded about Maisie as always. On Monday at the bank he got a note from Nora, thanking him for his kindness: her handwriting was small, neat and girlish, he noticed before screwing the note up into a ball and dropping it into the wastepaper basket.

Next day he stepped out of the bank at midday, on his way to a coffeehouse for a plate of lamb cutlets, and saw her walking along the street toward him. At first he did not recognize her, but simply thought what a nice face she had; then she smiled at him and he remembered. He doffed his hat and she stopped to talk. She worked as an assistant to a corset maker, she told him with a blush, and she was on her way back to the shop after visiting a client. A sudden impulse made him ask her to go dancing with him that night.

She said she would like to go but she did not have a respectable hat, so he took her to a milliner's shop and bought her one, and that settled the matter.

Much of their romance was conducted while shopping. She had never owned much and she took unashamed delight in Hugh's affluence. For his part he enjoyed buying her gloves, shoes, a coat, bracelets, and anything else she wanted. His sister, with all the wisdom of her twelve years, had announced that Nora only liked him for his money. He had laughed and said: "But who would love me for my looks?"

Maisie did not disappear from his mind—indeed, he still thought of her every day—but the memories no longer plunged him into despair. He had something to look forward to now, his next rendezvous with Nora.

In a few weeks she gave him back his joie de vivre.

On one of their shopping expeditions they met Maisie in a furrier's store in Bond Street. Feeling rather bashful, Hugh introduced the two women. Nora was bowled over to meet Mrs. Solomon Greenbourne. Maisie invited them to tea at the Piccadilly house. That evening Hugh saw Maisie again at a ball, and to his surprise Maisie was quite ungracious about Nora. "I'm sorry, but I don't like her," Maisie had said. "She strikes me as a hard-hearted grasping woman and I don't believe she loves you one bit. For God's sake don't marry her."

Hugh had been hurt and offended. Maisie was just jealous, he decided. Anyway, he was not thinking of marriage.

When the music-hall show came to an end they went outside into a fog, thick and swirling and tasting of soot. They wrapped scarves around their necks and over their mouths and set off for Nora's home in Camden Town.

It was like being underwater. All sound was muffled, and people and things loomed out of the fog suddenly, without warning: a whore soliciting beneath a gaslight, a drunk staggering out of a pub, a policeman on patrol, a crossing sweeper, a lamp-lit carriage creeping along the road, a damp dog in the gutter and a glint-eyed cat down an alley. Hugh and Nora held hands and stopped every now and again in the thickest darkness to pull down their scarves and kiss. Nora's lips were soft and responsive, and she let him slip his hand inside her coat and caress her breasts. The fog made everything hushed and secret and romantic.

He usually left her at the corner of her street but tonight, because of the fog, he walked her to the door. He wanted to kiss her again there, but he was afraid her father might open the door and see them. However, Nora surprised him by saying: "Would you like to come in?"

He had never been inside her house. "What will your papa think?" he said.

"He's gone to Huddersfield," she said, and she opened the door.

Hugh's heart beat faster as he stepped inside. He did not know what was going to happen next but it was sure to be exciting. He helped Nora out of her cloak, and his eyes rested longingly on the curves beneath her sky-blue gown.

The house was tiny, smaller even than his mother's house in Folkestone. The staircase took up most of the narrow hall. There were two doors off the hall, leading presumably to a front parlor and a back kitchen. Upstairs there must be two bedrooms. There would be a tin bath in the kitchen and a privy in the backyard.

Hugh hung his hat and coat on a stand. A dog was barking in the kitchen, and Nora opened the door to release a small black Scottish terrier with a blue ribbon around its neck. It greeted her enthusiastically then circled Hugh warily. "Blackie protects me when Pa's away," Nora said, and Hugh registered the double meaning.

He followed Nora into the parlor. The furniture was old and worn, but Nora had brightened the room with things they had bought together: gay cushions, a colorful rug and a painting of Balmoral Castle. She lit a candle and drew the curtains.

Hugh stood in the middle of the room, not knowing what to do with himself, until she put him out of his misery by saying: "See if you can get the fire going." There were a few embers in the hearth, and Hugh put on kindling and blew the fire back to life with a small bellows.

When he was done he turned around to see her sitting on the sofa with her hat off

and her hair let down. She patted the cush-
ion beside her and he sat down obediently.
Blackie glared jealously at him, and he wondered how soon he could get the dog out of
the room.

They held hands and looked into the fire.
Hugh felt at peace. He could not imagine
wanting to do anything else for the rest of
his life. After a while he kissed her again.
Tentatively he touched her breast. It was
firm, and filled his hand. He squeezed it
gently, and she sighed heavily. Hugh had
not felt this good for years, but he wanted
more. He kissed her harder, still touching
her breasts.

By degrees she leaned back until Hugh
was half lying on her. They both began to
breathe hard. He was sure she must be able
to feel his prick pressing against her plump
thigh. In the back of his mind the voice of
conscience told him he was taking advantage of a young girl in her father's absence,
but it was a faint voice and could not prevail
against the desire that welled up inside him
like a volcano.

He longed to touch her most intimate
places. He put his hand between her legs.
She stiffened immediately, and the dog
barked, sensing the tension. Hugh pulled

away a little and said: "Let's put the dog outside."

Nora looked troubled. "Perhaps we should stop."

Hugh could not bear the thought of stopping. However, the word "perhaps" encouraged him. "I can't stop now," he said. "Put the dog out."

"But . . . we're not even engaged, or anything."

"We could get engaged," he said without thinking.

She went slightly pale. "Do you mean it?"

He asked himself the same question. From the start he had thought of this as a dalliance, not a serious courtship; yet only a few moments ago he had been thinking how much he would like to spend the rest of his life holding hands with Nora in front of a fire. Did he really want to marry her? He realized that he did, in fact there was nothing he would like better. There would be trouble, of course. The family would say he was marrying beneath him. They could go to the devil. He was twenty-six years old, he earned a thousand pounds a year, and he was about to be made a partner in one of the most prestigious banks in the world: he could marry who the hell he liked. His mother would be troubled but supportive: she would worry, but she would be glad to see her son happy. And the rest of them could say what they pleased. They had never done anything for him.

He looked at Nora, pink and pretty and lovable, lying back on the old sofa with her hair around her bare shoulders. He wanted her badly, now, quickly. He had been alone too long. Maisie was thoroughly settled with Solly: she would never be his. It was time he had someone warm and soft to share his bed and his life. Why not Nora?

He snapped his fingers at the dog. "Come here, Blackie." It approached him warily. He stroked its head then grabbed the ribbon around its neck. "Come and guard the hall," he said, and he put the dog outside and closed the door. It barked twice and subsided into silence.

He sat beside Nora and took her hand. She looked wary. He said: "Nora, will you marry me?"

She flushed red. "Yes, I will."

He kissed her. She opened her mouth and kissed him back passionately. He touched her knee. She took his hand and guided it beneath the skirts of her dress, up between her legs to the fork of her thighs. Through the flannelette of her underwear he could feel the rough hair and soft flesh of her mound. Her lips tracked across his cheek to his ear, and she whispered: "Hugh, darling, make me yours, tonight, now."

"I will," he said hoarsely. "I will."

2

THE DUCHESS OF TENBIGH'S COSTUME BALL was the first great event of the 1879 London season. Everyone was talking about it weeks in advance. Fortunes were spent on fancy dress, and people would go to any length to get an invitation.

Augusta and Joseph Pilaster were not invited. That was hardly surprising: they did not belong in the very highest echelon of London society. But Augusta wanted to go, and she made up her mind she would be there.

As soon as she heard about the ball she mentioned it to Harriet Morte, who responded by looking embarrassed and saying nothing. As a lady-in-waiting to the Queen, Lady Morte had great social power; and on top of that she was a distant cousin of the duchess of Tenbigh. But she did not offer to get Augusta invited.

Augusta checked Lord Morte's account with Pilasters Bank and found that he had an overdraft of a thousand pounds. The next day he got a note asking him when he hoped to regularize the account.

Augusta called on Lady Morte the same day. She apologized, saying that the note had been an error and the clerk who sent it had been sacked. Then she mentioned the ball again.

Lady Morte's normally impassive face was momentarily animated by a glare of pure hatred as she understood the bargain that was being offered. Augusta was unmoved. She had no wish to be liked by Lady Morte, she just wanted to use her. And Lady Morte was confronted with a simple choice: exert her influence to get Augusta invited to the ball, or find a thousand pounds to pay off her overdraft. She took the easier option, and the invitation cards arrived the following day.

Augusta was annoyed that Lady Morte had not helped her willingly. It was hurtful that Lady Morte had to be coerced. Feeling spiteful, Augusta made her get Edward an invitation too.

Augusta was going as Queen Elizabeth and Joseph as the earl of Leicester. On the night of the ball they had dinner at home and changed afterwards. When she was dressed Augusta went into Joseph's room to help him with his costume and talk to him about his nephew Hugh.

She was incensed that Hugh was to be made a partner in the bank at the same time as Edward. Worse still, everyone knew that Edward had been made a partner only because he had married and been given a £250,000 investment in the bank, whereas Hugh was being made a partner because he had brought off a spectacularly profitable deal with Madler and Bell of New York. People were already talking of Hugh as a potential Senior Partner. The thought made Augusta grind her teeth.

Their promotion was to take place at the end of April, when the annual partnership agreement was formally renewed. But earlier in the month, to Augusta's delight, Hugh made the unbelievably foolish mistake of marrying a plump little working-class girl from Camden Town.

The Maisie episode six years ago had shown that he had a weakness for girls from the gutter, but Augusta had never dared to hope that he would marry one. He had done the deed quietly, in Folkestone, with just his mother and sister and the bride's father in attendance, then he had presented the family with a fait accompli.

As Augusta adjusted Joseph's Elizabethan ruff she said: "I presume you'll have to think again about Hugh's being made a partner, now that he's married a housemaid."

"She's not a housemaid, she's a corsetière. Or was. Now she's Mrs. Pilaster."

"All the same, a partner in Pilasters can hardly have a shopgirl as a wife."

"I must say I think he can marry whom he likes."

Augusta had been afraid he would take this line. "You wouldn't say that if she were ugly, bony and sour," she said acidly. "It's only because she's pretty and flirtatious that you're so tolerant."

"I just don't see the problem."

"A partner has to meet cabinet ministers, diplomats, leaders of great businesses. She won't know how to act. She could embarrass him at any moment."

"She can learn." Joseph hesitated, then added: "I sometimes think you forget your own background, my dear."

Augusta drew herself up to her full height. "My father had three shops!" she said vehemently. "How dare you compare me to that little trollop!"

He backed down instantly. "All right, I'm sorry."

Augusta was outraged. "Furthermore, I never worked in my father's shops," she said. "I was brought up to be a lady."

"I've apologized, let's say no more about it. It's time to go."

Augusta clamped her mouth shut but inside she was seething.

Edward and Emily were waiting for them in the hall, dressed as Henry II and Eleanor of Aquitaine. Edward was having trouble with his gold braid cross-garters, and he said: "You go on, Mother, and send the carriage back for us."

But Emily quickly put in: "Oh, no, I want to go now. Fix your garters on the way."

Emily had big blue eyes and the pretty face of a little girl, and she was very fetching in the embroidered twelfth-century gown and cloak, with a long wimple on her head. However, Augusta had discovered that she was not as timid as she looked. During the preparations for the wedding it had become clear that Emily had a will of her own. She had been happy to let Augusta take over the wedding breakfast, but she had insisted, rather stubbornly, on having her own way about her wedding dress and her bridesmaids.

As they got into their carriage and drove off, Augusta recalled vaguely that the marriage of Henry II and Eleanor had been stormy. She hoped Emily would not give Edward too much trouble. Since the wedding Edward had been bad-tempered, and Augusta suspected there was something wrong. She had tried to find out by questioning Edward delicately, but he would not say a word.

However, the important thing was that he was married and a partner in the bank. He was settled. Everything else could be worked out.

The ball began at half-past ten and the Pilasters arrived on time. Lights blazed from every window of Tenbigh House. There was already a crowd of onlookers outside, and in Park Lane a line of carriages waited to enter the courtyard. The crowd applauded each costume as the guests descended from their vehicles and mounted the steps to the door. Looking ahead as she waited, Augusta saw Anthony and Cleopatra, several Roundheads and Cavaliers, two Greek goddesses and three Napoleons enter the house.

At last her carriage reached the door and they got out. Once inside the house there was another queue, from the hall up the curving staircase to the landing where the duke and duchess of Tenbigh, dressed as Solomon and Sheba, were greeting their guests. The hall was a mass of flowers and a band played to entertain them while they waited.

The Pilasters were followed in by Micky Miranda—invited because of his diplomatic status—and his new wife Rachel. Micky looked more dashing than ever in the red silk of a Cardinal Wolseley outfit, and for a moment the sight of him made Augusta's heart flutter. She looked critically at his wife, who had chosen to come as a slave girl, rather surprisingly. Augusta had encouraged Micky to marry but she could not suppress a stab of resentment toward the plain girl who had won his hand. Rachel returned Augusta's stare coolly, and took Micky's arm possessively after he kissed Augusta's hand.

As they slowly mounted the stairs Micky said to Rachel: "The Spanish envoy is here —be sure to be nice to him."

"You be nice to him," Rachel said crisply. "I think he's a slug."

Micky frowned but said no more. With

her extreme views and forceful manner, Rachel would have made a good wife for a campaigning journalist or a Radical member of Parliament. Micky deserved someone less eccentric and more beautiful, Augusta felt.

Up ahead of them Augusta spotted another pair of newlyweds, Hugh and Nora. Hugh was a member of the Marlborough Set, because of his friendship with the Greenbournes, and to Augusta's chagrin he was invited to everything. He was dressed as an Indian rajah and Nora seemed to have come as a snake charmer, in a sequined gown cut away to reveal harem trousers. Artificial snakes were wound around her arms and legs, and one lay its papier-mâché head on her ample bosom. Augusta shuddered. "Hugh's wife really is impossibly vulgar," she murmured to Joseph.

He was inclined to be lenient. "It is a costume ball, after all."

"Not one of the other women here has been so tasteless as to show her legs."

"I don't see any difference between loose trousers and a dress."

He was probably enjoying the sight of Nora's legs, Augusta thought with distaste. It was so easy for such a woman to befuddle men's judgment. "I just don't think she's fit to be the wife of a partner in Pilasters Bank."

"Nora won't have to make any financial decisions."

Augusta could have screamed with frustration. Evidently it was not enough that Nora was a working-class girl. She would have to do something unforgivable before Joseph and his partners would turn against Hugh.

Now there was a thought.

Augusta's anger died down as quickly as it had flared. Perhaps, she thought, there was a way she could get Nora into trouble. She looked up the stairs again and studied her prey.

Nora and Hugh were talking to the Hungarian attaché, Count de Tokoly, a man of doubtful morals who was appropriately dressed as Henry VIII. Nora was just the kind of girl the count would be charmed by, Augusta thought biliously. Respectable ladies would cross the room to avoid speaking to him, but all the same he had to be invited everywhere because he was a senior diplomat. There was no sign of disapproval on Hugh's face as he watched his wife bat her eyelashes at the old roué. Indeed Hugh's expression showed nothing but adoration. He was still too much in love to find fault. That would not last. "Nora is talking to de Tokoly," Augusta murmured to Joseph. "She had better take care of her reputation."

"Now, don't you be rude to him," Joseph replied brusquely. "We're hoping to raise two million pounds for his government."

Augusta did not care a straw for de Tokoly. She continued to brood about Nora. The girl was most vulnerable right now, when everything was unfamiliar and she had not had time to learn upper-class manners. If she could be brought to disgrace herself somehow tonight, preferably in front of the Prince of Wales . . .

Just as she was thinking about the prince, a great cheer went up outside the house, indicating that the royal party had arrived.

A moment later the prince and Princess Alexandra came in, dressed as King Arthur and Queen Guinevere, followed by their entourage got up as knights in armor and medieval ladies. The band stopped abruptly in the middle of a Strauss waltz and struck up the national anthem. All the guests in the hall bowed and curtsied, and the queue on the staircase dipped like a wave as the royal party came up. The prince was getting fatter every year, Augusta thought as she curtsied to him. She was not sure whether there was any gray in his beard yet, but he was rapidly going bald on top. She always felt sorry for the pretty princess, who had a great deal to put up with from her spendthrift, philandering husband.

At the top of the stairs, the duke and duchess welcomed their royal guests and ushered them into the ballroom. The guests on the staircase surged forward to follow them.

Inside the long ballroom, masses of flowers from the hothouse at the Tenbigh's country home were banked up all around the walls, and the light from a thousand candles glittered back from the tall mirrors between the windows. The footmen handing round champagne were dressed as Elizabethan courtiers in doublet and hose. The prince and princess were ushered to a dais at the end of the room. It had been arranged that some of the more spectacular costumes should pass in front of the royal party in procession, and as soon as the royals were seated the first group came in from the salon. A crush formed near the dais, and Augusta found herself shoulder-to-shoulder with Count de Tokoly.

"What a delightful girl your nephew's wife is, Mrs. Pilaster," he said.

Augusta gave him a frosty smile. "How generous you are to say so, Count."

He raised an eyebrow. "Do I detect a note of dissent? No doubt you would have preferred young Hugh to choose a bride from his own class."

"You know the answer to that without my telling you."

"But her charm is irresistible."

"Doubtless."

"I shall ask her to dance later on. Do you think she will accept?"

Augusta could not resist an acid retort. "I am sure of it. She is not fastidious." She turned away. No doubt it was too much to hope for that Nora would cause some kind of incident with the count—

She was suddenly inspired.

The count was the critical factor. If she put him together with Nora the combination could be explosive.

Her mind was racing. Tonight was a perfect opportunity. She had to do it now.

Feeling a little breathless with excitement, Augusta looked around, spotted Micky, and went over to him. "There's something I want you to do for me, now, quickly," she said.

Micky gave her a knowing look. "Anything," he murmured.

She ignored the innuendo. "Do you know Count de Tokoly?"

"Indeed. All we diplomats know one another."

"Tell him that Nora is no better than she ought to be."

Micky's mouth curled in a half-smile. "Just that?"

"You may elaborate if you wish."

"Should I hint that I know this from, let us say, personal experience?"

This conversation was transgressing the boundaries of propriety, but Micky's idea was a good one and she nodded. "Even better."

"You know what he will do?" Micky said.

"I trust he will make an indecent suggestion to her."

"If that's what you want. . . ."

"Yes."

Micky nodded. "I am your slave, in this as in all things."

Augusta waved the compliment aside impatiently: she was too tense to listen to facetious gallantry. She looked for Nora and saw her staring around in wonderment at the lavish decor and the extravagant costumes: the girl had never seen anything like this in her life. She was quite off guard. Without further reflection Augusta made her way through the crowd to Nora's side.

She spoke into her ear. "A word of advice."

"Much obliged for it, I'm sure," Nora said.

Hugh had presumably given Nora a malevolent account of Augusta's character, but to the girl's credit she showed no sign of hostility. She appeared not to have made up her mind about Augusta, and was neither warm nor cold to her.

Augusta said: "I noticed you talking to Count de Tokoly."

"A dirty old man," Nora said immediately.

Augusta winced at her vulgarity but pressed on. "Be careful of him, if you value your reputation."

"Be careful?" Nora said. "What do you mean, exactly?"

"Be polite, of course—but whatever happens, don't let him take any liberties. The least encouragement is enough for him and if he is not set straight immediately he can be very embarrassing."

Nora nodded understanding. "Don't worry, I know how to deal with his type."

Hugh was standing nearby talking to the duke of Kingsbridge. Now he noticed Augusta, looked suspicious, and came to his wife's side. However, Augusta had already said all she needed to say, and she turned away to watch the procession. She had done her work: the seeds were planted. Now she had to wait anxiously and hope for the best.

Passing in front of the prince were some of the Marlborough Set, including the duke and duchess of Kingsbridge and Solly and Maisie Greenbourne. They were dressed as eastern potentates, shahs and pashas and sultanas, and instead of bowing and curtsying they knelt and salaamed, which drew a laugh from the portly prince and a round of applause from the crowd. Augusta loathed Maisie Greenbourne, but she hardly noticed. Her mind was rapidly turning over possibilities. There were a hundred ways her plot could go wrong: de Tokoly could be captivated by a different pretty face, Nora might deal with him graciously, Hugh might stay too close for de Tokoly to do anything offensive. But with a little luck the drama she had plotted would be played out—and then there would be ructions.

The procession was coming to an end when, to Augusta's dismay, she saw the face of David Middleton pushing through the crowd toward her.

She had last seen him six years ago, when he had questioned her about his brother Peter's death at Windfield School, and she had told him that the two witnesses, Hugh Pilaster and Antonio Silva, had gone abroad. But now Hugh was back and here was Middleton. How had a mere lawyer got invited to such a grand occasion? She recalled vaguely that he was a distant relation of the duke of Tenbigh. She could hardly have foreseen this. It was a potential disaster. I can't think of everything! she said to herself frenziedly.

To her horror Middleton walked straight up to Hugh.

Augusta edged closer through the crush. She heard Middleton say: "Hello, Pilaster, I heard you were back in England. Do you remember me? I'm Peter Middleton's brother."

Augusta turned her back so that he would not notice her and strained to hear over the hum of conversation around her.

"I do remember—you were at the inquest," Hugh said. "Allow me to present my wife."

"How do you do, Mrs. Pilaster," Middleton said perfunctorily, and returned his attention to Hugh. "I was never happy with that inquest, you know."

Augusta went cold. Middleton had to be obsessed to bluntly bring up such an inappropriate subject in the middle of a costume ball. This was insupportable. Would poor Teddy never be free of that old suspicion?

She could not hear Hugh's reply but his tone was guardedly neutral.

Middleton's voice was louder and she picked up what he said next. "You must know that the whole school disbelieved Edward's story about trying to rescue my brother from drowning."

Augusta was taut with fear of what Hugh might say, but he continued to be circumspect, and said something about its having taken place a long time ago.

Suddenly Micky was at Augusta's side. His face was a mask of relaxed urbanity but she could see the tension in the set of his shoulders. "Is that the Middleton fellow?" he murmured in her ear.

She nodded.

"I thought I recognized him."

"Hush, listen," she said.

Middleton had become slightly aggressive. "I think you know the truth about what happened," he said in a challenging voice.

"Do you, indeed?" Hugh grew audible as his tone became less friendly.

"Forgive me for being so blunt, Pilaster. He was my brother. For years I've wondered what happened. Don't you think I've a right to know?"

There was a pause. Augusta knew that such an appeal to the rights and wrongs of the case was just the kind of thing to move the sanctimonious Hugh. She wanted to intervene, to shut them up or change the subject or break up the group, but that would be tantamount to a confession that she had something to hide; so she stood helpless and terrified, rooted to the spot, straining her ears to hear over the murmur of the crowd.

At last Hugh replied. "I didn't see Peter die, Middleton. I can't tell you what happened. I don't know for certain, and it would be wrong to speculate."

"You have your suspicions, then? You can guess how it happened?"

"There's no room for guesswork in a case such as this. It would be irresponsible. You want the truth, you say. I'm all for that. If I knew the truth I'd consider myself duty-bound to tell it. But I don't."

"I think you're protecting your cousin."

Hugh was offended. "Damn it, Middleton, that's too strong. You're entitled to be upset, but don't cast doubt on my honesty."

"Well, somebody's lying," Middleton said rudely, and with that he went away.

Augusta breathed again. Relief made her weak at the knees and she surreptitiously leaned on Micky for support. Hugh's precious principles had worked in her favor. He suspected that Edward had contributed to the death of Peter, but because it was only a suspicion he would not say it. And now Middleton had put Hugh's back up. It was the mark of a gentleman never to tell a lie, and for young men such as Hugh the suggestion that they might not be speaking the truth was a serious insult. Middleton and Hugh were not likely to talk further.

The crisis had blown up suddenly, like a summer storm, scaring her badly; but it had vanished just as fast, leaving her feeling battered but safe.

The procession ended. The band struck up a quadrille. The prince led the duchess onto the floor, and the duke took the princess, to make the first foursome. Other groups rapidly followed suit. The dancing was rather sedate, probably because so many people were wearing heavy costumes and cumbersome headdresses.

Augusta said to Micky: "Perhaps Mr. Middleton is no longer a danger to us."

"Not if Hugh continues to keep his mouth shut."

"And so long as your friend Silva stays in Cordova."

"His family has less and less influence as the years go by. I don't expect to see him in Europe again."

"Good." Augusta's mind reverted to her plot. "Did you speak to de Tokoly?"

"I did."

"Good."

"I just hope you know what you're doing."

She gave him a reproving look.

"How foolish of me," he said. "You always know what you're doing."

The second dance was a waltz, and Micky asked her for the pleasure. When she was a girl the waltz had been considered indecent, because the partners were so close together, the man's arm going all the way around the woman's waist in an embrace. But nowadays even royalty waltzed.

As soon as Micky took her in his arms she felt changed. It was like being seventeen again, and dancing with Strang. When Strang danced he was thinking about his partner, not his feet, and Micky had the same talent. He made Augusta feel young and beautiful and carefree. She was aware of the smoothness of his hands, the masculine smell of tobacco and macassar oil, and the heat of his body as it pressed against hers. She felt a pang of envy toward Rachel, who shared his bed. Momentarily she recalled the scene in old Seth's bedroom six years ago, but it seemed unreal, like a dream she had once had, and she could never quite believe it had actually happened.

Some women in her position would have had a clandestine love affair, but although Augusta sometimes daydreamed of secret meetings with Micky, in reality she could not face the skulking in back streets, the hole-in-corner meetings, the furtive embraces, the evasions and excuses. And besides, such affairs were often found out. She was more likely to leave Joseph and run away with Micky. He might be willing. At any rate she could make him willing if she put her mind to it. But whenever she toyed with that dream she thought of all the things she would have to give up: her three houses, her carriage, her dress allowance, her social position, the entrée to balls such as this. Strang could have given her all that, but Micky could offer only his seductive self, and it was not enough.

"Look over there," Micky said.

She followed the direction of his nod and saw Nora dancing with Count de Tokoly. She tensed. "Let's get closer to them," she said.

It was not easy, for the royal group was in that corner, and everyone was trying to be near them; but Micky skillfully steered her through the crush until they were close.

The waltz ground on, endlessly repeating the same banal tune. So far Nora and the count looked like any other dancing couple. He made occasional remarks in a low voice; she nodded and smiled. Perhaps he was holding her a little too closely, but not enough to cause remark. As the orchestra played on, Augusta wondered whether she had misjudged her two victims. The worry made her tense and she danced badly.

The waltz began to wind up to its climax. Augusta continued to watch Nora and the count. Suddenly there was a change. Nora's face took on a look of frozen consternation: the count must have said something she did not like. Augusta's hopes rose. But whatever he had said clearly was not sufficiently offensive for Nora to make a scene, and they danced on.

Augusta was ready to give up hope, and the waltz was in its last few bars, when the explosion came.

Augusta was the only person to see how it started. The count put his lips close to Nora's ear and spoke. She colored up, then stopped dancing abruptly and pushed him away; but nobody except Augusta noticed this because the dance was just ending. However, the count pushed his luck and spoke again, his face creasing with a characteristic lascivious grin. At that second the music stopped, and in the momentary silence that followed, Nora slapped him.

The smack sounded throughout the ballroom like a gunshot. It was not a polite ladylike slap, designed for drawing room use, but the kind of blow that would deter a drunken groper in a saloon-bar. The count staggered back—and bumped into the Prince of Wales.

There was a collective gasp from the people around. The prince stumbled and was caught by the duke of Tenbigh. In the horrified silence, Nora's cockney accent rang out loud and clear: "Don't you ever come near me again, you filthy old reprobate!"

For another second they formed a still tableau: the outraged woman, the humiliated count and the startled prince. Augusta was possessed by jubilation. It had worked —it had worked better than she could have imagined!

Then Hugh appeared at Nora's side and took her arm; the count drew himself up to his full height and stalked out; and an anxious group clustered protectively around the prince, hiding him from view. Conversation broke out around the room like a roll of thunder.

Augusta looked triumphantly at Micky.

"Brilliant," he murmured with real admiration. "You're brilliant, Augusta." He squeezed her arm and led her off the dance floor.

Her husband was waiting for her. "That wretched girl!" he expostulated. "To cause a scene like that under the nose of the prince —she's brought disgrace on the whole family, and doubtless lost us a major contract too!"

It was just the reaction Augusta had

hoped for. "Now perhaps you'll believe that Hugh can't be made a partner," she said triumphantly.

Joseph gave her an appraising stare. For one dreadful moment she feared she had overplayed her hand, and he had guessed that she had orchestrated the whole incident. But if the thought crossed his mind he must have dismissed it, for he said: "You're right, my dear. You've been right all along."

Hugh was steering Nora to the door. "We're leaving, of course," he said neutrally as they passed.

"We'll all have to leave now," Augusta said. However, she did not want them to go immediately. If no more was said tonight, there was a danger that tomorrow when people cooled off they might say the incident was not as bad as it had seemed. To guard against that, Augusta wanted more of a row now: hot tempers, angry words, accusations that could not easily be forgotten. She put a detaining hand on Nora's arm. "I tried to warn you about Count de Tokoly," she said accusingly.

Hugh said: "When such a man insults a lady on the dance floor, there isn't much she can do other than cause a scene."

"Don't be ridiculous," Augusta snapped.

"Any well-bred young girl would have known exactly what to do. She should have said she felt unwell and sent for her carriage."

Hugh knew this was true and he did not try to deny it. Once again Augusta worried that everyone might calm down and the incident would fizzle out. But Joseph was still angry, and he said to Hugh: "Heaven knows how much damage you've done to the family and the bank tonight."

Hugh colored. "What precisely do you mean?" he said stiffly.

By challenging Joseph to back up the accusation Hugh was making things worse for himself, Augusta thought with satisfaction. He was too young to know that he should shut up and go home at this point.

Joseph grew more angry. "We've certainly lost the Hungarian account, and we'll never again be invited to a royal event."

"I know that perfectly well," Hugh said. "I meant to ask why you said the damage has been done by *me*."

"Because you brought into the family a woman who doesn't know how to behave!"

Better and better, Augusta thought with malicious glee.

Hugh was bright red now but he spoke

with controlled fury. "Let me get this straight. A Pilaster wife must be willing to suffer insult and humiliation at dances rather than do anything to jeopardize a business deal, is that your philosophy?"

Joseph was mightily offended. "You insolent young pup," he raged. "What I'm saying is that by marrying beneath yourself you have disqualified yourself from ever becoming a partner in the bank!"

He said it! Augusta thought jubilantly. He said it!

Hugh was jolted into silence. Unlike Augusta he had not thought ahead, had not worked out the implications of the row. Now the significance of what had happened was sinking in, and she watched his expression change from rage, through anxiety and comprehension, to despair.

She fought to conceal a victorious smile. She had what she wanted: she had won. Later Joseph might regret his pronouncement but it was most unlikely he would withdraw it—he was too proud.

"So that's it," Hugh said at last, and he was looking at Augusta rather than Joseph. To her surprise she saw that he was close to tears. "Very well, Augusta. You win. I don't know how it was done but I've no doubt you provoked this incident somehow." He turned to Joseph. "But you ought to reflect on it, Uncle Joseph. You should think about who genuinely cares about the bank . . ." He looked again at Augusta and finished: "And who are its real enemies."

3

THE NEWS OF HUGH'S FALL spread around the City in hours. By the following afternoon, people who had clamored to see him with money-making schemes for railways, steel mills, shipyards and suburban housing were canceling their appointments. In the bank, clerks who had venerated him now regarded him as just another manager. He found he could go into a coffeehouse in the streets around the Bank of England without immediately attracting a cluster of people eager to know his views on the Grand Trunk Railroad, the price of Louisiana bonds and the American national debt.

Within the Partners' Room there was a row. Uncle Samuel had been indignant when Joseph announced that Hugh could not be made a partner. However, Young William had sided with his brother Joseph, and Major Hartshorn did the same, so Samuel was outvoted.

It was Jonas Mulberry, the bald, lugubrious Principal Clerk, who told Hugh what had happened between the partners. "I must say I regret the decision, Mr. Hugh," he said with evident sincerity. "When you worked under me as a youngster you never tried to blame your mistakes on me—unlike certain other family members I have dealt with in the past."

"I wouldn't have dared, Mr. Mulberry," said Hugh with a smile.

Nora cried for a week. Hugh refused to blame her for what had happened. No one had forced him to marry her: he had to take responsibility for his own decisions. If his family had any decency they would stand by him in such a crisis, but he had never been able to count on them for that kind of support.

When Nora got over her upset she became rather unsympathetic, revealing a hard-hearted side that surprised Hugh. She could not understand the significance of the partnership to him. He realized, with a sense of disappointment, that she was not very good at imagining other people's feelings. He thought it must be because she had grown up poor and motherless, and had been forced to put her own interests first all her life. Although he was a little shaken by her attitude, he forgot about it every night when they climbed into the big soft bed together in their nightwear and made love.

Hugh's resentment grew inside him like an ulcer, but he now had a wife, a big new house and six servants to support, so he had to stay on at the bank. He had been given his own room, on the floor above the Partners' Room, and he put a big map of North America on the wall. Every Monday morning he wrote a summary of the previous week's North American business and cabled it to Sidney Madler in New York. On the second Monday after the duchess of Tenbigh's ball, in the telegraph office on the ground floor, he met a stranger, a dark-haired man of about twenty-one. Hugh smiled and said: "Hullo, who are you?"

"Simon Oliver," the man said in an accent that sounded vaguely Spanish.

"You must be new here," Hugh said, and stuck out his hand. "I'm Hugh Pilaster."

"How do you do," Oliver said. He seemed rather sulky.

"I work on North American loans," Hugh said. "What about you?"

"I'm clerk to Mr. Edward."

Hugh made a connection. "Are you from South America?"

"Yes, Cordova."

That made sense. As Edward's specialty was South America in general and Cordova in particular, it could be useful to have a native of that country to work with him, especially as Edward did not speak Spanish. "I was at school with the Cordovan Minister, Micky Miranda," Hugh said. "You must know him."

"He is my cousin."

"Ah." There was no family resemblance, but Oliver was immaculately groomed, his well-tailored clothes pressed and brushed, his hair oiled and combed, his shoes shiny: no doubt he modeled himself on his successful older cousin. "Well, I hope you enjoy working with us."

"Thank you."

Hugh was thoughtful as he returned to his own office on the next floor up. Edward needed all the help he could get, but Hugh was a little bothered at having a cousin of Micky's in such a potentially influential position at the bank.

His unease was vindicated a few days later.

Once again it was Jonas Mulberry who told him what was going on in the Partners' Room. Mulberry came into Hugh's room with a schedule of payments the bank had to make in London on behalf of the U.S. government, but his real reason was to talk. His spaniel face was longer than ever as he said: "I don't like it, Mr. Hugh. South American bonds have never been good."

"We're not launching a South American bond, are we?"

Mulberry nodded. "Mr. Edward proposed it and the partners have agreed."

"What's it for?"

"A new railroad from the capital city, Palma, to Santamaria Province."

"Where the provincial governor is Papa Miranda. . . ."

"The father of Mr. Edward's friend Señor Miranda."

"And the uncle of Edward's clerk Simon Oliver."

Mulberry shook his head disapprovingly. "I was a clerk here when the Venezuelan government defaulted on its bonds fifteen years ago. My father, God rest his soul, could remember the Argentine default of 1828. And look at Mexican bonds—they pay dividends now and again. Whoever heard of bonds that paid out now and again?"

Hugh nodded. "Anyway, investors who like railroads can get five and six percent on their money in the United States—why go to Cordova?"

"Exactly."

Hugh scratched his head. "Well, I'll try to find out what they're thinking about."

Mulberry flourished a bundle of papers. "Mr. Samuel asked for a summary of liabilities on Far East acceptances. You could take the figures to him."

Hugh grinned. "You think of everything." He took the papers and went down to the Partners' Room.

Only Samuel and Joseph were there. Joseph was dictating letters to a shorthand writer and Samuel was poring over a map of China. Hugh put the report on Samuel's table and said: "Mulberry asked me to give you this."

"Thank you." Samuel looked up and smiled. "Something else on your mind?"

"Yes. I'm wondering why we're backing the Santamaria railroad."

Hugh heard Joseph pause in his dictation, then resume.

Samuel said: "It's not the most attractive

investment we've ever launched, I grant you, but with the backing of the Pilaster name it should go off all right."

"You could say that of just about any issue that is proposed to us," Hugh objected. "The reason we have such a high reputation is that we never do offer the investors a bond that is only 'all right.'"

"Your uncle Joseph feels that South America may be ready for a revival."

Hearing his name, Joseph joined in. "This is a toe dipped into the water to feel the temperature."

"It's risky, then."

"If my great-grandfather had never taken a risk he would not have put all his money into one slave ship and there would be no such thing as Pilasters Bank today."

Hugh said: "But since then, Pilasters has always left it to smaller, more speculative houses to dip their toes into unknown waters."

Uncle Joseph did not like to be argued with and he replied in an irritated tone: "One exception will not harm us."

"But the willingness to make exceptions may harm us deeply."

"That's not for you to judge."

Hugh frowned. His instinct had been

right: the investment did not make commercial sense, and Joseph could not justify it. So why had they done it? As soon as he put the question to himself that way he saw the answer. "You've done this because it's Edward, haven't you? You want to encourage him, and this is the first deal he has come up with since you made him a partner, so you're letting him do it, even though it's a poor prospect."

"It's not your place to question my motives!"

"It's not your place to risk other people's money as a favor to your son. Small investors in Brighton and Harrogate will put up the money for this railroad, and they will lose everything if it fails."

"You're not a partner, so your opinion on these matters is not sought."

Hugh hated people to shift their ground during a discussion and he responded waspishly. "I'm a Pilaster, though, and when you damage the good name of the bank you injure me."

Samuel cut in: "I think you've probably said enough, Hugh—"

Hugh knew he should shut up but he could not restrain himself. "I'm afraid I haven't said enough." He heard himself shouting and tried to lower his voice. "You're dissipating the bank's reputation by doing this. Our good name is our greatest asset. To use it up in this way is like spending your capital."

Uncle Joseph was now beyond civility. "Don't you dare stand here in my bank and lecture me on the principles of investment, you insolent young whippersnapper. Get out of this room."

Hugh stared at his uncle for a long moment. He was furious and depressed. Foolish, weak Edward was a partner, and leading the bank into bad business deals with the help of his injudicious father, and there was nothing anyone could do about it. Boiling with frustration, Hugh turned and left the room, slamming the door.

Ten minutes later he went to ask Solly Greenbourne for a job.

He was not certain Greenbournes would take him on. He was an asset that any bank would covet, because of his contacts in the United States and Canada, but bankers felt it was not quite gentlemanly to pirate top managers from their rivals. In addition, the Greenbournes might fear that Hugh would tell secrets to his family at the dinner table, and the fact that he was not Jewish could only increase that fear.

However, Pilasters had become a dead-end street for him. He had to get out.

It had rained earlier but by midmorning the sun was out, and steam rose from the horse manure that carpeted the streets of London. The architecture of the City was a mixture of grand classical buildings and tumbledown old houses: the Pilaster building was the grand type, Greenbournes the other. You would not have guessed that Greenbournes Bank was bigger and more important than Pilasters from the appearance of the head office. The business had started, three generations ago, lending to fur importers out of two rooms of an old house in Thames Street. Whenever more space was needed they simply took over another house in the row, and now the bank occupied four adjacent buildings and three others nearby. But more business was done in these ramshackle houses than in the ostentatious splendor of the Pilaster building.

Inside there was none of the devotional hush of Pilasters' banking hall. Hugh had to fight his way through a crowd of people in the lobby, like petitioners waiting to see a medieval king, every one of them convinced that if only he could get a word with Ben Greenbourne, present his case or pitch his proposal, he could make a fortune. The zig-zag corridors and narrow staircases of the interior were obstructed by tin boxes of old files, cartons of stationery and demijohns of ink, and every spare cubbyhole had been made into an office for a clerk. Hugh found Solly in a large room with an uneven floor and a wonky window looking out over the river. Solly's bulk was half hidden behind a desk piled with papers. "I live in a palace and work in a hovel," Solly said ruefully. "I keep trying to persuade Father to commission a purpose-built office like yours, but he says there's no profit in property."

Hugh sat on a lumpy sofa and accepted a large glass of expensive sherry. He was uncomfortable, because in the back of his mind he was thinking about Maisie. He had seduced her before she became Solly's wife and he would have done it again afterwards if she had let him. But all that was over now, he told himself. Maisie had locked the door at Kingsbridge Manor, and he had married Nora. He did not intend to be an unfaithful husband.

Still he felt awkward.

"I came to see you here because I want to talk business," he said.

Solly made an openhanded gesture. "You have the floor."

"My area of expertise is North America, as you know."

"Don't I just! You've got it so well wrapped up that we can't get a look in."

"Exactly. And you're missing out on a good deal of profitable business as a result."

"No need to rub it in. Father asks me constantly why I'm not more like you."

"What you need is someone with North American experience to come in, set up a New York office for you, and go after the business."

"That and a fairy godmother."

"I'm serious, Greenbourne. I'm your man."

"You!"

"I want to work for you."

Solly was staggered. He peered over his glasses as if checking that it really was Hugh who had said that. After a moment he said: "It's because of that incident at the duchess of Tenbigh's ball, I suppose."

"They've said they won't make me a partner because of my wife." Solly would sympathize, Hugh thought, because he too had married a lower-class girl.

"I'm sorry to hear that," Solly said.

Hugh said: "But I'm not asking for kindness. I know what I'm worth and you'll have to pay my price if you want me. I'm earning a thousand a year now and I expect it to go up every year as long as I continue to make more and more money for the bank."

"That's no problem." Solly thought for a moment. "This could be a great coup for me, you know. I'm grateful for the offer. You're a good friend and a formidable businessman." Hugh, thinking of Maisie again, felt a guilty pang at the words "good friend." Solly continued: "There's nothing I'd like better than to have you working alongside me."

"I detect an unspoken 'but,' " Hugh said with trepidation in his heart.

Solly shook his owlish head. "No buts, as far as I'm concerned. Of course I can't hire you the way I'd hire a ledger clerk. I'll have to clear it with my father. But you know how it is in the world of banking: profit is an argument that outweighs all others. I don't see Father turning down the prospect of a chunk of the North American market."

Hugh did not want to seem too eager, but

he could not help saying: "When will you speak to him?"

"Why not now?" Solly said. He stood up. "I shan't be a minute. Have another glass of sherry." He went out.

Hugh sipped his sherry but he found it hard to swallow, he was so tense. He had never applied for a job before. It was unnerving that his future depended on the whim of old Ben Greenbourne. For the first time he understood the feelings of the scrubbed young men in starched collars whom he had occasionally interviewed for jobs as clerks. Restlessly he got up and went to the window. On the far side of the river a barge was unloading bales of tobacco into a warehouse: if it was Virginia tobacco, he had probably financed the transaction.

He had a doomy feeling, a bit like the sensation he had had when he boarded ship for Boston six years ago: a sense that nothing would ever be the same again.

Solly came back in with his father. Ben Greenbourne had the upright carriage and bullet-shaped head of a Prussian general. Hugh stood up to shake hands and looked anxiously at his face. It was solemn. Did that mean no?

Ben said: "Solly tells me your family has

decided not to offer you a partnership." His speech was coldly precise, the accent clipped. He was so different from his son, Hugh thought.

"To be exact, they offered it then withdrew the offer," Hugh said.

Ben nodded. He was a man who appreciated exactness. "It's not for me to criticize their judgment. However, if your North American expertise is for sale, as it were, then I'm certainly a buyer."

Hugh's heart leaped. That sounded like a job offer. "Thank you!" he said.

"But I shouldn't wish to take you on under false pretenses, so there's something I must make clear. It is not at all likely that you will ever become a partner here."

Hugh had not actually thought that far ahead, but all the same it was a blow. "I see," he said.

"I say this now so that you will never think it a reflection on your work. Many Christians are valued colleagues and dear friends, but the partners have always been Jews, and it will ever be so."

"I appreciate your frankness," Hugh said. He was thinking: By God, you're a coldhearted old man.

"Do you still want the job?"

"Yes, I do."

Ben Greenbourne shook his hand again. "Then I look forward to working with you," he said, and he left the room.

Solly smiled broadly. "Welcome to the firm!"

Hugh sat down. "Thank you," he said. His relief and pleasure were somewhat blighted by the thought that he would never be a partner, but he made an effort to put a good face on it. He would make a good salary, and live comfortably; it was just that he would never be a millionaire—to make that sort of money you had to be a partner.

"When can you start?" Solly said eagerly.

Hugh had not thought of that. "I probably should give ninety days notice."

"Make it less if you can."

"Of course. Solly, this is great. I can't tell you how pleased I am."

"Me too."

Hugh could not think what to say next, so he stood up to go, but Solly said: "Can I make another suggestion?"

"By all means." He sat down again.

"It's about Nora. I hope you won't take offense."

Hugh hesitated. They were old friends, but he really did not want to talk to Solly about his wife. His own feelings were too ambivalent. He was embarrassed about the scene she had made, yet he also felt she had been justified. He felt defensive about her accent, her manners and her low-class background, but he was also proud of her for being so pretty and charming.

However, he could hardly be touchy with the man who had just rescued his career, so he said: "Go ahead."

"As you know, I too married a girl who was . . . not used to high society."

Hugh nodded. He knew it perfectly well, but he did not know how Maisie and Solly had coped with the situation, for he had been abroad when they married. They must have handled it well, for Maisie had become one of London's leading society hostesses and if anyone remembered her humble origins they never spoke of it. This was unusual, but not unique: Hugh had heard of two or three celebrated working-class beauties who had been accepted by high society in the past.

Solly went on: "Maisie knows what Nora's going through. She could help her a lot: tell her what to do and say, what mistakes to avoid, where to get gowns and hats, how to manage the butler and the housekeeper, all that. Maisie's always been fond of you, Hugh, so I feel sure she'd be glad to help. And there's no reason Nora shouldn't pull off the trick Maisie did and end up as a pillar of society."

Hugh found himself moved almost to tears. This gesture of support from an old friend touched his heart. "I'll suggest it," he said, speaking rather curtly to hide his feelings. He stood up to go.

"I hope I haven't overstepped the mark," Solly said anxiously as they shook hands.

Hugh went to the door. "On the contrary. Damn it, Greenbourne, you're a better friend than I deserve."

When Hugh got back to Pilasters Bank there was a note waiting for him. It read:

10.30 a.m.
My dear Pilaster:
I must see you right away. You will find me in Plage's Coffee House around the corner. I will wait for you. Your old friend—Antonio Silva.

So Tonio was back! His career had been ruined when he lost more than he could pay in a card game with Edward and Micky. He had left the country in disgrace at about the same time as Hugh. What had happened to him since? Full of curiosity, Hugh went straight to the coffeehouse.

He found an older, shabbier, more subdued Tonio, sitting in a corner reading *The Times*. He still had a shock of carrot-colored hair, but otherwise there was nothing left of the mischievous schoolboy or the profligate young man. Although he was only Hugh's age, twenty-six, there were already tiny lines of worry around his eyes.

"I made a big success of Boston," Hugh said in answer to Tonio's first question. "I came back in January. But now I'm having trouble with my damned family all over again. How about you?"

"There have been a lot of changes in my country. My family is not as influential as it once was. We still control Milpita, the provincial city we come from, but in the capital others have come between us and President Garcia."

"Who?"

"The Miranda faction."

"Micky's family?"

"Absolutely. They took over the nitrate mines in the north of the country and that has made them rich. They also monopolize trade with Europe, because of their connection with your family's bank."

Hugh was surprised. "I knew Edward was doing a lot of business with Cordova, but I didn't realize it was all going through Micky. Still, I don't suppose it matters."

"But it does," said Tonio. He took a sheaf of papers from inside his coat. "Take a minute to read this. It's an article I've written for *The Times*."

Hugh took the manuscript and began to read. It was a description of conditions at a nitrate mine owned by the Mirandas. Because the trade was financed by Pilasters Bank, Tonio held the bank responsible for the ill-treatment of the miners. At first Hugh was unmoved: long hours, poor wages and child labor were features of mines all over the world. But as he read on he saw this was worse. At the Miranda mines, the overseers were armed with whips and guns, and they used them freely to enforce discipline. Laborers—including women and children—were flogged for being too slow, and if they tried to leave before they had worked out their contracts they could be shot. Tonio had eyewitness accounts of such "executions."

Hugh was horrified. "But this is murder!" he said.

"Exactly."

"Doesn't your president know about it?"

"He knows. But the Mirandas are his favorites now."

"And your own family . . ."

"Once upon a time we could have put a stop to it. Now it takes all our effort to retain control of our own province."

Hugh was mortified to think his own family and their bank were financing such a brutal industry, but for a moment he tried to put aside his feelings and think coolly about consequences. The article Tonio had written was just the kind of material *The Times* liked to publish. There would be speeches in Parliament and letters in the weekly journals. The social conscience of businessmen, many of whom were Methodists, would make them hesitate before getting involved with Pilasters. It would all be extremely bad for the bank.

Do I care? thought Hugh. The bank had treated him badly and he was about to leave it. But despite that, he could not ignore this problem. He was still an employee, he would draw his salary at the end of the month, and he owed Pilasters his loyalty at least until then. He had to do something.

What did Tonio want? The fact that he was showing Hugh the article before publishing it suggested that he wanted to make a deal. "What's your objective?" Hugh asked him. "Do you want us to stop financing the nitrate trade?"

Tonio shook his head. "If Pilasters pulled out, someone else would take over—another bank with a thicker hide. No, we must be more subtle."

"You've got something specific in mind."

"The Mirandas are planning a railway."

"Ah, yes. The Santamaria railroad."

"That railway will make Papa Miranda the wealthiest and most powerful man in the country, excepting only the president. And Papa Miranda is a brute. I want the railway stopped."

"And that's why you're going to publish this article."

"Several articles. And I'll hold meetings, make speeches, lobby members of Parliament, and try to get an appointment with the foreign secretary: anything to undermine the financing of this railway."

It might work, too, Hugh thought. Investors would shy away from anything controversial. It struck him that Tonio had changed a lot, from the young tearaway who couldn't stop gambling into the sober adult who campaigned against ill-treatment of miners. "So why have you come to me?"

"We could shortcut the process. If the bank decides not to underwrite the railway bonds, I won't publish the article. That way, you avoid a great deal of unpleasant publicity and I get what I want too." Tonio gave an embarrassed smile. "I hope you don't think of this as blackmail. It is a bit crude, I know, but nowhere near as crude as flogging children in a nitrate mine."

Hugh shook his head. "Not crude at all. I admire your crusading spirit. The consequences for the bank don't affect me directly—I'm about to resign."

"Really!" Tonio was astonished. "Why?"

"It's a long story. I'll tell you another time. However, the upshot is that all I can do is tell the partners that you've approached me with this proposition. They can decide how they feel about it and what they want to do. I'm quite sure they won't ask my opinion." He was still holding Tonio's manuscript. "May I keep this?"

"Yes. I have a copy."

The sheets of paper bore the letterhead

of the Hotel Russe, Berwick Street, Soho. Hugh had never heard of it: it was not one of London's fancy establishments. "I'll let you know what the partners say."

"Thank you." Tonio changed the subject. "I'm sorry our conversation has been all business. Let's get together and talk about the old days."

"You must meet my wife."

"I'd love to."

"I'll get in touch." Hugh left the coffee-house and walked back to the bank. When he looked at the big clock in the banking hall he was surprised it was not yet one o'clock: so much had happened this morning. He went straight to the Partners' Room, where he found Samuel, Joseph and Edward. He handed Tonio's article to Samuel, who read it and passed it on to Edward.

Edward became apoplectic with rage and was unable to finish it. He went red in the face, pointed his finger at Hugh and said: "You've cooked this up with your old school friend! You're trying to undermine our entire South American business! You're just jealous of me because you weren't made a partner!"

Hugh understood why he was so hysterical. The South American trade was Edward's only significant contribution to business. If that went he was useless. Hugh sighed. "You were Bonehead Ned at school, and you still are," he said. "The question is whether the bank wants to be responsible for increasing the power and influence of Papa Miranda, a man who apparently thinks nothing of flogging women and murdering children."

"I don't believe that!" Edward said. "The Silva family are enemies of the Mirandas. This is just malicious propaganda."

"I'm sure that's what your friend Micky will say. But is it true?"

Uncle Joseph looked suspiciously at Hugh. "You came in here just a few hours ago and tried to talk me out of this issue. I have to wonder whether this whole thing isn't some scheme to undermine Edward's first major piece of business as a partner."

Hugh stood up. "If you're going to cast doubt on my good faith I'll leave right away."

Uncle Samuel stepped in. "Sit down, Hugh," he said. "We don't have to find out whether this tale is true or not. We're bankers, not judges. The fact that the Santamaria railroad is going to be controversial makes the bond issue riskier, and that means we have to reconsider."

Uncle Joseph said aggressively: "I'm not willing to be bullied. Let this South American popinjay publish his article and go to the devil."

"That's one way to handle it," Samuel mused, treating Joseph's belligerence more seriously than it deserved. "We can wait and see what effect the article has on the price of existing South American stocks: there aren't many, but it's enough to serve as a gauge. If they crash, we'll cancel the Santamaria railroad. If not, we go ahead."

Joseph, somewhat mollified, said: "I don't mind submitting to the decision of the market."

"There is one other option we might consider," Samuel went on. "We could get another bank to come in with us on the issue of bonds, and float it jointly. That way, any hostile publicity would be enfeebled by having a divided target."

That made a lot of sense, Hugh thought. It was not what he would have done: he would prefer to cancel the bond issue. But the strategy worked out by Samuel would minimize the risk, and that was what banking was all about. Samuel was a much better banker than Joseph.

"All right," Joseph said with his usual impulsiveness. "Edward, see if you can find us a partner."

"Who should I approach?" Edward said anxiously. Hugh realized he had no idea how to go about something like this.

Samuel answered him. "It's a big issue. On reflection, not many banks would want such a big exposure to South America. You should go to Greenbournes: they might be the only people big enough to take the risk. You know Solly Greenbourne, don't you?"

"Yes. I'll see him."

Hugh wondered whether he should advise Solly to turn Edward down, and immediately thought better of it: he was being hired as an expert on North America, and it would seem presumptuous if he started out by passing judgment on a completely different area. He decided to have one more try at persuading Uncle Joseph to cancel the issue completely. "Why don't we just wash our hands of the Santamaria railroad?" he said. "It's low-grade business. The risk has always been high, and now we're threatened with bad publicity on top. Do we need this?"

Edward said petulantly: "The partners have made their decision and it's not for you to question them."

Hugh gave up. "You're quite right," he said. "I'm not a partner, and soon I won't be an employee either."

Uncle Joseph frowned at him. "What does that mean?"

"I'm resigning from the bank."

Joseph was jolted. "You can't do that!"

"I certainly can. I'm a mere employee, and you've treated me as such. So, like an employee, I'm leaving you for a better job elsewhere."

"Where?"

"As a matter of fact I shall be working at Greenbournes."

Uncle Joseph's eyes looked as if they would pop out. "But you're the one who knows all the North Americans!"

"I imagine that's why Ben Greenbourne was so keen to hire me," Hugh said. He could not help being pleased that Uncle Joseph was so irate.

"But you'll take business away from us!"

"You should have thought of that when you decided to go back on your offer of a partnership."

"How much are they paying you?"

Hugh stood up to leave. "That's not for you to ask," he said firmly.

Edward shrieked: "How dare you speak to my father that way!"

Joseph's indignation burst like a bubble, and to Hugh's surprise he suddenly calmed down. "Oh, shut up, Edward," he said mildly. "A certain amount of low cunning is part of what goes to make a good banker. There are times when I wish you were more like Hugh. He may be the black sheep of the family but at least he's got some spunk." He turned back to Hugh. "Go on, clear off," he said without malice. "I hope you'll come a cropper, but I'm not betting on it."

"No doubt that's the nearest to good wishes that I'm likely to get from your branch of the family," Hugh said. "Good day to you."

4

"AND HOW IS dear Rachel?" Augusta asked Micky as she poured tea.

"She's fine," Micky said. "She may come along later."

In fact he did not quite understand his wife. She had been a virgin when they married, but she acted like a whore. She submitted to him at any time, anywhere, and always with enthusiasm. One of the first things he had tried was tying her to the bedhead, to re-create the vision he had enjoyed when he first became attracted to her; and somewhat to his disappointment she had complied willingly. So far nothing he was able to do had succeeded in making her resist him. He had even taken her in the drawing room, where there was a constant risk that the servants would see; and she had seemed to enjoy it more than ever.

On the other hand, she was the opposite of submissive in every other area of life. She argued with him about the house, the servants, money, politics and religion. When he got fed up with contradicting her he tried ignoring her, then insulting her, but nothing made any difference. She suffered from the delusion that she had as much right to her point of view as a man.

"I hope she's a help to you in your work," Augusta said.

Micky nodded. "She's a good hostess at ministry functions," he said. "Attentive and gracious."

"I thought she did very well at the party you gave for Ambassador Portillo," Augusta said. Portillo was the Portuguese envoy and

Augusta and Joseph had attended the dinner.

"She has a stupid plan to open a maternity hospital for women without husbands," Micky said, allowing his irritation to show.

Augusta shook her head in disapproval. "It's impossible for a woman in her position in society. Besides, there are already one or two such hospitals."

"She says they're all religious institutions that tell women how wicked they are. Her place will help without preaching."

"Worse and worse," Augusta said. "Think what the press would say about that!"

"Exactly. I've been very firm with her about it."

"She's a lucky girl," Augusta said, and favored Micky with an intimate smile.

He realized that she was flirting and he was failing to respond. The truth was that he was too involved with Rachel. He certainly did not love her, but he was deeply engrossed by his relationship with her and she absorbed all his sexual energy. To compensate for his distraction he held Augusta's hand for a moment as she passed him a cup of tea. "You're flattering me," he said softly.

"No doubt I am. But something is worrying you, I can tell."

"Dear Mrs. Pilaster, as perceptive as always. Why do I ever imagine I can hide anything from you?" He released her hand and took his tea. "Yes, I'm a little tense about the Santamaria railroad."

"I thought the partners had agreed to that."

"They have, but these things take so long to organize."

"The financial world moves slowly."

"I understand that, but my family doesn't. Papa sends me cables weekly. I curse the day the telegraph reached Santamaria."

Edward came in bursting with news. "Antonio Silva's back!" he said before he had closed the door behind him.

Augusta paled. "How do you know?"

"Hugh saw him."

"That's a blow," she said, and Micky was surprised to see that her hand was shaking as she put down her cup and saucer.

"And David Middleton is still asking questions," said Micky, recalling Middleton's conversation with Hugh at the duchess of Tenbigh's ball. Micky was pretending to be worried, but in truth he was not altogether displeased. He liked to have Edward and Augusta reminded, from time to time, of the guilty secret they all shared.

"It's not just that," Edward said. "Antonio's trying to sabotage the Santamaria railroad bond issue."

Micky frowned. Tonio's family had opposed the railway scheme back home in Cordova, but they had been overruled by President Garcia. What could Tonio possibly do here in London?

The same question occurred to Augusta. "How can he do anything?"

Edward handed his mother a sheaf of papers. "Read that."

Micky said: "What is it?"

"An article Tonio plans to publish in *The Times* about your family's nitrate mines."

Augusta skimmed the pages rapidly. "He claims that life as a nitrate miner is unpleasant and dangerous," she said derisively. "Who ever supposed it was a garden party?"

Edward said: "He also reports that women are flogged and children shot for disobedience."

She said: "But what has this to do with your bond issue?"

"The railway is to carry nitrate to the capital. Investors don't like anything controversial. Many of them will already be wary of a South American bond. Something like this could scare them off completely."

Micky was shaken. This sounded like very bad news. He asked Edward: "What does your father say about all this?"

"We're trying to get another bank to come in with us on the deal, but basically we're going to let Tonio publish and see what happens. If the publicity causes a crash in South American stocks we'll have to abandon the Santamaria railroad."

Damn Tonio to hell. He was clever—and Papa was a fool, to run his mines like slave camps and then expect to raise money in the civilized world.

But what was to be done? Micky racked his brains. Tonio had to be silenced, but he would not be persuaded or bribed. A chill descended over Micky's heart as he realized he would have to use cruder, riskier methods.

He pretended to be calm. "May I see the article, please?"

Augusta handed it to him.

The first thing he noticed was the hotel address at the top of the paper. Putting on an air of insouciance that he did not feel, he said: "Why, this is no problem at all."

Edward protested: "But you haven't read it yet!"

"I don't need to. I've seen the address."

"So what?"

"Now that we know where to find him, we can deal with him," Micky said. "Leave it to me."

CHAPTER THREE

1

SOLLY LOVED TO WATCH Maisie getting dressed.

Each evening she would put on her dressing jacket and summon her maids to pin her hair up and thread it with flowers or feathers or beads; then she would dismiss the servants and wait for her husband.

Tonight they were going out, which they did most evenings. The only time they stayed in, during the London season, was when they were giving a party. Between Easter and the end of July they never dined alone.

He came in at half-past six, in his dress trousers and white waistcoat, carrying a large glass of champagne. Maisie's hair was decorated with yellow silk flowers tonight. She slipped out of her bedroom gown and stood naked in front of the mirror. She did a pirouette for Solly's benefit then began to dress.

First she put on a linen chemise with a neckline embroidered with flowers. It had silk tapes at the shoulders to tie it to her dress so that it would not be seen. Next she drew on fine white woolen stockings and fastened them just above her knees with elastic garters. She stepped into a pair of knee-length loose cotton lawn drawers with pretty braiding at the hems and a drawstring waist, then put on yellow silk evening slippers.

Solly picked up her corset from its frame and helped her into it, then drew the laces tight at the back. Most women were helped to dress by one or two maids, for it was impossible for a woman to manage the elaborate corset and gown alone. However, Solly had learned to perform these services himself rather than go without the pleasure of watching.

Crinolines and bustles were no longer in fashion, but Maisie put on a cotton petticoat with a flounced train and a ruffled hem to support the train of her gown. The petticoat was fastened at the back with a bow, and Solly tied it.

At last she was ready for the gown. It was of yellow-and-white striped silk taffeta. The bodice was loosely draped, which flattered her large bosom, and caught at the shoulder with a bow. The rest of the garment was similarly swagged and caught at the waist, knee and hem. It took a maid all day to iron it.

She sat on the floor and Solly lifted the dress over her so that she was sitting inside it like a tent. Then she stood up carefully, putting her hands through the armholes and her head through the neck. Together she and Solly arranged the folds of the drapery until they looked right.

She opened her jewelry box and took out a diamond-and-emerald necklace and matching earrings that Solly had given her on their first wedding anniversary. As she was putting them on he said: "We're going to be seeing a lot more of our old friend Hugh Pilaster from now on."

Maisie muffled a sigh. Solly's trusting nature could be tiresome. The normal suspicious-minded husband would have divined the attraction between Maisie and Hugh, and would be bad-tempered every time the other man's name was mentioned, but Solly was too innocent. He had no idea he was putting temptation in her way. "Why, what's happened?" she said neutrally.

"He's coming to work at the bank."

"Why is he leaving Pilasters? I thought he was doing so well."

"They refused him a partnership."

"Oh, no!" She knew Hugh better than anyone did, and she understood how badly he had suffered because of his father's bankruptcy and suicide. She could guess how broken he was by the refusal of a partnership. "The Pilasters are a mean-spirited family," she said with feeling.

"It's because of his wife."

Maisie nodded. "I'm not surprised." She had witnessed the incident at the duchess of Tenbigh's ball. Knowing the Pilasters as she did, she could not help wondering if Augusta had somehow stage-managed the whole incident in order to discredit Hugh.

"You have to feel sorry for Nora."

"Mmm." Maisie had met Nora, some weeks before the wedding, and had taken an instant dislike to her. Indeed, she had wounded Hugh by telling him Nora was a heartless gold digger and he should not marry her.

"Anyway, I suggested to Hugh that you might help her."

"What?" Maisie said sharply. She looked away from her mirror. "Help her?"

"Rehabilitate her. You know what it's like to be looked down on because of your background. You overcame all that prejudice."

"And now I'm supposed to work the same transformation on every other guttersnipe who marries into society?" Maisie snapped.

"I've obviously done something wrong," Solly said worriedly. "I thought you'd be glad to help, you've always been so fond of Hugh."

Maisie went to her cupboard for her gloves. "I wish you'd consulted me first." She opened the cupboard. On the back of the door, framed in wood, hung the old poster she had saved from the circus, showing her in tights, standing on the back of a white horse, over the legend "The Amazing Maisie." The picture jerked her out of her tantrum and she suddenly felt ashamed of herself. She ran to Solly and threw her arms around him. "Oh, Solly, how can I be so ungrateful?"

"There, there," he murmured, stroking her bare shoulders.

"You've been so kind and generous to me

and my family, of course I'll do this for you, if you wish."

"I'd hate to force you into something—"

"No, no, you're not forcing me. Why shouldn't I help her get what I got?" She looked at her husband's chubby face, creased now with lines of anxiety. She stroked his cheek. "Stop worrying. I was being horribly selfish for a minute but it's over. Go and put your jacket on. I'm ready." She stood on tiptoe and kissed his lips, then turned away and put on her gloves.

She knew what had really made her cross. The irony of the situation was bitter. She was being asked to train Nora for the role of Mrs. Hugh Pilaster—the position Maisie herself had longed to occupy. In her innermost heart she still wanted to be Hugh's wife, and she hated Nora for winning what she had lost. All in all it was a shameful attitude and Maisie resolved to drop it. She should be glad Hugh had married. He had been very unhappy, and it was at least partly her fault. Now she could stop worrying about him. She felt a sense of loss, if not grief, but she should keep those feelings locked away in a room no one ever entered. She would throw herself energetically into the task of bringing Nora Pilaster back into the good graces of London's high society.

Solly came back with his jacket on and they went along to the nursery. Bertie was in his nightshirt, playing with a wooden model of a railway train. He loved to see Maisie in her gowns and would be very disappointed if for some reason she went out in the evening without showing him what she was wearing. He told her what had happened in the park that afternoon—he had befriended a large dog—and Solly got down on the floor and played trains for a while. Then it was Bertie's bedtime, and Maisie and Solly went downstairs and got into their carriage.

They were going to a dinner party, then on to a ball afterwards. Both would take place within half a mile of their house in Piccadilly, but Maisie could not walk the streets in such an elaborate gown: the hem and train, and her silk shoes, would be filthy by the time she arrived. All the same she smiled to think that the girl who had once walked for four days to get to Newcastle could not now go half a mile without her carriage.

She was able to begin her campaign for Nora that very night. When they reached their destination and entered the drawing room of the marquis of Hatchford, the first person she saw was Count de Tokoly. She knew him quite well and he always flirted with her, so she felt free to be direct. "I want you to forgive Nora Pilaster for slapping you," she said.

"Forgive?" he said. "I'm flattered! To think that at my age I can still make a young woman slap my face—it's a great compliment."

That wasn't how you felt at the time, Maisie thought. However, she was glad he had decided to make light of the whole incident.

He went on: "Now, if she had refused to take me seriously—that would have been an insult."

It was exactly what Nora ought to have done, Maisie reflected. "Tell me something," she said. "Did Augusta Pilaster encourage you to flirt with her daughter-in-law?"

"Grisly suggestion!" he replied. "Mrs. Joseph Pilaster as a pander! She did nothing of the kind."

"Did anyone encourage you?"

He looked at Maisie through narrowed eyes. "You're clever, Mrs. Greenbourne; I've always respected you for that. Cleverer than Nora Pilaster. She'll never be what you are."

"But you haven't answered my question."

"I'll tell you the truth, as I admire you so much. The Cordovan Minister, Señor Miranda, told me that Nora was . . . what shall we say . . . susceptible."

So that was it. "And Micky Miranda was put up to it by Augusta, I'm sure of it. Those two are as thick as thieves."

De Tokoly was miffed. "I do hope I haven't been used as a pawn."

"That's the danger of being so predictable," Maisie said waspishly.

Next day she took Nora to her dressmaker.

As Nora tried on styles and fabrics Maisie found out a little more about the incident at the duchess of Tenbigh's ball. "Did Augusta say anything to you beforehand about the count?" she asked.

"She warned me not to let him take any liberties," Nora replied.

"So you were ready for him, so to speak."

"Yes."

"And if Augusta had said nothing, would you have behaved the same way?"

Nora looked thoughtful. "I probably wouldn't have slapped him—I wouldn't have had the nerve. But Augusta made me think it was important to take a stand."

Maisie nodded. "There you are. She wanted this to happen. She also got someone to tell the count you were easy."

Nora was amazed. "Are you sure?"

"He told me. She's a devious bitch and she has no scruples at all." Maisie realized she was speaking in her Newcastle accent, something that rarely happened nowadays. She reverted to normal. "Never underestimate Augusta's capacity for treachery."

"She doesn't scare me," Nora said defiantly. "I haven't got too many scruples myself."

Maisie believed her—and felt sorry for Hugh.

A polonaise was the perfect dress style for Nora, Maisie thought as the dressmaker pinned a gown around Nora's generous figure. The fussy details suited her pretty looks: the pleated frills, the front opening decorated with bows, and the tie-back skirt with flounces all looked sweet on her. Perhaps she was a little too voluptuous, but a long corset would restrain her tendency to wobble.

"Looking pretty is half the battle," she said as Nora admired herself in the mirror.

"As far as the men are concerned it's really all that matters. But you have to do more to get accepted by the women."

Nora said: "I've always got on better with men than women."

Maisie was not surprised: Nora was that type.

Nora went on: "You must be the same. That's why we've got where we are."

Are we the same? wondered Maisie.

"Not that I put myself on the same level as you," Nora added. "Every ambitious girl in London envies you."

Maisie winced at the thought that she was looked up to as a hero by fortune-hunting women, but she said nothing because she probably deserved it. Nora had married for money, and she was quite happy to admit it to Maisie because she assumed that Maisie had done the same. And she was right.

Nora said: "I'm not complaining, but I did pick the black sheep of the family, the one with no capital. You married one of the richest men in the world."

How surprised you would be, Maisie thought, if you knew how willingly I'd swap.

She put the thought out of her mind. All right, she and Nora were two of a kind. She would help Nora win the acceptance of the snobs and shrews who ruled society.

"Never talk about how much anything costs," she began, remembering her own early mistakes. "Always remain calm and unruffled, no matter what happens. If your coachman has a heart attack, your carriage crashes, your hat blows off and your drawers fall down, just say: 'Goodness me, such excitement,' and get in a hansom. Remember that the country is better than the town, idleness is superior to work, old is preferable to new and rank is more important than money. Know a little about everything, but never be an expert. Practice talking without moving your mouth—it will improve your accent. Tell people that your great-grandfather farmed in Yorkshire: Yorkshire is too big for anyone to check, and agriculture is an honorable way to become poor."

Nora struck a pose, looked vague, and said languidly: "Goodness me, *such* a lot to remember, how shall I *ever* manage?"

"Perfect," said Maisie. "You'll do very well indeed."

2

MICKY MIRANDA STOOD IN A DOORWAY in Berwick Street, wearing a light overcoat to keep out the chill of a spring evening. He was smoking a cigar and watching the street. There was a gas lamp nearby but he stood in the shadow so that his face could not easily be seen by passersby. He felt anxious, dissatisfied with himself, soiled. He disliked violence. It was Papa's way, Paulo's way. For Micky it always seemed such an admission of failure.

Berwick Street was a narrow, filthy passage of cheap pubs and lodging houses. Dogs rummaged in the gutters and small children played in the gaslight. Micky had been there since nightfall and he had not seen a single policeman. Now it was almost midnight.

The Hotel Russe was across the street. It had seen better days, but still it was a cut above its surroundings. There was a light over the door and inside Micky could see a lobby with a reception counter. However, there did not appear to be anyone there.

Two other men loitered on the far pavement, one on either side of the hotel entrance. All three of them were waiting for Antonio Silva.

Micky had pretended to be calm in front of Edward and Augusta but in fact he was desperately worried about Tonio's article appearing in *The Times*. He had put so much effort into getting Pilasters to launch the Santamaria railroad. He had even married that bitch Rachel for the sake of the damn bonds. His entire career depended on its success. If he let his family down over this, his father would be not only raging but vengeful. Papa had the power to get Micky fired as minister. With no money and no position he could hardly stay in London: he would have to return home and face humiliation and disgrace. Either way, the life he had enjoyed for so many years would be over.

Rachel had demanded to know where he was planning to spend this evening. He had laughed at her. "Never try to question me," he had said.

She had surprised him by saying: "Then I shall go out for the evening, too."

"Where?"

"Never try to question me."

Micky had locked her in the bedroom. When he got home she would be in-

candescent with wrath, but that had happened before. On previous occasions when
she had raged at him he had thrown her on
the bed and torn off her clothes, and she
had always submitted to him eagerly. She
would do it yet again tonight, he felt sure.

He wished he could feel as sure of Tonio.

He was not even certain the man was still
living at this hotel, but he could not go in
and ask without arousing suspicion.

He had moved as quickly as possible, but
still it had taken forty-eight hours to locate
and hire two ruthless toughs, reconnoiter
the location and set up the ambush. In that
time Tonio might have moved. Then Micky
would be in trouble.

A careful man would move hotels every
few days. But a careful man would not use
notepaper that bore an address. Tonio was
not the cautious type. On the contrary, he
had always been reckless. In all probability
he was still at this hotel, Micky thought.

He was right.

A few minutes after midnight, Tonio appeared.

Micky thought he recognized the walk as
the figure turned into the far end of Berwick
Street, coming from the direction of
Leicester Square. He tensed, but resisted

the temptation to move right away. Restraining himself with an effort, he waited until the man passed a gas lamp, when the face became clearly visible for a moment. Then there was no doubt: it was Tonio. Micky could even see the carroty color of the side-whiskers. He felt relief and heightened anxiety at the same time: relief that he had Tonio in his sights, anxiety about the crude, dangerous attack he was about to make.

Then he saw the policemen.

It was the worst possible luck. There were two of them, coming down Berwick Street from the opposite direction, helmeted and caped, their truncheons hanging from their belts, shining their bull's-eye lanterns into dark corners. Micky stood stock still. There was nothing he could do. They saw Micky, noted his top hat and his cigar, and nodded deferentially: it was none of their business what an upper-class man might be doing loitering in a doorway—they were after criminals, not gentlemen. They passed Tonio fifteen or twenty yards from the hotel door. Micky fidgeted in frustration. Another few moments and Tonio would be safe inside his hotel.

Then the two policemen turned a corner and were gone from sight.

Micky gestured to his two accomplices.

They moved fast.

Before Tonio reached the door of his hotel, the two men seized him and bundled him into the alley alongside the building. He shouted once, but after that his cries were muffled.

Throwing away the remains of his cigar, Micky crossed the road and entered the alley. They had stuffed a scarf into Tonio's mouth, to prevent his making a noise, and they were beating him with iron bars. His hat had fallen off, and his head and face were already covered with blood. His body was protected by a coat, but they slashed at his knees and shins and his unprotected hands.

The sight made Micky feel ill. "Stop it, you fools!" he hissed at them. "Can't you see he's had enough?" Micky did not want them to kill Tonio. As things stood, the incident looked like a routine robbery, accompanied by a savage beating. A murder would create a great deal more fuss—and the policemen had seen Micky's face, however briefly.

With apparent reluctance the two thugs

stopped hitting Tonio, who slumped to the ground and lay still.

"Empty his pockets!" Micky whispered.

Tonio did not move as they took from him a watch and chain, a pocketbook, some coins, a silk handkerchief and a key.

"Give me the key," Micky said. "The rest is yours."

The older of the two men, Barker—humorously known as Dog—said: "Give us the money."

He gave them each ten pounds in gold sovereigns.

Dog gave him the key. Tied to it with a small piece of thread was a slip of card with the number 11 scrawled on it. It was all Micky needed.

He turned to leave the alley—and saw that they were being watched. A man stood in the street staring at them. Micky's heart raced.

Dog saw him a moment later. He grunted an oath and raised his iron bar as if to strike the man down. Suddenly Micky realized something and grabbed Dog's arm. "No," he said. "That won't be necessary. Look at him."

The watching man had a slack mouth and a empty look in his eyes: he was an idiot.

Dog lowered his weapon. "He'll do us no harm," he said. "He's two sticks short of a bundle."

Micky pushed past him into the street. Looking back, he saw Dog and his companion taking off Tonio's boots.

Micky walked away, hoping he would never see them again.

He turned into the Hotel Russe. To his relief the desk in the little lobby was still unoccupied. He went up the stairs.

The hotel consisted of three houses knocked together, and it took Micky a while to find his way around, but two or three minutes later he let himself into room number 11.

It was a cramped, grimy room stuffed with furniture that had once been pretentious but was now merely shabby. Micky put his hat and cane on a chair and began to search quickly and methodically. In the writing desk he found a copy of the article for *The Times,* which he took. However, it was not worth much. Tonio either had copies or could rewrite it from memory. But in order to get the article published he would have to produce some kind of evidence, and it was the evidence that Micky was looking for.

In the chest of drawers he found a novel

called *The Duchess of Sodom* which he was tempted to steal, but he decided it was an unnecessary risk. He tipped Tonio's shirts and underwear out of the drawers onto the floor. There was nothing hidden there.

He had not really expected to find it in an obvious place.

He looked behind and underneath the chest, the bed and the wardrobe. He climbed on the table so that he could look on top of the wardrobe: there was nothing there but thick dust.

He pulled the sheets off the bed, probed the pillows for something hard, and examined the mattress. He finally found what he wanted underneath the mattress.

Inside a large envelope was a wad of papers tied together with lawyers' ribbons.

Before he could examine the documents he heard footsteps in the hall.

He dropped the bundle and stood behind the door.

The footsteps went past and faded.

He untied the ribbons and scanned the documents. They were in Spanish, and bore the stamp of a lawyer in Palma. They were the sworn affidavits of witnesses who had seen floggings and executions at Micky's family's nitrate mines.

Micky lifted the sheaf of papers to his lips and kissed them. They were the answer to his prayers.

He stuffed them into the bosom of his coat. Before destroying them he had to make a note of the names and addresses of the witnesses. The lawyers would have copies of the affidavits, but the copies were no use without the witnesses. And now that Micky knew who the witnesses were, their days were numbered. He would send their addresses to Papa, and Papa would silence them.

Was there anything else? He looked around the room. It was a mess. There was nothing more for him here. He had what he needed. Without proof, Tonio's article was worthless.

He left the room and went down the stairs.

To his surprise there was a clerk at the desk in the lobby. The man looked up and said challengingly: "May I ask your business?"

Micky made an instant decision. If he ignored the clerk, the man would probably just think he was rude. To stop and give an account of himself would allow the clerk to study his face. He said nothing and went out. The clerk did not follow.

As he passed the alley he heard a feeble cry for help. Tonio was crawling toward the street, leaving a trail of blood. The sight made Micky want to throw up. Disgusted, he grimaced, looked away and walked on.

3

IN THE AFTERNOONS, wealthy ladies and idle gentlemen called on one another. It was a tiresome practice and four days of the week Maisie told her servants to say she was not at home. On Fridays she received people, and there might be twenty or thirty during the course of an afternoon. It was always more or less the same crowd: the Marlborough Set, the Jewish set, women with "advanced" ideas such as Rachel Bodwin, and a few wives of Solly's more important business acquaintances.

Emily Pilaster was in the last category. Her husband Edward was involved in a deal with Solly about a railway in Cordova, and Maisie assumed it was on the strength of that that Emily called. But she stayed all afternoon and at half-past five, when everyone else had gone, she was still there.

A pretty girl with big blue eyes, she was only about twenty years old and anyone could tell she was miserable, so Maisie was not surprised when she said: "Please can I talk to you about something personal?"

"Of course, what is it?"

"I do hope you won't be offended but there's no one I can discuss it with."

This sounded like a sexual problem. It would not be the first time that a well-bred girl had come to Maisie for advice on a subject she could not discuss with her mother. Perhaps they had heard rumors about her racy past, or perhaps they just found her approachable. "It's hard to offend me," Maisie said. "What do you want to discuss?"

"My husband hates me," she said, and she burst into tears.

Maisie felt sorry for her. She had known Edward in the old Argyll Rooms days and he had been a pig then. No doubt he had got worse since. She could sympathize with anyone unfortunate enough to have married him.

"You see," Emily said between sobs, "his parents wanted him to marry, but he didn't want to, so they offered him a huge settlement, and a partnership in the bank, and that persuaded him. And I agreed because my parents wanted me to and he seemed as good as anyone and I wanted to have babies. But he never liked me and now that he's got his money and his partnership he can't stand the sight of me."

Maisie sighed. "This may sound hard, but you're in the same position as thousands of women."

Emily wiped her eyes with a handkerchief and made an effort to stop crying. "I know, and I don't want you to think I'm feeling sorry for myself. I've got to make the best of it. And I know I could cope with the situation if only I could have a baby. That's all I ever really wanted."

Children were the consolation of most unhappy wives, Maisie reflected. "Is there any reason why you shouldn't have babies?"

Emily was shifting restlessly on the couch, almost writhing with embarrassment, but her childlike face was set in lines of determination. "I've been married for two months and *nothing's happened.*"

"Early days yet—"

"No, I don't mean I expected to be pregnant by now."

Maisie knew it was difficult for such girls to be specific, so she led her with questions. "Does he come to your bed?"

"He did at first, but not anymore."

"When he did, what went wrong?"

"The trouble is, I'm not sure what's supposed to happen."

Maisie sighed. How could mothers allow their daughters to walk up the aisle in such ignorance? She recalled that Emily's father was a Methodist minister. That did not help. "What's supposed to happen is this," she began. "Your husband kisses and touches you, his doodle gets long and stiff, and he puts it into your cunny. Most girls like it."

Emily blushed scarlet. "He did the kissing and touching, but nothing else."

"Did his doodle get stiff?"

"It was dark."

"Didn't you feel it?"

"He made me rub it once."

"And what was it like? Rigid, like a candle, or limp, like an earthworm? Or in between, like a sausage before it's cooked?"

"Limp."

"And when you rubbed it, did it stiffen?"

"No. It made him very angry and he slapped me and said I was no good. *Is* it my fault, Mrs. Greenbourne?"

"No, it's not your fault, though men generally blame women. It's a common problem and it's called impotence."

"What causes it?"

"Lots of different things."

"Does it mean I can't have a baby?"

"Not until you can make his doodle stiff."

Emily looked as if she might cry. "I do so want a baby. I'm so lonely and unhappy but if I had a baby I could put up with every-thing else."

Maisie wondered what Edward's problem was. He certainly had not been impotent in the old days. Was there anything she could do to help Emily? She could probably find out whether Edward was impotent all the time or just with his wife. April Tilsley would know. Edward had still been a regu-lar customer at Nellie's brothel last time Maisie spoke to April—although that had been years ago: it was difficult for a society lady to remain close friends with London's leading madam. "I know someone close to Edward," she said cautiously. "She might be able to shed some light on the problem."

Emily swallowed. "Do you mean that he has a mistress? Please tell me—I must face the facts."

She was a determined girl, Maisie thought. She may be ignorant and naive but she's going to get what she wants. "This woman isn't his mistress. But if he has one she might know."

Emily nodded. "I'd like to meet your friend."

"I don't know that you personally should—"

"I want to. He's my husband, and if there's something bad to be told I want to hear it." Her face took on that set, stubborn look again, and she said: "I'll do anything, you must believe me—anything. My whole life is going to be a wasteland unless I save myself."

Maisie decided to test her resolve. "My friend's name is April. She owns a brothel near Leicester Square. It's two minutes from here. Are you prepared to go there with me now?"

"What's a brothel?" said Emily.

The hansom pulled up outside Nellie's. Maisie peeked out, scanning the street. She did not want to be seen going into a brothel by anyone she knew. However, this was the hour when most people of her class were dressing for dinner, and there were only a few poor people on the street. She and Emily got out of the cab. She had paid the driver in advance. The door to the brothel was not locked. They went inside.

Daylight was not kind to Nellie's. At night it might have a certain seedy glamor, Maisie thought, but at the moment it looked threadbare and grubby. The velvet upholstery was faded, the tables were scarred by cigar burns and glass rings, the silk wallpaper was peeling and the erotic paintings just looked vulgar. An old woman with a pipe in her mouth was sweeping the floor. She did not appear surprised to see two society ladies in expensive dresses. When Maisie asked for April, the old woman jerked a thumb at the staircase.

They found April in an upstairs kitchen, drinking tea at the table with several other women, all in dressing gowns or housecoats: obviously it was some hours before business would begin. At first April did not recognize Maisie and they stared at each other for a long moment. Maisie found her old friend little changed: still thin, hard-faced and sharp-eyed; a little weary-looking, perhaps, from too many late nights and too much cheap champagne; but with the confident, assertive air of a successful business woman. "What can we do for you?" she said.

"Don't you know me, April?" said

Maisie; and at once April shrieked with delight and jumped up and threw her arms around her.

When they had embraced and kissed, April turned to the other women in the kitchen and said: "Girls, this is the woman who did what we all dream of. Formerly Miriam Rabinowicz, later Maisie Robinson, she is now Mrs. Solomon Greenbourne!"

The women all cheered as if Maisie were some kind of hero. She felt bashful: she had not anticipated that April would give such a frank account of her story—especially in front of Emily Pilaster—but it was too late now.

"Let's have a gin to celebrate," April said. They sat down and one of the women produced a bottle and some glasses and poured them drinks. Maisie had never enjoyed gin, and now that she was accustomed to the best champagne she liked it even less, but she knocked it back to be companionable. She saw Emily sip hers and grimace. Their glasses were immediately recharged.

"Well, what brings you here?" April said.

"A marital problem," Maisie said. "My friend here has an impotent husband."

"Bring him here, my love," April said to Emily. "We'll sort him out."

"He's already a customer, I suspect," Maisie said.

"What's his name?"

"Edward Pilaster."

April was startled. "My God." She stared hard at Emily. "So you're Emily. You poor cow."

"You know my name," Emily said. She looked mortified. "That means he speaks to you about me." She drank some more gin.

One of the other women said: "Edward's not impotent."

Emily blushed.

"I'm sorry," the woman said. "Only he usually asks for me." She was a tall girl with dark hair and a deep bosom. Maisie thought she did not look very impressive in her grubby robe, smoking a cigarette like a man; but perhaps she was attractive when she was dressed up.

Emily recovered her composure. "It's so strange," she said. "He's my husband, but you know more about him than I do. And I don't even know your name."

"Lily."

There was a moment of awkward silence. Maisie sipped her drink: the second gin tasted better than the first. This was a very bizarre scene: the kitchen, the women in *déshabillé,* the cigarettes and gin, and Emily, who an hour ago had not been sure what sexual intercourse consisted of, discussing her husband's impotence with his favorite whore.

"Well," April said briskly, "now you know the answer to the question. Why is Edward impotent with his wife? Because Micky's not around. He can never get hard if he's alone with a woman."

"Micky?" said Emily incredulously. "Micky Miranda? The Cordovan Minister?"

April nodded. "They do everything together, especially here. Once or twice Edward has come in on his own but it never works."

Emily was looking bewildered. Maisie asked the obvious question: "What, exactly, do they do?"

It was Lily who answered. "Nothing very complicated. Over the years they've tried several variations. At the moment what they like is, the two of them go to bed with one girl, usually me or Muriel."

Maisie said: "But Edward really does it, properly, does he? I mean, he gets hard, and everything?"

Lily nodded. "No question of that."

"Do you think that's the only way he could ever manage it?"

Lily frowned. "I don't think it matters much exactly what happens, how many girls and so on. If Micky is there, it works, and if he's not, it doesn't."

Maisie said: "Almost as if Micky is the one Edward really loves."

Emily said faintly: "I feel as if I'm in a dream, or something." She took a long swallow of gin. "Can all this be true? Do these things really go on?"

April said: "If you but knew. Edward and Micky are tame by comparison with some of our customers."

Even Maisie was startled. The thought of Edward and Micky in bed together with a woman was so odd it made her want to laugh out loud, and she had to make an effort to suppress the chuckle that bubbled up in her throat.

She recalled the night Edward had discovered her and Hugh making love. Edward had been uncontrollably aroused, she remembered; and she had felt intuitively that what inflamed him was the idea of fucking her immediately after Hugh. "A buttered bun!" she said.

Some of the women giggled.

"That's right," April laughed.

Emily smiled and looked puzzled. "I don't understand."

April said: "Some men like a buttered bun." The whores laughed louder. "It means a woman who's just been fucked by another man."

Emily started to giggle, and in a moment they were all laughing hysterically. It was a combination of the gin, the weird situation, and the talk of men's peculiar sexual preferences, Maisie thought. Her use of the vulgar phrase had released the tension. Every time the laughter eased one of them would say "A buttered bun!" and they would all collapse into giggles again.

At last they were too exhausted to laugh anymore. When they quietened down, Maisie said: "But where does this leave Emily? She wants to have a baby. She can hardly invite Micky to bed with her and her husband."

Emily looked miserable.

April caught her eye and held it. "How determined are you, Emily?" she said.

"I'll do anything," said Emily. "Really, anything in the world."

"If you mean that," said April slowly, "there is something we could try."

4

JOSEPH PILASTER FINISHED OFF a large plate of grilled lamb's kidneys and scrambled eggs, and began to butter a slice of toast. Augusta often wondered whether the customary bad temper of middle-aged men had to do with the amount of meat they ate. The thought of kidneys for breakfast made her feel quite ill.

"Sidney Madler has come to London," he said. "I have to see him this morning."

For a moment Augusta was not sure who he was talking about. "Madler?"

"From New York. He's angry about Hugh's not being a partner."

"What is it to do with him?" Augusta said. "The insolence!" She spoke superciliously but she was bothered.

"I know what he'll say," Joseph said. "When we formed our joint enterprise with Madler and Bell there was an implicit understanding that the London end of the operation would be run by Hugh. Now Hugh has resigned, as you know."

"But you did not wish Hugh to resign."

"No, but I could keep him by offering him a partnership."

There was some risk of Joseph's weakening, Augusta could see. The thought scared her. She had to stiffen his nerve. "I trust you won't allow outsiders to decide who shall and who shall not be a partner in Pilasters Bank."

"Indeed I won't."

A thought occurred to Augusta. "Can Mr. Madler terminate the joint enterprise?"

"He could, though he hasn't threatened to, so far."

"Is it worth a lot money?"

"It was. But when Hugh goes to work at Greenbournes he's likely to take most of the business with him."

"So it really makes very little difference what Mr. Madler thinks."

"Perhaps not. But I'll have to tell him something. He's come all the way from New York just to make a fuss about this."

"Tell him Hugh has married an impossible wife. He can hardly fail to understand that."

"Of course." Joseph stood up. "Goodbye, dear."

Augusta stood up and kissed her husband on the lips. "Don't be bullied, Joseph," she said.

His shoulders straightened and his mouth set in a stubborn line. "I shan't."

When he had gone she sat at the table

sipping coffee for a while, wondering how serious this threat was. She had tried to bolster Joseph's resistance but there was a limit to how much she could do. She would have to keep a very close eye on that situation.

She was surprised to hear that Hugh's departure would cost the bank a lot of money. It had not occurred to her that in promoting Edward and undermining Hugh she was also losing money. For a moment she wondered whether she might be endangering the bank that was the foundation of all her hopes and schemes. But that was ridiculous. Pilasters Bank was hugely wealthy: nothing she could do would threaten it.

While she was finishing her breakfast Hastead sidled in to tell her that Mr. Fortescue had called. She immediately put Sidney Madler out of her mind. This was much more important. Her heart beat faster.

Michael Fortescue was her tame politician. Having won the Deaconridge by-election with financial help from Joseph, he was now a member of Parliament, and indebted to Augusta. She had made it very clear how he could repay that debt: by helping her to get a peerage for Joseph. The by-election had cost five thousand pounds, enough to buy the finest house in London, but that was a cheap price to pay for a title. The afternoon was the time for calls, so morning visitors generally had urgent business. She felt sure Fortescue would not have called so early unless he had news of the peerage, and her heart beat faster. "Put Mr. Fortescue in the lookout," she told the butler. "I shall be with him directly." She sat still for a few moments, trying to make herself calm.

Her campaign had gone according to plan so far. Arnold Hobbes had published a series of articles in his journal *The Forum* calling for peerages for commercial men. Lady Morte had talked to the queen about it, and had sung Joseph's praises; and she said Her Majesty had seemed impressed. And Fortescue had told Prime Minister Disraeli that there was a groundswell of public opinion in favor of the idea. Now perhaps the whole effort was about to bear fruit.

The tension was almost too much for her, and she felt a little breathless as she hurried up the stairs, her head full of the phrases she hoped soon to hear: *Lady Whitehaven . . . the earl and countess Whitehaven . . . very good, m'lady . . . as your ladyship pleases. . . .*

The lookout was a curious room. It was over the front lobby, and was reached by a door halfway up the stairs. It had a bay window over the street, but that was not what gave the room its name. What was unusual about it was an interior window that looked down into the main hall. People in the hall did not suspect they were observed, and over the years Augusta had seen some strange sights from that vantage point. The room was informal, small and cozy, with a low ceiling and a fireplace. Augusta received visitors there in the morning.

Fortescue looked a little tense. Augusta sat close to him on the window seat and gave him a warm, reassuring smile.

"I've just been with the prime minister," he said.

Augusta could hardly speak. "Did you talk about peerages?"

"We did indeed. I've managed to convince him that it is time the banking industry was represented in the House of Lords, and he's now minded to grant a peerage to a City man."

"Wonderful!" said Augusta. But Fortescue had an uncomfortable expression, not at all like the bringer of glad tidings. "So why do you look so glum?" she said uneasily.

"There's also bad news," Fortescue said, and suddenly he looked a little frightened.

"What?"

"I'm afraid he wants to give the peerage to Ben Greenbourne."

"No!" Augusta felt as if she had been punched. "How can that be?"

Fortescue became defensive. "I suppose he can give peerages to whomever he pleases. He is the prime minister."

"But I didn't go to all this trouble for the benefit of Ben Greenbourne!"

"I agree it's ironic," Fortescue said languidly. "But I did my best."

"Don't be so smug," she snapped. "Not if you want my help in future elections."

Rebellion flashed in his eyes, and for a moment she thought she had lost him, thought he was going to say that he had repaid the debt and now he no longer needed her; but then he dropped his gaze and said: "I assure you I'm devastated by this news—"

"Be quiet, let me think," she said, and she began to pace up and down the little room. "We must find a way to change the prime minister's mind. . . . We must make it into a scandal. What are Ben Greenbourne's weaknesses? His son is married to a gutter-snipe, but that's not really enough. . . ." It occurred to her that if Greenbourne got a title it would be inherited by his son Solly, which would mean that Maisie would eventually be a countess. The thought was sickening. "What are Greenbourne's politics?"

"None known."

She looked at the young man and saw that he was sulking. She had spoken too harshly to him. She sat down beside him and took one of his big hands in both her own. "Your political instincts are remarkable, in fact that's what first made me notice you. Tell me what your guess would be."

Fortescue melted immediately, as men generally did when she took the trouble to be nice to them. "If pressed he would probably be Liberal. Most businessmen are Liberal, and so are most Jews. But as he has never expressed any opinion publicly, it will be hard to make him out to be an enemy of the Conservative government—"

"He's a Jew," Augusta said. "That's the key."

Fortescue looked dubious. "The prime minister himself is a Jew by birth, and he has now been made Lord Beaconsfield."

"I know, but he's a practicing Christian. Besides . . ."

Fortescue raised an inquiring eyebrow.

"I have instincts too," Augusta said.

"Mine tell me that Ben Greenbourne's Jewishness is the key to it all."

"If there is anything I can do . . ."

"You've been wonderful. There's nothing for the moment. But when the prime minister begins to have doubts about Ben Greenbourne, just remind him that there is a safe alternative in Joseph Pilaster."

"Rely on me, Mrs. Pilaster."

Lady Morte lived in a house in Curzon Street which her husband could not afford. The door was opened by a liveried footman in a powdered wig. Augusta was shown into a morning room crowded with costly knickknacks from Bond Street shops: gold candelabra, silver picture-frames, porcelain ornaments, crystal vases, and an exquisite antique jeweled inkstand that must have cost as much as a young racehorse. Augusta despised Harriet Morte for her weakness in spending money she did not have; but at the same time she was reassured by these signs that the woman was as extravagant as ever.

She paced up and down the room as she waited. A feeling of panic grew over her every time she faced the prospect that Ben Greenbourne would get the honor instead of Joseph. She did not think she could mount a campaign like this a second time. And it made her squirm to think that the result of all her efforts might be that the title of countess would eventually go to that little sewer rat Maisie Greenbourne. . . .

Lady Morte came in, saying distantly: "What a lovely surprise to see you at this time of day!" It was a reproof to Augusta for calling before lunch. Lady Morte's iron-gray hair looked hastily combed, and Augusta guessed she had not been fully dressed.

But you had to receive me, didn't you? thought Augusta. You were afraid I might be calling about your bank account, so you had no choice.

However, she spoke in a subservient tone that would flatter the woman. "I've come to ask your advice over something urgent."

"Anything I can do . . ."

"The prime minister has agreed to give a peerage to a banker."

"Splendid! I mentioned it to Her Majesty, as you know. Doubtless that had its effect."

"Unfortunately, he wants to give it to Ben Greenbourne."

"Oh, dear. That is unfortunate."

Augusta could tell that Harriet Morte was secretly pleased by this news. She hated Augusta. "It's more than unfortunate," Augusta said. "I've expended a good deal of effort over this and now its seems the benefits will go to my husband's greatest rival!"

"I do see that."

"I wish we could prevent it happening."

"I'm not sure what we can do."

Augusta pretended to be thinking aloud. "Peerages have to be approved by the queen, don't they?"

"Yes, indeed. Technically it is she who grants them."

"Then she could do something, if you asked her."

Lady Morte gave a little laugh. "My dear Mrs. Pilaster, you overestimate my power." Augusta held her tongue and ignored the condescending tone. Lady Morte went on: "Her Majesty is not likely to take my advice over that of the prime minister. Besides, what would be my grounds of objection?"

"Greenbourne is a Jew."

Lady Morte nodded. "There was a time when that would have finished it. I remember when Gladstone wanted to make Lionel Rothschild a peer: the queen refused point-blank. But that was ten years ago. Since then we have had Disraeli."

"But Disraeli is a Christian. Greenbourne is a practicing Jew."

"I wonder if that would make a difference," Lady Morte mused. "It might, you know. And she's constantly criticizing the Prince of Wales for having so many Jews among his friends."

"Then if you were to mention to her that the prime minister is proposing to ennoble one of them . . ."

"I can bring it up in conversation. I'm not sure it will be enough to effect your purpose."

Augusta thought hard. "Is there anything we can do to make the whole question a matter of more concern to Her Majesty?"

"If there were to be some public protest —questions in Parliament, perhaps, or articles in the press . . ."

"The press," Augusta said. She thought of Arnold Hobbes. "Yes!" she said. "I think that could be arranged."

Hobbes was splendidly discombobulated by Augusta's presence in his cramped, inky office. He could not make up his mind whether to tidy up, attend to her or get rid of her. Consequently he did all three in a hysterical muddle: he moved sheets of paper and bundles of proofs from the floor to the table and back again; he fetched her a chair, a glass of sherry and a plate of biscuits; and at the same time he proposed that they go elsewhere to talk. She let him run wild for a minute or two then said: "Mr. Hobbes, please sit down and listen to me."

"Of course, of course," he said, and he subsided into a chair and peered at her through his grimy spectacles.

She told him in a few crisp sentences about Ben Greenbourne's peerage.

"Most regrettable, most regrettable," he blabbered nervously. "However, I don't think *The Forum* could be accused of lack of enthusiasm in promoting the cause which you so kindly suggested to me."

And in exchange for which you got two lucrative directorships of companies controlled by my husband, Augusta thought. "I know it's not your fault," she said irritably. "The point is, what can you do about it?"

"My journal is in a difficult position," he said worriedly. "Having campaigned so vociferously for a banker to get a peerage, it's hard for us to turn around and protest when it actually happens."

"But you never intended for a Jew to be so honored."

"True, true, although so many bankers are Jews."

"Couldn't you write that there are enough Christian bankers for the prime minister to choose from?"

He remained reluctant. "We might. . . ."

"Then do so!"

"Excuse me, Mrs. Pilaster, but it's not quite enough."

"I don't understand you," she said impatiently.

"A professional consideration, but I need what we journalists call a slant. For instance, we could accuse Disraeli—or Lord Beaconsfield, as he now is—of partiality to members of his own race. Now that would be a slant. However, he is in general a man so upright that that particular charge might not stick."

Augusta hated dithering, but she reined in her impatience because she could see there was a genuine problem here. She thought for a moment and was struck by an idea. "When Disraeli took his seat in the House of Lords, was the ceremony normal?"

"In every way, I believe."

"He took the oath of loyalty on a Christian Bible?"

"Indeed."

"Old and New Testament?"

"I begin to see your drift, Mrs. Pilaster. Would Ben Greenbourne swear on a Christian Bible? From what I know of him, I doubt it."

Augusta shook her head dubiously. "He might, though, if nothing were said about it. He's not a man to look for a confrontation. But he's very stiff-necked when challenged. If there were to be a noisy public demand for him to swear the same way as everyone else he might well rebel. He wouldn't let people say he had been pushed into anything."

"A noisy public demand," Hobbes mused. "Yes . . ."

"Could you create that?"

Hobbes warmed to the idea. "I see it already," he said excitedly. " 'Blasphemy in the House of Lords.' Now that, Mrs. Pilaster, is what we call a slant. You're quite brilliant. You ought to be a journalist yourself!"

"How flattering," she said. The sarcasm was lost on him.

Hobbes suddenly looked pensive. "Mr. Greenbourne is a very powerful man."

"So is Mr. Pilaster."

"Of course, of course."

"Then I may rely on you?"

Hobbes rapidly weighed the risks and decided to back the Pilaster cause. "Leave everything to me."

Augusta nodded. She was beginning to feel better. Lady Morte would turn the queen against Greenbourne, Hobbes would make an issue of it in the press, and Fortescue was standing by to whisper into the ear of the prime minister the name of a blameless alternative: Joseph. Once again the prospects looked good.

She stood up to go, but Hobbes had more to say. "If I might venture a question on another topic?"

"By all means."

"I've been offered a printing press rather cheaply. At present, you know, we use outside printers. If we had our own press it would reduce our costs, and we could perhaps make a little extra by printing other publications as a service."

"Obviously," Augusta said impatiently.

"I was wondering whether Pilasters Bank might be persuaded into a commercial loan."

It was the price of his continuing support. "How much?"

"A hundred and sixty pounds."

It was a peppercorn. And if he campaigned against peerages for Jews with as much energy and bile as he had brought to his campaign in favor of peerages for bankers, it would be well worth it.

He said: "A bargain, I assure—"

"I'll speak to Mr. Pilaster." He would assent, but she did not want to let Hobbes have it too easily. He would value it more highly if it was granted reluctantly.

"Thank you. Always a pleasure to meet with you, Mrs. Pilaster."

"Doubtless," she said, and she went out.

CHAPTER FOUR

1

THE CORDOVAN MINISTRY was quiet. The offices on the first floor were empty, the three clerks having gone home hours ago. Micky and Rachel had given a dinner party in the second-floor dining room for a small group —Sir Peter Mountjoy, an under-secretary at the Foreign Office, and his wife; the Danish Minister; and the Chevalier Michele from the Italian embassy—but the guests had left and the domestic staff had cleared away. Micky was about to go out.

The novelty of being married was beginning to wear off. He had tried and failed to shock or disgust his sexually inexperienced wife. Her unfailing enthusiasm for whatever perversion he proposed was beginning to

unnerve him. She had decided that whatever he wanted was all right with her, and
when she made a decision like that there
was no moving her. He had never met a
woman who could be so implacably logical.

She would do anything he asked in bed,
but she believed that outside the bedroom a
woman should not be a slave to her husband, and she was equally rigid about both
rules. Consequently they were always fighting about domestic issues. Sometimes Micky
could turn one situation into the other. In
the middle of a row about servants or
money he would say: "Lift up your dress
and lie on the floor," and the quarrel would
end in a passionate embrace. But that no
longer worked every time: sometimes she
would recommence the argument as soon as
he rolled off her.

Lately he and Edward had been spending
more and more evenings in their old haunts.
Tonight was Mask Night at Nellie's brothel.
This was one of April's innovations: all the
women would be wearing masks. April
claimed that sexually frustrated high-society
ladies came in and mingled with the regular
girls on Mask Nights. Certainly some of the
women were not regulars, but Micky suspected the strangers were in fact middle-

class women in desperate financial straits, rather than bored aristocrats in search of degenerate thrills. Whatever the truth of the matter, Mask Night never failed to be interesting.

He combed his hair and filled his cigar case, then he went downstairs. To his surprise, Rachel was standing in the hall, barring the way to the door. Her arms were folded and she wore a determined expression. Micky braced himself for a fight.

"It's eleven o'clock in the evening," she said. "Where are you going?"

"To the devil," he replied. "Get out of my way." He picked up his hat and cane.

"Are you going to a brothel called Nellie's?"

He was startled enough to be silenced for a moment.

"I see you are," she said.

"Who have you been talking to?" he said.

She hesitated, then said: "Emily Pilaster. She told me that you and Edward go there regularly."

"You shouldn't listen to women's gossip."

Her face was white. She was scared. That was unusual. Perhaps this fight would be different.

"You must stop going there," she said.

"I've told you, don't try to give orders to your master."

"It's not an order. It's an ultimatum."

"Don't be silly. Get out of my way."

"Unless you promise not to go there any-more, I shall leave you. I'll go away from this house tonight and never come back."

She meant it, he saw. That was why she looked scared. She even had her outdoor shoes on, ready. "You're not leaving," he said. "I shall lock you in your room."

"You'll find that difficult. I've collected all the room keys and thrown them away. There isn't a single room in this house that can be locked."

That was clever of her. It seemed this was going to be one of their more interesting contests. He grinned at her and said: "Take off your knickers."

"That won't work tonight, Micky," she said. "I used to think it meant you loved me. Now I've realized sex is just your way of controlling people. I doubt whether you even enjoy it."

He reached out and grasped her breast. It was warm and heavy in his hand, despite the layers of clothing. He caressed it, watching her face, but her expression did not change. She was not going to give in to passion tonight. He squeezed hard, hurting her, then let go. "What's got into you?" he said with genuine curiosity.

"Men catch infectious diseases at places such as Nellie's."

"The girls there are very clean—"

"Please, Micky—don't pretend to be stupid."

She was right. There was no such thing as a clean prostitute. In fact he had been very lucky: he had only caught one mild case of the pox during many years of visiting brothels. "All right," he conceded. "I might catch an infectious disease."

"And give it to me."

He shrugged. "It's one of the hazards of being a wife. I might give you the measles, too, if I catch it."

"But syphilis can be hereditary."

"What are you driving at?"

"I might give it to our children, if we have any. And that is what I am not willing to do. I will not bring a child into the world with such a dreadful disease." She was breathing in short gasps, a sign of severe tension. She means it, he thought. She finished: "So I'm going to leave you, unless you agree to cease all contact with prostitutes."

There was no point in further discussion.

"We'll see whether you can leave with a broken nose," he said, and he raised his cane to strike her.

She was ready for him. She dodged the blow and ran to the door. To Micky's surprise it was ajar—she must have opened it earlier, in anticipation of violence, he thought—and she slipped outside in a flash.

Micky went after her. Another surprise awaited him outside: there was a carriage at the curb. Rachel jumped into it. Micky was amazed at how meticulously she had planned everything. He was about to leap into the carriage after her when his way was blocked by a large figure in a top hat. It was her father, Mr. Bodwin, the lawyer.

"I take it you refuse to mend your ways," he said.

"Are you abducting my wife?" Micky replied. He was angry at having been outmaneuvered.

"She's leaving of her own free will." Bodwin's voice was a little shaky, but he stood his ground. "She will return to you whenever you agree to give up your vicious habits. Subject of course to a satisfactory medical examination."

For a moment Micky was tempted to strike him—but only for a moment. Anyway, the lawyer would undoubtedly charge him with assault, and such a scandal could blight a diplomatic career. Rachel was not worth that.

It was a standoff. What am I fighting for? he asked himself. "You can keep her," he said. "I've finished with her." He went back into the house and slammed the door.

He heard the carriage drive away. To his surprise he found himself regretting Rachel's departure. He had married her purely for convenience, of course—it had been a way of persuading Edward to marry—and it some respects life would be simpler without her. But in a curious way he had enjoyed the daily clash of wits. He had never had that with a woman. However, it was often tiresome too, and he told himself that on balance he would be better off alone.

When he had caught his breath, he put on his hat and went out. It was a mild summer night with a clear sky and bright stars. London's air always tasted better in summer, when people did not need to burn coal to warm their houses.

As he walked down Regent Street he turned his mind to business. Since he had had Tonio Silva beaten up a month ago he had heard no more of his article about the

nitrate mines. Tonio was probably still re-
covering from his wounds. Micky had sent
Papa a coded telegram with the names and
addresses of the witnesses who had signed
Tonio's affidavits, and they were probably
dead by now. Hugh had been made to look
foolish, for having started an unnecessary
scare, and Edward was delighted.

Meanwhile, Edward had got Solly Greenbourne to agree in principle to float the
Santamaria railroad bonds jointly with Pilasters. It had not been easy: Solly was as suspicious of South America as most investors
were. Edward had been obliged to offer a
higher commission and take a share in a
speculative scheme of Solly's before the deal
could be closed. Edward had also played on
the fact that they were old school friends,
and Micky suspected it was Solly's softheart-
edness that had tipped the balance in the
end.

Now they were drawing up contracts. It
was a painfully slow business. What made
life difficult for Micky was that Papa could
not understand why these things could not
be done in a few hours. He was demanding
the money right away.

However, when Micky thought of the ob-
stacles he had overcome he was quite

pleased with himself. After Edward turned him down flat the task had seemed impossible. But with Augusta's help he had maneuvered Edward into marriage and a partnership in the bank. Then he had dealt with opposition from Hugh Pilaster and Tonio Silva. Now the fruits of all his efforts were about to fall into his hands. Back home the Santamaria railroad would always be Micky's railroad. Half a million pounds was a vast sum, greater than the military budget of the entire country. This one achievement would count for more than everything his brother Paulo had ever done.

A few minutes later he stepped into Nellie's. The party was in full swing: every table was occupied, the air was thick with cigar smoke, and ribald banter and raucous laughter could be heard over the sound of a small orchestra playing loud dance tunes. All the women wore masks. Some were simple dominoes but most were more elaborate, and a few were entire headdresses covering everything but the eyes and mouth.

Micky pushed his way through the crowd, nodding at acquaintances and kissing some of the girls. Edward was in the card room, but he got up as soon as Micky walked in.

"April's got a virgin for us," he said thickly. It was late, and he had drunk a lot.

Virginity had never been Micky's particular obsession, but there was always something stimulating about a girl who was frightened, and he was titillated. "How old?"

"Seventeen."

Which probably meant twenty-three, Micky thought, knowing how April estimated the ages of her girls. Still, he was intrigued. "Have you seen her?"

"Yes. She's masked, of course."

"Of course." Micky wondered what her story was. She might be a provincial girl who had run away from home and found herself destitute in London; she might have been abducted from a farm; she might just be a housemaid fed up with slaving sixteen hours a day for six shillings a week.

A woman in a little black domino touched his arm. The mask was no more than a token, and he recognized April. "A genuine virgin," April said.

No doubt she was charging Edward a small fortune for the privilege of taking the girl's maidenhead. "Have you put your own hand up her, to feel her hymen?" Micky said skeptically.

April shook her head. "I don't need to. I know when a girl is telling the truth."

"If I don't feel it pop you won't get paid," he said, even though they both knew Edward would be paying.

"Agreed."

"What's her story?"

"She's an orphan, brought up by an uncle. He was eager to get her off his hands as soon as possible, and arranged for her to marry an older man. When she refused he put her out on the street. I rescued her from a life of drudgery."

"You're an angel," Micky said sarcastically. He did not believe a word of it. Even though he could not read April's expression behind the mask he had the strongest feeling that she was up to something. He gave her a skeptical look. "Tell me the truth," he said.

"I have," April said. "If you don't want her, there are six other men here who'll pay just as much as you."

Edward said impatiently: "We want her. Stop arguing, Micky. Let's have a look at her."

"Room three," April said. "She's waiting for you."

Micky and Edward made their way up the

stairs, which were littered with embracing couples, and went into room three.

The girl stood in the corner. She wore a simple muslin gown, and her entire head was covered with a hood, leaving only slits for the eyes and an opening for the mouth. Once again Micky was seized by suspicion. They could see nothing of her face and head: she might be hideously ugly, perhaps deformed. Was this some kind of prank?

He realized, as he stared at her, that she was trembling with fear, and he put his doubts aside as he felt a stirring of desire in his loins. To frighten her more he crossed the room quickly, pulled the neckline of her gown aside, and plunged his hand into her bosom. She flinched, and there was terror in her bright blue eyes, but she stood her ground. She had small, firm breasts.

Her fear made him want to be brutal. Normally he and Edward would toy with a woman for a while, but he decided to take this one suddenly. "Kneel on the bed," he told her.

She did as he said. He got behind her and pulled up her skirt. She gave a little cry of fright. She was wearing nothing underneath.

It was easier to penetrate her than he had expected: April must have given her some cream to lubricate herself. He felt the obstruction of her maidenhead. He grabbed her hips and pulled her roughly to him as he thrust deep inside her, and the membrane broke. She began to sob, and that excited him so much that he reached his climax immediately.

He withdrew to make way for Edward. There was blood on his prick. He felt dissatisfied, now that it was over, and he wished he had stayed at home and gone to bed with Rachel. Then he remembered that she had left him and he felt worse.

Edward turned the girl over onto her back. She almost rolled off the bed, and he grabbed her ankles and pulled her back into the middle. As he did so her hood came partly off.

Edward said: "Good God!"

"What's the matter?" Micky said without much interest.

Edward was kneeling between the girl's thighs with his prick in his hand, staring at her half-revealed face. Micky decided that the girl must be someone they knew. He watched, fascinated, as she tried to tug the hood down again. Edward prevented her, and pulled it right off.

Then Micky saw the big blue eyes and childlike face of Edward's wife, Emily.

"I never heard of such a thing!" he said, and he started to laugh.

Edward gave a roar of rage. "You filthy cow!" he yelled. "You did this to shame me!"

"No, Edward, no!" she cried. "To help you—to help us!"

"Now they all know!" he shouted, and he punched her face.

She screamed and struggled, and he hit her again.

Micky laughed all the more. It was the funniest thing he had ever seen: a man going into a whorehouse and meeting his own wife!

April came rushing in, in response to the screams. "Leave her alone!" she yelled, and she tried to pull Edward off.

He pushed her aside. "I'll chastise my own wife if I please!" he roared.

"You great big fool, she only wants to have a baby!"

"She'll have my fist instead!"

They struggled for a moment. Edward punched his wife again, then April punched him on the ear. He gave cry of pain and surprise, making Micky collapse with hysterical laughter.

At last April managed to haul Edward off his wife.

Emily got off the bed. Astonishingly, she did not immediately rush out. Instead she spoke to her husband. "Please don't give up, Edward. I'll do anything you want, anything!"

He lunged at her again. April clung to his legs and tripped him up. He fell to his knees. April said: "Get out, Emily, before he kills you!"

Emily rushed out, weeping.

Edward was still raging. "I'll never come to this poxy whorehouse again!" he yelled, wagging his finger at April.

Micky fell on the sofa, holding his sides, laughing fit to bust.

2

MAISIE GREENBOURNE'S MIDSUMMER BALL was one of the fixtures of the London season. She always had the best band, the most delicious food, outrageously extravagant decorations, and endless champagne. But the main reason everyone wanted to go was that the Prince of Wales always came.

This year Maisie decided to use the occasion to launch the new Nora Pilaster.

It was a high-risk strategy, for if it went wrong both Nora and Maisie would be humiliated. But if it went well no one would ever dare to snub Nora again.

Maisie gave a small dinner for twenty-four people earlier in the evening, before the ball. The prince could not come to the dinner. Hugh and Nora were there, and Nora looked quite bewitching in a gauzy sky-blue gown covered with little satin bows. The off-the-shoulder style made the most of her pink skin and voluptuous figure.

The other guests were surprised to see her at the table, but assumed Maisie knew what she was doing. She hoped they were right. She understood how the prince's mind worked, and she was fairly sure she could predict his reactions; but now and again he defied expectations and turned on his friends, particularly if he felt he was being used. If that happened Maisie would end up like Nora, cold-shouldered by London society. When she thought about it she was amazed that she had allowed herself to take that risk merely for the sake of Nora. But it was not for Nora, it was for Hugh.

Hugh was working out his notice at Pilasters Bank. It was now two months since he had resigned. Solly was impatient for Hugh to start at Greenbournes, but the Pilasters partners had insisted he stay the full three months. No doubt they wanted to postpone as long as possible the moment when Hugh went to work for their rivals.

After dinner Maisie talked briefly to Nora as the ladies used the bathroom. "Stay as close to me as you can," she said. "When the moment comes for me to present you to the prince, I won't be able to go looking for you: you'll have to be right there."

"I'll stick to you like a Scotchman to a five-pound note," Nora said in her cockney accent, then she changed to an upper-class drawl and said: "Never fear! I shan't run off!"

The guests began to arrive at ten-thirty. Maisie did not normally invite Augusta Pilaster, but she had this year, wanting Augusta to see Nora's triumph, if triumph it should be. She had half expected Augusta to decline, but she was among the first to arrive. Maisie had also invited Hugh's New York mentor, Sidney Madler, a charming man of about sixty with a white beard. He turned up in a distinctly American version

of evening dress, with a short jacket and a
black tie.

Maisie and Solly stood shaking hands for
an hour, then the prince arrived. They escorted him into the ballroom and presented
Solly's father. Ben Greenbourne bowed
stiffly from the waist, as straight-backed as a
Prussian guardsman. Then Maisie danced
with the prince.

"I've a splendid titbit of gossip for you,
sir," she said as they waltzed. "Although I
hope it won't make you cross."

He held her closer and spoke in her ear.
"How intriguing, Mrs. Greenbourne—do go
on."

"It's about the incident at the duchess of
Tenbigh's ball."

She felt him go stiff. "Ah, yes. Faintly embarrassing, I do confess." He lowered his
voice. "When that girl called de Tokoly a
filthy old reprobate I thought for a minute
she was talking to me!"

Maisie laughed gaily, as if the idea were
absurd, although she knew that quite a lot
of people had made the same assumption.

"But do go on," said the prince. "Was
there more to it than met the eye?"

"It seems so. De Tokoly had been told,

quite falsely, that the young woman was, how shall I put it, open to invitation."

"Open to invitation!" He chuckled fruitily. "I must remember that one."

"And she, for her part, had been warned to slap him instantly if he tried to take liberties."

"So there was almost certain to be a scene. Cunning. Who was behind it all?"

Maisie hesitated momentarily. She had never before used her friendship with the prince to do someone down. But Augusta was wicked enough to deserve it. "Do you know who I mean by Augusta Pilaster?"

"Indeed. Matriarch of the *other* banking family."

"It was she. The girl, Nora, is married to Augusta's nephew, Hugh. Augusta did it to spite Hugh, whom she hates."

"What a snake she must be! But she ought not to cause such scenes when I am present. I rather feel like punishing her."

This was the moment Maisie had been leading up to. "All you would have to do is notice Nora, to show that she is forgiven," she said; and she held her breath for his reply.

"And ignore Augusta, perhaps. Yes, I think I might do that."

The dance ended. Maisie said: "Shall I present Nora to you? She's here tonight."

He looked at her shrewdly. "Did you plan all this, you little minx?"

She had been afraid of this. He was not stupid and he could guess that she had been scheming. It would be better not to deny it. She looked bashful and did her best to blush. "You have found me out. How foolish of me to think I might pull the wool over *your* eagle eyes." She changed her expression and favored him with a direct, candid gaze. "What shall I do for a penance?"

A lascivious smile passed over his face. "Don't tempt me. Come, I forgive you."

Maisie breathed easier: she had got away with it. Now it was up to Nora to charm him.

"Where is this Nora?" he said.

She was hovering close by, as instructed. Maisie caught her eye and she approached instantly. Maisie said: "Your Royal Highness, may I present Mrs. Hugh Pilaster."

Nora curtsied and batted her eyelashes.

The prince eyed her bare shoulders and plump, rosy bosom. "Charming," he said enthusiastically. "Quite charming."

*

Hugh watched in astonishment and delight as Nora chatted happily with the Prince of Wales.

Yesterday she had been a social outcast, living proof that you can't make a silk purse out of a sow's ear. She had lost the bank a big contract and run Hugh's career into a brick wall. Now she was the envy of every woman in the room: her clothes were perfect, her manners were charming and she was flirting with the heir to the throne. And the transformation had been brought about by Maisie.

Hugh glanced at his aunt Augusta, standing near him, with Uncle Joseph by her side. She was staring at Nora and the prince. Augusta was trying to look unconcerned, but Hugh could see she was horrified. How it must gall her, Hugh thought, to know that Maisie, the working-class girl she derided six years ago, is now so much more influential than she is.

With perfect timing, Sidney Madler came over. Looking incredulous, he said to Joseph: "Is *that* the woman you say is hopelessly unsuitable to be a banker's wife?"

Before Joseph could reply, Augusta spoke. In a deceptively mild voice she said: "She did lose the bank a major contract."

Hugh said: "As a matter of fact, she didn't. That loan is going through."

Augusta turned on Joseph. "Count de Tokoly didn't interfere?"

"He seems to have got over his fit of pique rather quickly," Joseph said.

Augusta had to pretend to be pleased. "How fortunate," she said, but her insincerity was transparent.

Madler said: "Financial need generally outweighs social prejudice in the end."

"Yes," said Joseph. "So it does. I think I may have been too hasty in denying Hugh a partnership."

Augusta interrupted in a voice of deadly sweetness. "Joseph, what are you saying?"

"This is business, my dear—men's talk," he said firmly. "You need not concern yourself with it." He turned to Hugh. "We certainly don't want you working for Greenbournes."

Hugh did not know what to say. He knew that Sidney Madler had made a fuss, and that Uncle Samuel had backed him—but it was almost unknown for Uncle Joseph to admit a mistake. And yet, he thought with mounting excitement, why else was Joseph raising the subject? "You know why I'm going to Greenbournes, Uncle," he said.

"They'll never make you a partner, you know," Joseph said. "You have to be Jewish for that."

"I'm well aware of it."

"Given that, wouldn't you rather work for the family?"

Hugh felt let down: after all, Joseph was only trying to talk him into staying on as an employee. "No, I wouldn't rather work for the family," he said indignantly. He saw that his uncle was taken aback by his strength of feeling. He went on: "To be quite honest, I'd prefer to work for the Greenbournes, where I would be free from family intrigues"—he darted a defiant glance at Augusta—"and where my responsibilities and rewards would depend on nothing but my ability as a banker."

Augusta said in a scandalized tone: "You prefer Jews to your own family?"

"Keep out of this," Joseph told her brusquely. "You know why I'm saying all this, Hugh. Mr. Madler feels that we have let him down, and all the partners are worried about your taking our North American business with you when you go."

Hugh tried to steady his nerves. It was time to drive a hard bargain. "I wouldn't come back if you doubled my salary," he said, burning his boats. "There's only one thing you can offer me that would make me change my mind, and that's a partnership."

Joseph sighed. "You're the very devil to negotiate with."

Madler put in: "As every good banker should be."

"Very well," Joseph said at last. "I'm offering you a partnership."

Hugh felt weak. They've backed down, he thought. They've given in. I've won. He could hardly believe it had really happened.

He glanced at Augusta. Her face was a rigid mask of self-control, but she said nothing: she knew she had lost.

"In that case," he said, and he hesitated, savoring the moment. He took a deep breath. "In that case, I accept."

Augusta finally lost her composure. She turned red and her eyes seemed to bulge. "You're going to regret this for the rest of your lives!" she spat. Then she stalked off.

She cut a swath through the crowd in the ballroom as she headed for the door. People stared at her and looked nervous. She realized her rage was showing on her face, and she wished she could hide her feelings, but she was too distraught. All the people she loathed and despised had triumphed. The guttersnipe Maisie, the underbred Hugh and the appalling Nora had thwarted her and got what they wanted. Her stomach was twisted in knots of frustration and she felt nauseated.

At last she reached the door and passed out onto the second-floor landing, where the crowd was thinner. She buttonholed a passing footman. "Call Mrs. Pilaster's carriage instantly!" she commanded. He went off at a run. At least she could still intimidate footmen.

She left the party without speaking to anyone else. Her husband could go home in a hansom. She fumed all the way to Kensington.

When she got to the house her butler Hastead was waiting in the hall. "Mr. Hobbes is in the drawing room, ma'am," he said sleepily. "I told him you might not be back until dawn, but he insisted on waiting."

"What the dickens does he want?"

"He didn't say."

Augusta was in no mood to see the editor of *The Forum*. What was he doing here in the early hours of the morning? She was tempted to ignore him and go straight to her room, but then she thought of the peerage and decided she had better talk to him.

She went into the drawing room. Hobbes was asleep by the dying fire. "Good morning!" Augusta said loudly.

He started and sprang to his feet, peering at her through his smeared spectacles. "Mrs. Pilaster! Good—ah, yes, morning."

"What brings you here so late?"

"I thought you would like to be the first to see this," he said, and he handed her a journal.

It was the new number of *The Forum,* still smelling of the printing press. She opened it to the title page and read the headline over the leading article:

CAN A JEW BE A LORD?

Her spirits lifted. Tonight's fiasco was only one defeat, she reminded herself. There were other battles to be fought.

She read the first few lines:

> *We trust there is no truth in the rumours, currently circulating at Westminster and in the London clubs, that the Prime Minister is contemplating the grant*

of a peerage to a prominent banker of the Jewish race and faith.

We have never favoured per-secution of heathen religions. However, tolerance can go too far. To give the highest acco-lade to one who openly rejects Christian salvation would be perilously close to blasphemy.

Of course, the Prime Minis-ter himself is a Jew by race. But he has been converted, and took his oath of allegiance to Her Majesty on the Christian Bible. No constitutional ques-tion was therefore raised by his ennoblement. But we have to ask whether the unbaptised banker of whom rumour speaks would be prepared so far to compromise his faith as to swear on the combined Old and New Testaments. If he were to insist on the Old Testament alone, how could the bishops in the House of Lords stand by without protest?

We have no doubt that the

*man himself is a loyal citizen
and an honest man of business. . . .*

There was much more of the same. Augusta was pleased. She looked up from the page. "Well done," she said. "That should cause a stir."

"I hope so." With a quick, birdlike gesture, Hobbes reached inside his jacket and pulled out a sheet of paper. "I have taken the liberty of contracting to buy the printing press I mentioned to you. The bill of sale—"

"Go to the bank in the morning," Augusta snapped, ignoring the proffered paper. Somehow she could never bring herself to be civil to Hobbes for long, even when he had served her well. Something about his manner irritated her. She made an effort to be more pleasant. In a softer voice she said: "My husband will give you a cheque."

Hobbes bowed. "In that case I will take my leave." He went out.

Augusta breathed a sigh of satisfaction. This would show them all. Maisie Greenbourne thought she was the leader of London society. Well, she could dance with the Prince of Wales all night long, but she couldn't fight the power of the press. It would take the Greenbournes a long time to recover from this onslaught. And meanwhile Joseph would have his peerage.

Feeling better, she sat down to read the article again.

3

ON THE MORNING AFTER THE BALL Hugh woke up feeling jubilant. His wife had been accepted into high society and he was going to be made a partner in Pilasters Bank. The partnership gave him the chance to make not just thousands of pounds but, over the years, hundreds of thousands. One day he would be rich.

Solly would be disappointed that Hugh would not be working for him after all. But Solly was nothing if not easygoing: he would understand.

He put on his robe. From his bedside drawer he took a gift-wrapped jeweler's box and slipped it into his pocket. Then he went into his wife's bedroom.

Nora's room was large but it always felt cramped. The windows, the mirrors and the bed were all draped with patterned silk; the floor was covered with rugs two and three deep; the chairs were piled with embroidered cushions; and every shelf and tabletop was crowded with framed pictures, china dolls, miniature porcelain boxes and other knickknacks. The predominant colors were her favorite pink and blue, but just about every other color was represented some- where, in the wallpapers, bedclothes, cur- tains or upholstery.

Nora was sitting up in bed, surrounded by lace pillows, sipping tea. Hugh perched on the edge of the bed and said: "You were wonderful last night."

"I showed them all," she said, looking pleased with herself. "I danced with the Prince of Wales."

"He couldn't stop looking at your bo- som," Hugh said. He reached over and ca- ressed her breasts through the silk of her high-buttoned nightdress.

She pushed his hand aside irritably. "Hugh! Not now."

He felt hurt. "Why not now?"

"It's the second time this week."

"When we were first married we used to do it constantly."

"Exactly—when we were first married. A girl doesn't expect to have to do it every day forever."

Hugh frowned. He would have been per-

fectly happy to do it every day forever—
wasn't that what marriage was all about?
But he did not know what was normal. Perhaps he was overactive. "How often do you
think we should do it, then?" he said uncer-
tainly.

She looked pleased to have been asked,
as if she had been waiting for an opportunity to clear this up. "Not more than once a
week," she said firmly.

"Really?" His feeling of exultation went
away and he suddenly felt very cast down. A
week seemed an awfully long time. He
stroked her thigh through the sheets. "Perhaps a little more than that."

"No!" she said, moving her leg.

Hugh was upset. Once upon a time she
had seemed enthusiastic about lovemaking.
It had been something they enjoyed together. How had it become a chore she performed for his benefit? Had she never really
liked it, but just pretended? There was
something dreadfully depressing about that
idea.

He no longer felt like giving her his gift,
but he had bought it and he did not want to
take it back to the shop. "Well, anyway, I
got you this, to commemorate your triumph

at Maisie Greenbourne's ball," he said rather dolefully, and he gave her the box.

Her manner changed instantly. "Oh, Hugh, you know how I love presents!" she said. She tore off the ribbon and opened the box. It contained a pendant in the shape of a spray of flowers, made of rubies and sapphires on gold stems. The pendant hung from a fine gold chain. "It's beautiful," she said.

"Put it on, then."

She put it over her head.

The pendant did not show to best advantage against the front of her nightdress. "It will look better with a low-cut evening gown," Hugh said.

Nora gave him a coquettish look and began to unbutton her nightdress. Hugh watched hungrily as she exposed more and more of her chest. The pendant hung in the swelling of her cleavage like a drop of rain on a rosebud. She smiled at Hugh and carried on undoing buttons, then she pulled the nightdress open, showing him her bare breasts. "Do you want to kiss them?" she said.

Now he did not know what to think. Was she toying with him or did she want to make love? He leaned over and kissed her breasts with the jewelry nestling between them. He took her nipple into his mouth and sucked it gently.

"Come to bed," she said.

"I thought you said—"

"Well . . . a girl has to show she's grateful, doesn't she?" She drew back the covers.

Hugh felt sick. It was the jewelry that had changed her mind. All the same he could not resist the invitation. He shrugged out of his dressing gown, hating himself for being so weak, and climbed in beside her.

When he came, he felt like crying.

With his morning mail there was a letter from Tonio Silva.

Tonio had vanished shortly after Hugh met him in the coffeehouse. No article had appeared in *The Times*. Hugh had looked rather foolish, having made such a fuss about the danger to the bank. Edward had taken every opportunity to remind the partners of Hugh's false alarm. However, the incident had been eclipsed by the drama of Hugh's threatened move to Greenbournes.

Hugh had written to the Hotel Russe but got no reply. He had been worried about his friend, but there was no more he could do.

He opened the letter anxiously. It came

from a hospital, asking Hugh to visit. The letter finished: "Whatever you do, *tell no one where I am.*"

What had happened? Tonio had been in perfect health two months ago. And why was he in a public hospital? Hugh was dismayed. Only the poor went to hospitals, which were grim, unsanitary places: anyone who could afford it had doctors and nurses come to the house, even for operations.

Mystified and concerned, Hugh went straight to the hospital. He found Tonio in a dark, bare ward of thirty close-packed beds. His ginger hair had been shaved and his face and head were scarred. "Dear God!" Hugh said. "Have you been run over?"

"Beaten up," said Tonio.

"What happened?"

"I was attacked in the street outside the Hotel Russe a couple of months ago."

"You were robbed, I suppose."

"Yes."

"You're a mess!"

"It's not quite as bad as it looks. I had a broken finger and a cracked ankle, but otherwise it was only cuts and bruises—although rather a lot of them. However, I'm almost better now."

"You should have contacted me before.

We must get you out of here. I'll send my doctor to you, and arrange a nurse—"

"No, thanks, old boy. I appreciate your generosity. But money isn't the only reason I stayed here. It's also safer. Other than you, only one person knows where I am: a trusted colleague who brings me beefsteak pies and brandy and messages from Cordova. I hope you didn't tell anyone you were coming."

"Not even my wife," Hugh said.

"Good."

Tonio's old recklessness seemed to have vanished, Hugh thought; in fact he was going to the other extreme. "But you can't stay in hospital for the rest of your life to hide from street ruffians."

"The people who attacked me were not just thieves, Pilaster."

Hugh took off his hat and sat on the edge of the bed. He tried to ignore the intermittent groaning of the man in the next bed. "Tell me what happened," he said.

"It wasn't a routine theft. My key was taken and the thieves used it to get into my room. Nothing of value was stolen but all the papers pertaining to my article for *The Times* were taken, including the affidavits signed by the witnesses."

Hugh was horrified. It chilled his heart to think that the immaculately respectable transactions taking place in the hushed halls of Pilasters should have any link with violent crime in the streets and the battered face in front of him. "It almost sounds as if the bank is under suspicion!"

"Not the bank," Tonio said. "Pilasters is a powerful institution, but I don't believe it could organize murders in Cordova."

"Murders?" This was getting worse and worse. "Who has been murdered?"

"All the witnesses whose names and addresses were on the affidavits that were stolen from my hotel room."

"I can hardly believe it."

"I'm lucky to be alive myself. They would have killed me, I think, were it not that murders are investigated more thoroughly here in London than they are back at home, and they were afraid of the fuss."

Hugh was still dazed and disgusted by the revelation that people had been murdered because of a bond issue by Pilasters Bank. "But who is behind all this?"

"Micky Miranda."

Hugh shook his head incredulously. "I'm not fond of Micky, as you know, but I can't believe he would do this."

"The Santamaria railroad is vital to him. It will make his family the second most powerful in the land."

"I realize that, and I don't doubt that Micky would bend a lot of rules to achieve his aims. But he's not a killer."

"Yes, he is," Tonio said.

"Come on."

"I know it for sure. I haven't always acted as if I knew—in fact I've been a damn fool about Miranda. But that's because he has a devilish charm. For a while he made me think he was my friend. The truth is that he's evil through and through and I've known it since school."

"How could you?"

Tonio shifted in the bed. "I know what really happened thirteen years ago, the afternoon Peter Middleton drowned in the swimming hole at Bishop's Wood."

Hugh was electrified. He had been wondering about this for years. Peter Middleton had been a strong swimmer: it was most unlikely that he had died by accident. Hugh had long been convinced that there had been some kind of foul play. Perhaps at last he was going to learn the truth. "Go on, man," he said. "I can't wait to hear this."

Tonio hesitated. "Could you give me a little wine?" he said. There was a bottle of Madeira on the floor beside the bed. Hugh poured some into a glass. While Tonio sipped it, Hugh recalled the heat of that day, the stillness of the air in Bishop's Wood, the scarred rock walls of the swimming hole, and the cold, cold water.

"The coroner was told that Peter was in difficulty in the pool. He was never told that Edward was ducking him repeatedly."

"I knew that much," Hugh interrupted. "I had a letter from Hump Cammel in the Cape Colony. He was watching from the far side of the pool. But he didn't stay to see the end."

"That's right. You escaped and Hump ran away. That left me, Peter, Edward and Micky."

"What happened after I left?" Hugh said impatiently.

"I got out and threw a stone at Edward. It was a lucky shot: it hit him square in the middle of the forehead, and drew blood. It caused him to leave off tormenting Peter and come after me. I scrambled up the side of the quarry, trying to get away from him."

"Edward was never light on his feet, even then," Hugh observed.

"That's right. I got well ahead of him,

then halfway up I looked back. Micky was continuing to bully Peter. Peter had swum to the side and was trying to get out of the water, but Micky kept pushing his head under. I only glanced at them for a moment, but I could see very clearly what was going on. Then I continued to climb."

He took another sip of the wine. "When I got to the rim of the quarry I looked back again. Edward was still coming after me but he was a long way behind and I had time to catch my breath." Tonio paused, and an expression of revulsion crossed his scarred face. "By this time Micky was in the water with Peter. What I saw—perfectly clearly, and I can see it in my memory now as if it were yesterday—was Micky holding Peter under the water. Peter was thrashing about, but Micky had Peter's head under his arm and Peter couldn't break the hold. Micky was drowning him. There is absolutely no doubt about it. It was straightforward murder."

"Dear God," Hugh breathed.

Tonio nodded. "It makes me feel ill to think of it even now. I stared at them for I don't know how long. Edward almost caught me. Peter had stopped thrashing about, and was just struggling feebly, when Edward reached the rim of the quarry and I had to run away."

"So that's how Peter died." Hugh was stunned and horrified.

"Edward followed me through the woods a little way, but he was puffed out and I shook him off. Then I found you."

Hugh remembered the thirteen-year-old Tonio wandering through Bishop's Wood, naked, wet, carrying his clothes and sobbing. The memory brought back the shock and pain he had suffered later that same day, when he learned that his father was dead. "But why did you never tell anyone what you had seen?"

"I was afraid of Micky—afraid he'd do to me what he did to Peter. I'm still afraid of Micky—look at me now! You should be afraid of him too."

"I am, don't worry." Hugh was thoughtful. "You know, I don't believe Edward and his mother know the truth about this."

"What makes you say so?"

"They had no reason to cover up for Micky."

Tonio looked dubious. "Edward might have, out of friendship."

"Perhaps—although I doubt he could have kept the secret more than a day or two.

Anyway, Augusta knew that the story they told, about Edward trying to rescue Peter, was a lie."

"How did she know that?"

"My mother told her, and I told my mother. Which means that Augusta was involved in covering up the truth. Now, I can believe that Augusta would tell any amount of lies for the sake of her son—but not for Micky. In those days she didn't even know him."

"So what do you think happened?"

Hugh frowned. "Imagine this. Edward gives up chasing you and goes back to the swimming hole. He finds Micky dragging Peter's body out of the water. As Edward arrives, Micky says: 'You fool, you've killed him!' Remember, Edward hasn't seen Micky holding Peter's head under. Micky pretends that Peter was so exhausted by Edward's ducking that he could swim no longer and he just drowned. 'What am I going to do?' says Edward. Micky says: 'Don't worry. We'll say it was an accident. In fact, we'll say you jumped in and tried to rescue him.' Micky thereby covers up his own crime and earns the undying gratitude of both Edward and Augusta. Does that make sense?"

Tonio nodded. "By God, I think you're right."

"We must go to the police," Hugh said angrily.

"To what purpose?"

"You're witness to a murder. The fact that it happened thirteen years ago makes no difference. Micky must be brought to book."

"You're forgetting something. Micky has diplomatic immunity."

Hugh had not thought of that. As the Cordovan Minister, Micky could not be put on trial in Britain. "He could still be disgraced and sent home."

Tonio shook his head. "I'm the only witness. Micky and Edward will both tell a different story. And it's well known that Micky's family and mine are sworn enemies back home. If it had happened yesterday we'd have trouble convincing anyone." Tonio paused. "But you might want to tell Edward that he's not a murderer."

"I don't think he'd believe me. He'd suspect me of trying to stir up trouble between him and Micky. There is one person I must tell, though."

"Who?"

"David Middleton."

"Why?"

"I think he's entitled to know how his brother died," Hugh said. "He questioned me about it at the duchess of Tenbigh's ball. He was rather rude, in fact. But I said that if I knew the truth I would be honor-bound to tell him. I'll go and see him today."

"Do you think he'll go to the police?"

"I assume he'll see that it would be pointless, as you and I have realized." Suddenly he felt oppressed by the drab hospital ward and the grim talk of past murder. "I'd better go to work." He stood up. "I'm going to be made a partner in the bank."

"Congratulations! I'm sure you deserve it." Tonio suddenly looked hopeful. "Will you be able to stop the Santamaria railroad?"

Hugh shook his head. "I'm sorry, Tonio. Much as I dislike the project, I can't do anything about it now. Edward has made a deal with Greenbournes Bank to float the bonds jointly. The partners of both banks have approved the issue and contracts are being drawn up. I'm afraid we've lost that battle."

"Damn." Tonio was crestfallen.

"Your family will have to find other ways to oppose the Mirandas."

"I fear they may be unstoppable."

"I'm sorry," Hugh repeated. A new thought struck him and he frowned in puzzlement. "You know, you've solved a mystery for me. I couldn't understand how Peter drowned when he was such a good swimmer. But your answer is an even greater mystery."

"I'm not sure I follow you."

"Think about it. Peter was innocently swimming; Edward ducked him, just out of general nastiness; we all ran away; Edward gave chase—and then Micky cold-bloodedly killed Peter. *It has nothing to do with what went before.* Why did it happen? What had Peter done?"

"I see what you mean. Yes, it's puzzled me for years."

"Micky Miranda murdered Peter Middleton . . . but why?"

CHAPTER FIVE

1

AUGUSTA WAS LIKE A HEN that had laid an egg on the day Joseph's peerage was announced. Micky went to the house at teatime as usual and found the drawing room crowded with people congratulating her on becoming Countess Whitehaven. Her butler Hastead was wearing a smug smile and saying "my lady" and "your ladyship" at every opportunity.

She was amazing, Micky thought as he watched everyone buzzing around her like the bees in the sunny garden outside the open windows. She had planned her campaign like a general. At one point there had been a rumor that Ben Greenbourne was to get the peerage, but that had been killed by an eruption of anti-Jewish sentiment in the press. Augusta was not admitting, even to Micky, that she had been behind the press coverage, but he was sure of it. In some ways she reminded him of his father: Papa had the same remorseless determination. But Augusta was cleverer. Micky's admiration for her had grown as the years went by.

The only person who had ever defeated her ingenuity was Hugh Pilaster. It was astonishing how difficult he was to crush. Like a persistent garden weed, he could be stamped on time and time again and he would always grow back straighter and stronger than ever.

Happily, Hugh had been unable to stop the Santamaria railroad. Micky and Edward had proved too strong for Hugh and Tonio. "By the way," Micky said to Edward over the teacups, "when are you going to sign the contract with Greenbournes?"

"Tomorrow."

"Good!" Micky would be relieved when the deal was finally sewn up. It had dragged on for half a year, and Papa was now sending angry cables twice a week asking irascibly if he would ever get the money.

That evening Edward and Micky dined at the Cowes Club. Throughout the meal Edward was interrupted every few minutes by people congratulating him. One day he would inherit the title, of course. Micky was pleased. His association with Edward and the Pilasters had been a key factor in everything he had achieved, and greater prestige for the Pilasters would mean more power for Micky.

After dinner they moved to the smoking room. They were among the earliest diners and for a while they had the room to themselves. "I have come to the conclusion that Englishmen are terrified of their wives," said Micky as they lit their cigars. "It is the only possible explanation for the phenomenon of the London club."

"What the devil are you talking about?" said Edward.

"Look around you," Micky said. "This place is exactly like your home, or mine. Expensive furniture, servants everywhere, boring food and unlimited drink. We can eat all our meals here, get our mail, read the newspapers, take a nap, and if we get too drunk to fall into a cab we can even get a bed for the night. The only difference between an Englishman's club and his home is that there are no women in his club."

"Don't you have clubs in Cordova, then?"

"Certainly not. No one would join. If a Cordovan man wants to get drunk, play cards, hear political gossip, talk about his whores, smoke and belch and fart in comfort he does it in his own home; and if his wife is foolish enough to object he slaps her until she sees reason. But an English gentleman is so frightened of his wife that he has to leave the house to enjoy himself. That's why there are clubs."

"You don't seem to be frightened of Rachel. You've got rid of her, haven't you?"

"Sent her back to her mother," Micky said airily. It had not happened quite that way but he was not going to tell Edward the truth.

"People must notice that she doesn't appear at ministry functions anymore. Don't they comment?"

"I tell them she's in poor health."

"But everyone knows she's trying to start a hospital for unmarried women to have babies. It's a public scandal."

"It doesn't matter. People sympathize with me for having a difficult wife."

"Will you divorce her?"

"No. That would be a real scandal. A diplomat can't be divorced. I'm stuck with her as long as I'm the Cordovan Minister, I'm afraid. Thank God she didn't get pregnant before she left." It was a miracle she hadn't, he thought. Perhaps she was infertile. He waved at a waiter and ordered brandy. "Speaking of wives," he said tentatively, "what about Emily?"

Edward looked embarrassed. "I see as little of her as you see of Rachel," he said. "You know I bought a country house in Leicestershire a while ago—she spends all her time there."

"So, we're both bachelors again."

Edward grinned. "We were never anything else, really, were we?"

Micky glanced across the empty room and saw the bulky form of Solly Greenbourne in the doorway. For some reason the sight of him made Micky feel nervous—which was odd, because Solly was the most harmless man in London. "Here comes another friend to congratulate you," Micky said to Edward as Solly approached.

When Solly was closer Micky realized he was not wearing his usual amiable smile. In fact he looked positively angry. That was rare. Micky felt intuitively that there was some problem with the Santamaria railroad deal. He told himself that he was worrying like an old woman. But Solly was never angry. . . .

Anxiety made Micky fatuously amicable. "Hello, Solly, old boy—how's the genius of the Square Mile?"

Solly was not interested in Micky, however. Without even acknowledging the greeting, he rudely turned his vast back on Micky and faced Edward. "Pilaster, you're a damned cad," he said.

Micky was astonished and horrified. Solly and Edward were on the point of signing the deal. This was very grave—Solly never quarreled with people. What on earth had brought it about?

Edward was equally mystified. "What the devil are you talking about, Greenbourne?"

Solly reddened and he could hardly speak. "I've discovered that you and that witch you call Mother are behind those filthy articles in *The Forum.*"

"Oh, no!" Micky said to himself in dismay. This was a catastrophe. He had suspected Augusta's involvement, although he had no evidence—but how on earth had Solly found out?

The same question occurred to Edward. "Who's been filling your fat head with such rot?"

"One of your mother's cronies is a lady-in-waiting to the queen," Solly replied. Micky guessed he was speaking of Harriet Morte: Augusta seemed to have some kind of hold over her. Solly went on: "She let the cat out of the bag—she told the Prince of Wales. I've just been with him."

Solly must be practically insane with anger to speak so indiscreetly about a private conversation with royalty, Micky thought. It was a case of a gentle soul being pushed too far. He could not see how a quarrel such as this could possibly be patched up—certainly not in time for the signing of the contract tomorrow.

He tried desperately to cool the temperature. "Solly, old man, you can't be sure this story is true—"

Solly rounded on him. His eyes were bulging and he was perspiring. "Can't I? When I read in today's newspaper that Joseph Pilaster has got the peerage that was expected to go to Ben Greenbourne?"

"All the same—"

"Can you imagine what this means to my father?"

Micky began to understand how the armor of Solly's amiability had been breached. It was not for himself that he was angry, but for his father. Ben Greenbourne's grandfather had arrived in London with a bale of Russian furs, a five-pound note and a hole in his boot. For Ben to take a seat in the House of Lords would be the ultimate badge of acceptance into English society. No doubt Joseph too would like to crown his career with a peerage—his family had also risen by their own efforts—but it would be much more of an achievement for a Jew. Greenbourne's peerage would have been a triumph not just for himself and his family but for the entire Jewish community in Britain.

Edward said: "I can't help it if you're a Jew."

Micky butted in quickly. "You two shouldn't let your parents come between you. After all, you're partners in a major business enterprise—"

"Don't be a damn fool, Miranda," Solly said with a savagery that made Micky flinch. "You can forget about the Santamaria railroad, or any other joint venture with Greenbournes Bank. After our partners hear this story, they'll never do business with the Pilasters again."

*

Micky tasted bile in his throat as he watched Solly leave the room. It was easy to forget how very powerful these bankers were—especially the unprepossessing Solly. Yet in a moment of fury he could wipe out all Micky's hopes with one simple sentence.

"Damned insolence," Edward said feebly. "Typical Jew."

Micky almost told him to shut up. Edward would survive the collapse of this deal but Micky might not. Papa would be disappointed and angry and would look for someone to punish, and Micky would bear the brunt of his rage.

Was there really no hope? He tried to stop feeling destroyed and start thinking. Was there anything he could do to prevent Solly canceling the deal? If there were, it would have to be done quickly, for once Solly told the other Greenbournes what he had learned, they would all turn against the deal.

Could Solly be talked around?

Micky had to try.

He stood up abruptly.

"Where are you going?" Edward said.

Micky decided not to tell Edward what he had in mind. "To the card room," he replied. "Don't you want to play?"

"Yes, of course." Edward heaved himself out of his chair and they walked out of the room.

At the foot of the stairs Micky turned aside toward the toilets, saying: "You go on up—I'll catch you."

Edward went upstairs. Micky stepped into the cloakroom, grabbed his hat and cane, and dashed out through the front door.

He looked up and down Pall Mall, terrified that Solly might already be out of sight. It was dusk, and the gaslights were being lit. Micky could not see Solly anywhere. Then, a hundred yards away, he spotted him, a big figure in evening dress and a top hat heading toward St. James's at a brisk waddle.

Micky went after him.

He would explain to Solly how important the railroad was to him and to Cordova. He would say that Solly was punishing millions of impoverished peasants on account of something Augusta had done. Solly was softhearted: if only he would calm down he might yet be talked around.

He had said he had just been with the Prince of Wales. That meant he might not yet have had time to tell anyone else the secret he had learned from the prince—that Augusta had arranged the anti-Jewish propaganda in the press. No one had overheard the row in the club: the smoking room had been empty but for the three of them. In all probability Ben Greenbourne did not yet know who had cheated him out of his peerage.

Of course the truth might come out eventually. The Prince might tell someone else. But the contract was to be signed tomorrow. If the secret could be kept until then, all would be well. After that, the Greenbournes and the Pilasters could quarrel until kingdom come: Papa would have his railroad.

Pall Mall was crowded with prostitutes strolling along the pavements, men going in and out of the clubs, lamplighters doing their work, and carriages and hansom cabs bowling along the road. Micky had trouble catching up. Panic bubbled up inside him. Then Solly turned up a side street, heading toward his house in Piccadilly.

Micky followed. The side street was less busy. Micky broke into a run. "Greenbourne!" he called. "Wait!"

Solly stopped and turned, breathing hard. He recognized Micky and turned away again.

Micky grabbed his arm. "I must talk to you!"

Solly was so breathless he could hardly speak. "Take your damned hands off me," he panted. He broke away from Micky and walked on.

Micky went after him and grabbed him again. Solly tried to pull his arm away but this time Micky held on. "Listen to me!"

"I told you to leave me alone!" Solly said fiercely.

"Just a minute, damn it!" Micky was getting angry now.

But Solly would not listen. He struggled furiously, jerked himself violently out of Micky's grasp, and turned away.

Two steps later he came to a cross-street and was forced to stop at the curb as a carriage went by fast. Micky took the opportunity to speak to him again. "Solly, calm down!" he said. "I only want to reason with you!"

"Go to the devil!" Solly shouted.

The road cleared. To stop his moving away again Micky grabbed Solly's lapels. Solly struggled to free himself but Micky held on. "Listen to me!" he yelled.

"Let me go!" Solly got one hand free and punched Micky on the nose.

The blow stung and Micky tasted blood. He lost his temper. "Damn you!" he cried.

He let go of Solly's coat and punched him back, hitting him on the cheek.

Solly turned and stepped into the road. At that moment they both saw a carriage coming toward them, being driven very fast. Solly jumped back to avoid being hit.

Micky saw a chance.

If Solly were dead, Micky's troubles would be over.

There was no time to reckon the odds, no room for hesitation and forethought.

Micky gave Solly a mighty shove, pushing him into the road in front of the horses.

The coachman yelled and hauled on the reins. Solly stumbled, saw the horses almost on top of him, fell to the ground and screamed.

For a frozen moment Micky saw the charging horses, the heavy carriage wheels, the terrified coachman and the huge help-less form of Solly, flat on his back in the road.

Then the horses charged over Solly. Micky saw the fat body twist and writhe as the ironclad hooves pounded it. Then the front nearside wheel of the carriage struck Solly's head a mighty blow, and he slumped unconscious. A split second later the rear wheel ran over his face and crushed his skull like an eggshell.

Micky turned away. He thought he was going to vomit but he managed to control the urge. Then he began to shake. He felt weak and faint, and he had to lean on the wall.

He forced himself to look at the motionless body in the road. Solly's head was smashed, his face unrecognizable, blood and something else smeared over the road beside him. He was dead.

And Micky was saved.

Now Ben Greenbourne need never know what Augusta had done to him; the deal could go ahead; the railroad would be built; and Micky would be a hero in Cordova.

He felt a warm trickle on his lip. His nose was bleeding. He pulled out a handkerchief and dabbed at it.

He stared a moment longer at Solly. You only lost your temper once in your life, and it killed you, he thought.

He looked up and down the street in the gaslight. There was no one around. Only the coachman had seen what happened.

The carriage juddered to a halt thirty yards down the road. The coachman leaped down and a woman looked out of the window. Micky turned and walked quickly away, heading back toward Pall Mall.

A few seconds later he heard the coachman call after him: "Hey! You!"

He walked faster and turned the corner into Pall Mall without looking back. A moment later he was lost in the crowd.

By God, I did it, he thought. Now that he could no longer see the mangled body, the sense of disgust was passing, and he began to feel triumphant. Quick thinking and bold action had enabled him to overcome yet another obstacle.

He hurried up the steps of the club. With luck nobody would have noticed his absence, he hoped; but as he passed through the front door he had the bad fortune to bump into Hugh Pilaster going out.

Hugh nodded to him and said: "Evening, Miranda."

"Evening, Pilaster," said Micky; and he went in, cursing Hugh under his breath.

He went to the cloakroom. His nose was red from Solly's punch but otherwise he just appeared a little rumpled. He straightened his clothing and brushed his hair. As he did so he thought about Hugh Pilaster. If Hugh had not been right there on the doorstep at the wrong moment, nobody would have known Micky had even left the club—he had been gone for only a few minutes. But did it really matter? No one was going to suspect Micky of killing Solly, and if they did, the fact that he had left his club for a few minutes would not prove anything. Still, he no longer had a watertight alibi, and that worried him.

He washed his hands thoroughly and hurried up the stairs to the card room.

Edward was already playing baccarat and there was an empty seat at the table. Micky sat down. No one commented on the length of time he had been away.

He was dealt a hand. "You look a bit seasick," said Edward.

"Yes," he said calmly. "I think the fish soup may not have been perfectly fresh tonight."

Edward waved at a waiter. "Bring this man a glass of brandy."

Micky looked at his cards. He had a nine and a ten, the perfect hand. He bet a sovereign.

He just could not lose today.

2

HUGH WENT TO SEE MAISIE two days after Solly died.

He found her alone, sitting quiet and still on a sofa, neatly dressed in a black gown, looking small and insignificant in the splendor of the drawing room at the palatial Piccadilly house. Her face was lined with grief and she looked as if she had not slept. His heart ached for her.

She threw herself into his arms and said: "Oh, Hugh, he was the best of us!"

When she said that, Hugh himself could not keep the tears back. Until this moment he had been too stunned to cry. It was a dreadful fate to die as Solly had, and he deserved it less than any man Hugh could name. "There was no malice in him," he said. "He seemed incapable of it. I knew him for fifteen years and I can't remember a single time when he was unkind to someone."

"Why do such things happen?" Maisie said miserably.

Hugh hesitated. Just a few days ago he had learned, from Tonio Silva, that Micky Miranda had killed Peter Middleton all those years ago. Because of that, Hugh could not help wondering whether Micky had had something to do with the death of Solly. The police were looking for a well-dressed man who had been arguing with Solly just before he was run over. Hugh had seen Micky entering the Cowes Club at around the time Solly died, so he had certainly been in the neighborhood.

But there was no motive: quite the reverse. Solly had been on the point of closing the Santamaria railroad deal that was so close to Micky's heart. Why would he kill his benefactor? Hugh decided to say nothing to Maisie about his unfounded suspicions. "It seems to have been a tragic accident," he said.

"The coachman thinks Solly was pushed. Why would the witness run away if he wasn't guilty?"

"He may have been attempting to rob Solly. That's what the newspapers are saying, anyway." The papers were full of the story. It was a sensational case: the grisly death of a prominent banker, one of the richest men in the world.

"Do thieves wear evening dress?"

"It was almost dark. The coachman may have been mistaken about the man's clothing."

Maisie detached herself from Hugh and sat down again. "And if you had only waited a little longer you could have married me instead of Nora," she said.

Hugh was startled by her frankness. The same thought had come to him within seconds of hearing the news—but he was ashamed of it. It was typical of Maisie to come right out and say what they were both thinking. He was not sure how to respond, so he made a foolish joke. "If a Pilaster married a Greenbourne, it would be not so much a wedding as a merger."

She shook her head. "I'm not a Greenbourne. Solly's family never really accepted me."

"You must have inherited a big chunk of the bank, though."

"I've inherited nothing, Hugh."

"But that's impossible!"

"It's true. Solly had no money of his own. His father gave him a huge monthly allowance, but he never settled any capital on him, because of me. Even this house is rented. I own my clothes, furniture and jewelry, so I'll never starve. But I'm not the heir to the bank—and neither is little Bertie."

Hugh was astonished—and angry that

anyone should be so mean to Maisie. "The old man won't even provide for your son?"

"Not a penny. I saw my father-in-law this morning."

It was a shabby way to treat her, and Hugh as her friend felt personally affronted. "It's disgraceful," he said.

"Not really," Maisie said. "I gave Solly five years of happiness, and in return I had five years of the high life. I can go back to normal. I'll sell my jewelry, invest the money and live quietly on the income."

It was hard to take in. "Will you go and live with your parents?"

"In Manchester? No, I don't think I can go quite that far back. I'll stay in London. Rachel Bodwin is opening a hospital for unmarried mothers: I might work with her."

"There's a lot of fuss about Rachel's hospital. People think it's scandalous."

"Then it should suit me very well!"

Hugh was still hurt and worried by Ben Greenbourne's ill-treatment of his daughter-in-law. He decided he would have a word with Greenbourne and try to change the man's mind. He would not mention it to Maisie beforehand, though. He did not want to raise her hopes and then disappoint them. "Don't make any sudden decisions, will you?" he counseled.

"Such as?"

"Don't move out of the house, for example. Greenbourne might try to confiscate your furniture."

"I won't."

"And you need a lawyer of your own, to represent your interests."

She shook her head. "I no longer belong to the class of people who call in a lawyer the way they summon a footman. I have to count the cost. I shan't see a lawyer unless I feel sure I'm being cheated. And I don't think that will happen. Ben Greenbourne isn't dishonest. He's just hard: as hard as iron, and as cold. It's amazing that he fathered someone as warmhearted as Solly."

"You're very philosophical," Hugh said. He admired her courage.

Maisie shrugged. "I've had an amazing life, Hugh. I was destitute at eleven and fabulously wealthy at nineteen." She touched a ring on her finger. "This diamond is probably worth more money than my mother has ever seen. I gave the best parties in London; I met everyone who was anyone; I danced with the Prince of Wales. I've no regrets. Except that you married Nora."

"I'm very fond of her," he said unconvincingly.

"You were angry because I wouldn't have an affair with you," Maisie said brutally. "You were desperate for sexual release. And you picked Nora because she reminded you of me. But she's not me, and now you're unhappy."

Hugh winced as if he had been struck. All this was painfully near to the truth. "You never liked her," he said.

"And you may say I'm jealous, and you may be right, but I still say she never loved you and she married you for your money. I'll bet you've found that to be true since the wedding, haven't you?"

Hugh thought of how Nora refused to make love more than once a week, and how she changed her tune if he bought her gifts; and he felt miserable and looked away. "She's always been deprived," he said. "It's not surprising that she became materialistic."

"She was not as deprived as I was," Maisie said scornfully. "Even you were taken out of school for want of money, Hugh. It's no excuse for false values. The world is full of poor people who understand that love and friendship are more important than riches."

Her scorn made Hugh defensive. "She's not as bad as you make out."

"All the same you're not happy."

Feeling confused, Hugh fell back on what he knew to be right. "Well, I've married her now, and I won't leave her," he said. "That's what the vows mean."

Maisie smiled tearfully. "I knew you would say that."

Hugh had a sudden vision of Maisie naked, her round freckled breasts and the bush of red-gold hair at her groin, and he wished he could take back his high-principled words. Instead he stood up to go.

Maisie stood up too. "Thank you for coming, dear Hugh," she said.

He intended to shake her hand but instead he bent to kiss her cheek; and then somehow he found himself kissing her lips. It was a soft, tender kiss that lingered for a long moment and almost destroyed Hugh's resolve; but then at last he tore himself away and left the room without another word.

Ben Greenbourne's house was another palace a few yards along Piccadilly. Hugh went straight there after seeing Maisie. He was glad to have something to do, some way of taking his mind off the turmoil in his heart. He asked for the old man. "Say it's a matter of great urgency," he told the butler. While he waited he noticed that the mirrors in the hall were covered, and he guessed this was part of the Jewish mourning ritual.

Maisie had thrown him off balance. When he saw her his heart had filled with love and longing. He knew he could never be truly happy without her. But Nora was his wife. She had brought warmth and affection into his life after Maisie rejected him, and that was why he had married her. What was the point of making promises in a wedding cere-mony if you were going to change your mind later?

The butler showed Hugh into the library. Six or seven people were just going, leaving Ben Greenbourne alone. He had no shoes on and sat on a plain wooden stool. A table was piled with fruit and pastries for visitors.

Greenbourne was past sixty—Solly had been a late child—and he looked old and worn, but he showed no sign of tears. He stood up, straight-backed and formal as ever, and shook hands, then waved Hugh to another stool.

Greenbourne had an old letter in his

hand. "Listen to this," he said, and he began to read. " 'Dear Papa, We have a new Latin teacher, Reverend Green, and I am getting on much better, ten out of ten every day last week. Waterford caught a rat in the broom cupboard and he is trying to train it to eat out of his hand. The food here is too little, can you send me a cake? Your loving son, Solomon.' " He folded the letter. "He was fourteen when he wrote that."

Hugh saw that Greenbourne was suffering despite his rigid self-control. "I remember that rat," he said. "It bit Waterford's forefinger off."

"How I wish I could turn back the years," Greenbourne said, and Hugh saw that the old man's self-control was weakening.

"I must be one of Solly's oldest friends," Hugh said.

"Indeed. He always admired you, although you were younger."

"I can't think why. But he was always ready to think the best of people."

"He was too soft."

Hugh did not want the conversation to go that way. "I've come here not just as Solly's friend, but as Maisie's too."

Greenbourne stiffened immediately. The sad look went from his face and he became the caricature of the upright Prussian again. Hugh wondered how anyone could so hate a woman as beautiful and full of fun as Maisie.

Hugh went on: "I met her soon after Solly did. I fell in love with her myself, but Solly won her."

"He was richer."

"Mr. Greenbourne, I hope you will allow me to be frank. Maisie was a penniless girl looking for a rich husband. But after she married Solly she kept her part of the bargain. She was a good wife to him."

"And she has had her reward," Greenbourne said. "She has enjoyed the life of a lady for five years."

"Funnily enough, that's what she said. But I don't think it's good enough. What about little Bertie? Surely you don't want to leave your grandson destitute?"

"Grandson?" said Greenbourne. "Hubert is no relation to me."

Hugh had an odd premonition that something momentous was about to happen. It was like a nightmare in which a frightening but nameless horror was about to strike. "I don't understand," he said to Greenbourne. "What do you mean?"

"That woman was already with child when she married my son."

Hugh gasped.

"Solly knew it, and he knew the child was not his," Greenbourne went on. "He took her all the same—against my will, I need hardly add. People generally don't know this, of course: we went to great lengths to keep it secret, but there's no need to any longer, now that—" He broke off, swallowed hard, and continued. "They went around the world after the wedding. The child was born in Switzerland; they gave out a false birth date; by the time they came home, having been away for almost two years, it was hard to tell that the baby was actually four months older than they said."

Hugh felt as if his heart had stopped. There was a question he had to ask, but he was terrified of the answer. "Who—who was the father?"

"She would never say," Greenbourne said. "Solly never knew."

But Hugh did.

The child was his.

He stared at Ben Greenbourne, unable to speak.

He would talk to Maisie, and make her tell the truth, but he knew she would confirm his intuition. She had never been promiscuous, despite appearances. She had been a virgin when he seduced her. He had made her pregnant, on that first night. Then Augusta had contrived to split them up, and Maisie had married Solly.

She had even called the baby Hubert, a name closely similar to Hugh.

"It is appalling, of course," Greenbourne said, seeing his consternation and misunderstanding the reason for it.

I have a child, Hugh thought. A son. Hubert. Called Bertie. The thought wrenched at his heart.

"However, I'm sure you now see why I don't wish to have anything more to do with the woman or her child, now that my dear son has passed away."

"Oh, don't worry," Hugh said distractedly. "I'll take care of them."

"You?" Greenbourne said, mystified. "Why should it be any concern of yours?"

"Oh . . . well, I'm all they've got, now, I suppose," Hugh said.

"Don't get sucked in, young Pilaster," Greenbourne said kindly. "You've got a wife of your own to worry about."

Hugh did not want to explain and he was too dazed to make up a story. He had to get away. He stood up. "I must go. My deepest condolences, Mr. Greenbourne. Solly was the best man I ever knew."

Greenbourne bowed his head. Hugh left him.

In the hall with the shrouded mirrors he took his hat from the footman and went out into the sunshine of Piccadilly. He walked west and entered Hyde Park, heading for his home in Kensington. He could have taken a hansom but he wanted time to think.

Everything was different now. Nora was his legal wife but Maisie was the mother of his son. Nora could look after herself—and so could Maisie, for that matter—but a child needed a father. Suddenly the question of what he was to do with the rest of his life was open again.

No doubt a clergyman would say that nothing had changed and he should stay with Nora, the woman he had married in church; but clergymen did not know much. The strict Methodism of the Pilasters had passed Hugh by: he had never been able to believe that the answer to every modern moral dilemma could be found in the Bible. Nora had seduced and married him for cold-hearted gain—Maisie was right about that—and all there was between them was a piece of paper. That was very little, weighed against a child—the child of a love so strong that it had persisted for many years and through many trials.

Am I just making excuses, he wondered? Is all this no more than a specious justification for giving in to a desire I know to be wrong?

He felt torn in two.

He tried to consider the practicalities. He had no grounds for divorce, but he felt sure that Nora would be willing to divorce him, if she were offered enough money. However, the Pilasters would ask him to resign from the bank: the social stigma of divorce was too great to allow him to continue as a partner. He could get another job but no respectable people in London would entertain him and Maisie as a couple even after they married. They would almost certainly have to go abroad. But that prospect attracted him and he felt it would appeal to Maisie too. He could return to Boston or, better still, go to New York. He might never be a millionaire but what was that balanced against the joy of being with the woman he had always loved?

He found himself outside his own house. It was part of an elegant new red-brick terrace in Kensington, half a mile from his aunt Augusta's much more extravagant place at Kensington Gore. Nora would be in her overdecorated bedroom, dressing for lunch. What was to stop him walking in and announcing that he was leaving her?

That was what he wanted to do, he knew that now. But was it right?

It was the child that made the difference. It would be wrong to leave Nora for Maisie; but it was right to leave Nora for the sake of Bertie.

He wondered what Nora would say when he told her, and his imagination gave him the answer. He pictured her face set in lines of hard determination, and he heard the unpleasant edge to her voice, and he could guess the exact words she would use: "It will cost you every penny you've got."

Oddly enough, that decided him. If he had pictured her bursting into tears of sadness he would have been unable to go through with it, but he knew his first intuition was right.

He went into the house and ran up the stairs.

She was in front of the mirror, putting on the pendant he had given her. It was a bitter reminder that he had to buy her jewelry to persuade her to make love.

She spoke before he did. "I've got some news," she said.

"Never mind that now—"

But she would not be put off. She had an odd expression on her face: half triumphant, half sulky. "You'll have to stay out of my bed for a while, anyway."

He saw that he was not going to be allowed to speak until she had had her say. "What on earth are you talking about?" he said impatiently.

"The inevitable has happened."

Suddenly Hugh guessed. He felt as if he had been hit by a train. It was too late: he could never leave her now. He felt revulsion, and the pain of loss: loss of Maisie, loss of his son.

He looked into her eyes. There was defiance there, almost as if she had guessed what he had been planning. Perhaps she had.

He forced himself to smile. "The inevitable?"

Then she said it. "I'm going to have a baby."

PART III

1890

CHAPTER ONE

1

JOSEPH PILASTER DIED in September 1890, having been Senior Partner of Pilasters Bank for seventeen years. During that period Britain had grown steadily richer, and so had the Pilasters. They were now almost as rich as the Greenbournes. Joseph's estate came to more than two million pounds, including his collection of sixty-five antique jeweled snuffboxes—one for each year of his life—which was worth a hundred thousand pounds on its own, and which he left to his son Edward.

All the family kept all their capital invested in the business, which paid them an infallible five percent interest when ordinary depositors were getting about one and a half percent on their money most of the time. The partners got even more. As well as five percent on their invested capital they shared out the profits between them, according to complicated formulas. After a decade of such profit shares, Hugh was halfway to being a millionaire.

On the morning of the funeral Hugh inspected his face in his shaving mirror, looking for signs of mortality. He was thirty-seven years old. His hair was going gray, but the stubble he was scraping off his face was still black. Curly moustaches were fashionable and he wondered whether he should grow one to make himself look younger.

Uncle Joseph had been lucky, Hugh thought. During his tenure as Senior Partner the financial world had been stable. There had been only two minor crises: the failure of the City of Glasgow Bank in 1878 and the crash of the French bank Union Générale in 1882. In both cases the Bank of England had contained the crisis by raising interest rates briefly to six percent, which was still a long way below panic level. In Hugh's opinion, Uncle Joseph had committed the bank much too heavily to investment in South America—but the crash which Hugh constantly feared had not come, and

as far as Uncle Joseph was concerned it now
never would. However, having risky investments was like owning a tumbledown house
and renting it to tenants: the rent would
keep coming in until the very end, but when
the house finally fell down there would be
no more rent and no more house either.
Now that Joseph was gone Hugh wanted to
put the bank on a sounder footing by selling
or repairing some of those tumbledown
South American investments.

When he had washed and shaved he put
on his dressing gown and went into Nora's
room. She was expecting him: they always
made love on Friday mornings. He had long
ago accepted her once-a-week rule. She had
become very plump, and her face was
rounder than ever, but as a result she had
very few lines, and she still looked pretty.

All the same, as he made love to her he
closed his eyes and imagined he was with
Maisie.

Sometimes he felt like giving up altogether. But these Friday-morning sessions
had so far given him three sons whom he
loved to distraction: Tobias, named for
Hugh's father; Samuel, for his uncle; and
Solomon, for Solly Greenbourne. Toby, the
eldest, would start at Windfield School next

year. Nora produced babies with little difficulty but once they were born she lost interest in them, and Hugh gave them a lot of
attention to compensate for their mother's
coldness.

Hugh's secret child, Maisie's son Bertie,
now sixteen, had been at Windfield for
years, and was a prizewinning scholar and
star of the cricket team. Hugh paid his fees,
visited the school on Speech Day, and generally acted like a godfather. Perhaps this
led a few cynical people to suspect that he
was Bertie's real father. But he had been
Solly's friend, and everyone knew that
Solly's father refused to support the boy, so
most people assumed he was simply being
generously faithful to the memory of Solly.

As he rolled off Nora she said: "What
time is the ceremony?"

"Eleven o'clock at Kensington Methodist
Hall. And lunch afterwards at Whitehaven
House."

Hugh and Nora still lived in Kensington,
but they had moved to a bigger house when
the boys started coming. Hugh had left the
choice to Nora, and she had picked a big
house in the same ornate, vaguely Flemish
style as Augusta's—a style that had become
the height of fashion, or at any rate the

height of suburban fashion, since Augusta
built her place.

Augusta had never been satisfied with
Whitehaven House. She wanted a Piccadilly
palace like the Greenbournes. But there was
still a measure of Methodist puritanism in
the Pilasters, and Joseph had insisted that
Whitehaven House was enough luxury for
anyone, no matter how rich. Now the house
belonged to Edward. Perhaps Augusta
would persuade him to sell it and buy her
something grander.

When Hugh went down to breakfast his
mother was already there. She and Dotty
had come up from Folkestone yesterday.
Hugh kissed his mother and sat down, and
she said without preamble: "Do you think
he really loves her, Hugh?"

Hugh did not have to ask whom she was
talking about. Dotty, now twenty-three, was
engaged to Lord Ipswich, eldest son of the
duke of Norwich. Nick Ipswich was heir to a
bankrupt dukedom, and Mama was afraid
he only wanted Dotty for her money, or
rather her brother's money.

Hugh looked fondly at his mother. She
still wore black, twenty-four years after the
death of his father. Her hair was now white,

but in his eyes she was as beautiful as ever. "He loves her, Mama," he said.

As Dotty did not have a father, Nick had come to Hugh to ask formal permission to marry her. In such cases it was usual for the lawyers on both sides to draw up the marriage settlement before the engagement was confirmed, but Nick had insisted on doing things the other way around. "I've told Miss Pilaster that I'm a poor man," he had said to Hugh. "She says she has known both affluence and poverty, and she thinks happiness comes from the people you are with, not the money you have." It was all very idealistic, and Hugh would certainly give his sister a generous dowry; but he was happy to know that Nick genuinely loved her for richer or poorer.

Augusta was enraged that Dotty was marrying so well. When Nick's father died, Dotty would be a duchess, which was far superior to a countess.

Dotty came down a few minutes later. She had grown up in a way Hugh would never have expected. The shy, giggly little girl had become a sultry woman, dark-haired and sensual, strong-willed and quick-tempered. Hugh guessed that quite a lot of young men were intimidated by her, which was probably why she had reached the age of twenty-three without getting married. But Nick Ipswich had a quiet strength that did not need the prop of a compliant wife. Hugh thought they would have a passionate, quarrelsome marriage, quite the opposite of his own.

Nick called, by appointment, at ten, while they were still sitting around the breakfast table. Hugh had asked him to come. Nick sat next to Dotty and took a cup of coffee. He was an intelligent young man, twenty-two years old, just down from Oxford where, unlike most young aristocrats, he had actually sat examinations and got a degree. He had typically English good looks, fair hair and blue eyes and regular features, and Dotty looked at him as if she wanted to eat him with a spoon. Hugh envied their simple, lustful love.

Hugh felt too young to be playing the role of head of the family, but he had asked for this meeting, so he plunged right in. "Dotty, your fiancé and I have had several long discussions about money."

Mama got up to leave, but Hugh stopped her. "Women are supposed to understand money nowadays, Mama—it's the modern way." She smiled at him as if he were being a foolish boy, but she sat down again.

Hugh went on: "As you all know, Nick had been planning a professional career, and thinking of reading for the bar, as the dukedom no longer provides a living." As a banker Hugh understood exactly how Nick's father had lost everything. The duke had been a progressive landowner, and in the agricultural boom of the midcentury he had borrowed money to finance improvements: drainage schemes, the grubbing up of miles of hedges, and expensive steam-powered machinery for threshing, mowing and reaping. Then in the 1870s had come the great agricultural depression which was still going on now in 1890. The price of farmland had slumped and the duke's lands were worth less than the mortgages he had taken on them.

"However, if Nick could get rid of the mortgages that hang around his neck, and rationalize the dukedom, it could still generate a very considerable income. It just needs to be managed well, like any enterprise."

Nick added: "I'm going to sell quite a lot of outlying farms and miscellaneous property, and concentrate on making the most of what's left. And I'm going to build houses on the land we own at Sydenham in south London."

Hugh said: "We've worked out that the finances of the dukedom can be transformed, permanently, with about a hundred thousand pounds. So that is what I'm going to give you as a dowry."

Dotty gasped, and Mama burst into tears. Nick, who had known the figure in advance, said: "It is remarkably generous of you." Dotty threw her arms around her fiancé and kissed him, then came around the table and kissed Hugh. Hugh felt a little awkward, but all the same he was glad to be able to make them so happy. And he was confident that Nick would use the money well and provide a secure home for Dotty.

Nora came down dressed for the funeral in purple-and-black bombazine. She had taken breakfast in her room, as always. "Where are those boys?" she said irritably, looking at the clock. "I told that wretched governess to have them ready—"

She was interrupted by the arrival of the governess and the children: eleven-year-old Toby; Sam, who was six; and Sol, four. They were all in black morning coats and black ties and carried miniature top hats. Hugh felt a glow of pride. "My little soldiers," he said. "What was the Bank of England's discount rate last night, Toby?"

"Unchanged at two and a half percent, sir," said Tobias, who had to look it up in *The Times* every morning.

Sam, the middle one, was bursting with news. "Mamma, I've got a pet," he said excitedly.

The governess looked anxious. "You didn't tell me. . . ."

Sam took a matchbox from his pocket, held it out to his mother, and opened it. "Bill the spider!" he said proudly.

Nora screamed, knocked the box from his hand, and jumped away. "Horrible boy!" she yelled.

Sam scrabbled on the floor for the box. "Bill's gone!" he cried, and burst into tears.

Nora turned on the governess. "How could you let him do such a thing!" she yelled.

"I'm sorry, I didn't know—"

Hugh intervened. "There's no harm done," he said, trying to cool the temperature. He put an arm around Nora's shoulders. "You were taken by surprise, that's all." He ushered her out into the hall. "Come on, everyone, it's time to leave."

As they left the house he put a hand on

Sam's shoulder. "Now, Sam, I hope you've learned that you must always take care not to frighten ladies."

"I lost my pet," Sam said miserably.

"Spiders don't really like living in matchboxes anyway. Perhaps you should have a different kind of pet. What about a canary?"

He brightened immediately. "Could I?"

"You'd have to make sure it was fed and watered regularly, or it would die."

"I would, I would!"

"Then we'll look for one tomorrow."

"Hooray!"

They drove to Kensington Methodist Hall in closed carriages. It was pouring rain. The boys had never been to a funeral. Toby, who was a rather solemn child, said: "Are we expected to cry?"

Nora said: "Don't be so stupid."

Hugh wished she could be more affectionate with the boys. She had been a baby when her own mother died, and he guessed that was why she found it so difficult to mother her own children: she had never learned how. All the same she might try harder, he thought. He said to Toby: "But you can cry if you feel like it. It's allowed at funerals."

"I don't think I shall. I didn't love Uncle Joseph very much."

Sam said: "I loved Bill the spider."

Sol, the youngest, said: "I'm too big to cry."

Kensington Methodist Hall expressed in stone the ambivalent feelings of prosperous Methodists, who believed in religious simplicity but secretly longed to display their wealth. Although it was called a hall, it was as ornate as any Anglican or Catholic church. There was no altar, but there was a magnificent organ. Pictures and statues were banned, but the architecture was baroque, the moldings were extravagant and the decor was elaborate.

This morning the hall was packed to the galleries, with people standing in the aisles and at the back. The employees of the bank had been given the day off to attend, and representatives had come from every important financial institution in the City. Hugh nodded to the governor of the Bank of England, the First Lord of the Treasury, and Ben Greenbourne, more than seventy years old but still as straight-backed as a young guardsman.

The family were ushered to reserved seats in the front row. Hugh sat next to his uncle

Samuel, who was as immaculate as ever in a black frock coat, a wing collar and a fashionably knotted silk tie. Like Greenbourne, Samuel was in his seventies, and he too was alert and fit.

Samuel was the obvious choice as Senior Partner, now that Joseph was dead. He was the oldest and most experienced of the partners. However, Augusta and Samuel hated each other, and she would oppose him fiercely. She would probably back Joseph's brother Young William, now forty-two years old.

Among the other partners, two would not be considered because they did not bear the Pilaster name: Major Hartshorn and Sir Harry Tonks, husband of Joseph's daughter Clementine. The remaining partners were Hugh and Edward.

Hugh wanted to be Senior Partner—he wanted it with all his heart. Although he was the youngest of the partners, he was the ablest banker of them all. He knew he could make the bank bigger and stronger than it had ever been and at the same time reduce its exposure to the risky kind of loans Joseph had relied on. However, Augusta would oppose him even more bitterly than she would oppose Samuel. But he could not bear to wait until Augusta was old, or dead, before he took control. She was only fifty-eight: she could easily be around in another fifteen years, as vigorous and spiteful as ever.

The other partner was Edward. He was sitting next to Augusta in the front row. He was heavy and red-faced in middle age, and he had recently developed some kind of skin rash which was very unsightly. He was neither intelligent nor hardworking and in seventeen years he had managed to learn very little about banking. He arrived at work after ten and left for lunch around noon, and he quite often failed to return at all in the afternoon. He drank sherry for breakfast and was never quite sober all day, and he relied on his clerk, Simon Oliver, to keep him out of trouble. The idea of his being Senior Partner was unthinkable.

Edward's wife was sitting next to him, which was a rare event. They led quite separate lives. He lived at Whitehaven House with his mother, and Emily spent all her time at their country house, coming to London only for ceremonial occasions such as funerals. Emily had once been very pretty, with big blue eyes and a childlike smile, but over the years her face had set in lines of disappointment. They had no children and it seemed to Hugh that they hated each other.

Next to Emily was Micky Miranda, fiendishly debonair in a gray coat with a black mink collar. Ever since finding out that Micky had murdered Peter Middleton, Hugh had been frightened of him. Edward and Micky were still as thick as thieves. Micky was involved in many of the South American investments the bank had backed over the last ten years.

The service was long and tedious, then the procession from the hall to the cemetery, in the relentless September rain, took more than an hour, because of the hundreds of carriages following the hearse.

Hugh studied Augusta as her husband's coffin was lowered into the ground. She stood under a big umbrella held by Edward. Her hair was all silver, and she looked magnificent in a huge black hat. Surely now, when she had lost the companion of a lifetime, she would seem human and pitiable? But her proud face was carved in stern lines, like a marble sculpture of a Roman senator, and she showed no grief.

After the burial there was a lunch at Whitehaven House for the whole Pilaster extended family, including all the partners with their wives and children, plus close business associates and long-time hangers-on such as Micky Miranda. So that they could all eat together Augusta had put two dining tables end-to-end in the long drawing room.

Hugh had not been inside the house for a year or two, and since his last visit it had been redecorated yet again, this time in the newly fashionable Arab style. Moorish arches had been inserted in the doorways, all the furniture featured carved fretwork, the upholstery was in colorful abstract Islamic designs, and here in the drawing room were a Cairo screen and a Koran stand.

Augusta sat Edward in his father's chair. Hugh thought that was a bit tactless. Putting him at the head of the table cruelly emphasized how incapable he was of filling his father's shoes. Joseph had been an erratic leader but he had not been a fool.

However, Augusta had a purpose as always. Toward the end of the meal she said, with her customary abruptness: "There must be a new Senior Partner as soon as possible, and obviously it will be Edward."

Hugh was horrified. Augusta had always had a blind spot about her son, but all the same this was totally unexpected. He felt sure she could not possibly get her way, but it was unnerving that she should even make the suggestion.

There was a silence, and he realized that everyone was waiting for him to speak. He was regarded by the family as the opposition to Augusta.

He hesitated while he considered how best to handle it. He decided to try for a standoff. "I think the partners should discuss the question tomorrow," he said.

Augusta was not going to let him off that easily. She said: "I'll thank you not to tell me what I may and may not discuss in my own house, young Hugh."

"If you insist." He collected his thoughts rapidly. "There's nothing obvious about the decision, although you, dear Aunt, clearly don't understand the subtleties of the question, perhaps because you have never worked at the bank, or indeed worked at all—"

"How dare you—"

He raised his voice and overrode her. "The oldest surviving partner is Uncle Samuel," he said. He realized he was sounding too aggressive and he softened his voice again. "I'm sure we would all agree that he would be a wise choice, mature and experienced and highly acceptable to the financial community."

Uncle Samuel inclined his head in acknowledgment of the compliment but did not say anything.

Nobody contradicted Hugh—but nobody supported him either. He supposed they did not want to antagonize Augusta: the cowards preferred that he do it on their behalf, he thought cynically.

So be it. He went on: "However, Uncle Samuel has declined the honor once before. If he should do so again, the eldest Pilaster would be Young William, who is also widely respected in the City."

Augusta said impatiently: "It is not the City that has to make the choice—it is the Pilaster family."

"The Pilaster partners, to be exact," Hugh corrected her. "But just as the partners need the confidence of the rest of the family, so the bank needs to be trusted by the wider financial community. If we lose that trust we are finished."

Augusta seemed to be getting angry. "We have the right to choose whom we like!"

Hugh shook his head vigorously. Nothing annoyed him more than this kind of irresponsible talk. "We have no rights, only duties," he said emphatically. "We're entrusted with millions of pounds of other people's money. We can't do what we like: we have to do what we must."

Augusta tried another tack. "Edward is the son and heir."

"It's not a hereditary title!" Hugh said indignantly. "It goes to the most able."

It was Augusta's turn to be indignant. "Edward is as good as anyone!"

Hugh looked around the table, dramatically holding the gaze of each man for a moment before moving on. "Is there anyone here who will put his hand on his heart and say that Edward is the most able banker among us?"

No one spoke for a long minute.

Augusta said: "Edward's South American bonds have made a fortune for the bank."

Hugh nodded. "It's true that we have sold many millions of pounds' worth of South American bonds in the last ten years, and Edward has handled all that business. But it's dangerous money. People bought the bonds because they trust Pilasters. If one of those governments should default on interest payments, the price of all South American bonds will go through the floor—and

Pilasters will be blamed. Because of Edward's success in selling South American bonds our reputation, which is our most precious asset, is now in the hands of a set of brutish despots and generals who can't read." Hugh found himself becoming emotional as he said this. He had helped to build up the reputation of the bank by his own brains and hard work, and it made him angry that Augusta was willing to jeopardize it.

"You sell North American bonds," Augusta said. "There's always a risk. That's what banking is about." She spoke triumphantly, as if she had caught him out.

"The United States of America has a modern democratic government, vast natural wealth and no enemies. Now that they've abolished slavery, there's no reason why the country shouldn't be stable for a hundred years. By contrast, South America is a collection of warring dictatorships that may not be the same for the next ten days. There is a risk in both cases, but in the north it's much smaller. Banking is about *calculating* risk."

"You're just envious of Edward—you always were," she said.

Hugh wondered why the other partners were so silent. As soon as he asked himself the question, he realized that Augusta must have spoken to them beforehand. But surely she could not have persuaded them to accept Edward as Senior Partner? He began to feel seriously worried.

"What has she said to you?" he said abruptly. He looked at each of them in turn. "William? George? Harry? Come on, out with it. You've discussed this earlier and Augusta has nobbled you."

They all looked a little foolish. Finally William said: "Nobody has been nobbled, Hugh. But Augusta and Edward have made it clear that unless Edward becomes Senior Partner, they . . ." He seemed embarrassed.

"Out with it," Hugh said.

"They will withdraw their capital from the business."

"What?" Hugh was stunned. Withdrawing your capital was a cardinal sin in this family: his own father had done it and had never been forgiven. That Augusta should be willing even to threaten such a step was astonishing—and showed that she was deadly serious.

Between them, she and Edward controlled about forty percent of the bank's capital, over two million pounds. If they withdrew the money at the end of the financial year, as they were legally entitled to do, the bank would be crippled.

It was startling that Augusta should make such a threat—and even worse that the partners were ready to give in to her. "You're surrendering all authority to her!" he said. "If you let her get away with it this time she'll do it again. Anytime she wants something she can just threaten to withdraw her capital and you'll cave in. You might as well make *her* Senior Partner."

Edward blustered: "Don't you dare speak of my mother like that—mind your manners!"

"Manners be damned," Hugh said rudely. He knew he was doing his cause no good by losing his temper, but he was too angry to stop. "You're about to ruin a great bank. Augusta's blind, Edward is stupid and the rest of you are too cowardly to stop them." He pushed back his chair and stood up, throwing his napkin down on the table like a challenge. "Well, here's one person who won't be bullied."

He stopped and took a breath, realizing he was about to say something that would change the course of the rest of his life.

Around the table they all stared at him. He had no alternative. "I resign," he said.

As he turned from the table he caught Augusta's eye, and saw on her face a victorious smile.

Uncle Samuel came to see him that evening.

Samuel was an old man now, but no less vain than he had been twenty years ago. He still lived with Stephen Caine, his "secretary." Hugh was the only Pilaster who ever went to their home, which was a house in raffish Chelsea, decorated in the fashionable aesthetic style and full of cats. Once, when they were halfway down a bottle of port, Stephen had said he was the only Pilaster wife who was not a harridan.

When Samuel called, Hugh was in his library, where he generally retired after dinner. He had a book on his knee but had not been reading it. Instead he had been staring into the fire, thinking about the future. He had plenty of money, enough to live comfortably for the rest of his life without working, but he would never be Senior Partner now.

Uncle Samuel looked weary and sad. "I was at odds with my cousin Joseph for most of his life," he said. "I wish it had been otherwise."

Hugh offered him a drink and he asked for port. Hugh called his butler and ordered a bottle decanted.

"How do you feel about it all?" Samuel asked.

"I was angry before, but now I'm just despondent," Hugh replied. "Edward is so hopelessly unsuited to be Senior Partner, but there's nothing to be done. How about you?"

"I feel as you do. I shall resign, too. I shan't withdraw my capital, at least not right away, but I shall go at the end of the year. I told them so after you made your dramatic exit. I don't know whether I should have spoken up earlier. It wouldn't have made any difference."

"What else did they say?"

"Well, that's why I'm here, really, dear boy. I regret to say I'm a sort of messenger from the enemy. They asked me to persuade you not to resign."

"Then they're damn fools."

"That they certainly are. However, there is one thing you ought to think about. If you resign immediately, everyone in the City will know why. People will say that if Hugh Pilaster believes Edward can't run the bank he's probably right. It could cause a loss of confidence."

"Well, if the bank has weak leadership people ought to lose confidence in it. Otherwise they'll lose their money."

"But what if your resignation creates a financial crisis?"

Hugh had not thought of that. "Is it possible?"

"I think so."

"I wouldn't want to do that, needless to say." A crisis might bring down other, perfectly sound businesses, the way the collapse of Overend Gurney had destroyed Hugh's father's firm in 1866.

"Perhaps you ought to stay until the end of the financial year, like me," Samuel said. "It's only a few months. By then Edward will have been in charge for a while and people will be used to it, and you can go with no fuss."

The butler came back with the port. Hugh sipped it thoughtfully. He felt he had to agree to Samuel's proposal, much as he disliked the idea. He had given them all a lecture about their duty to their depositors and the wider financial community, and he had to heed his own words. If he were to allow the bank to suffer just because of his own feelings, he would be no better than Augusta. Besides, the postponement would give him time to think about what to do with the rest of his life.

He sighed. "All right," he said at last. "I'll stay until the end of the year."

Samuel nodded. "I thought you would," he said. "It's the right thing to do—and you always do the right thing, in the end."

2

BEFORE MAISIE GREENBOURNE finally said goodbye to high society, eleven years before, she had gone to all her friends—who were many and rich—and persuaded them to give money to Rachel's Southwark Female Hospital. Consequently, the hospital's running costs were covered by the income from its investments.

The money was managed by Rachel's father, the only man involved in the running of the hospital. At first Maisie had wanted to handle the investments herself, but she had found that bankers and stockbrokers refused to take her seriously. They would ignore her instructions, ask for authority from her husband, and withhold information from her. She might have fought them, but in setting up the hospital she and Rachel had too many other fights on their hands, and they had let Mr. Bodwin take over the finances.

Maisie was a widow, but Rachel was still married to Micky Miranda. Rachel never saw her husband but he would not divorce her. For ten years she had been carrying on a discreet affair with Maisie's brother Dan Robinson, who was a member of Parliament. The three of them lived together in Maisie's house in suburban Walworth.

The hospital was in a working-class area, in the heart of the city. They had taken a long lease on a row of four houses near Southwark Cathedral and had knocked internal doors through the walls on each level to make their hospital. Instead of rows of beds in cavernous wards they had small, comfortable rooms, each with only two or three beds.

Maisie's office, a cozy sanctuary near the main entrance, had two comfortable chairs, flowers in a vase, a faded rug and bright curtains. On the wall was the framed poster of "The Amazing Maisie." The desk was unobtrusive, and the ledgers in which she kept her records were stowed in a cupboard.

The woman sitting opposite her was bare-foot, ragged and nine months pregnant. In her eyes was the wary, desperate look of a starving cat that walks into a strange house hoping to be fed. Maisie said: "What's your name, dear?"

"Rose Porter, mum."

They always called her "mum," as if she were a grand lady. She had long ago given up trying to make them call her Maisie. "Would you like a cup of tea?"

"Yes, please, mum."

Maisie poured tea into a plain china cup and added milk and sugar. "You look tired."

"I've walked all the way from Bath, mum."

It was a hundred miles. "It must have taken you a week!" said Maisie. "You poor thing."

Rose burst into tears.

This was normal, and Maisie was used to it. It was best to let them cry as long as they wanted to. She sat on the arm of Rose's chair, put her arm around her shoulders and hugged her.

"I know I've been wicked." Rose sobbed.

"You aren't wicked," Maisie said. "We're all women here, and we understand. We don't talk of wickedness. That's for clergy-men and politicians."

After a while Rose calmed down and drank her tea. Maisie took the current ledger from the cupboard and sat at her writing table. She kept notes on every woman admitted to the hospital. The records were often useful. If some self-righ-teous Conservative got up in Parliament and said that most unmarried mothers were prostitutes, or that they all wanted to aban-don their babies, or some such rot, she would refute him with a careful, polite, fac-tual letter, and repeat the refutation in the speeches she made up and down the coun-try.

"Tell me what happened," she said to Rose. "How were you living, before you fell pregnant?"

"I was cook for a Mrs. Freeman in Bath."

"And how did you meet your young man?"

"He came up and spoke to me in the street. It was my afternoon off, and I had a new yellow parasol. I looked a treat, I know I did. That yellow parasol was the undoing of me."

Maisie coaxed the story out of her. It was typical. The man was an upholsterer, respectable and prosperous working class. He had courted her and they had talked of marriage. On warm evenings they had caressed each other, sitting in the park after dark, surrounded by other couples doing the same thing. Opportunities for sexual intercourse were few, but they had managed it four or five times, when her employer was away or his landlady was drunk. Then he had lost his job. He moved to another town, looking for work; wrote to her once or twice; and vanished out of her life. Then she found she was pregnant.

"We'll try to get in touch with him," Maisie said.

"I don't think he loves me anymore."

"We'll see." It was surprising how often such men were willing to marry the girl, in the end. Even if they had run away on learning she was pregnant, they might regret their panic. In Rose's case the chances were high. The man had gone away because he had lost his job, not because he had fallen out of love with Rose; and he did not yet know he was going to be a father. Maisie always tried to get them to come to the hospital and see the mother and child. The sight of a helpless baby, their own flesh and blood, sometimes brought out the best in them.

Rose winced, and Maisie said: "What's the matter?"

"My back hurts. It must be all the walking."

Maisie smiled. "It's not backache. Your baby's coming. Let's get you to a bed."

She took Rose upstairs and handed her over to a nurse. "It's going to be all right," she said. "You'll have a lovely bonny baby."

She went into another room and stopped beside the bed of the woman they called Miss Nobody, who refused to give any details about herself, not even her name. She was a dark-haired girl of about eighteen. Her accent was upper-class and her underwear was expensive, and Maisie was fairly sure she was Jewish. "How do you feel, my dear?" Maisie asked her.

"I'm comfortable—and so grateful to you, Mrs. Greenbourne."

She was as different from Rose as could be—they might have come from opposite ends of the earth—but they were both in the same predicament, and they would both give birth in the same painful, messy way.

When Maisie got back to her room she

resumed the letter she had been writing to the editor of *The Times.*

> *The Female Hospital*
> *Bridge Street*
> *Southwark*
> *London, S.E.*
> *September 10th, 1890*
> *To the Editor of* The Times
> *Dear Sir,*
> *I read with interest the letter from Dr Charles Wickam on the subject of women's physical inferiority to men.*

She had not been sure how to go on, but the arrival of Rose Porter had given her inspiration.

> *I have just admitted to this hospital a young woman in a certain condition who has walked here from Bath.*

The editor would probably delete the words "in a certain condition" as being vulgar, but Maisie was not going to do his censoring for him.

> *I note that Dr Wickham writes from the Cowes Club, and I cannot help but*

wonder how many members of the club could walk from Bath to London?

Of course as a woman I have never been inside the club, but I often see its members on the steps, hailing hansom cabs to take them distances of a mile or less, and I am bound to say that most of them look as if they would find it diffi-cult to walk from Piccadilly Circus to Parliament Square.

They certainly could not work a twelve-hour shift in an East End sweat-shop, as thousands of Englishwomen do every day—

She was interrupted again by a knock at the door. "Come in," she called.

The woman who entered was neither poor nor pregnant. She had big blue eyes and a girlish face, and she was richly dressed. She was Emily, the wife of Edward Pilaster.

Maisie got up and kissed her. Emily Pilaster was one of the hospital's supporters. The group included a surprising diversity of women—Maisie's old friend April Tilsley, now the owner of three London brothels, was a member. They gave cast-off clothes, old furniture, surplus food from their kitchens, and odd supplies such as paper and ink. They could sometimes find employment for the mothers after confinement. But most of all they gave moral support to Maisie and Rachel when they were vilified by the male establishment for not having compulsory prayers, hymn-singing and sermons on the wickedness of unmarried motherhood.

Maisie felt partly responsible for Emily's disastrous visit to April's brothel on Mask Night, when she had failed to seduce her own husband. Since then Emily and the loathsome Edward had led the discreetly separate lives of wealthy couples who hated each other.

This morning Emily was bright-eyed and excited. She sat down, then got up again and checked that the door was firmly shut. Then she said: "I've fallen in love."

Maisie was not sure this was unqualified good news, but she said: "How wonderful! Who with?"

"Robert Charlesworth. He's a poet and he writes articles about Italian art. He lives in Florence most of the year but he's renting a cottage in our village; he likes England in September."

It sounded to Maisie as if Robert Charlesworth had enough money to live well without doing any real work. "He sounds madly romantic," she said.

"Oh, he is, he's so soulful, you'd love him."

"I'm sure I would," Maisie said, although in fact she could not stand soulful poets with private incomes. However, she was happy for Emily, who had had more bad luck than she deserved. "Have you become his mistress?"

Emily blushed. "Oh, Maisie, you always ask the most embarrassing questions! Of course not!"

After what had happened on Mask Night, Maisie found it astonishing that Emily could be embarrassed about anything. However, experience had taught her that it was she, Maisie, who was peculiar in this respect. Most women were able to close their eyes to just about anything if they really wanted to. But Maisie had no patience with polite euphemisms and tactful phrases. If she wanted to know something she asked. "Well," she said brusquely, "you can't be his wife, can you?"

The answer took her by surprise. "That's why I came to see you," Emily said. "Do you know anything about getting a marriage annulled?"

"Goodness!" Emily thought for a moment. "On the grounds that the marriage has never been consummated, I presume?"

"Yes."

Maisie nodded. "I do know about it, yes." It was no surprise that Emily had come to her for legal advice. There were no women lawyers, and a man would probably have gone straight to Edward and spilled the beans. Maisie was a campaigner for women's rights and had studied the existing law on marriage and divorce. "You would have to go to the Probate, Divorce and Admiralty Division of the High Court," she said. "And you would have to prove that Edward is impotent under all circumstances, not just with you."

Emily's face fell. "Oh, dear," she said. "We know that's not so."

"Also, the fact that you're not a virgin would be a major problem."

"Then it's hopeless," Emily said miserably.

"The only way to do it would be to persuade Edward to cooperate. Do you think he would?"

Emily brightened. "He might."

"If he would sign an affidavit saying that he was impotent, and agree not to contest the annulment, your evidence won't be challenged."

"Then I'll find a way to make him sign." Emily's face took on a stubborn set and Maisie remembered how unexpectedly strong-willed the girl could be.

"Be discreet. It's against the law for a husband and wife to conspire in this way, and there's a man called the Queen's Proctor who acts as a kind of divorce policeman."

"Will I be able to marry Robert afterwards?"

"Yes. Nonconsummation is grounds for a full divorce under church law. It will take about a year for the case to come to court, and then there's a waiting-period of six months before the divorce becomes final, but in the end you will be allowed to remarry."

"Oh, I hope he'll do it."

"How does he feel about you?"

"He hates me."

"Do you think he'd like to get rid of you?"

"I don't think he cares, so long as I stay out of his way."

"And if you didn't stay out of his way?"

"You mean if I were to make a nuisance of myself?"

"That's what I had in mind."

"I suppose I could."

Maisie was sure Emily could make an unbearable nuisance of herself once she put her mind to it.

"I'll need a lawyer to write the letter for Edward to sign," Emily said.

"I'll ask Rachel's father, he's a lawyer."

"Would you?"

"Certainly." Maisie glanced at the clock. "I can't see him today, it's the first day of term at Windfield School and I have to take Bertie. But I'll see him in the morning."

Emily stood up. "Maisie, you're the best friend a woman ever had."

"I'll tell you what, this is going to stir up the Pilaster family. Augusta will have a fit."

"Augusta doesn't scare me," said Emily.

Maisie Greenbourne attracted a lot of attention at Windfield School. She always did. She was known to be the widow of the fabulously wealthy Solly Greenbourne, although she had very little money herself. She was also notorious as an "advanced" woman who believed in women's rights and, it was said, encouraged parlormaids to have illegitimate babies. And then, when she brought Bertie to school, she was always accompanied by Hugh Pilaster, the handsome banker who paid her son's fees: no doubt the more sophisticated among the other parents suspected that Hugh was Bertie's real father. But the main reason, she thought, was that at thirty-five she was still pretty enough to turn men's heads.

Today she was wearing a tomato-red outfit, a dress with a short jacket over it and a hat with a feather. She knew she looked pretty and carefree. In fact these visits to the school with Bertie and Hugh broke her heart.

It was seventeen years since she had spent a night with Hugh, and she loved him as much as ever. Most of the time she immersed herself in the troubles of the poor girls who came to her hospital, and forgot her own grief; but two or three times a year she had to see Hugh, and then the pain came back.

He had known for eleven years that he was Bertie's real father. Ben Greenbourne had given him a hint, and he had confronted her with his suspicions. She told him the truth. Since then he had done everything he could for Bertie, short of acknowledging him as his son. Bertie believed his father was the late, lovable Solomon Greenbourne, and to tell him the truth would just cause unnecessary pain.

His name was Hubert, and calling him Bertie had been a sly compliment to the Prince of Wales, who was also a Bertie. Maisie never saw the prince now. She was no longer a society hostess and the wife of a millionaire: she was just a widow living in a modest house in the south London suburbs, and such women did not feature in the prince's circle of friends.

She had chosen to call her son Hubert because the name sounded like Hugh, but she had quickly become embarrassed by the similarity, and that was another reason for calling the boy Bertie. She told her son that Hugh was his dead father's best friend. Luckily there was no obvious likeness between Bertie and Hugh. In fact Bertie was like Maisie's father, with soft dark hair and sad brown eyes. He was tall and strong, a good athlete and a hardworking student, and Maisie was so proud of him that she sometimes felt her heart would burst.

On these occasions Hugh was scrupulously polite to Maisie, playing the role of family friend, but she could tell that he felt the bittersweetness of the situation as painfully as she did.

Maisie knew, from Rachel's father, that Hugh was considered a prodigy in the City. When he talked about the bank his eyes sparkled and he was interesting and amusing. She could tell that his work was challenging and fulfilling. But if ever their conversation strayed into the domestic field he became sour and uncommunicative. He did not like to talk about his house, his social life, or—least of all—his wife. The only aspect of his family life he told her about was his three sons, whom he loved to distraction. But there was a streak of regret even when he spoke of them, and Maisie had gathered that Nora was not a loving mother. Over the years she had watched him resign himself to a cold, sexually frustrating marriage.

Today he had on a silver-gray tweed suit that matched his silver-streaked hair, and a bright blue tie the color of his eyes. He was heavier than he used to be but he still had a mischievous grin which appeared now and again. They made an attractive couple—but they were not a couple, and the fact that they looked and acted like one was what made her so sad. She took his arm as they walked into Windfield School, and she thought she would give her soul to be with him every day.

They helped Bertie unpack his trunk, then he made them tea in his study. Hugh had brought a cake which would probably feed the sixth form for a week. "My boy Toby will be coming here next half," Hugh said as they drank their tea. "I wonder if you'd keep an eye on him for me?"

"I'll be glad to," Bertie said. "I'll make sure he doesn't go swimming in Bishop's Wood." Maisie frowned at him, and he said: "Sorry. Bad joke."

"They still talk about that, do they?" Hugh said.

"Every year the head tells the story of how Peter Middleton drowned, to try and frighten chaps. But they still go swimming."

After tea they said good-bye to Bertie, Maisie feeling tearful as always about leaving her little boy behind, even though he was now taller than she. They walked back into the town and took the train to London. They had a first-class compartment to themselves.

As they watched the scenery flash by, Hugh said: "Edward is going to be Senior Partner at the bank."

Maisie was startled. "I didn't think he had the brains!"

"He hasn't. I shall resign at the end of the year."

"Oh, Hugh!" Maisie knew how much he cared for that bank. All his hopes were tied up in it. "What will you do?"

"I don't know. I'm staying on until the end of the financial year, so I've got time to think about it."

"Won't the bank go to ruin under Edward?"

"I'm afraid it may."

Maisie felt very sad for Hugh. He had had more bad luck than he deserved, while Edward had far too much good. "Edward is Lord Whitehaven, too. Do you realize that if the title had gone to Ben Greenbourne, as it should have, Bertie would be in line to inherit it now?"

"Yes."

"But Augusta put a stop to all that."

"Augusta?" said Hugh with a puzzled frown.

"Yes. She was behind all that rubbish in the newspapers about 'Can a Jew be a peer?' Do you remember?"

"I do, but how can you be so sure that Augusta was behind it?"

"The Prince of Wales told us."

"Well, well." Hugh shook his head. "Augusta never ceases to amaze me."

"Anyway, poor Emily is Lady Whitehaven now."

"At least she got something out of that wretched marriage."

"I'm going to tell you a secret," Maisie said. She lowered her voice even though there was no one within earshot. "Emily is about to ask Edward for an annulment."

"Good for her! On the grounds of non-consummation, I presume?"

"Yes. You don't seem surprised."

"You can tell. They never touch. They're so awkward with each other, it's hard to believe they're man and wife."

"She's been leading a false life all these years and she's decided to put an end to it."

"She'll have trouble with my family," Hugh said.

"With Augusta, you mean." That had been Maisie's reaction too. "Emily knows that. But she's got a streak of obstinacy that should serve her well."

"Does she have a lover?"

"Yes. But she won't become his mistress. I can't think why she should be so scrupulous. Edward spends every night in a brothel."

Hugh smiled at her, a sad, loving smile. "You were scrupulous, once."

Maisie knew he was talking about the night at Kingsbridge Manor when she had locked her bedroom door against him. "I was married to a good man and you and I were about to betray him. Emily's situation is quite different."

Hugh nodded. "All the same I think I understand how she feels. It's the lying that makes adultery shameful."

Maisie disagreed. "People should grab happiness where they can. You only have one life."

"But when you grab happiness you may let go of something even more valuable—your integrity."

"Too abstract for me," Maisie said dismissively.

"No doubt it was for me, that night at Kingo's house, when I would have betrayed Solly's trust willingly, if you had let me. But it's become more concrete to me over the years. Now I think I value integrity more than anything else."

"But what is it?"

"It means telling the truth, keeping promises, and taking responsibility for your mistakes. It's the same in business as it is in everyday life. It's a matter of being what you claim to be, doing what you say you'll do. And a banker of all people can't be a liar. After all, if his wife can't trust him, who can?"

Maisie was getting angry with Hugh and she wondered why. She sat back in silence for a while, looking out of the window at the London suburbs in the dusk. Now that he was leaving the bank, what was there left in his life? He did not love his wife and his wife did not love their children. Why should he not find happiness in the arms of Maisie, the woman he had always loved?

At Paddington Station he escorted her to the cab stand and helped her into a hansom. As they said good-bye she held his hands and said: "Come home with me."

He looked sad and shook his head.

"We love each other—we always have," she pleaded. "Come with me, and to hell with the consequences."

"But life is consequences, isn't it?"

"Hugh! Please!"

He withdrew his hands and stepped back. "Good-bye, dear Maisie."

She stared at him helplessly. Years of suppressed yearning caught up with her. If she had been strong enough she would have seized him and dragged him into the cab by force. She felt maddened by frustration.

She would have stayed there forever, but he nodded to the cabbie and said: "Drive on."

The man touched the horse with his whip, and the wheels turned.

A moment later Hugh was gone from her sight.

3

HUGH SLEPT BADLY that night. He kept waking up and running over his conversation with Maisie. He wished he had given in and gone home with her. He could be sleeping in her arms now, his head on her breasts, instead of tossing and turning alone.

But something else was bothering him, too. He had a feeling she had said something momentous, something surprising and sinister, the significance of which had escaped him at the time. It still eluded him.

They had talked about the bank, and Edward's becoming Senior Partner; Edward's title; Emily's plan to seek an annulment; the night at Kingsbridge Manor when they had almost made love; the conflicting values of integrity and happiness. . . . Where was the momentous revelation?

He tried running over the conversation backwards: *Come home with me. . . . People should grab happiness where they can. . . . Emily is about to ask Edward for an annulment. . . . Emily is Lady Whitehaven now. . . . Do you realize that if the title had gone to Ben Greenbourne, as it should have, Bertie would be in line to inherit it now?*

No, he had missed something. Edward had got the title that should have gone to Ben Greenbourne—but Augusta had put a stop to all that. She had been behind all the nasty propaganda about whether a Jew could be a lord. Hugh had not realized that, although looking back he thought he should have been able to guess. But the Prince of Wales had known, somehow, and he had told Maisie and Solly.

Hugh turned over restlessly. Why should that be such a momentous revelation? It was just another example of Augusta's ruthlessness. It had been kept quiet at the time. But Solly had known. . . .

Suddenly Hugh sat up in bed, staring into the darkness.

Solly had known.

If Solly knew that the Pilasters were responsible for a press campaign of racial hatred against his father, he would never again do business with Pilasters Bank. In particular, he would have canceled the Santamaria railroad issue. He would have told Edward that he was canceling it. And Edward would have told Micky.

"Oh, my God," Hugh said aloud.

He had always wondered whether Micky had something to do with the death of Solly. He knew Micky had been in the neighborhood. But the motive had always puzzled him. As far as he knew, Solly had been about to consummate the deal and give Micky what he wanted; and if that was right Micky had every motive for keeping Solly alive. But if Solly had been about to cancel, Micky might have killed him to save the deal. Had Micky been the well-dressed man quarreling with Solly a few seconds before he was run over? The coachman had always claimed Solly was pushed into his path. Had Micky shoved Solly under the wheels of that carriage? The thought was horrifying and disgusting.

Hugh got out of bed and turned up the gaslight. He would not go back to sleep tonight. He put on a dressing gown and sat by the dying embers of the fire. Had Micky murdered *two* of his friends, Peter Middleton and Solly Greenbourne?

And if he had, what was Hugh going to do about it?

He was still agonizing over the question the next day when something happened that gave him the answer.

He spent the morning at his desk in the Partners' Room. He had once longed to sit here, in the quiet, luxurious center of power, making decisions about millions of pounds, under the eyes of his ancestors' portraits; but now he was used to it. And soon he would be giving it up.

He was tying up loose ends, completing projects he had already begun but not starting new ones. His mind kept returning to Micky Miranda and poor Solly. It maddened him to think that a man as good as Solly had been done away with by a reptile and parasite such as Micky. What he really wanted to do was strangle Micky with his bare hands. But he could not kill him; in fact there was not even any point in reporting his beliefs to the police, for he had no proof.

His clerk, Jonas Mulberry, had been looking agitated all morning. Mulberry had come into the Partners' Room four or five times on different pretexts but had not said what was on his mind. Eventually Hugh divined that the man had something to say that he did not want the other partners to hear.

A few minutes before midday Hugh went along the corridor to the telephone room. They had had the phone installed two years before, and they were already regretting the decision not to put it in the Partners' Room: each of them was called to the instrument several times a day.

On the way he met Mulberry in the corridor. He stopped him and said: "Is there something on your mind?"

"Yes, Mr. Hugh," said Mulberry with evident relief. He lowered his voice. "I happened to see some papers being drawn up by Simon Oliver, Mr. Edward's clerk."

"Come in here for a moment." Hugh stepped into the telephone room and closed the door behind them. "What was in the papers?"

"A proposal for a loan issue to Cordova —for two million pounds!"

"Oh, no!" said Hugh. "This bank needs

less exposure to South American debt—not more.”

“I knew you’d feel that way.”

“What is it for, specifically?”

“To build a new harbor in Santamaria Province.”

“Another scheme of Señor Miranda’s.”

“Yes. I’m afraid that he and his cousin Simon Oliver have a great deal of influence over Mr. Edward.”

“All right, Mulberry. Thank you very much for letting me know. I’ll try to deal with it.”

Forgetting his phone call, Hugh returned to the Partners’ Room. Would the other partners let Edward do this? They might. Hugh and Samuel no longer had much influence, as they were leaving. Young William did not share Hugh’s fear of a South American collapse. Major Hartshorn and Sir Harry would do as they were told. And Edward was Senior Partner now.

What was Hugh going to do about it? He had not left yet, and he was still earning his share of the profits, so his responsibilities were not at an end.

The trouble was that Edward was not rational: as Mulberry had said, he was completely under the influence of Micky Miranda.

Was there any way Hugh could weaken that influence? He could tell Edward that Micky was a murderer. Edward would not believe him. But he began to feel that he had to try. He had nothing to lose. And he badly needed to do something about the dreadful revelation he had had in the night.

Edward had already left for lunch. On impulse, Hugh decided to follow him.

Guessing Edward's destination, he took a hansom to the Cowes Club. He spent the journey from the City to Pall Mall trying to think of words that would be plausible and inoffensive, to help convince Edward. But all the phrases he thought of sounded artificial, and when he arrived he decided to tell the unvarnished truth and hope for the best.

It was still early, and he found Edward alone in the smoking room of the club, drinking a large glass of Madeira. Edward's skin rash was getting worse, he noticed: where his collar chafed his neck it was red and raw.

Hugh sat down at the same table and ordered tea. When they were boys, Hugh had hated Edward passionately, for being a beast and a bully. But in recent years he had

come to see his cousin as a victim. Edward
was the way he was because of the influence
of two wicked people, Augusta and Micky.
Augusta had suffocated him and Micky had
corrupted him. However, Edward had not
softened toward Hugh, and he now made no
bones about showing that he had no wish
for Hugh's company. "You didn't have to
come this far for a cup of tea," he said.
"What do you want?"

It was a bad start, but nothing could be
done about that. Feeling pessimistic, Hugh
began. "I have something to say that will
shock and horrify you."

"Really?"

"You'll have trouble believing it, but all
the same it's true. I think Micky Miranda is
a murderer."

"Oh, for God's sake," Edward said angrily. "Don't bother me with such nonsense."

"Listen to me before you dismiss the idea
out of hand," Hugh said. "I'm leaving the
bank, you're Senior Partner, I have nothing
left to fight for. But I discovered something
yesterday. Solly Greenbourne knew that
your mother was behind that press campaign to stop Ben Greenbourne's getting a
peerage."

Edward gave an involuntary start, as if what Hugh had said chimed with something he already knew.

Hugh felt more hopeful. "I'm on the right track, am I not?" he said. Guessing, he went on: "Solly threatened to cancel the Santamaria railroad deal, didn't he?"

Edward nodded.

Hugh sat forward, trying to contain his excitement.

Edward said: "I was sitting at this very table, with Micky, when Solly came in, angry as the devil. But—"

"And that night Solly died."

"Yes—but Micky was with me all night. We played cards here, then went on to Nellie's."

"He must have left you, just for a few minutes."

"No—"

"I saw him coming into the club about the time Solly died."

"That must have been earlier."

"He may have gone to the toilet, or something."

"That hardly gives him enough time." Edward's face settled into an expression of decided skepticism.

Hugh's hopes faded again. For a moment

he had succeeded in creating a doubt in Edward's mind, but it had not lasted.

"You've lost your senses," Edward went on. "Micky's not a murderer. The notion is absurd."

Hugh decided to tell him about Peter Middleton. It was an act of desperation, for if Edward refused to believe that Micky might have killed Solly eleven years ago, why would he believe that Micky had killed Peter twenty-four years ago? But Hugh had to try. "Micky killed Peter Middleton, too," he said, knowing that he was in danger of sounding wild.

"This is ridiculous!"

"You think you killed him, I know that. You ducked him repeatedly, then went chasing after Tonio; and you think that Peter was too exhausted to swim to the side, and drowned. But there's something you don't know."

Despite his skepticism, Edward was intrigued. "What?"

"Peter was a very strong swimmer."

"He was a weed!"

"Yes—but he had been practicing swimming every day that spring. He was a weed all right, but he could swim for miles. He swam to the side without difficulty—Tonio saw it."

"What . . ." Edward swallowed. "What else did Tonio see?"

"While you were climbing up the side of the quarry, Micky held Peter's head under the water until he drowned."

To Hugh's surprise, Edward did not spurn the idea. Instead he said: "Why have you waited so long to tell me this?"

"I didn't think you'd believe me. I'm only telling you now out of desperation, to try to dissuade you from this latest Cordovan investment." He studied Edward's expression, and went on: "But you do believe me, don't you?"

Edward nodded.

"Why?"

"Because I know why he did it."

"Why?" said Hugh. He was inflamed by curiosity. He had wondered about this for years. "Why did Micky kill Peter?"

Edward took a long swallow of his Madeira, then he went silent. Hugh was afraid he would refuse to say any more. But eventually he spoke. "In Cordova the Mirandas are a wealthy family, but their dollars don't buy much over here. When Micky came to Windfield he spent his entire year's allowance in a few weeks. But he had boasted of his family's riches, and he was much too proud to admit the truth. So, when he ran out of money . . . he stole."

Hugh remembered the scandal that had rocked the school in June of 1866. "The six gold sovereigns that were stolen from Mr. Offerton," he said wonderingly. "Micky was the thief?"

"Yes."

"Well, I'm damned."

"And Peter knew."

"How?"

"He saw Micky coming out of Offerton's study. When the theft was reported he guessed the truth. He said he would tell unless Micky owned up. We thought it was a piece of luck to catch him at the pool. When I ducked him I was trying to frighten him into silence. But I never thought . . ."

"That Micky would kill him."

"And all these years he's let me think it was my fault, and he was covering up for me," Edward said. "The swine."

Hugh realized that, against the odds, he had succeeded in shaking Edward's faith in Micky. He was tempted to say *Now that you know what he's like, forget about the Santamaria harbor.* But he had to be careful not to overplay his hand. He decided he had said enough: Edward should be left to draw his own conclusions. Hugh stood up to go. "I'm sorry to have given you such a blow," he said.

Edward was deep in thought, rubbing his neck where the rash itched. "Yes," he said vaguely.

"I must go."

Edward said nothing. He seemed to have forgotten Hugh's existence. He was staring into his glass. Hugh looked hard at him and saw, with a jolt, that he was crying.

He went out quietly and closed the door.

4

AUGUSTA LIKED being a widow. For one thing, black suited her. With her dark eyes, silver hair and black eyebrows she was quite striking in mourning clothes.

Joseph had been dead for four weeks and it was remarkable how little she missed him. She found it a little odd that he was not there to complain if the beef was underdone or the library was dusty. She dined alone once or twice a week but she had always been able to enjoy her own company. She no longer had the status of wife of the Senior Partner, but she was the mother of the new Senior Partner. And she was the dowager countess of Whitehaven. She had everything Joseph had ever given her, without the nuisance of having Joseph himself.

And she might marry again. She was fifty-eight, and no longer capable of bearing children; but she still had the desires that she thought of as girlish feelings. In fact they had got worse since Joseph's death. When Micky Miranda touched her arm, or looked into her eyes, or let his hand rest on her hip as he ushered her into a room, she felt more strongly than ever that sensation of pleasure combined with weakness that made her head spin.

Looking at herself in the drawing room mirror, she thought: We are so alike, Micky and I, even in our coloring. We would have had such pretty dark-eyed babies.

As she was thinking it, her blue-eyed, fair-haired baby came in. He was not looking well. He had gone from being stout to positively fat, and he had some kind of skin problem. He was often bad-tempered around teatime, as the effects of the wine he had drunk at lunch wore off.

But she had something important to say to him and was in no mood to go easy on him. "What's this I hear about Emily's asking you for an annulment?" she said.

"She wants to marry someone else," Edward said dully.

"She can't—she's married to you!"

"Not really," Edward said.

What on earth was he talking about? Much as she loved him, he could be deeply irritating. "Don't be silly," she snapped. "Of course she's married to you."

"I only married her because you wanted me to. And she only agreed because her parents made her. We never loved each other, and . . ." He hesitated, then blurted: "We never consummated the marriage."

So that was what he was getting at. Augusta was astonished that he had the nerve to refer directly to the sexual act: such things were not said in front of women. However, she was not surprised to learn that the marriage was a sham: she had guessed it for years. All the same she was not going to let Emily get away with this. "We can't have a scandal," she said firmly.

"It wouldn't be a scandal—"

"Of course it would," she barked, exasperated by his shortsightedness. "It would be the talk of London for a year, and it would be in all the cheap newspapers, too."

Edward was Lord Whitehaven now, and a
sexual sensation involving a peer was just
the kind of thing featured in the weekly
newspapers that servants bought.

Edward said miserably: "But don't you
think Emily has a right to her freedom?"

Augusta ignored that feeble appeal to justice. "Can she force you?"

"She wants me to sign a document admitting that the marriage was never consummated. Then, apparently, it's straightforward."

"And if you don't sign?"

"Then it's more difficult. These things are
not easy to prove."

"That settles it. We have nothing to worry
about. Let's speak no more about this embarrassing topic."

"But—"

"Tell her she can't have an annulment. I
absolutely will not hear of it."

"Very well, Mother."

She was taken aback by his rapid capitula-
tion. Although she generally got her way in
the end, he normally put up more of a fight
than this. He must have other problems on
his mind. "What's the matter, Teddy?" she
said in a softer voice.

He sighed heavily. "Hugh told me the devil of a thing," he said.

"What?"

"He says Micky killed Solly Greenbourne."

Augusta felt a shiver of horrid fascination. "How? Solly was run over."

"Hugh says Micky pushed him in front of that carriage."

"Do you believe it?"

"Micky was with me that evening, but he might have slipped out for a few minutes. It's possible. Do you believe it, Mother?"

Augusta nodded. Micky was dangerous and bold: it was what made him so magnetic. She had no doubt he was capable of committing such a daring murder—and getting away with it.

"I find it hard to accept," Edward said. "I know Micky is wicked in some ways, but to think he would kill. . . ."

"He would, though," Augusta said.

"How can you be sure?"

Edward looked so pathetic that Augusta was tempted to share her own secret knowledge with him. Would it be wise? It could do no harm. The shock of Hugh's revelation seemed to have made Edward more thoughtful than usual. Perhaps the truth would be good for him. It might make him more serious. She decided to tell him. "Micky killed your uncle Seth," she said.

"Good God!"

"He suffocated him with a pillow. I caught him red-handed." Augusta felt a flush of heat in her loins as she remembered the scene that had followed.

Edward said: "But why would Micky kill Uncle Seth?"

"He was in such a hurry to get those rifles shipped to Cordova, don't you remember?"

"I remember." Edward was silent for a few moments. Augusta closed her eyes, reliving that long, wild embrace with Micky, in the room with the dead man.

Edward brought her out of her reverie. "There's something else, and it's even worse. You remember that boy Peter Middleton?"

"Certainly." Augusta would never forget him. His death had haunted the family ever since. "What about him?"

"Hugh says Micky killed him."

Now Augusta was shocked. "What? No— I can't believe that."

Edward nodded. "Deliberately held his head under the water and drowned him."

It was not the murder itself but the idea

of Micky's betrayal that horrified her. "Hugh must be lying."

"He says Tonio Silva saw the whole thing."

"But that would mean Micky has been wickedly deceiving us all these years!"

"I think it's true, Mother."

Augusta realized, with a growing sense of dread, that Edward would not give credence to such a wild story without a reason. "Why are you so willing to believe what Hugh says?"

"Because I knew something Hugh didn't know, something that confirms the story. You see, Micky had stolen some money from one of the masters. Peter knew and was threatening to tell. Micky was desperate to find some way of shutting him up."

"Micky was always short of money," Augusta recalled. She shook her head in incredulity. "And all these years we've thought—"

"That it was my fault Peter died."

Augusta nodded.

Edward said: "And Micky let us think it. I can't take it in, Mother. I believed I was a killer, and Micky knew I wasn't, but he said nothing. Isn't that a terrible betrayal of friendship?"

Augusta looked sympathetically at her son. "Will you throw him over?"

"Inevitably." Edward was grief-stricken. "But he's my only friend, really."

Augusta felt close to tears. They sat looking at each other, thinking about what they had done, and why.

Edward said: "For nearly twenty-five years we've treated him as a member of the family. And he's a monster."

A monster, Augusta thought. It was true.

And yet she loved him. Even if he had killed three people, she loved Micky Miranda. Despite the way he had deceived her, she knew that if he walked into the room at this moment she would long to take him in her arms.

She looked at her son. Reading his face, she saw he felt the same way. She had known it in her heart but now her mind acknowledged it.

Edward loved Micky too.

CHAPTER TWO

1

MICKY MIRANDA was worried. He sat in the lounge of the Cowes Club smoking a cigar, wondering what he had done to offend Edward. Edward was avoiding him. He stayed away from the club, he did not go to Nellie's, and he did not even appear in Augusta's drawing room at teatime. Micky had not seen him for a week.

He had asked Augusta what was wrong but she said she did not know. She was a little odd with him and he suspected that she knew but would not say.

This had not happened in over twenty years. Every now and again Edward would take offense at something Micky did and go into a sulk, but it never lasted more than a day or two. This time it was serious—and that meant it could jeopardize the Santamaria harbor money.

In the last decade, Pilasters Bank had issued Cordovan bonds about once a year. Some of the money had been capital for railways, waterworks and mines; some had been simple loans to the government. All of it had benefited the Miranda family directly or indirectly, and Papa Miranda was now the most powerful man in Cordova, after the president.

Micky had taken a commission on everything—although nobody at the bank knew this—and he was now personally very rich. More significantly, his ability to raise the money had made him one of the most important figures in Cordovan politics and the unquestioned heir to his father's power.

And Papa was about to start a revolution.

The plans were laid. The Miranda army would dash south by rail and lay siege to the capital. There would be a simultaneous attack on Milpita, the port on the Pacific coast that served the capital.

But revolutions cost money. Papa had instructed Micky to raise the biggest loan yet, two million pounds sterling, to buy weapons and supplies for a civil war. And Papa had promised a matchless reward. When Papa was president, Micky would be prime minister, with authority over everyone except Papa himself. And he would be designated Papa's successor, to become president when Papa died.

It was everything he had ever wanted.

He would return to his own country a conquering hero, the heir to the throne, the president's right-hand man, and lord over his cousins and uncles and—most gratifyingly—his older brother.

And now all of that had been put at risk by Edward.

Edward was essential to the plan. Micky had given Pilasters an unofficial monopoly of trade with Cordova, in order to boost Edward's prestige and power at the bank. It had worked: Edward was now Senior Partner, something he could never have achieved without help. But no one else in London's financial community had got a chance to develop any expertise in Cordovan trade. Consequently the other banks felt they did not know enough to invest there. And they were doubly suspicious of any project Micky brought to them because they assumed it had already been turned down by Pilasters. Micky had tried raising money for Cordova through other banks, but they had always turned him down.

Edward's sulk was therefore deeply disquieting. It was giving Micky sleepless nights. With Augusta unwilling or unable to shed any light on the problem Micky had no one to ask: he himself was Edward's only close friend.

While he sat smoking and worrying, he spotted Hugh Pilaster. It was seven o'clock, and Hugh was in evening dress, having a drink alone, presumably on his way to meet people for dinner.

Micky did not like Hugh and he knew the feeling was mutual. However, Hugh might know what was going on. And Micky had nothing to lose by asking him. So he stood up and went over to Hugh's table. "Evening, Pilaster," he said.

"Evening, Miranda."

"Have you seen your cousin Edward lately? He seems to have vanished."

"He comes to the bank every day."

"Ah." Micky hesitated. When Hugh did not invite him to take a seat he said: "May I join you?" and sat down without waiting for a reply. In a lower voice he said: "Would you happen to know whether I've done anything to offend him?"

Hugh had looked thoughtful for a moment, then said: "I can't think of any reason why I shouldn't tell you. Edward has discovered that you killed Peter Middleton, and you've been lying to him about it for twenty-four years."

Micky almost jumped out of his chair. How the devil had that come out? He almost asked the question, then remembered he could not without admitting his guilt. Instead he feigned anger and stood up abruptly. "I shall forget you ever said that," he said, and he left the room.

It took him only a few moments to realize that he was in no more danger from the police than he had ever been. No one could prove what he had done and it had all happened so long ago that there would be no point in reopening the investigation. The real danger he faced was that Edward would refuse to raise the two million pounds Papa needed.

He had to win Edward's forgiveness. And to do that he had to see him.

That night he could do nothing, for he was engaged to go to a diplomatic reception at the French embassy and a supper party with some Conservative members of Parliament. But the next day he went to Nellie's at lunchtime, woke April up, and persuaded her to send Edward a note, promising him "something special" if he would come to the brothel that night.

Micky took April's best room and booked Edward's current favorite, Henrietta, a slim girl with short dark hair. He instructed her to dress in a man's evening clothes with a top hat, an outfit Edward found sexy.

By half-past nine in the evening he was waiting for Edward. The room had a huge four-poster bed, two sofas, a big ornate fireplace, the usual washstand, and a series of vividly obscene paintings set in a mortuary, showing the slavering attendant performing various sexual acts on the pale corpse of a beautiful young girl. Micky reclined on a velvet sofa, wearing nothing but a silk robe, sipping brandy, with Henrietta beside him.

She quickly got bored. "Do you like these pictures?" she asked him.

He shrugged and did not answer. He did not want to talk to her. He had very little interest in women for their own sake. The sexual act itself was a humdrum mechanical process. What he liked about sex was the power it gave him. Women and men had always fallen in love with him and he never tired of using their infatuation to control, exploit and humiliate them. Even his youthful passion for Augusta Pilaster had been in part the desire to tame and ride a spirited wild mare.

From that point of view, Henrietta offered him nothing: it was no challenge to control her, she had nothing worth exploiting her for, and there was no satisfaction in humiliating someone as low down on the scale as a prostitute. So he smoked his cigar and worried about whether Edward would come.

An hour went by, and then another. Micky began to lose hope. Was there some other way to reach Edward? It was very difficult to get to a man who really did not want to be seen. He could be "not at home" at his house and unavailable at his place of work. Micky could hang around outside the bank to catch Edward leaving for lunch, but that was undignified, and anyway Edward could easily just ignore him. Sooner or later they would meet at some social occasion, but it might not happen for weeks, and Micky could not afford to wait that long.

Then, just before midnight, April put her head around the door and said: "He's arrived."

"At last," Micky said with relief.

"He's having a drink but he says he doesn't want to play cards. He'll be with you in a few minutes, I'd guess."

Micky's tension mounted. He was guilty of a betrayal about as bad as could be imagined. He had allowed Edward to suffer for a quarter of a century under the illusion that he had killed Peter Middleton when in fact Micky had been the guilty one all along. It was a lot to ask Edward to forgive.

But Micky had a plan.

He posed Henrietta on the sofa. He made her sit with the hat over her eyes and her legs crossed, smoking a cigarette. He turned the gaslights down low then went and sat on the bed, behind the door.

A few moments later Edward came in. In the dim light he did not notice Micky sitting on the bed. He stopped in the doorway, looking at Henrietta, and said: "Hullo— who are you?"

She looked up and said: "Hello, Edward."

"Oh, it's you," he said. He shut the door and came inside. "Well, what's the 'something special' April has been talking about? I've seen you in a tailcoat before."

"It's me," Micky said, and stood up.

Edward frowned. "I don't wish to see you," he said, and turned toward the door.

Micky stood in his way. "At least tell me why. We've been friends too long."

"I've found out the truth about Peter Middleton."

Micky nodded. "Will you give me a chance to explain?"

"What is there to explain?"

"How I came to make such an awful mistake, and why I never had the courage to admit it."

Edward looked mulish.

Micky said: "Sit down, just for a minute, by Henrietta, and let me speak."

Edward hesitated.

Micky said: "Please?"

Edward sat on the sofa.

Micky went to the sideboard and poured him a brandy. Edward took it with a nod. Henrietta moved close to him on the sofa and took his arm. Edward sipped his drink, looked around, and said: "I hate these paintings."

"Me too," said Henrietta. "They give me the shivers."

"Shut up, Henrietta," said Micky.

"Sorry I spoke, I'm sure," she said indignantly.

Micky sat on the opposite sofa and addressed Edward. "I was wrong, and I betrayed you," he began. "But I was sixteen years old, and we've been best friends for most of our lives. Are you really going to throw that away for a schoolboy peccadillo?"

"But you could have told me the truth at any time in the last twenty-five years!" Edward said indignantly.

Micky made his face sad. "I could have, and I should have, but once a lie like that is told, it's hard to take it back. It would have ruined our friendship."

"Not necessarily," Edward said.

"Well, it has now . . . hasn't it?"

"Yes," Edward said, but there was a tremor of uncertainty in his voice.

Micky realized the time had come to go all out.

He stood up and slipped off his robe.

He knew he looked good: his body was still lean, and his skin was smooth except for the curly hair at his chest and groin.

Henrietta immediately got up from the sofa and knelt in front of him. Micky watched Edward. Desire flickered in his eyes, but then he glowered obstinately and looked away.

In desperation Micky played his last card. "Leave us, Henrietta," he said.

She looked startled, but she got up and went out.

Edward stared at Micky. "Why did you do that?" he said.

"What do we need her for?" Micky replied. He stepped closer to the sofa, so that his groin was just inches from Edward's face. He put out a tentative hand, touched Edward's head, and gently stroked his hair. Edward did not move.

Micky said: "We're better off without her . . . aren't we?"

Edward swallowed hard and said nothing.

"Aren't we?" Micky persisted.

At last Edward replied. "Yes," he whispered. "Yes."

The following week, Micky entered for the first time the hushed dignity of the Partners' Room at Pilasters Bank.

He had been bringing them business for seventeen years, but whenever he came to the bank he was shown to one of the other rooms, and a walker would fetch Edward from the Partners' Room. He suspected that an Englishman would have been admitted to the inner sanctum a lot faster. He loved

London but he knew he would always be an outsider here.

Feeling nervous, he spread out the plan for Santamaria harbor on the big table in the middle of the room. The drawing showed an entirely new port on the Atlantic coast of Cordova, with ship repair facilities and a rail link.

None of it would ever be built, of course. The two million pounds would go straight into the Miranda war chest. But the survey was genuine and the plans were professionally drawn, and if it had been an honest proposal it might even have made money.

Being a dishonest proposal it probably ranked as the most ambitious fraud in history.

While Micky explained it to them, talking of building materials, labor costs, customs duties and income projections, he struggled to maintain an appearance of calm. His entire career, the future of his family and the destiny of his country depended on the decision made in this room today.

The partners were also tense. All six were there: the two in-laws, Major Hartshorn and Sir Harry Tonks; Samuel, the old queen; Young William; and Edward and Hugh.

There would be a battle, but the odds

were on Edward's side. He was Senior Partner. Major Hartshorn and Sir Harry always did what their Pilaster wives told them, and the wives got their orders from Augusta, so they would back Edward. Samuel would probably back Hugh. Young William was the only unpredictable one.

Edward was enthusiastic, as expected. He had forgiven Micky, they were the best of friends again, and this was his first major project as Senior Partner. He was pleased to have brought in such a big piece of business to launch his term of office.

Sir Harry spoke next. "The proposal is carefully thought out, and we've been doing well with Cordova bonds for a decade. It looks an attractive proposition to me."

As anticipated, the opposition came from Hugh. It was Hugh who had told Edward the truth about Peter Middleton, and his motive had surely been to prevent this loan issue. "I've been looking at what has happened to the last few South American issues we've handled," he said, and he handed round copies of a table.

Micky studied the table while Hugh continued. "The interest rate offered has gone up from six percent three years ago to seven and a half percent last year. Despite that increase, the number of bonds remaining unsold has been higher each time."

Micky knew enough about finance to understand what that meant: investors were finding South American bonds less and less attractive. Hugh's calm exposition and relentless logic made Micky fume.

Hugh went on: "Also, in each of the last three issues, the bank has been obliged to buy bonds in the open market to keep the price up artificially." Which meant, Micky realized, that the figures in the table understated the problem.

"The consequence of our persistence in this saturated market is that we now hold almost a million pounds' worth of Cordova bonds. Our bank is gravely overexposed to that one sector."

It was a powerful argument. Trying to stay cool, Micky reflected that if he were a partner he would now vote against the issue. But it would not be decided purely by the financial reasoning. There was more at stake here than money.

For a few seconds no one spoke. Edward looked angry, but he was restraining himself, knowing it would appear better if one of the other partners contradicted Hugh.

At last Sir Harry said: "Point taken,

Hugh, but I think you may be overstating the case a little."

George Hartshorn concurred. "We're all agreed that the plan itself is sound. The risk is small and the profits are considerable. I think we should accept."

Micky had known in advance that those two would support Edward. He was waiting for Young William's verdict.

But it was Samuel who spoke next. "I understand that you're all reluctant to veto the first major proposal brought in by a new Senior Partner," he said. His tone suggested that they were not enemies divided into opposing camps, but reasonable men who could not help but agree given a little goodwill. "Perhaps you're not inclined to place much reliance on the views of two partners who have already announced their resignations. But I've been in the business twice as long as anyone else in this room, and Hugh is probably the most successful young banker in the world, and we both feel this project is more dangerous than it looks. Don't let personal considerations lead you to dismiss that advice out of hand."

Samuel was eloquent, Micky thought, but his position had been known in advance. Everyone now looked at Young William.

At last he spoke. "South American bonds have always seemed more risky," he began. "If we had allowed ourselves to be frightened of them we would have missed out on a great deal of profitable business during the last few years." This sounded good, Micky thought. William went on: "I don't think there's going to be a financial collapse. Cordova has gone from strength to strength under President Garcia. I believe we can anticipate increasing profits from our business there in future. We should be looking for more such business, not less."

Micky let his breath out in a long, silent sigh of relief. He had won.

Edward said: "Four partners in favor, then, and two against."

"Just a minute," said Hugh.

God forbid that Hugh should have something up his sleeve, Micky thought. He clenched his jaw. He wanted to cry out a protest but he had to suppress his feelings.

Edward looked crossly at Hugh. "What is it? You're outvoted."

"A vote has always been a last resort in this room," Hugh said. "When there is disagreement between the partners we try to reach a compromise that everyone can assent to."

Micky could see that Edward was ready to squash this idea, but William said: "What have you got in mind, Hugh?"

"Let me ask Edward something," Hugh said. "Are you confident that we can sell all or most of this issue?"

"Yes, if we price it right," Edward said. It was clear from his expression that he did not know where this was heading. Micky had a dreadful premonition that he was about to be outmaneuvered.

Hugh went on: "Then why don't we sell the bonds on a commission basis, rather than underwriting the issue."

Micky muffled a curse. That was not what he wanted. Normally, when the bank launched, say, a million pounds' worth of bonds, it agreed to buy any unsold bonds itself, thereby guaranteeing that the borrower would receive the full million. In return for that guarantee, the bank took a fat percentage. The alternative method was to offer the bonds for sale with no guarantee. The bank took no risk and received a much lower percentage, but if only ten thousand of the million bonds were sold, the borrower would get only ten thousand pounds. The risk remained with the borrower—and at this stage Micky did not want any risks.

William grunted. "Hmm. That's an idea."

Hugh had been cunning, Micky thought despondently. If he had continued to oppose the scheme outright, he would have been overruled. But he had suggested a way of reducing the risk. Bankers, being a conservative breed, loved to reduce their risks.

Sir Harry said: "If we do sell them all, we still make about sixty thousand pounds, even at the reduced commission. And if we don't sell them all we shall have avoided a considerable loss."

Say something, Edward! thought Micky. Edward was losing control of the meeting. But he seemed not to know how to get it back.

Samuel said: "And we can record a unanimous decision of the partners—always a pleasant outcome."

There was a general murmur of assent.

In desperation, Micky said: "I can't promise that my principals will agree to that. In the past the bank has always underwritten Cordovan bonds. If you decide to change your policy . . ." He hesitated. "I may have to go to another bank." It was an empty threat, but would they know that?

William was offended. "That's your privilege. Another bank may take a different view of the risks."

Micky saw that his threat had only served to consolidate the opposition. Hastily he added: "The leaders of my country value their relationship with Pilasters Bank and would not wish to jeopardize that."

Edward said: "And we reciprocate their feelings."

"Thank you." Micky realized there was no more to be said.

He began to roll up the map of the harbor. He had been defeated, but he was not ready to give up yet. That two million pounds was the key to the presidency of his country. He had to have it.

He would think of something.

Edward and Micky had arranged to have lunch together in the dining room of the Cowes Club. It was planned as a celebration of their triumph, but now they had nothing to celebrate.

By the time Edward arrived, Micky had worked out what he had to do. His only chance now was to persuade Edward secretly to go against the decision of the partners, and underwrite the bonds without telling them. It was an outrageous, foolhardy and probably criminal act. But there was no alternative.

Micky was already sitting at the table when Edward came in. "I'm very disappointed about what happened at the bank this morning," Micky said right away.

"It was the fault of my damned cousin Hugh," Edward said as he sat down. He waved at a waiter and said: "Bring me a big glass of Madeira."

"The trouble is, if the issue isn't underwritten, there's no guarantee the harbor will be built."

"I did my best," Edward said plaintively. "You saw that, you were there."

Micky nodded. Unfortunately it was true. If Edward had been a brilliant manipulator of other people—like his mother—he might have defeated Hugh. But if Edward had been that sort of person he would not be Micky's pawn.

Pawn though he was, he might resist the proposal Micky had in mind. Micky cudgeled his brains for ways of persuading or coercing him.

They ordered their lunch. When the waiter had left Edward said: "I've been thinking that I might get a place of my own. I've been living with my mother too long."

Micky made an effort to be interested. "You'd buy a house?"

"A small one. I don't want a palace, with dozens of parlormaids running around putting coal on fires. A modest house that can be run by a good butler and a handful of servants."

"But you've got everything you need at Whitehaven House."

"Everything but privacy."

Micky began to see what he was driving at. "You don't want your mother to know everything you do. . . ."

"You might want to stay with me overnight, for example," Edward said, giving Micky a very direct look.

Micky suddenly saw how he could exploit this idea. He feigned sadness and shook his head. "By the time you get the house I shall probably have left London."

Edward was devastated. "What the devil do you mean?"

"If I don't raise the money for the new harbor, I'm sure to be recalled by the president."

"You can't go back!" Edward said in a frightened voice.

"I certainly don't want to. But I may not have the choice."

"The bonds will sell out, I'm sure," Edward said.

"I hope so. If they don't . . ."

Edward hit the table with his fist, making the glasses shake. "I wish Hugh had let me underwrite the issue!"

Micky said nervously: "I suppose you have to abide by the decision of the partners."

"Of course—what else?"

"Well . . ." He hesitated. He tried to sound casual. "You couldn't just ignore what was said today, and simply have your staff draw up an underwriting deal, without telling anyone, could you?"

"I could, I suppose," Edward said worriedly.

"After all, you are Senior Partner. That ought to mean something."

"It damn well should."

"Simon Oliver would do the paperwork discreetly. You can trust him."

"Yes."

Micky could hardly believe Edward was agreeing so readily. "It might make the difference between my staying in London and my being recalled to Cordova."

The waiter brought their wine and poured them each a glass.

Edward said: "It would all come out, eventually."

"By then it will be too late. And you can pass it off as a clerical error." Micky knew this was implausible and he doubted if Edward would swallow it.

But Edward ignored it. "If you stay . . ." He paused and dropped his eyes.

"Yes?"

"If you stay in London, will you spend nights at my new house sometimes?"

That was the only thing Edward was interested in, Micky realized with a surge of triumph. He gave his most winning smile. "Of course."

Edward nodded. "That's all I want. I'll speak to Simon this afternoon."

Micky picked up his wineglass. "To friendship," he said.

Edward clinked glasses and smiled shyly. "To friendship."

2

WITHOUT WARNING, Edward's wife Emily moved into Whitehaven House.

Although everyone still thought of it as Augusta's house, Joseph had in fact bequeathed it to Edward. Consequently they could not throw Emily out: it would probably have been grounds for divorce, and that was just what Emily wanted.

In fact Emily was technically mistress of the house, and Augusta just a mother-in-law living there on sufferance. If Emily had openly confronted Augusta there would have been a mighty clash of wills. Augusta would have relished that, but Emily was too adroit to fight her openly. "It is your home," Emily would say sweetly. "You must do whatever you wish." The condescension was enough to make Augusta flinch.

Emily even had Augusta's title: as Edward's wife she was the countess of Whitehaven now, and Augusta was the dowager countess.

Augusta continued to give orders to the servants as if she were still mistress of the house, and whenever she got the chance she would countermand Emily's instructions. Emily never complained. However, the servants became subversive. They liked Emily better than Augusta—because she was foolishly soft on them, Augusta thought—and they found ways to make Emily's life comfortable despite Augusta's efforts.

The most powerful weapon an employer had was the threat of dismissing a servant without a character reference. No one else would give the servant a job thereafter. But Emily had taken this weapon away from Augusta with an ease that was almost frightening. One day Emily ordered sole for lunch. Augusta changed it to salmon, sole was served, and Augusta dismissed the cook. But Emily gave the cook a glowing reference and she was hired by the duke of Kingsbridge at a better wage. And for the first time ever, Augusta's servants were not terrified of her.

Emily's friends would call at Whitehaven House in the afternoon. Tea was a ritual presided over by the mistress of the house. Emily would smile sweetly and beg Augusta to take charge, but then Augusta would have to be polite to Emily's friends, which was almost as bad as letting Emily play the role of mistress.

Dinner was worse. Augusta would have to suffer her guests telling her how sweet Lady Whitehaven was to defer to her mother-in-law by letting her sit at the head of the table.

Augusta had been outmaneuvered, a new experience for her. Normally she held over people's heads the ultimate deterrent of expulsion from the circle of her favor. But expulsion was what Emily wanted, and that made her impossible to frighten.

Augusta became all the more determined never to give in.

People began to invite Edward and Emily to social functions. Emily would go, whether Edward accompanied her or not. People began to notice. When Emily had hidden herself away in Leicestershire, her estrangement from her husband could be overlooked; but with both of them living in town it became embarrassing.

Once upon a time Augusta had been indifferent to the opinion of high society. It was a tradition among commercial people to regard the aristocracy as frivolous if not degenerate, and to ignore their opinions, or at least to pretend to. But Augusta had long ago left behind that simple middle-class pride. She was the dowager countess of Whitehaven and she craved the approval of London's elite. She could not allow her son churlishly to decline invitations from the very best people. So she forced him to go.

Tonight was a case in point. The marquis of Hocastle was in London for a debate in the House of Lords, and the marchioness was giving a dinner party for such few of her friends as were not in the country hunting and shooting. Edward and Emily were going, and so was Augusta.

But when Augusta came downstairs in her black silk gown she found Micky Miranda in evening dress drinking whisky in the drawing room. Her heart leaped at the sight of him, so dashing in his white waistcoat and high collar. He stood up and kissed her hand. She was glad she had chosen this gown, which had a low bodice that showed off her bosom.

Edward had dropped Micky after finding out the truth about Peter Middleton, but it had only lasted a few days, and they were now closer friends than ever before. Augusta was glad. She could not be angry with Micky. She had always known he was dangerous: it made him even more desirable. She sometimes felt frightened of him, knowing he had killed three people, but her fear was exciting. He was the most immoral person she had ever met, and she wished he would throw her to the floor and ravish her.

Micky was still married. He could probably divorce Rachel if he wanted to—there were persistent rumors about her and Maisie Robinson's brother Dan, the Radical member of Parliament—but it could not be done while he was the minister.

Augusta sat on the Egyptian sofa, intending that he should sit beside her, but to her disappointment he sat opposite. Feeling spurned, she said: "What are you here for?"

"Edward and I are going to a prizefight."

"No, you're not. He's dining with the marquis of Hocastle."

"Ah." Micky hesitated. "I wonder if I made a mistake . . . or he did."

Augusta was quite sure Edward was responsible and she doubted whether it was a mistake. He loved to watch prizefighting and he was probably intending to slide out of the dinner engagement. She would soon put a stop to that. "You'd better go on your own," she said to Micky.

A rebellious look came into his eye, and for a moment she thought he was going to defy her. Was she losing her power over this young man, she wondered? But he stood up, albeit slowly, and said: "I'll slope off, then, if you'll explain to Edward."

"Of course."

But it was too late. Before Micky reached the door Edward came in.

Augusta noticed that his skin rash was inflamed tonight. It covered his throat and the back of his neck and reached up to one ear.

It troubled her, but he said the doctor insisted it was nothing to worry about.

Rubbing his hands in anticipation, he said: "I'm looking forward to this."

Augusta said in her most authoritative voice: "Edward, you cannot go the prizefight."

He looked like a child who has been told that Christmas is canceled. "Why not?" he said plaintively.

For a moment Augusta felt sorry for him and almost backed down. Then she hardened her heart and said: "You know perfectly well that we are engaged to dine with the marquis of Hocastle."

"That's not tonight, is it?"

"You know it is."

"I shan't go."

"You must!"

"But I dined out with Emily last night!"

"Then tonight will make two civilized dinners in a row."

"Why the deuce are we invited anyway?"

"Don't swear in front of your mother! We're invited because they are friends of Emily's."

"Emily can go to the—" He caught Augusta's look and stopped short. "Tell them I've been taken ill," he said.

"Don't be ridiculous."

"I think I should be able to go where I like, Mother."

"You cannot offend high-ranking people!"

"I want to see the fights!"

"You may not go!"

At that moment Emily came in. She could not help but notice the charged atmosphere in the room, and she said immediately: "What's wrong?"

Edward said: "Go and fetch me that blasted bit of paper you're always asking me to sign!"

"What are you talking about?" Augusta said. "What bit of paper?"

"My agreement to the annulment," he said.

Augusta was horrified—and she realized with sudden rage that none of this was accidental. Emily had planned it exactly this way. Her aim had been to irritate Edward so much that he would sign anything just to be rid of her. Augusta had even helped her, inadvertently, by insisting that Edward fulfill his social obligations. She felt a fool: she had allowed herself to be manipulated. And now Emily's plan was on the brink of succeeding.

Augusta said: "Emily! Stay here!"

Emily smiled sweetly and went out.

Augusta turned on Edward. "You are not to consent to an annulment!"

Edward said: "I'm forty years old, Mother. I'm head of the family business and this is my own house. You ought not to tell me what to do."

He had a sulky, stubborn look on his face, and the dreadful thought occurred to Augusta that he might actually defy her for the first time in his life.

She began to feel scared.

"Come and sit here, Teddy," she said in a softer voice.

Reluctantly he sat beside her.

She reached out to stroke his cheek, but he flinched away.

"You can't take care of yourself," she said. "You've never been able to. That's why Micky and I have always looked after you, ever since you were at school."

He looked even more obstinate. "Perhaps it's time you stopped."

A feeling of panic began to creep over Augusta. It was almost as if she was losing her grip.

Before she could say any more, Emily came back with a legal-looking document.

She put it on the Moorish writing table, where pens and ink were already laid out.

Augusta looked at her son's face. Could it be that he was more afraid of his wife than of his mother? Augusta thought wildly about snatching the document away, throwing the pens on the fire and spilling the ink. She got a grip on herself. Better perhaps to give in and pretend it was of no great consequence. But the pretense would be useless: she had made a stand and forbidden this annulment, and everyone would know she had been defeated.

She said to Edward: "You'll have to resign from the bank if you sign that document."

"I don't see why," he replied. "It's not like a divorce."

Emily said: "The church has no objection to an annulment if the grounds are genuine." It sounded like a quotation: she had obviously checked.

Edward sat at the table, selected a quill, and dipped its point into a silver inkwell.

Augusta fired her last shot. "Edward!" she said in a voice quivering with rage. "If you sign that I will never speak to you again!"

He hesitated, then put the pen to paper.

Everyone was silent. His hand moved, and the scratch of the quill on the paper sounded like thunder.

Edward put down the pen.

"How could you treat your mother this way?" Augusta said, and the sob in her voice was genuine.

Emily sanded the signature and picked up the document.

Augusta moved between Emily and the door.

Both Edward and Micky looked on, bemused and motionless, as the two women faced each other.

Augusta said: "Give me that paper."

Emily stepped closer, hesitated in front of Augusta, and then, astonishingly, she slapped Augusta's face.

The blow stung. Augusta cried out with surprise and pain and staggered back.

Emily stepped past her quickly, opened the door, and left the room, still clutching the document.

Augusta sat down heavily in the nearest chair and began to cry.

She heard Edward and Micky leave the room.

She felt old, defeated and alone.

3

THE ISSUE OF TWO MILLION POUNDS' WORTH of Santamaria harbor bonds was a flop, much worse than Hugh had feared. By the deadline date Pilasters Bank had sold only four hundred thousand pounds' worth, and on the following day the price immediately fell. Hugh was deeply glad he had forced Edward to sell the bonds on commission rather than underwriting them.

On the following Monday morning Jonas Mulberry brought in the summary of the previous week's business that was handed to all the partners. Before the man had left the room Hugh noticed a discrepancy. "Just a minute, Mulberry," he said. "This can't be right." There was a huge fall in cash on deposit, well over a million pounds. "There hasn't been a big withdrawal, has there?"

"Not that I know of, Mr. Hugh," said Mulberry.

Hugh looked around the room. All the partners were there except Edward, who had not yet arrived. "Does anyone recall a big withdrawal last week?"

Nobody did.

Hugh stood up. "Let's check," he said to Mulberry.

They went up the stairs to the senior clerks' room. The item they were looking for was too big to have been a cash withdrawal. It had to be an interbank transaction. Hugh recalled from his days as a clerk that there was a journal of such transactions updated daily. He sat at a table and said to Mulberry: "Find me the interbank book, please."

Mulberry pulled a big ledger from a shelf and set it in front of him. Another clerk piped up: "Is there anything I can do to assist, Mr. Hugh? I keep that ledger." He had a worried look and Hugh realized he was afraid he might have made an error.

Hugh said: "You're Clemmow, aren't you?"

"Yes, sir."

"What big withdrawals were there last week—a million pounds or more?"

"Only one," the clerk said immediately. "The Santamaria Harbor Company withdrew one million, eight hundred thousand— the amount of the bond issue, less commission."

Hugh shot to his feet. "But they didn't have that much—they only raised four hundred thousand!"

Clemmow turned pale. "The issue was two million pounds' of bonds—"

"But it wasn't underwritten, it was a commission sale!"

"I checked their balance—it was a million eight."

"Damnation!" Hugh shouted. All the clerks in the room stared at him. "Show me the ledger!"

Another clerk on the other side of the room pulled down a huge book, brought it over to Hugh and opened it at a page marked: "Santamaria Harbor Board."

There were only three entries: a credit of two million pounds, a debit of two hundred thousand pounds commission to the bank, and a transfer to another bank of the balance.

Hugh was livid. The money was gone. If it had simply been credited to the account in error, the mistake could have been rectified easily. But the money had been withdrawn from the bank the next day. That suggested a carefully planned fraud. "By God, someone is going to jail for this," he said wrathfully. "Who wrote these entries?"

"I did, sir," said the clerk who had brought him the book. He was shaking with fear.

"On what instructions?"

"The usual paperwork. It was all in order."

"Where did it come from?"

"From Mr. Oliver."

Simon Oliver was a Cordovan and the cousin of Micky Miranda. Hugh instantly suspected he was behind the fraud.

Hugh did not want to continue this inquiry in front of twenty clerks. He was already regretting that he had let them all know about the problem. But when he started he had not known he was going to uncover a massive embezzlement.

Oliver was Edward's clerk, and worked on the partners' floor alongside Mulberry. "Find Mr. Oliver right away and bring him to the Partners' Room," Hugh said to Mulberry. He would continue the investigation there, with the other partners.

"Right away, Mr. Hugh," said Mulberry. "All of you get back to your work, now," he said to the rest of them. They returned to their desks and picked up their pens, but before Hugh was out of the room a buzz of excited conversation broke out.

Hugh returned to the Partners' Room. "There's been a major fraud," he said grimly. "The Santamaria Harbor Company has been paid the full amount of the bond issue even though we only sold four hundred thousand."

They were all horrified. "How the devil did it happen?" said William.

"The amount was credited to their account and then immediately transferred to another bank."

"Who's responsible?"

"I think it was done by Simon Oliver, Edward's clerk. I've sent for him, but my guess is the swine is already on a ship headed for Cordova."

Sir Harry said: "Can we get the money back?"

"I don't know. They may have moved it out of the country by now."

"They can't build a harbor with stolen money!"

"Perhaps they don't want to build a harbor. The whole thing could have been a damned swindle."

"Good God."

Mulberry came in—and, to Hugh's surprise, he was accompanied by Simon Oliver. That suggested that Oliver had not stolen the money. He had a thick contract in his hand. He looked scared: no doubt Hugh's remark about someone going to jail had been repeated to him.

Without preamble Oliver said: "The Santamaria issue was underwritten—the contract says so." He held the document out to Hugh with a trembling hand.

Hugh said: "The partners agreed that these bonds were to be sold on a commission basis."

"Mr. Edward told me to draw up an underwriting contract."

"Can you prove it?"

"Yes!" He gave Hugh another sheet of paper. This was a contract brief, a short note of the terms of an agreement, given by a partner to the clerk who was to draw up the full contract. It was in Edward's handwriting and it quite clearly said that the loan was to be underwritten.

That settled it. Edward was responsible. There had been no fraud, and there was no way the money could be got back. The whole transaction was perfectly legitimate. Hugh was dismayed and enraged.

"All right, Oliver, you can go," he said.

Oliver stood his ground. "I hope I may take it that no suspicion attaches to me, Mr. Hugh."

Hugh was not convinced that Oliver was

totally innocent, but he was obliged to say: "You are not to be blamed for anything you did under Mr. Edward's orders."

"Thank you, sir." Oliver went out.

Hugh looked at his partners. "Edward went against our collective decision," he said bitterly. "He changed the terms of the issue behind our backs. And it has cost us one million, four hundred thousand pounds."

Samuel sat down heavily. "How dreadful," he said.

Sir Harry and Major Hartshorn just looked bewildered.

William said: "Are we bankrupt?"

Hugh realized the question was addressed to him. Well, were they bankrupt? It was unthinkable. He reflected for a moment. "Technically, no," he said. "Although our cash reserve has gone down by one million four hundred thousand pounds, the bonds appear on the other side of our balance sheet, valued at nearly their purchase price. So our assets match our liabilities, and we're solvent."

Samuel added: "As long as the price doesn't collapse."

"Indeed. If something happened to cause a fall in South American bonds we would be in deep trouble." To think that the mighty Pilasters Bank was so weak made him feel sick with rage at Edward.

Sir Harry said: "Can we keep this quiet?"

"I doubt it," Hugh replied. "I'm afraid I made no attempt to hide it up in the senior clerks' room. It's gone around the building by now and it will be all over the City by the end of the lunch hour."

Jonas Mulberry interjected a practical question. "What about our liquidity, Mr. Hugh? We'll need a large deposit before the end of the week to meet routine withdrawals. We can't sell the harbor bonds—it would depress the price."

That was a thought. Hugh worried at the problem for a moment then said: "I'll borrow a million from the Colonial Bank. Old Cunliffe will keep it quiet. That should tide us over." He looked around at the others. "That takes care of the immediate emergency. However, the bank is dangerously weak. In the medium term we have to correct the position just as fast as we can."

William said: "What about Edward?"

Hugh knew what Edward had to do: resign. But he wanted someone else to say it, so he remained silent.

Eventually Samuel said: "Edward must

resign from the bank. None of us could ever trust him again."

William said: "He may withdraw his capital."

"He can't," Hugh said. "We haven't got the cash. That threat has lost its power."

"Of course," William said. "I hadn't thought of that."

Sir Harry said: "Then who will be Senior Partner?"

There was a moment of silence. Samuel broke it by saying: "Oh, for goodness' sake, can there be any question? Who uncovered Edward's deceit? Who took charge in the crisis? Who have you all looked to for guidance? During the last hour all the decisions have been made by one person. The rest of you have just asked questions and looked helpless. You *know* who the new Senior Partner must be."

Hugh was taken by surprise. His mind had been on the problems facing the bank, and he had not given a thought to his own position. Now he saw that Samuel was right. The others had all been more or less inert. Ever since he noticed the discrepancy in the weekly summary he had been acting as if he were the Senior Partner. And he knew he was the only one capable of steering the bank through the crisis.

Slowly it dawned on him that he was about to achieve his life's ambition: he was going to be Senior Partner of Pilasters Bank. He looked at William, Harry and George. They all had a shamefaced air. They had brought about this disaster by allowing Edward to become Senior Partner. Now they knew Hugh had been right all along. They were wishing they had listened to him before, and they wanted to make up for their error. He could see in their faces that they wanted him to take over.

But they had to say it.

He looked at William, who was the most senior Pilaster after Samuel. "What do you think?"

He hesitated only for a second. "I think you should be Senior Partner, Hugh," he said.

"Major Hartshorn?"

"I agree."

"Sir Harry?"

"Certainly—and I hope you'll accept."

It was done. Hugh could hardly believe it.

He took a deep breath. "Thank you for your confidence. I will accept. I hope I can bring us all through this calamity with our reputation and our fortunes intact."

At that moment Edward came in.

There was a dismayed silence. They had been discussing him almost as if he were dead, and it was a shock to see him in the room.

At first he did not notice the atmosphere. "This whole place is in turmoil," he said. "Juniors running around, senior clerks whispering in the corridors, hardly anyone doing any work—what the devil is going on?"

Nobody spoke.

Consternation spread over his face, then a look of guilt. "What's wrong?" he said, but his expression told Hugh that he could guess. "You'd better tell me why you're all staring at me," he persisted. "After all, I am the Senior Partner."

"No, you're not," said Hugh. "I am."

CHAPTER THREE

1

MISS DOROTHY PILASTER married Viscount Nicholas Ipswich at Kensington Methodist Hall on a cold, bright morning in November. The service was simple though the sermon was long. Afterwards a lunch of hot consommé, Dover sole, roast grouse and peach sherbet was served to three hundred guests in a vast heated tent in the garden of Hugh's house.

Hugh was very happy. His sister was radiantly beautiful and her new husband was charming to everyone. But the happiest person there was Hugh's mother. Smiling beatifically, she sat beside the groom's father, the duke of Norwich. For the first time in twenty-four years she was not wearing black:

she had on a blue-gray cashmere outfit that set off her thick silver hair and calm gray eyes. Her life had been blighted by his father's suicide, and she had suffered years of scrimping poverty, but now in her sixties she had everything she wanted. Her beautiful daughter was Viscountess Ipswich and would one day be the duchess of Norwich, and her son was rich and successful and the Senior Partner of Pilasters Bank. "I used to think I had been unlucky," she murmured to Hugh in between courses. "I was wrong." She put her hand on his arm in a gesture like a blessing. "I'm very fortunate." It made Hugh want to cry.

Because none of the women wanted to wear white (for fear of competing with the bride) or black (because it was for funerals) the guests made a colorful splash. They seemed to have chosen hot colors to ward off the autumn chill: bright orange, deep yellow, raspberry-red and fuchsia-pink. The men were wearing black, white and gray, as always. Hugh had on a frock coat with velvet lapels and cuffs: it was black, but as usual he defied convention by wearing a bright blue silk tie, his only eccentricity. He was so respectable nowadays that he sometimes felt nostalgic for the time when he had been the black sheep of the family.

He took a sip of Château Margaux, his favorite red wine. It was a lavish wedding breakfast for a special couple, and Hugh was glad he could afford it. But he also felt a twinge of guilt about spending all that money when Pilasters Bank was so weak. They still had one million four hundred thousand pounds' worth of Santamaria harbor bonds, plus other Cordova bonds valued at almost a million pounds; and they could not sell them without causing a drop in the price, which was the very thing Hugh feared. It was going to take him at least a year to strengthen the balance sheet. However, he had steered the bank through the immediate crisis, and they now had enough cash to meet normal withdrawals for the foreseeable future. Edward no longer came to the bank at all, although technically he would remain a partner until the end of the financial year. They were safe from everything except some unexpected catastrophe such as war, earthquake or plague. On balance he felt he was entitled to give his only sister an expensive wedding.

And it was good for Pilasters Bank. Everyone in the financial community knew that the bank was down more than a million on Santamaria harbor. This big party boosted confidence by assuring people that the Pilasters were still unimaginably rich. A cheap wedding would have aroused suspicion.

Dotty's dowry of a hundred thousand pounds had been made over to her husband, but it remained invested in the bank, earning five percent. Nick could withdraw it, but he did not need it all at once. He would draw money gradually as he paid off his father's mortgages and reorganized the estate. Hugh was glad he did not want all the cash right away, for large withdrawals put a strain on the bank at present.

Everyone knew about Dotty's huge dowry. Hugh and Nick had not been able to keep it completely secret, and it was the kind of thing that got around very quickly. Now it was the talk of London. Hugh guessed it was being discussed this very moment at half the tables at least.

Looking around, he caught the eye of one guest who was not happy—indeed, she wore a miserable, cheated look, like a eunuch at an orgy: Aunt Augusta.

"London society has degenerated completely," Augusta said to Colonel Mudeford.

"I fear you may be right, Lady Whitehaven," he murmured politely.

"Breeding counts for nothing anymore," she went on. "Jews are admitted everywhere."

"Quite so."

"I was the first countess of Whitehaven, but the Pilasters were a distinguished family for a century before being honored with a title; whereas today a man whose father was a navvy can get a peerage simply because he made a fortune selling sausages."

"Indeed." Colonel Mudeford turned to the woman on his other side and said: "Mrs. Telston, may I hand you some more red-currant sauce?"

Augusta lost interest in him. She was seething at the spectacle she had been forced to attend. Hugh Pilaster, son of bankrupt Tobias, giving Château Margaux to three hundred guests; Lydia Pilaster, widow of Tobias, sitting next to the duke of Norwich; Dorothy Pilaster, daughter of Tobias, married to Viscount Ipswich with the biggest dowry anyone had ever heard of. Whereas her son, dear Teddy, the offspring of the great Joseph Pilaster, had been summarily dismissed as Senior Partner and was soon to have his marriage annulled.

There were no rules anymore! Anyone could enter society. As if to prove the point she caught sight of the greatest parvenu of them all: Mrs. Solly Greenbourne, formerly Maisie Robinson. It was amazing that Hugh had the gall to invite her, a woman whose whole life had been scandal. First she had been practically a prostitute, then she had married the richest Jew in London, and now she ran a hospital where women who were no better than herself could give birth to their bastards. But there she was, sitting at the next table in a dress the color of a new copper penny, chatting earnestly to the governor of the Bank of England. She was probably talking about unmarried mothers. And he was listening!

"Put yourself in the position of an unmarried servant girl," Maisie said to the governor. He looked startled, and she suppressed a grin. "Think of the consequences if you become a mother: you will lose your job and your home, you will have no means of support, and your child will have no father. Would you then think to yourself: 'Oh, but I can be delivered at Mrs. Greenbourne's nice hospital in Southwark, so I may as well go ahead and do it?' Of course not. My hospital does nothing to encourage girls into immorality. I just save them from giving birth in the gutter."

Dan Robinson, sitting on his sister's other side, joined in. "It's rather like the banking bill I'm proposing in Parliament, which would oblige banks to take out insurance for the benefit of small depositors."

"I know of it," the governor said.

Dan went on: "Some critics say it would encourage bankruptcy by making it less painful. But that's nonsense. No banker would want to fail, under any circumstances."

"Indeed not."

"When a banker is making a deal he does not think that he may make a widow in Bournemouth penniless by his rashness—he worries about his own wealth. Similarly, making illegitimate children suffer does nothing to discourage unscrupulous men from seducing servant girls."

"I do see your point," the governor said with a pained expression. "A most . . . ah . . . original parallel."

Maisie decided they had tormented him enough, and turned away, letting him concentrate on his grouse.

Dan said to her: "Have you ever noticed

how peerages always go to the wrong people? Look at Hugh and his cousin Edward. Hugh is honest, talented and hardworking, where Edward is foolish, lazy and worthless —yet Edward is the earl of Whitehaven and Hugh is just plain Mr. Pilaster."

Maisie was trying not to look at Hugh. Although she was glad to have been invited, she found it painful to see him in the bosom of his family. His wife, his sons, his mother and his sister made a closed family circle that left her outside. She knew his marriage to Nora was unhappy: it was obvious from the way they spoke to one another, never touching, never smiling, never affectionate. But that was no consolation. They were a family and she would never be part of it.

She wished she had not come to the wedding.

A footman came to Hugh's side and said quietly: "There's a telephone call for you from the bank, sir."

"I can't speak now," Hugh said.

A few minutes later his butler came out. "Mr. Mulberry from the bank is on the telephone, sir, asking for you."

"I can't speak now!" Hugh said irritably.

"Very good, sir." The butler turned away.

"No, wait a minute," Hugh said. Mulberry knew Hugh would be in the middle of the wedding breakfast. He was an intelligent and responsible man. He would not insist on speaking to Hugh unless something was wrong.

Very wrong.

Hugh felt a chill of fear.

"I'd better speak to him," he said. He stood up, saying: "Please excuse me, Mother, Your Grace—something I have to attend to."

He hurried out of the tent, across the lawn and into the house. The telephone was in his library. He picked up the instrument and said: "Hugh Pilaster speaking."

He heard the voice of his clerk. "It's Mulberry, sir. I'm sorry to—"

"What's happened?"

"A telegram from New York. War has broken out in Cordova."

"Oh, no!" It was catastrophic news for Hugh, his family and the bank. Nothing could be worse.

"Civil war, in fact," Mulberry went on. "A rebellion. The Miranda family has attacked the capital city, Palma."

Hugh's heart was racing. "Any indication of how strong they are?" If the rebellion could be crushed quickly there was still hope.

"President Garcia has fled."

"The devil he has." That meant it was serious. He cursed Micky and Edward bitterly. "Anything else?"

"There's another cable from our Cordova office, but it's still being decoded."

"Telephone to me again as soon as it's ready."

"Very good, sir."

Hugh cranked the machine, got the operator, and gave the name of the stockbroker used by the bank. He waited while the man was called to the telephone. "Danby, this is Hugh Pilaster. What's happening to Cordovan bonds?"

"We're offering them at half par and getting no takers."

Half price, Hugh thought. Pilasters was already bankrupt. Despair filled his heart. "What will they fall to?"

"They'll go to zero, I should think. No one pays interest on government bonds in the middle of a civil war."

Zero. Pilasters had just lost two and a half million pounds. There was no hope now of gradually returning the balance sheet to strength. Clutching at straws, Hugh said:

"Suppose the rebels are wiped out in the next few hours—what then?"

"I shouldn't think anyone will buy the bonds even then," said Danby. "Investors will wait and see. At the very best it will take five or six weeks before confidence begins to return."

"I see." Hugh knew Danby was right. The broker was only confirming Hugh's own instincts.

"I say, Pilaster, your bank will be all right, won't it?" Danby said worriedly. "You must have quite a lot of these bonds. It was noised about that you hardly sold any of the Santamaria harbor issue."

Hugh hesitated. He hated to tell lies. But the truth would destroy the bank. "We've got more Cordovan bonds than I'd like, Danby. But we've got a lot of other assets as well."

"Good."

"I must get back to my guests." Hugh had no intention of going back to his guests, but he wanted to give an impression of calm. "I'm giving lunch to three hundred people —my sister got married this morning."

"So I heard. Congratulations."

"Good-bye."

Before he could ask for another number,

Mulberry called again. "Mr. Cunliffe from the Colonial Bank is here, sir," he said, and Hugh could hear the panic in his voice. "He is asking for repayment of the loan."

"Damn him," Hugh said fervently. The Colonial had lent Pilasters a million pounds to tide them over the crisis, but the money was repayable on demand. Cunliffe had heard the news and seen the sudden slump in Cordova bonds, and he knew Pilasters must be in trouble. Naturally he wanted to get his money out before the bank went bust.

And he was only the first. Others would be close behind. Tomorrow morning depositors would be queuing outside the doors, wanting cash. And Hugh would not be able to pay them.

"Have we got a million pounds, Mulberry?"

"No, sir."

The weight of the world descended on Hugh's shoulders, and he felt old. This was the end. It was the banker's nightmare: people came for their money, and the bank did not have it. And it was happening to Hugh.

"Tell Mr. Cunliffe that you have been unable to get authorization to sign the cheque, because all the partners are at the wedding," he said.

"Very good, Mr. Hugh."

"And then . . ."

"Yes, sir?"

Hugh paused. He knew he had no choice, but still he hesitated to say the dreadful words. He shut his eyes. Better get it over with.

"And then, Mulberry, you must close the doors of the bank."

"Oh, Mr. Hugh."

"I'm sorry, Mulberry."

There was an odd noise down the line, and Hugh realized that Mulberry was crying.

He put down the phone. Staring at the bookshelves of his library, he saw instead the grand facade of Pilasters Bank, and imagined the closing of the ornate iron doors. He saw passersby stop and look. Before long a crowd would gather, pointing at the closed doors and chattering excitedly. The word would go around the City faster than a fire in an oil store: Pilasters has crashed.

Pilasters has crashed.

Hugh buried his face in his hands.

2

"WE ARE ALL absolutely penniless," said Hugh.

They did not understand, at first. He could tell by their faces.

They gathered in the drawing room of his house. It was a cluttered room, decorated by his wife, Nora, who loved to drape every stick of furniture with flowered fabrics and crowd every surface with ornaments. The guests had gone, at last—Hugh had not told anyone the bad news until the party was over—but the family were still in their wedding finery. Augusta sat with Edward, both of them wearing scornful, disbelieving expressions. Uncle Samuel sat next to Hugh. The other partners, Young William, Major Hartshorn and Sir Harry, stood behind a sofa on which sat their wives Beatrice, Madeleine and Clementine. Nora, flushed from lunch and champagne, sat in her usual chair beside the fire. The bride and groom, Nick and Dotty, held hands, looking frightened.

Hugh felt most sorry for the newlyweds. "Dotty's dowry is gone, Nick. I'm afraid all our plans have come to nothing."

Aunt Madeleine said shrilly: "You're the Senior Partner—it must be your fault!"

She was being stupid and malicious. It was a predictable reaction, yet all the same Hugh was wounded. It was so unfair that she should blame him after he had fought so hard to prevent this.

However, William, her younger brother, corrected her with surprising sharpness. "Don't talk rot, Madeleine," he said. "Edward deceived us all and burdened the bank with huge amounts of Cordova bonds which are now worthless." Hugh was grateful to him for being honest. William went on: "The blame lies with those of us who let him become Senior Partner." He looked at Augusta.

Nora looked bewildered. "We can't be *penniless*," she said.

"But we are," Hugh said patiently. "All our money is in the bank and the bank has failed." There was some excuse for his wife's not understanding: she had not been born into a banking family.

Augusta stood up and went to the fireplace. Hugh wondered whether she would try to defend her son, but she was not that foolish. "Never mind whose fault it is," she said. "We must salvage what we can. There must be quite a lot of cash in the bank still, gold and bank notes. We must get it out and hide it somewhere safe before the creditors move in. Then—"

Hugh interrupted her. "We'll do no such thing," he said sharply. "It's not our money."

"Of course it's our money!" she cried.

"Be quiet and sit down, Augusta, or I'll have the footmen throw you out."

She was sufficiently surprised to shut up, but she did not sit down.

Hugh said: "There is cash at the bank, and as we have not officially been declared bankrupt, we can choose to pay some of our creditors. You'll all have to dismiss your servants; and if you send them to the side door of the bank with a note of how much they are owed I will pay them off. You should ask all tradesmen with whom you have accounts to give you a statement, and I will see that they are paid too—but only up to today's date: I will not pay any debts you incur from now on."

"Who are you to tell me to dismiss my servants?" Augusta said indignantly.

Hugh was prepared to feel sympathy for their plight, even though they had brought it on themselves; but this deliberate obtuseness was very wearying, and Hugh snapped at her: "If you don't dismiss them they will leave anyway, because they won't get paid. Aunt Augusta, try to understand that *you haven't got any money.*"

"Ridiculous," she muttered.

Nora spoke again. "I can't dismiss our servants. It's not possible to live in a house like this with no servants."

"That need not trouble you," Hugh said. "You won't be living in a house like this. I will have to sell it. We will all have to sell our houses, furniture, works of art, wine cellars and jewelry."

"This is absurd!" Augusta cried.

"It's the law," Hugh retorted. "Each partner is personally liable for all the debts of the business."

"I'm not a partner," said Augusta.

"But Edward is. He resigned as Senior Partner but he remained a partner, on paper. And he owns your house—Joseph left it to him."

Nora said: "We have to live somewhere."

"First thing tomorrow we must all look for small, cheap houses to rent. If you pick something modest our creditors will sanction it. If not you will have to choose again."

Augusta said: "I have absolutely no intention of moving house, and that's final. And I imagine the rest of the family feel the same." She looked at her sister-in-law. "Madeleine?"

"Quite right, Augusta," said Madeleine. "George and I will stay where we are. All this is foolishness. We can't possibly be destitute."

Hugh despised them. Even now, when their arrogance and foolishness had ruined them, they still refused to listen to reason. In the end they would have to give up their illusions. But if they tried to cling to wealth that was no longer theirs, they would destroy the family's reputation as well as its fortune. He was determined to make them behave with scrupulous honesty, in poverty as in wealth. It was going to be an uphill struggle but he would not give in.

Augusta turned to her daughter. "Clementine, I'm sure you and Harry will take the same view as Madeleine and George."

Clementine said: "No, Mother."

Augusta gasped. Hugh was equally startled. It was not like his cousin Clementine to go against her mother. At least one family member had some common sense, he thought.

Clementine said: "It was listening to you that got us all into this trouble. If we had made Hugh Senior Partner, instead of Edward, we would all still be as rich as Croesus."

Hugh began to feel better. Some of the family understood what he had tried to do.

Clementine went on: "You were wrong, Mother, and you've ruined us. I'm never going to heed your advice again. Hugh was right, and we had better let him do all he can to guide us through this dreadful disaster."

William said: "Quite right, Clementine. We should do whatever Hugh advises."

The battle lines were drawn. On Hugh's side were William, Samuel, and Clementine, who ruled her husband Sir Harry. They would try to behave decently and honestly. Against him were Augusta, Edward, and Madeleine, who spoke for Major Hartshorn: they would try to snatch what they could and let the family's reputation go to hell.

Then Nora said defiantly: "You'll have to carry me out of this house."

There was a bitter taste in Hugh's mouth. His own wife was joining the enemy. "You're the only person in the room who has gone against their husband or wife," he said sadly. "Don't you owe me any loyalty at all?"

She tossed her head. "I didn't marry you to live in poverty."

"All the same you *will* leave this house," he said grimly. He looked at the other die-hards: Augusta, Edward, Madeleine and Major Hartshorn. "You will all have to give in, eventually," he said. "If you don't do it now, with dignity, you'll do it later, in disgrace, with bailiffs and policemen and newspaper reporters in attendance, vilified by the gutter press and slighted by your unpaid servants."

"We shall see about that," said Augusta.

When they had all gone Hugh sat staring into the fire, racking his brains for some way to pay the bank's creditors.

He was determined not to let Pilasters go into formal bankruptcy. The idea was almost too painful to contemplate. All his life he had lived under the shadow of his father's bankruptcy. His whole career had been an attempt to prove he was not tainted. In his heart of hearts he feared that if he suffered the same fate as his father, he too might be driven to take his own life.

Pilasters was finished as a bank. It had closed its doors on its depositors, and that was the end. But in the long term it ought to be able to repay its debts, especially if the partners were scrupulous about selling all their valuable possessions.

As the afternoon faded into twilight, the outlines of a plan began to form in his mind, and he allowed himself the faintest glimmer of hope.

At six P.M. he went to see Ben Greenbourne.

Greenbourne was past seventy, but still fit, and he continued to run the business. He had a daughter, Kate, but Solly had been his only son; so when he retired he would have to hand over to his nephews, and he seemed reluctant to do that.

Hugh called at the mansion in Piccadilly. The house gave the impression not just of prosperity but of limitless wealth. Every clock was a jewel, every stick of furniture a priceless antique; every panel was exquisitely carved, every carpet specially woven. Hugh was shown into the library, where gaslights blazed and a fire roared. In this room he had first learned that the boy called Bertie Greenbourne was his son.

Wondering if the books were just for show, he glanced at several while he was waiting. Some might have been chosen for their fine bindings, he thought, but others were well thumbed, and several languages were represented. Greenbourne's learning was genuine.

The old man appeared fifteen minutes later, and apologized for keeping Hugh waiting. "A domestic problem detained me," he said with clipped Prussian courtesy. His family had never been Prussian; they had copied the manners of upper-class Germans then retained them through a hundred years of living in England. He held himself as straight as ever, but Hugh thought he looked tired and worried. Greenbourne did not say what the domestic problem was and Hugh did not ask.

"You know that Cordovan bonds have crashed this afternoon," Hugh said.

"Yes."

"And you probably heard that my bank has closed its doors as a result."

"Yes. I am very sorry."

"It's twenty-four years since the last time an English bank failed."

"That was Overend and Gurney. I remember it well."

"So do I. My father went broke and hanged himself in his office in Leadenhall Street."

Greenbourne was embarrassed. "I am

most terribly sorry, Pilaster. That dreadful fact had slipped my mind."

"A lot of firms went down in that crisis. But much worse will happen tomorrow." Hugh leaned forward on his stool and began his big pitch. "In the last quarter of a century the business done in the City has increased tenfold. And because banking has become so sophisticated and complex, we are all more closely intertwined than ever. Some of the people whose money we have lost will be unable to pay their debts, so they will go bust too—and so on. Next week *dozens* of banks will fail, hundreds of businesses will be forced to close, and thousands upon thousands of people will suddenly find themselves destitute—unless we take action to prevent it."

"Action?" said Greenbourne with more than a hint of irritation. "What action can be taken? Your only remedy is to pay your debts; you cannot do so; therefore you are helpless."

"Alone, yes, I'm helpless. But I am hoping that the banking community will do something."

"Do you propose to ask other bankers to pay your debts? Why should they?" He was getting ready to be angry.

"You'll agree, surely, that it would be better for all of us if Pilasters' creditors could be paid in full."

"Obviously."

"Suppose a syndicate of bankers were formed to take over both the assets and the liabilities of Pilasters. The syndicate would guarantee to pay any creditor on demand. At the same time, it would begin to liquidate Pilasters' assets in an orderly fashion."

Suddenly Greenbourne was interested, and his irritability vanished as he considered this novel proposal. "I see. If the members of the syndicate were sufficiently respected and prestigious, their guarantee might be enough to reassure everyone, and creditors might not demand their cash immediately. With luck, the flow of money coming in from the sale of assets might cover the payments to creditors."

"And a dreadful crisis would be averted."

Greenbourne shook his head. "But in the end, the members of the syndicate would lose money, for Pilasters' liabilities are greater than its assets."

"Not necessarily."

"How so?"

"We have more than two million pounds' worth of Cordova bonds which are today valued at nothing. However, our other assets are substantial. A lot depends on how much we can raise by the sale of the partners' houses, and so on; but I estimate that even today the shortfall is only a million pounds."

"So the syndicate must expect to lose a million."

"Perhaps. But Cordova bonds may not be worthless forever. The rebels may be defeated. Or the new government may resume interest payments. At some point the price of Cordova bonds will rise."

"Possibly."

"If the bonds came up to just half their previous level, the syndicate would break even. And if they did better than that, the syndicate would actually make a profit."

Greenbourne shook his head. "It might work, but for those Santamaria harbor bonds. That Cordovan Minister, Miranda, strikes me as an out-and-out thief; and his father is apparently the leader of the rebels. My guess is that the whole two million pounds has gone to pay for guns and ammunition. In which case investors will never see a penny."

The old boy was as sharp as always, Hugh thought: he had exactly the same fear. "I'm afraid you may be right. All the same there's a chance. And if you allow a financial panic you're sure to lose money in other ways."

"It's an ingenious plan. You always were the cleverest of your family, young Pilaster."

"But the plan depends on you."

"Ah."

"If you agree to head the syndicate, the City will follow your lead. If you refuse to be part of it, the syndicate will not have the prestige to reassure creditors."

"I see that." Greenbourne was not the man for false modesty.

"Will you do it?" Hugh held his breath.

The old man was silent for several seconds, thinking, then he said firmly: "No, I won't."

Hugh slumped in his chair. It was his last shot and it had failed. He felt a great weariness descend on him, as if his life were over and he were a tired old man.

Greenbourne said: "All my life I have been cautious. Where other men see high profits, I see high risks, and I resist the temptation. Your uncle Joseph was not like me. He would take the risk—and he pocketed the profits. His son Edward was worse. I say nothing about you: you have only just taken over. But the Pilasters must pay the price for their years of high profits. I didn't take those profits—why should I pay your debts? If I spend money to rescue you now, the foolish investor will be rewarded and the careful one will suffer. And if banking were run that way, why should anyone be cautious? We might as well all take risks, for there is no risk when failed banks can always be rescued. But there is always risk. Banking cannot be run your way. There will always be crashes. They are necessary to remind good and bad investors that risk is real."

Hugh had wondered, before coming here, whether to tell the old man that Micky Miranda had murdered Solly. Now he considered it again, but he came to the same conclusion: it would shock and distress the old man but it would do nothing to persuade him to rescue Pilasters.

He was casting about for something to say, some last attempt to change Greenbourne's mind, when the butler came in and said: "Pardon me, Mr. Greenbourne, but you asked to be called the moment the detective arrived."

Greenbourne stood up immediately, looking agitated, but his courtesy would not let him rush out without an explanation.

"I'm sorry, Pilaster, but I must leave you. My granddaughter Rebecca has . . . disappeared . . . and we are all distraught."

"I'm so sorry to hear that," Hugh said. He knew Solly's sister Kate, and he had a vague memory of her daughter, a pretty dark-haired girl. "I hope you find her safe and well."

"We don't believe she has suffered violence—in fact we're quite sure she has only run off with a boy. But that's bad enough. Please excuse me."

"By all means."

The old man went out, leaving Hugh amid the ruins of his hopes.

3

MAISIE SOMETIMES WONDERED if there was something infectious about going into labor. It often happened, in a ward full of women nine months pregnant, that days would go by without incident, but as soon as one started labor the others would follow within hours.

It had been like that today. It had started at four o'clock in the morning and they had been delivering babies ever since. The midwives and nurses did most of the work, but

when they were overstretched Maisie and
Rachel had to leave their pens and ledgers
and scurry around with towels and blankets.

By seven o'clock, however, it was all over,
and they were enjoying a cup of tea in
Maisie's office with Rachel's lover, Maisie's
brother Dan, when Hugh Pilaster came in.
"I bring very bad news, I'm afraid," he said
right away.

Maisie was pouring tea but his tone of
voice shocked her and she stopped. Looking
hard at his face she saw that he was grief-
stricken, and she thought someone must
have died. "Hugh, what has happened?"

"I think you keep all the hospital's money
in an account at my bank, don't you?"

If it was only money, Maisie thought, the
news could not be that bad.

Rachel answered Hugh's question. "Yes.
My father handles the money, but he has
kept his own private account with you ever
since he became the bank's lawyer, and I
suppose he found it convenient to do the
same with the hospital's account."

"And he invested your money in Cordova
bonds."

"Did he?"

Maisie said: "What's wrong, Hugh? For
goodness' sake tell us!"

"The bank has failed."

Maisie's eyes filled with tears, not for herself but for him. "Oh, Hugh!" she cried. She knew how much he was hurting. For him this was almost like the death of a loved one, for he had invested all his hopes and dreams in the bank. She wished she could take some of the pain into herself, to ease his suffering.

Dan said: "Good God. There will be a panic."

"All your money has gone," Hugh said. "You'll probably have to close the hospital. I can't tell you how sorry I am."

Rachel was white with shock. "That's not possible!" she said. "How can our money be gone?"

Dan answered her. "The bank can't pay its debts," he said bitterly. "That's what bankruptcy means, it means you owe people money and you can't pay them."

In a flash of recollection Maisie saw her father, a quarter of a century earlier looking much as Dan did today, saying exactly the same thing about bankruptcy. Dan had spent much of his life trying to protect ordinary people from the effects of these financial crises—but so far he had achieved nothing. "Perhaps now they'll pass your Banking Bill," she said to him.

Rachel said to Hugh: "But what have you *done* with our money?"

Hugh sighed. "Essentially this happened because of something Edward did while he was Senior Partner. It was a mistake, a huge mistake, and he lost a lot of money, more than a million pounds. I've been trying to hold everything together since then, but today my luck ran out."

"I just didn't know this could happen!" said Rachel.

Hugh said: "You should get some of your money back but not for a year or more."

Dan put his arm around Rachel but she would not be consoled. "And what is going to happen to all the wretched women who come here for help?"

Hugh looked so wounded that Maisie wanted to tell Rachel to shut up. "I would gladly give you the money out of my own pocket," he said. "But I've lost everything too."

"Surely something can be done?" she persisted.

"I did try. I've just come from Ben Greenbourne's house. I asked him to rescue the bank and pay the creditors, but he refused.

He has troubles of his own, poor man: apparently his granddaughter Rebecca has run off with her boyfriend. Anyway, without his support nothing can be done."

Rachel stood up. "I think I'd better go and see my father."

"I must go to the House of Commons," Dan said.

They went out.

Maisie's heart was full. She was dismayed at the prospect of closing the hospital, and rocked by the sudden destruction of all she had worked for; but most of all she ached for Hugh. She recalled, as if it were yesterday, the night seventeen years ago, after the Goodwood races, when Hugh had told her his life story; and she could hear now the agony in his voice when he told her that his father had gone bankrupt and taken his own life. He had said then that he was going to be the cleverest, most conservative and richest banker in the world one day—as if he believed that would ease the pain of his loss. And perhaps it would have. But instead he had suffered the same fate as his father.

Their eyes met across the room. Maisie read a silent appeal in his look. Slowly she got up and went to him. Standing beside his chair, she took his head in her hands and cradled it on her bosom, stroking his hair. Tentatively he put his arm around her waist, touching her gingerly at first, then hugging her to him hard. And then, at last, he began to cry.

When Hugh had gone Maisie made a tour of the wards. Now she saw everything with new eyes: the walls they had painted themselves, the beds they had bought in junk shops, the pretty curtains Rachel's mother had sewn. She remembered the superhuman efforts that had been required of her and Rachel to get the hospital opened: their battles with the medical establishment and the local council, the tireless charm they had used on the respectable householders and censorious clergy of the neighborhood, the sheer dogged persistence that had enabled them to pull through. She consoled herself with the thought that they had, after all, been victorious, and the hospital had been open for eleven years and had given comfort to hundreds of women. But she had wanted to make a permanent change. She had seen this as the first of dozens of Female Hospitals all over the country. In that she had failed.

She spoke to each of the women who had

given birth today. The only one she was worried about was Miss Nobody. She was a slight figure and her baby had been very small. Maisie guessed she had been starving herself to help conceal her pregnancy from her family. Maisie was always astonished that girls managed to do this—she herself had ballooned when pregnant and could not have hidden it after five months—but she knew from experience that it happened all the time.

She sat down on the edge of Miss Nobody's bed. The new mother was nursing her child, a girl. "Isn't she beautiful?" she said.

Maisie nodded. "She's got black hair, just like yours."

"My mother has the same hair."

Maisie reached out and stroked the tiny head. Like all babies, this one looked like Solly. In fact—

Maisie was jolted by a sudden revelation.

"Oh my God, I know who you are," she said.

The girl stared at her.

"You're Ben Greenbourne's granddaughter Rebecca, aren't you? You kept your pregnancy secret as long as you could, then ran away to have the baby."

The girl's eyes widened. "How did you know? You haven't seen me since I was two years old!"

"But I knew your mother so well. I was married to her brother, after all." Kate had not been as snobbish as the rest of the Greenbournes and had been kind to Maisie when the rest were not around. "And I remember when you were born. You had black hair, just like your daughter."

Rebecca was scared. "Promise you won't tell them?"

"I promise I won't do anything without your consent. But I think you ought to send word to your family. Your grandfather is distraught."

"He's the one I'm frightened of."

Maisie nodded. "I can understand why. He's a hard-hearted old curmudgeon, as I know from personal experience. But if you let me talk to him I think I can make him see sense."

"Would you?" said Rebecca in a voice full of youthful optimism. "Would you do that?"

"Of course," Maisie said. "But I won't tell

him where you are unless he promises to be kind."

Rebecca looked down. Her baby's eyes had closed and she had stopped sucking. "She's asleep," Rebecca said.

Maisie smiled. "Have you chosen a name for her yet?"

"Oh, yes," Rebecca said. "I'm going to call her Maisie."

Ben Greenbourne's face was wet with tears as he came out of the ward. "I've left her with Kate for a while," he said in a choked voice. He pulled a handkerchief from his pocket and dabbed ineffectually at his cheeks. Maisie had never seen her father-in-law lose his self-possession. He made a rather pathetic sight, but she felt it would do him a lot of good.

"Come to my room," she said. "I'll make you a cup of tea."

"Thank you."

She led him to her room and told him to sit down. He was the second man to weep in that chair this evening, she thought.

"All those young women," the old man said. "Are they all in the same position as Rebecca?"

"Not all," Maisie said. "Some are widows.

Some have been abandoned by their husbands. Quite a lot have run away from men who beat them. A woman will suffer a lot of pain, and stay with a husband even if he injures her; but when she gets pregnant she worries that his blows will damage the child, and that's when she leaves. But most of our women are like Rebecca, girls who have simply made a stupid mistake."

"I didn't think life had much more to teach me," he said. "Now I find I have been foolish and ignorant."

Maisie handed him a cup of tea. "Thank you," he said. "You're very kind. I was never kind to you."

"We all make mistakes," she said briskly.

"What a good thing you are here," he said to her. "Otherwise where would these poor girls go?"

"They would have their babies in ditches and alleyways," Maisie said.

"To think that might have happened to Rebecca."

"Unfortunately the hospital has to close," Maisie said.

"Why is that?"

She looked him in the eye. "All our

money was in Pilasters Bank," she said. "Now we are penniless."

"Is that so?" he said, and he looked very thoughtful.

Hugh undressed for bed but he felt far from sleepy, so he sat up in his dressing gown, staring into the fire, brooding. He went over and over the bank's situation in his mind, but he could think of no way to ameliorate it. Yet he could not stop thinking.

At midnight he heard a loud, determined knocking at the front door. He went downstairs in his nightclothes to answer it. There was a carriage at the curb and a liveried footman on the doorstep. The man said: "I beg pardon for knocking so late, sir, but the message is urgent." He handed over an envelope and left.

As Hugh closed the door his butler came down the stairs. "Is everything all right, sir?" he said worriedly.

"Just a message," Hugh said. "You can go back to bed."

"Thank you, sir."

Hugh opened the envelope and saw the neat, old-fashioned writing of a fussy elderly man. The words made his heart leap with joy.

12, Piccadilly
London, S.W.
November 23rd, 1890
Dear Pilaster,
On further reflection I have decided to
consent to your proposal. Yours, etc.
B. Greenbourne.

He looked up from the letter and grinned at the empty hall. "Well, I'll be blowed," he said delightedly. "I wonder what made the old man change his mind?"

4

AUGUSTA SAT IN THE BACK ROOM of the best jeweler's shop in Bond Street. Bright gaslights flared, making the jewelry glitter in the glass cases. The room was full of mirrors. An obsequious assistant padded across the room and placed in front of her a black velvet cloth bearing a diamond necklace.

The manager of the shop was standing beside her. "How much?" she asked him.

"Nine thousand pounds, Lady Whitehaven." He breathed the price piously, like a prayer.

The necklace was simple and stark, just a plain row of identical large square-cut dia-

monds set in gold. It would look very striking against her black widow's gowns, she
thought. But she was not buying it to wear.

"It's a wonderful piece, my lady; quite the
loveliest thing we have in the shop."

"Don't rush me, I'm thinking," she replied.

This was her last desperate attempt to
raise money. She had tried going openly to
the bank and demanding a hundred pounds
in gold sovereigns: the clerk, an insolent dog
called Mulberry, had refused her. She had
tried to have the house transferred from Edward's name into her own, but that had not
worked either: the deeds were in the safe of
old Bodwin, the bank's lawyer, and he had
been got at by Hugh. Now she was going to
try to buy diamonds on credit and sell them
for cash.

Edward had at first been her ally, but now
even he refused to help her. "What Hugh is
doing is for the best," he had said stupidly.
"If word gets around that family members
are trying to grab what they can, the syndicate could fall apart. They've been persuaded to put up money to avert a financial
crisis, not to keep the Pilaster family in luxury." It was a long speech for Edward. A
year ago it would have shaken her to the

core to have her son go against her, but since his rebellion over the annulment he was no longer the sweet, biddable boy she loved. Clementine had turned against her too, supporting Hugh's plans to turn them all into paupers. It made her shake with rage when she thought about it. But they would not get away with it.

She looked up at the shop manager. "I'll take it," she said decisively.

"A wise choice, I have no doubt, Lady Whitehaven," he said.

"Send the bill to the bank."

"Very good, my lady. We will deliver the necklace to Whitehaven House."

"I'll take it with me," Augusta said. "I want to wear it tonight."

The manager looked as if he were in pain. "You put me in an impossible position, my lady."

"What on earth are you talking about? Wrap it up!"

"I fear I cannot release the jewelry until payment has been received."

"Don't be ridiculous. Do you know who I am?"

"Yes—but the newspapers say the bank has closed its doors."

"This is an insult."

"I am very, very sorry."

Augusta stood up and picked up the necklace. "I refuse to listen to this nonsense. I shall take it with me."

Perspiring, the manager moved between her and the door. "I beg you not to," he said.

She moved toward him but he stood his ground. "Get out of my way!" she blazed.

"I shall have to have the shop door locked and send for the police," he said.

It dawned on Augusta that although the man was practically gibbering with terror he had not conceded one inch. He was afraid of her, but he was more frightened of losing nine thousand pounds' worth of diamonds. She realized she was defeated. Enraged, she threw the necklace on the floor. The man scooped it up with no attempt at dignity. Augusta opened the door herself, stalked through the shop, and went out to where her carriage waited.

She held her head high but she was mortified. The man had practically accused her of stealing. A small voice in the back of her mind said that stealing was exactly what she had been trying to do, but she stifled it. She rode home in a rage.

As she entered the house Hastead tried

to detain her, but she had no patience for domestic trivia at this moment, and she silenced him, saying: "Bring me a glass of warm milk." She had a pain in her stomach.

She went to her room. She sat at her dressing table and opened her jewelry box. There was very little in it. What she had was worth only a few hundred pounds. She pulled out the bottom tray, took out a piece of folded silk and unwrapped it to reveal the serpent-shaped gold ring that Strang had given her. As always, she slipped it on her finger and brushed the jeweled head against her lips. She would never sell this. How different everything would have been if she had been allowed to marry Strang. For a moment she felt like crying.

Then she heard strange voices outside her bedroom door. A man . . . two men, perhaps . . . and a woman. They did not sound like servants and anyway her staff would not have the temerity to stand around conversing on the landing. She stepped outside.

The door to her late husband's room was open and the voices came from in there. When she went in Augusta saw a young man, obviously a clerk, and an older, well-dressed couple of her own class. She had never set eyes on any of them before. She said: "In heaven's name who are you?"

The clerk said deferentially: "Stoddart, from the agents, my lady. Mr. and Mrs. de Graaf are very interested in buying your beautiful house—"

"Get out!" she said.

The clerk's voice rose to a squeak. "We have received instructions to put the house on the market—"

"Get out this minute! My house is not for sale!"

"But I personally spoke—"

Mr. de Graaf touched Stoddart's arm and silenced him. "An embarrassing mistake, quite obviously, Mr. Stoddart," he said mildly. He turned to his wife. "Shall we leave, my dear?" The two of them walked out with a quiet dignity that made Augusta seethe, and Stoddart scurried after them, spilling apologies everywhere.

Hugh was responsible. Augusta did not have to make inquiries to establish that. The house was the property of the syndicate that had rescued the bank, he said, and they naturally wished to sell it. He had told Augusta to move out, but she had refused. His response was to send prospective buyers to view the place anyway.

She sat down in Joseph's chair. Her butler came in with her hot milk. She said: "You are not to admit any more such people, Hastead—the house is not for sale."

"Very good, my lady." He set down her drink and hovered.

"Is there something else?" she asked him.

"M'lady, the butcher called personally today about his bill."

"Tell him he will be paid at Lady Whitehaven's convenience, not his own."

"Very good, m'lady. And both the footmen left today."

"You mean they gave notice?"

"No, they just went."

"Wretched people."

"My lady, the rest of the staff are asking when they will get their wages."

"Anything else?"

He looked bewildered. "But what shall I tell them?"

"Tell them I did not answer your question."

"Very good." He hesitated, then said: "I beg to give notice that I shall be leaving at the end of the week."

"Why?"

"All the rest of the Pilasters have dismissed their staff. Mr. Hugh told us we would be paid up to last Friday, but no more, regardless of how long we stay on."

"Get out of my sight, you traitor."

"Very good, my lady."

Augusta told herself she would be glad to see the back of Hastead. She was well rid of the lot of them, rats leaving the sinking ship.

She sipped her milk but the pain in her stomach did not ease.

She looked around the room. Joseph had never let her redecorate it, so it was still done out in the style she had chosen back in 1873, with leather-paper on the walls and heavy brocade curtains, and Joseph's collection of jeweled snuffboxes in a lacquered display cabinet. The room seemed dead, as he was. She wished she could bring him back. None of this would have happened if he were still alive. She had a momentary vision of him standing by the bay window, holding one of his favorite snuffboxes, turning it this way and that to see the play of light on the precious stones. She felt an unfamiliar choking sensation in her throat, and she shook her head to make the vision go away.

Soon Mr. de Graaf or someone like him would move into this bedroom. No doubt he would tear down the curtains and the wallpaper and redecorate, probably in the currently fashionable arts-and-crafts style, with oak paneling and hard rustic chairs.

She would have to move out. She had accepted this, although she pretended otherwise. But she was not going to move to a cramped modern house in St. John's Wood or Clapham, as Madeleine and Clementine had. She could not bear to live in reduced circumstances in London, where she could be seen by people she had once looked down upon.

She was going to leave the country.

She was not sure where to go. Calais was cheap but too close to London. Paris was elegant, but she felt too old to begin a new social life in a strange city. She had heard people talk of a place called Nice, on the Mediterranean coast of France, where a big house and servants could be had for next to nothing, and there was a quiet community of foreigners, many her own age, enjoying the mild winters and the sea air.

But she could not live on nothing a year. She had to have enough for rent and staff wages, and although she was prepared to live frugally she could not manage without a carriage. She had very little cash, no more than fifty pounds. Hence her desperate attempt to buy diamonds. Nine thousand pounds was not really enough, but it might have sufficed for a few years.

She knew she was jeopardizing Hugh's plans. Edward had been right about that. The goodwill of the syndicate depended on the family's being serious about paying off their debts. A family member running off to the Continent with her luggage full of jewelry was just the thing to upset a fragile coalition. In a way, that made the prospect more attractive: she would be happy to trip up the self-righteous Hugh.

But she had to have a stake. The rest would be easy: she would pack a single trunk, go to the steamship office to book passage, call a cab early in the morning, and slip away to the railway station without warning. But what could she use for money?

Looking around her husband's room she noticed a small notebook. She opened it, idly curious, and saw that someone—presumably Stoddart, the agent's clerk—had been making an inventory of the house contents. It angered her to see her possessions listed in a clerk's notebook and casually valued: *dining table £9; Egyptian screen 30s; portrait of a woman by Joshua Reynolds, £100.* There must be a few thousand pounds' worth of paintings in the house, but she could not pack those in a trunk. She turned the page and read *65 snuffboxes—refer to jewelry department.* She looked up. There in front of her, in the cabinet she had bought seventeen years ago, was the solution to her problem. Joseph's collection of jeweled snuffboxes was worth thousands, perhaps as much as a hundred thousand pounds. She could pack it into her luggage easily: the boxes themselves were tiny, designed to fit into a man's waistcoat pocket. They could be sold one by one, as money was needed.

Her heart beat faster. This could be the answer to her prayers.

She reached out to open the cabinet. It was locked.

She suffered a moment of panic. She was not sure she could break it open: the wood was stout, the panes of glass small and thick.

She calmed herself. Where would he keep the key? In the drawer of his writing table, probably. She went to the table and pulled open the drawer. In it was a book with the horrifying title of *The Duchess of Sodom,* which she hastily pushed to the back, and a small silver-colored key. She snatched up the key.

With a trembling hand she tried it in the

lock of the cabinet. As she turned it she heard a bolt click, and a moment later the door opened.

She breathed deeply and waited until her hands stopped shaking.

Then she began to remove the boxes from the shelves.

CHAPTER FOUR

1

THE PILASTER CRASH was the society scandal of
the year. The cheap newspapers reported
every development breathlessly: the sale of
the great Kensington mansions; the auctions
of the paintings, antique furniture, and
cases of port; the cancellation of Nick and
Dotty's planned six-month honeymoon in
Europe; and the modest suburban houses
where the proud and mighty Pilasters now
peeled potatoes for themselves and washed
their own undergarments.

Hugh and Nora rented a small house with
a garden in Chingford, a village nine miles
from London. They left all their servants behind, but a muscular fourteen-year-old girl
from a nearby farm came in the afternoons

to scrub floors and wash windows. Nora, who had not done housework for twelve years, took it very badly, and shuffled about in a grubby apron, halfheartedly sweeping floors and preparing indigestible dinners, complaining constantly. The boys liked it better than London because they could play in the woods. Hugh traveled into the City every day by train and continued to go to the bank, where his work consisted of disposing of Pilasters' assets on behalf of the syndicate.

Each partner received a small monthly allowance from the bank. In theory they were not entitled to anything. But the syndicate members were bankers just like the Pilasters, and in their hearts they thought *There but for the grace of God go I.* Besides, the cooperation of the partners was helpful in selling off the assets, and it was worth a small payment to retain their goodwill.

Hugh watched the progress of the civil war in Cordova with an anxious heart. The outcome would determine how much money the syndicate would lose. Hugh badly wanted them to make a profit. He wanted one day to be able to say that no one had lost money rescuing Pilasters Bank. But the possibility seemed remote.

At first the Miranda faction seemed set to win the war. By all accounts their attack was well planned and bloodily executed. President Garcia was forced to flee the capital and take refuge in the fortified city of Campanario, in the south, his home region. Hugh was dispirited. If the Mirandas won they would run Cordova like a private kingdom, and would never pay interest on loans made to the previous regime; and Cordova bonds would be worthless for the foreseeable future.

But then came an unexpected development. Tonio's family, the Silvas, who for some years had been the mainstay of the small and ineffectual liberal opposition, joined in the fighting on the president's side, in return for promises of free elections and land reform when the president regained control. Hugh's hopes rose again.

The revitalized presidential army won a lot of popular support and fought the usurpers to a standstill. The forces were evenly balanced. So were the financial resources: the Mirandas had spent their war chest on a fierce all-out initial assault. The north had nitrate mines and the south had silver, but neither side could get its exports financed or insured, since Pilasters was no longer in business and no other banks would take on a customer who might vanish tomorrow.

Both sides appealed to the British government for recognition, in the hope that it would help them get credit. Micky Miranda, still officially the Cordovan Minister in London, furiously lobbied Foreign Office officials, government ministers and members of Parliament, pressing for Papa Miranda to be recognized as the new president. But so far the prime minister, Lord Salisbury, refused to favor either side.

Then Tonio Silva arrived in London.

He turned up at Hugh's suburban home on Christmas Eve. Hugh was in the kitchen, giving the boys hot milk and buttered toast for breakfast. Nora was still getting dressed: she was going into London to do her Christmas shopping, although she would have very little money to spend. Hugh had agreed to stay at home and take care of the boys: there was nothing urgent for him to do at the bank today.

He answered the doorbell himself, an experience that reminded him of the old days with his mother in Folkestone. Tonio had grown a beard and moustache, no doubt to hide the scars of the beating he had been given by Micky's thugs eleven years earlier;

but Hugh instantly recognized the carrot-colored hair and reckless grin. It was snowing, and there was a dusting of white on Tonio's hat and the shoulders of his coat.

Hugh took his old friend into the kitchen and gave him tea. "How did you find me?" he asked.

"It wasn't easy," Tonio replied. "There was no one at your old house and the bank was closed. But I went to Whitehaven House and saw your aunt Augusta. She hasn't changed. She didn't know your address, but she remembered Chingford. The way she said the name, it sounded like a prison camp, like Van Diemen's Land."

Hugh nodded. "It's not so bad. The boys are fine. Nora finds it hard."

"Augusta hasn't moved house."

"No. She's more to blame than anyone else for the mess we're in. Yet she of all of them is the one who refuses to accept reality. She'll find out that there are worse places than Chingford."

"Cordova, for instance," said Tonio.

"How is it?"

"My brother was killed in the fighting."

"I'm sorry."

"The war has reached a stalemate. Everything depends on the British government now. The side that wins recognition will be able to get credit, resupply its army, and overrun the opposition. That's why I'm here."

"Have you been sent by President Garcia?"

"Better than that. I am now officially the Cordovan Minister in London. Miranda has been dismissed."

"Splendid!" Hugh was pleased that at last Micky had been sacked. It had irked him to see a man who had stolen two million pounds from him walking around London, going to clubs and theatres and dinner parties as if nothing had happened.

Tonio added: "I brought letters of accreditation with me and lodged them at the Foreign Office yesterday."

"And you're hoping to persuade the prime minister to support your side."

"Yes."

Hugh looked at him quizzically. "How?"

"Garcia is the president—Britain ought to support the legitimate government."

That was a bit feeble, Hugh thought. "We haven't so far."

"I shall just tell the prime minister that you should."

"Lord Salisbury is busy trying to keep the

lid on a boiling cauldron in Ireland—he's got no time for a distant South American civil war." Hugh did not mean to sound negative, but an idea was forming in his mind.

Tonio said rather irritably: "Well, my job is to persuade Salisbury that he should pay attention to what is going on in South America, even if he does have other things on his mind." But he could see the weakness of this approach, and after a moment he said: "Well, all right. You're English, what do you think would engage his attention?"

Hugh said immediately: "You could promise to protect British investors from loss."

"How?"

"I'm not sure, I'm thinking aloud." Hugh shifted in his chair. Four-year-old Sol was building a castle of wooden blocks around his feet. It was odd to be deciding the future of a whole country here in the tiny kitchen of a cheap suburban house. "British investors put two million pounds into the Santamaria Harbor Corporation—Pilasters Bank being the biggest contributor. All the directors of the corporation were members or associates of the Miranda family and I have no doubt the entire two million went

straight into their war chest. We need to get
it back."

"But it's all been spent on weapons."

"All right. But the Miranda family must
have assets worth millions."

"Indeed—they own the country's nitrate
mines."

"If your side won the war, could President
Garcia hand over the mines to the Santamaria Harbor Corporation, in compensation for the fraud? The bonds would be
worth something then."

Tonio said firmly: "I have been told by the
president that I can promise anything—*anything*—that will get the British to side with
the government forces in Cordova."

Hugh began to feel excited. Suddenly the
prospect of paying off all the Pilasters' debts
seemed closer. "Let me think," he said. "We
ought to lay the groundwork before you actually make your pitch. I believe I could persuade old Ben Greenbourne to put in a
good word with Lord Salisbury, telling him
he ought to support the British investor. But
what about the Opposition in Parliament?
We could go to see Dan Robinson, Maisie's
brother—he's a member of Parliament, and
he's obsessed with bank failures. He ap-
proves of my rescue scheme for Pilasters

and he wants it to work. He might make
sure the Opposition supports us in the
House of Commons." He drummed his fingers on the kitchen table. "This is beginning
to look possible!"

"We should act fast," Tonio said.

"We'll go into town right away. Dan
Robinson lives with Maisie in south London. Greenbourne will be at his country
house, but I can telephone him from the
bank." Hugh stood up. "Let me tell Nora."
He extricated his feet from Sol's wood-block
castle and went out.

Nora was in the bedroom, putting on an
elaborate hat with fur trimmings. "I have to
go into town," Hugh said as he put on a
collar and tie.

"Who's going to look after the boys,
then?" she said.

"You, I hope."

"No!" she screeched. "I'm going shopping!"

"I'm sorry, Nora, but this is very important."

"I'm important too!"

"Of course you are, but you can't have
your way about this. I have to speak to Ben
Greenbourne urgently."

"I'm sick of this," she said disgustedly.

"Sick of the house, sick of this boring village, sick of the children and sick of you. My father lives better than we do!" Nora's father had opened a pub, with a loan from Pilasters Bank, and was doing extremely well. "I ought to go and live with him, and work as a barmaid," she said. "I'd have more fun and I'd be paid for doing drudgery!"

Hugh stared at her. Suddenly he knew he would never share her bed again. There was nothing left of his marriage. Nora hated him, and he despised her. "Take your hat off, Nora," he said. "You're not going shopping today." He put on his suit jacket and went out.

Tonio was waiting impatiently in the hall. Hugh kissed the boys, picked up his hat and coat, and opened the door. "There's a train in a few minutes," he said as they went out.

He put on his hat and shrugged into his coat as they hurried down the short garden path and out through the gate. It was snowing harder and there was a layer an inch thick on the grass. Hugh's home was one of twenty or thirty identical houses built in a row on what had been a turnip field. They walked along a gravel road toward the village. "We'll call on Robinson first," Hugh said, planning their schedule. "Then I can tell Greenbourne that the Opposition is already on our side. . . . Listen!"

"What?"

"That's our train. We'd better hurry."

They quickened their pace. Fortunately the station was on the near side of the village. The train came into sight as they crossed a bridge over the line.

A man was leaning on the parapet, watching the approaching train. As they passed him he turned, and Hugh recognized him: it was Micky Miranda.

And he had a revolver in his hand.

After that everything happened very quickly.

Hugh cried out, but his shout was a whisper compared to the noise of the train. Micky pointed the gun at Tonio and fired at point-blank range. Tonio staggered and fell. Micky turned the gun on Hugh—but as he did so, steam and smoke from the engine billowed over the bridge in a dense cloud, and suddenly they were both blind. Hugh threw himself to the snowy ground. He heard the gun again, twice, but he felt nothing. He rolled sideways and got to his knees, peering into the fog.

The smoke began to clear. Hugh

glimpsed a figure in the mist and rushed at him. Micky saw him and turned, but too late: Hugh cannoned into him. Micky fell and the gun flew from his hand and sailed in an arc over the parapet and down onto the railway line. Hugh fell on top of Micky and rolled clear.

They both struggled to their feet. Micky stooped to pick up his walking cane. Hugh rushed at him again and knocked him down, but Micky kept hold of the cane. As Micky scrambled to his feet again Hugh lashed out at him. But Hugh had not punched anyone for twenty years and he missed. Micky struck at him with the cane and hit his head. The blow hurt. Micky hit him again. The second blow maddened Hugh and he roared with rage, rushed at Micky and butted his face. They both staggered back, breathing hard.

Then there was a whistle from the station, indicating that the train was leaving, and panic showed on Micky's face. Hugh guessed that Micky had planned to escape by train, and could not afford to be stuck in Chingford for another hour so close to the scene of his crime. The guess was right: Micky turned and ran to the station.

Hugh gave chase.

Micky was no sprinter, having spent too many nights drinking in brothels; but Hugh had passed his adult life sitting behind a desk, and he was not in much better shape. Micky ran into the station as the train was pulling out. Hugh followed him, blowing hard. When they charged onto the platform a railwayman shouted: "Oy! Where's your tickets?"

By way of reply Hugh yelled: "Murder!"

Micky ran along the platform, trying to catch the receding rear end of the train. Hugh charged after him, doing his best to ignore the stabbing pain in his side. The railwayman joined in the chase. Micky caught up with the train, grabbed a handle and jumped on a step. Hugh dived after him, caught him by the ankle and lost his grip. The railwayman tripped over Hugh and went flying.

When Hugh got to his feet the train was out of reach. He stared after it in despair. He saw Micky open the door of the carriage and move gingerly from the step into the train, closing the door behind him.

The railwayman got up, brushing snow off his clothes, and said: "What the 'ell was all that about?"

Hugh bent over, breathing like a leaky bellows, too weak to speak.

"A man has been shot," he said when he caught his breath. As soon as he felt strong enough to move he walked back toward the station entrance, beckoning the railwayman to follow. He led the man to the bridge where Tonio lay.

Hugh knelt by the body. Tonio had been hit between the eyes, and there was not much left of his face. "My God, what a mess," said the railwayman. Hugh swallowed hard, fighting down nausea. He forced himself to slide his hand under Tonio's coat and feel for a heartbeat. As he had expected there was none. He remembered the mischievous boy with whom he had splashed around in the swimming hole at Bishop's Wood twenty-four years earlier, and he felt a wave of grief that pushed him close to tears.

Hugh's head was clearing, and he could see, with anguished clarity, how Micky had planned this. Micky had friends in the Foreign Office, as did every halfway competent diplomat. One of those friends must have whispered in his ear, perhaps at a reception or dinner party last night, that Tonio was in London. Tonio had lodged his letters of accreditation already, so Micky knew his days were numbered. But if Tonio were to die the situation would become muddled again. There would be no one in London to negotiate on behalf of President Garcia, and Micky would be the de facto minister. It was Micky's only hope. But he had to act fast and take chances, for he had only a day or two.

How had Micky known where to find Tonio? Perhaps he had people following Tonio—or maybe Augusta had told him that Tonio had been there, asking where to find Hugh. Either way, he had followed Tonio to Chingford.

To seek out Hugh's house would have meant talking to too many people. However, he had known that Tonio had to come back to the railway station sooner or later. So he had lurked near the station, planning to kill Tonio—and any witnesses to the murder—and escape by train.

Micky was a desperate man, and it was a fearfully risky scheme—but it had almost worked. He had needed to kill Hugh as well as Tonio, but the smoke from the engine had spoiled his aim. If things had gone according to plan no one would have recognized him. Chingford had neither telegraph nor telephone, and there was no means of transport faster than the train, so he would have been back in London before the crime could be reported. No doubt one of his employees would have given him an alibi, too.

But he had failed to kill Hugh. And—Hugh suddenly realized—technically Micky was no longer the Cordovan Minister, so he had lost his diplomatic immunity.

He could hang for this.

Hugh stood up. "We must report the murder as soon as possible," he said.

"There's a police station in Walthamstow, a few stops down the line."

"When's the next train?"

The railwayman took a large watch from his waistcoat pocket. "Forty-seven minutes," he said.

"We should both get on it. You go to the police in Walthamstow and I'll go on to town and report it to Scotland Yard."

"There's no one to mind the station. I'm on my own, being Christmas Eve."

"I'm sure your employer would want you to do your public duty."

"Right you are." The man seemed grateful to be told what to do.

"We'd better put poor Silva somewhere. Is there a place in the station?"

"Only the waiting room."

"We'd better carry him there and lock it up." Hugh bent and took hold of the body under the arms. "You take his legs." They lifted Tonio and carried him into the station.

They laid him on a bench in the waiting room. Then they were not sure what to do. Hugh felt restive. He could not grieve—it was too soon. He wanted to catch the murderer, not mourn. He paced up and down, consulting his watch every few minutes, and rubbing the sore place on his head where Micky's cane had struck him. The railwayman sat on the opposite bench, staring at the body with fearful fascination. After a while Hugh sat beside him. They stayed like that, silent and watchful, sharing the cold room with the dead man, until the train came in.

2

MICKY MIRANDA was fleeing for his life.

His luck was running out. He had committed four murders in the last twenty-four years, and he had got away with the first three, but this time he had stumbled. Hugh Pilaster had seen him shoot Tonio Silva in broad daylight, and there was no way to escape the hangman but by leaving England.

Suddenly he was on the run, a fugitive in the city that had been his home for most of his life. He hurried through Liverpool Street Railway Station, avoiding the eyes of policemen, his heart racing and his breath coming in shallow gasps, and dived into a hansom cab.

He went straight to the office of the Gold Coast and Mexico Steamship Company.

The place was crowded, mainly with Latins. Some would be trying to return to Cordova, others trying to get relatives out, and some might just be asking for news. It was noisy and disorganized. Micky could not afford to wait for the riffraff. He fought his way to the counter, using his cane indiscriminately on men and women to get through. His expensive clothes and upper-class arrogance got the attention of a clerk, and he said: "I want to book passage to Cordova."

"There's a war on in Cordova," said the clerk.

Micky suppressed a sarcastic retort. "You haven't suspended all sailings, I take it."

"We're selling tickets to Lima, Peru. The ship will go on to Palma if political conditions permit: the decision will be made when it reaches Lima."

That would do. Micky mainly needed to get out of England. "When is the next departure?"

"Four weeks from today."

His heart sank. "That's no good, I have to go sooner!"

"There's a ship leaving Southampton tonight, if you're in a hurry."

Thank God! His luck had not quite run out just yet. "Reserve me a stateroom—the best available."

"Very good, sir. May I have the name?"

"Miranda."

"Beg pardon, sir?"

The English were deaf when a foreign name was spoken. Micky was about to spell his name when he changed his mind. "Andrews," he said. "M. R. Andrews." It had occurred to him that the police might check passenger lists, looking for the name Miranda. Now they would not find it. He was grateful for the insane liberalism of Britain's laws, which permitted people to enter and leave the country without passports. It would not have been so easy in Cordova.

The clerk began to make out his ticket. Micky watched restlessly, rubbing the sore place on his face where Hugh Pilaster had butted him. He realized he had another problem. Scotland Yard could circulate his description to all port towns by cable. Damn the telegraph. Within an hour they would have local policemen checking all passengers. He needed some kind of disguise.

The clerk gave him his ticket and he paid with bank notes. He pushed impatiently through the crowd and went out into the snow, still worrying.

He hailed a hansom and directed it to the Cordovan Ministry, but then he had second thoughts. It was risky to go back there, and anyway he was short of time.

The police would be looking for a well-dressed man of forty, traveling alone. One way to get past them would be to appear as an older man with a companion. In fact, he could pretend to be an invalid, and be taken on board in a wheelchair. But for that he would need an accomplice. Whom could he use? He was not sure he could trust any of his employees, especially now that he was no longer the minister.

That left Edward.

"Drive to Hill Street," he told the cabbie.

Edward had a small house in Mayfair. Unlike the other Pilasters, he rented his home, and he had not been obliged to move out yet because his rent was paid three months in advance.

Edward did not seem to care that Micky had destroyed Pilasters Bank and brought ruin to his family. He had only become more dependent on Micky. As for the rest of the Pilasters, Micky had not seen them since the crash.

Edward answered the door in a stained silk dressing gown and took Micky up to his bedroom, where there was a fire. He was smoking a cigar and drinking whisky at eleven o'clock in the morning. The skin rash was all over his face now, and Micky had second thoughts about using him as an accomplice: the rash made him conspicuous. But there was no time to be choosy. Edward would have to do.

"I'm leaving the country," Micky said.

Edward said: "Oh, take me with you," and burst into tears.

"What the devil is the matter with you?" Micky said unsympathetically.

"I'm dying," Edward said. "Let's go somewhere quiet and live together in peace until I'm gone."

"You're not dying, you damn fool— you've only got a skin disease."

"It's not a skin disease, it's syphilis."

Micky gasped in horror. "Jesus and Mary, I might have it too!"

"It's no wonder, the amount of time we've spent at Nellie's."

"But April's girls are supposed to be clean!"

"Whores are never clean."

Micky fought down panic. If he delayed in London to see a doctor he might die at the end of a rope. He had to leave the country today. But the ship went via Lisbon: he could see a doctor there in a few days' time. That would have to do. He might not have the disease at all: he was much healthier than Edward generally, and he always washed himself after sex, whereas Edward was not so fastidious.

But Edward was in no state to help smuggle him out of the country. Anyway, Micky was not going to take a terminal syphilis case back to Cordova with him. Still he needed an accomplice. And there was only one candidate left: Augusta.

He was not as sure of her as he was of Edward. Edward had always been willing to do anything Micky asked. Augusta was independent. But she was his last chance.

He turned to go.

"Don't leave me," Edward pleaded.

There was no time for sentiment. "I can't take a dying man with me," he snapped.

Edward looked up, and his face took on a malicious expression. "If you don't . . ."

"Well?"

"I'll tell the police that you killed Peter Middleton, and Uncle Seth, and Solly Greenbourne."

Augusta must have told him about old Seth. Micky stared at Edward. He made a pathetic figure. How have I put up with him for so long, Micky wondered? He suddenly realized how happy he would be to leave him behind. "Tell the police," he said. "They're already after me for killing Tonio Silva, and I might as well be hanged for four murders as for one." He went out without looking back.

He let himself out of the house and got a hansom in Park Lane. "Kensington Gore," he told the cabbie. "Whitehaven House." On the way he worried about his health. He had none of the symptoms: no skin problems, no unexplained lumps on his genitals. But he would have to wait to be sure. Damn Edward to hell.

He also worried about Augusta. He had not seen her since the crash. Would she help him? He knew she had always struggled to control her sexual hunger for him; and on that one bizarre occasion she had actually yielded to her passion. In those days Micky had burned for her too. Since then Micky's fire had abated, but he felt that hers had grown hotter. He hoped so: he was going to ask her to run away with him.

Augusta's door was opened not by her butler but by a slovenly woman in an apron. Passing through the hall, Micky noticed that the place was not very clean. Augusta was in difficulties. So much the better: it would make her more inclined to go along with his plan.

However, she appeared her usual imperious self as she came into the drawing room in a purple silk blouse with leg-of-mutton sleeves and a black flared skirt with a tiny pinched waist. She had been a breathtakingly beautiful young woman and now, at fifty-eight, she could still turn heads. He recalled the lust he had felt for her as a boy of sixteen, but there was none left. He would have to fake it.

She did not offer him her hand. "Why have you come here?" she said coldly. "You've brought ruin to me and my family."

"I didn't intend to—"

"You must have known that your father was about to launch a civil war."

"But I didn't know that Cordovan bonds would become valueless because of the war," he said. "Did you?"

She hesitated. Obviously she had not.

A crack had opened in her armor and he tried to widen it. "I wouldn't have done it if I'd known—I would have cut my own throat before harming you." He could tell that she wanted to believe this.

But she said: "You persuaded Edward to deceive his partners so that you could have your two million pounds."

"I thought there was so much money in the bank that it could never be harmed."

She looked away. "So did I," she said quietly.

He pressed his advantage. "Anyway, it's all irrelevant now—I'm leaving England today, and I will probably never come back."

She looked at him with sudden fear in her eyes, and he knew he had her. "Why?" she said.

There was no time for beating about the bush. "I have just shot and killed a man and the police are chasing me."

She gasped and took his hand. "Who?"

"Antonio Silva."

She was excited as well as shocked. Her face colored a little and her eyes became bright. "Tonio! Why?"

"He was a threat to me. I've booked passage on a steamer leaving Southampton tonight."

"So soon!"

"I have no choice."

"And so you've come to say good-bye," she said, and she looked downcast.

"No."

She looked up at him. Was that hope in her eyes? He hesitated, then took the plunge. "I want you to come with me."

Her eyes widened. She took a step back.

He kept hold of her hand. "Having to leave—and so quickly—has made me realize something I should have admitted to myself a long time ago. I think you have always known it. I love you, Augusta."

As he acted his part he watched her face, reading it the way a sailor reads the surface of the sea. For a moment she tried to put on a look of astonishment, but she abandoned it almost immediately. She gave the hint of a gratified smile, then a faint blush of embarrassment that was almost maidenly; and then a calculating look that told him she was reckoning up what she had to gain and lose.

He saw she was still undecided.

He put his hand on her corseted waist and drew her gently toward him. She did not resist, but her face still wore that appraising look which told him she had not made up her mind.

When their faces were close and her breasts were touching the lapels of his coat, he said: "I can't live without you, dear Augusta."

He could feel her trembling beneath his touch. In a shaky voice she said: "I'm old enough to be your mother."

He spoke into her ear, brushing her face with his lips. "But you aren't," he said, making his voice almost a whisper. "You're the most desirable woman I've ever met. I've longed for you all these years, you know that. Now . . ." He moved his hand up from her waist until he was almost touching her breast. "Now I can hardly keep my hands under control. Augusta . . ." He paused.

"What?" she said.

He almost had her, but not quite. He had to play his last card.

"Now that I'm no longer minister, I can divorce Rachel."

"What are you saying?"

He whispered into her ear: "Will you marry me?"

"Yes," she said.

He kissed her.

3

APRIL TILSLEY BURST INTO Maisie's office at the Female Hospital, dressed to the nines in scarlet silk and fox fur, carrying a newspaper and saying: "Have you heard what's happened?"

Maisie stood up. "April! What on earth is it?"

"Micky Miranda shot Tonio Silva!"

Maisie knew who Micky was, but it took her a moment to remember that Tonio had been one of that crowd of boys around Solly and Hugh when they were young. He had been a gambler in those days, she recalled, and April had been very sweet on him until she discovered that he always lost what little money he had in wagers. "Micky *shot* him?" she said in amazement. "Is he dead?"

"Yes. It's in the afternoon paper."

"I wonder why?"

"It doesn't say. But it also says—" April hesitated. "Sit down, Maisie."

"Why? Tell me!"

"It says the police want to question him about three other murders—Peter Middleton, Seth Pilaster and . . . Solomon Greenbourne."

Maisie sat down heavily. "Solly!" she said, and she felt faint. "Micky killed Solly? Oh, poor Solly." She closed her eyes and buried her face in her hands.

"You need a sip of brandy," April said. "Where do you keep it?"

"We don't have any here," Maisie said. She tried to pull herself together. "Show me that paper."

April handed her the newspaper.

Maisie read the first paragraph. It said the police were hunting for the former Cordovan Minister, Miguel Miranda, to question him about the murder of Antonio Silva.

April said: "Poor Tonio. He was one of the nicest men I ever opened my legs for."

Maisie read on. The police also wanted to question Miranda about the deaths of Peter Middleton, at Windfield School in 1866; Seth Pilaster, the Senior Partner of Pilasters Bank, in 1873; and Solomon Greenbourne, who was pushed under a speeding carriage in a side street off Piccadilly in July of 1879.

"And Seth Pilaster—Hugh's uncle Seth?"

Maisie said agitatedly. "Why did he kill all these people?"

April said: "The newspapers never tell you what you really want to know."

The third paragraph jolted Maisie yet again. The shooting had taken place in northeast London, near Walthamstow, at a village called Chingford. Her heart missed a beat. "Chingford!" she gasped.

"I've never heard of it—"

"It's where Hugh lives!"

"Hugh Pilaster? Are you still carrying a torch for him?"

"He must have been involved, don't you see? It can't be a coincidence! Oh, dear God, I hope he's all right."

"I expect the paper would say if he had been hurt."

"It only happened a few hours ago. They may not know." Maisie could not bear this uncertainty. She stood up. "I must find out if he's all right," she said.

"How?"

She put on her hat and stuck a pin in it. "I'll go to his house."

"His wife won't like it."

"His wife's a *paskudniak*."

April laughed. "What's that?"

"A shitbag." Maisie put on her coat.

April stood up. "My carriage is outside. I'll take you to the railway station."

When they got into April's carriage they realized that neither of them knew which London terminus they should go to for a train to Chingford. Fortunately the coachman, who was also the doorman at Nellie's brothel, was able to tell them it was Liverpool Street.

When they got there Maisie thanked April perfunctorily and dashed into the station. It was packed with Christmas travelers and shoppers returning to their suburban homes. The air was full of smoke and dirt. People shouted greetings and farewells over the screech of steel brakes and the explosive exhalations of the steam engines. She fought her way to the booking office through a throng of women with armfuls of parcels, bowler-hatted clerks going home early, black-faced engineers and firemen, children and horses and dogs.

She had to wait fifteen minutes for a train. On the platform she watched a tearful farewell between two young lovers, and envied them.

The train puffed through the slums of Bethnal Green, the suburbs of Walthamstow and the snow-covered fields of Woodford, stopping every few minutes. Although it was twice as fast as a horse-drawn carriage it seemed slow to Maisie as she bit her finger-nails and wondered if Hugh was all right.

When she got off the train at Chingford she was stopped by the police and asked to step into the waiting room. A detective asked her if she had been in the locality that morning. Obviously they were looking for witnesses to the murder. She told him she had never been to Chingford before. On im-pulse she said: "Was anyone else hurt, other than Antonio Silva?"

"Two people received minor cuts and bruises in the fracas," the detective replied.

"I'm worried about a friend of mine who knew Mr. Silva. His name is Hugh Pilaster."

"Mr. Pilaster grappled with the assailant and was struck on the head," the man said. "His injuries are not serious."

"Oh, thank God," said Maisie. "Can you direct me to his house?"

The detective told her where to go. "Mr. Pilaster was at Scotland Yard earlier in the day—whether he has returned yet, I couldn't say."

Maisie wondered whether she should go back to London right away, now that she was fairly sure Hugh was all right. It would avoid a meeting with the ghastly Nora. But she would feel happier if she saw him. And she was not afraid of Nora. She set off for his house, trudging through two or three inches of snow.

Chingford was a brutal contrast to Kensington, she thought as she walked down the new street of cheap houses with their raw front gardens. Hugh would be stoical about his comedown, she guessed, but she was not so sure of Nora. The bitch had married Hugh for his money and she would not like being poor again.

Maisie could hear a child crying inside when she knocked on the door of Hugh's house. It was opened by a boy of about eleven years. "You're Toby, aren't you," Maisie said. "I've come to see your father. My name is Mrs. Greenbourne."

"I'm afraid Father's not at home," the boy said politely.

"When do you expect him back?"

"I don't know."

Maisie felt let down. She had been looking forward to seeing Hugh. Disappointed, she said: "Perhaps you would just say that I saw the newspaper and I called to make sure he was all right."

"Very well, I'll tell him."

There was no more to be said. She might as well go back to the station and wait for the next train into London. She turned away, disappointed. At least she had escaped an altercation with Nora.

Something in the boy's face bothered her: a look almost of fear. On impulse she turned back and said: "Is your mother in?"

"No, I'm afraid she's not."

That was odd. Hugh could no longer afford a governess. Maisie had a feeling that something was wrong. She said: "Might I speak to whoever is looking after you?"

The boy hesitated. "Actually, there isn't anybody here but me and my brothers."

Maisie's intuition had been right. What was going on? How had three small boys been left totally alone? She hesitated to interfere, knowing she would catch hell from Nora Pilaster. On the other hand she could not simply walk away and leave Hugh's children to fend for themselves. "I'm an old friend of your father . . . and mother," she said.

"I saw you at Auntie Dotty's wedding," said Toby.

"Ah, yes. Um . . . may I come in?"

Toby looked relieved. "Yes, please do," he said.

Maisie stepped inside. She followed the sound of the crying child to the kitchen at the back of the house. There was a four-year-old squatting on the floor bawling, and a six-year-old sitting on the kitchen table looking as if he were ready to burst into tears at any moment.

She picked up the youngest. She knew that he was named Solomon, after Solly Greenbourne, but they called him Sol. "There, there," she murmured. "What's the matter?"

"I want my mama," he said, and cried louder.

"Hush, hush," Maisie murmured, rocking him. She felt dampness penetrate her clothing and she realized the little boy had wet himself. Looking around, she saw that the place was a mess. The table was covered with breadcrumbs and spilled milk, there were dirty dishes in the sink, and there was mud on the floor. It was cold, too: the fire had gone out. It almost looked as if the children had been abandoned.

"What's going on here?" she said to Toby.

"I gave them some lunch," he said. "I made bread and butter and cut some ham. I tried to make tea but I burned my hand on the kettle." He was trying to be brave but he was on the brink of tears. "Do you know where my father might be?"

"No, I don't." The baby had asked for his mama, but the older boy wanted his father, Maisie noted. "What about your mother?"

Toby took an envelope from the mantelpiece and handed it to her. It was addressed simply *Hugh*.

"It's not sealed," Toby said. "I read it."

Maisie opened it and took out a single sheet of paper. One word was written on it in large, angry capital letters:

GOOD-BYE

Maisie was horrified. How could a mother walk out on three small children—and leave them to fend for themselves? Nora had given birth to each of these boys, and held them to her breast as helpless babies. Maisie thought of the mothers in the Southwark Female Hospital. If one of them were given a three-bedroom house in Chingford she would think herself in heaven.

She put such thoughts out of her mind for the moment. "Your father will be back tonight, I'm sure," she said, praying it was true. She addressed the four-year-old in her arms. "But we wouldn't want him to find the house a mess, would we?"

Sol shook his head solemnly.

"We're going to wash the dishes, clean the kitchen, light the fire and make some supper." She looked at the six-year-old. "Do you think that's a good idea, Samuel?"

Samuel nodded. "I like buttered toast," he added helpfully.

"Then that's what we'll have."

Toby was not reassured. "What time do you think Father will come home?"

"I'm not sure," she said candidly. There was no point in lying: children always knew. "But I tell you what. You can stay up until he gets here, no matter how late. How's that?"

The boy looked somewhat relieved. "All right," he said.

"Now, then. Toby, you're the strongest, you can bring in a bucket of coal. Samuel, I believe I can trust you to do a job properly, you can wipe the kitchen table clean with a rag. Sol, you can sweep up because—you're the smallest, so you're closer to the floor. Come on, boys, let's start work!"

4

HUGH WAS IMPRESSED by the way Scotland Yard responded to his report. The case was assigned to Detective-Inspector Magridge, a sharp-faced man of about Hugh's age, meticulous and intelligent, the kind who would have made it to chief clerk in a bank. Within an hour he had circulated a description of Micky Miranda and set a watch on all the ports.

He also sent a detective-sergeant to interview Edward Pilaster, at Hugh's suggestion; and the man came back with the report that Miranda was leaving the country.

Edward had also said that Micky was implicated in the deaths of Peter Middleton, Seth Pilaster and Solomon Greenbourne. Hugh was shaken by the suggestion that Micky had killed Uncle Seth, but he told Magridge that he already suspected Micky of killing Peter and Solly.

The same detective was dispatched to see Augusta. She was still living at Whitehaven House. With no money she could not hold out indefinitely, but so far she had succeeded in preventing the sale of the house or its contents.

A police constable assigned to check London steamship offices reported that a man answering the description but calling himself M. R. Andrews had booked passage on the *Aztec* sailing from Southampton tonight. The Southampton police were instructed to have men at the railway station and at the dockside.

The detective sent to see Augusta came back to report there was no answer when he rang and knocked at the door of Whitehaven House.

"I have a key," Hugh said.

Magridge said: "She's probably out—and I want the sergeant to go to the Cordovan Ministry. Why don't you check Whitehaven House yourself?"

Glad of something to do, Hugh took a cab to Kensington Gore. He rang and knocked, but there was no answer. The last of the servants had left, obviously. He let himself in.

The house was cold. Hiding was not Augusta's style, but he decided to search the rooms anyway, just in case. The first floor was deserted. He went up to the second floor and checked her bedroom.

What he saw surprised him. The wardrobe doors were ajar, the drawers of the chest were open, and there were discarded clothes on the bed and chairs. This was not like Augusta: she was a tidy person with an ordered mind. At first he thought she had been robbed. Then another thought struck him.

He ran up two flights of stairs to the servants' floor. When he had lived here, seventeen years ago, the suitcases and trunks had been kept jam-packed in a big closet known as the box room.

He found the door open. The room contained a few suitcases and no steamer trunk.

Augusta had run away.

He quickly checked all the other rooms of the house. As he expected he saw no one. The servants' rooms and the guest bedrooms were already acquiring the musty air of disuse. When he looked into the room that had been Uncle Joseph's bedroom, he was surprised to see that it looked exactly as it always had, although the rest of the house had been redecorated several times. He was about to leave when his eye fell on the lacquered display cabinet that held Joseph's valuable collection of snuffboxes.

The cabinet was empty.

Hugh frowned. He knew the snuffboxes had not been lodged with the auctioneers: Augusta had so far prevented the removal of any of her possessions.

That meant she had taken them with her.

They were worth a hundred thousand pounds—she could live comfortably for the rest of her life on that money.

But they did not belong to her. They belonged to the syndicate.

He decided to go after her.

He ran down the stairs and out into the street. There was a cabstand a few yards along the road. The drivers were chatting in a group, stamping their feet to keep warm. Hugh ran up to them, saying: "Did any of you drive Lady Whitehaven this afternoon?"

"Two of us did," said a cabbie. "One for her luggage!" The others chortled.

Hugh's deduction was confirmed. "Where did you take her?"

"Waterloo Station, for the one o'clock boat train."

The boat train went to Southampton—where Micky was sailing from. Those two had always been cronies. Micky smarmed all over her like a cad, kissing her hand and flattering her. Despite the eighteen years' difference in their ages, they made a plausible couple.

"But they missed the train," the cabbie added.

"They?" Hugh said. "There was someone with her?"

"An elderly chap in a wheelchair."

Not Micky, evidently. Who, then? No one in the family was frail enough to use a wheelchair. "They missed the train, you say. Do you know when the next boat train leaves?"

"At three."

Hugh looked at his watch. It was two-thirty. He could catch it.

"Take me to Waterloo," he said, and jumped into the cab.

He reached the station just in time to get a ticket and board the boat train.

It was a corridor train with interconnecting coaches, so he could walk along it. As it pulled out of the station and picked up speed through the tenements of south London, he set out to look for Augusta.

He did not have to look far. She was in the next coach.

With a quick glance he hurried past her compartment so that she would not see him.

Micky was not with her. He must have gone by an earlier train. The only other person in her compartment was an elderly man with a rug over his knees.

He went to the next coach and found a

seat. There was not much point in confronting Augusta right away. She might not have the snuffboxes with her—they could be in one of her cases in the luggage van. To speak to her now would serve only to forewarn her. Better to wait until the train arrived at Southampton. He would jump off, find a policeman, then challenge her as her bags were unloaded.

Suppose she denied she had the snuffboxes? He would insist that the police search her luggage. They were obliged to investigate a reported theft, and the more Augusta protested the more suspicious they would be.

Suppose she claimed the snuffboxes were hers? It was hard to prove anything on the spot. If that happened, Hugh decided he would propose that the police take custody of the valuables while they investigated the contradictory claims.

He controlled his impatience as the white fields of Wimbledon sped by. A hundred thousand pounds was a big chunk of the money Pilasters Bank owed. He was not going to let Augusta steal it. The snuffboxes also symbolized the family's determination to pay off its debts. If Augusta was allowed to make off with them, people would say the

Pilasters were grabbing what they could, just like any ordinary embezzlers. The thought made Hugh angry.

It was still snowing when the train reached Southampton. Hugh was leaning out of the carriage window as the engine puffed into the station. There were uniformed policemen everywhere. That meant Micky had not yet been caught, Hugh inferred.

He jumped off while the train was still moving and got to the ticket barrier before anyone else. He spoke to a police inspector. "I'm the Senior Partner of Pilasters Bank," he said, giving the inspector his card. "I know you're looking for a murderer, but there's a woman on this train who is carrying stolen property worth a hundred thousand pounds belonging to the bank. I believe she is planning to leave the country on the *Aztec* tonight, taking it with her."

"What property would that be, Mr. Pilaster?" said the inspector.

"A collection of jeweled snuffboxes."

"And the name of the woman?"

"She's the dowager countess of Whitehaven."

The policeman raised his eyebrows. "I do

read the newspapers, sir. I take it this is all to do with the failure of the bank."

Hugh nodded. "Those snuffboxes must be sold to help pay people who have lost their money."

"Can you point out Lady Whitehaven to me?"

Hugh looked along the platform, peering through the falling snow. "That's her, by the luggage van, in the big hat with bird's wings on it." She was supervising the unloading of her bags.

The inspector nodded. "Very well. Stay here with me at the ticket barrier. We'll detain her as she passes through."

Hugh was tense as he watched the passengers stream off the train and out. Although he was fairly certain Micky was not on the train, nevertheless he scrutinized the face of every passenger.

Augusta was the last to leave. Three porters were carrying her luggage. When she saw Hugh at the ticket barrier she turned pale.

The inspector was all politeness. "Pardon me, Lady Whitehaven. May I have a word?"

Hugh had never seen Augusta so frightened, but she had not lost her queenly manner. "I'm afraid I can't spare the time, officer," she said coolly. "I have to board a ship that is sailing tonight."

"I guarantee the *Aztec* won't leave without you, my lady," the inspector said smoothly. He glanced at the porters and said: "You can put those down for a minute, lads." He turned back to Augusta. "Mr. Pilaster here claims you have in your possession some very valuable snuffboxes that belong to him. Is that so?"

She began to look less alarmed—which puzzled Hugh. It worried him, too: he was afraid she might have something up her sleeve. "I don't see why I should answer such impertinent questions," she said arrogantly.

"If you don't, I shall have to look through your bags."

"Very well, I do have the snuffboxes," she said. "But they belong to me. They were my husband's."

The inspector turned to Hugh. "What do you say to that, Mr. Pilaster?"

"They were her husband's, but he left them to his son Edward Pilaster; and Edward's possessions are forfeit to the bank. Lady Whitehaven is trying to steal them."

The inspector said: "I must ask you both

to come to the police station while these allegations are investigated."

Augusta looked panicky. "But I can't miss my sailing!"

"In that case, the only thing I can suggest is that you leave the disputed property in the care of the police. It will be returned to you if your claims are verified."

Augusta hesitated. Hugh knew it would break her heart to part with so much wealth. But surely she could see it was inevitable? She had been caught red-handed and she was lucky she was not going to jail.

"Where are the snuffboxes, my lady?" said the inspector.

Hugh waited.

Augusta pointed to a suitcase. "They're all in there."

"The key, please?"

Again she hesitated; again she gave in. She took out a small ring of luggage keys, selected one, and handed it over.

The inspector opened the case. It was full of shoe bags. Augusta pointed to one of the bags. The inspector opened it and drew out a light wooden cigar box. He lifted the lid to reveal numerous small objects carefully wrapped in paper. Selecting one at random, he unwrapped it. It was a small gold box inlaid with diamond chips in the design of a lizard.

Hugh let out a long sigh of relief.

The inspector looked at Hugh. "Do you know how many there should be, sir?"

Everyone in the family did. "Sixty-five," said Hugh. "One for every year of Uncle Joseph's life."

"Would you like to count them?"

Augusta said: "They're all there."

Hugh counted them anyway. There were sixty-five. He began to feel the pleasure of victory.

The inspector took the box and passed it to another policeman. "If you would like to go with Constable Neville to the police station, he will give you an official receipt for the goods, my lady."

"Send it to the bank," she said. "May I go now?"

Hugh was uneasy. Augusta was disappointed, but not devastated. It was almost as if there was something else she was worried about, something more important to her than the snuffboxes. And where was Micky Miranda?

The inspector bowed, and Augusta went out, followed by her three heavily laden porters.

"Thank you very much, Inspector," said Hugh. "I'm only sorry you didn't catch Miranda as well."

"We will, sir. He won't get aboard the *Aztec* unless he's learned how to fly."

The guard from the luggage van came along the platform pushing a wheelchair. He stopped in front of Hugh and the inspector and said: "Now what am I supposed to do with this?"

"What's the problem?" the inspector said patiently.

"That woman with all the luggage and the bird on her hat."

"Lady Whitehaven, yes."

"She was with an old gent at Waterloo. Puts him in a first-class compartment and then asks me to take the bath chair in the luggage van. Glad to oblige, says I. Gets off at Southampton and pretends she don't know what I'm talking about. 'You must have mistaken me for somebody else,' she goes. 'Not likely—there's only one hat like that,' says I."

Hugh said: "That's right—the cabbie said she was with a man in a wheelchair . . . and there was an old fellow in the compartment with her."

868

KEN FOLLETT

"There you are," the guard said triumphantly.

The inspector suddenly lost his avuncular air and rounded on Hugh. "Did you see the old man pass through the ticket barrier?"

"No, I didn't. And I looked at every passenger. Aunt Augusta was the last." Then it hit him. "Good God! Do you think it was Micky Miranda in disguise?"

"Yes, I do. But where is he now? Could he have got off at an earlier stop?"

The guard said: "No—it's an express train, nonstop from Waterloo to Southampton."

"Then we'll search the train. He must be on it still."

But he was not.

5

THE *AZTEC* WAS FESTOONED with colored lanterns and paper streamers. The Christmas party was in full swing when Augusta boarded: a band played on the main deck, and passengers in evening dress drank champagne and danced with friends who had come to say good-bye.

A steward led Augusta up the grand staircase to a stateroom on an upper deck. She had spent all her cash on the best cabin available, thinking that with the snuffboxes in her suitcase she need not worry about money. The room opened directly onto the deck. Inside it had a wide bed, a full-size washbasin, comfortable chairs and electric lights. There were flowers on the dresser, a box of chocolates beside the bed and a bottle of champagne in a bucket of ice on the low table. Augusta was about to tell the steward to take the champagne away, then changed her mind. She was beginning a new life: perhaps she would drink champagne from now on.

She was only just in time. She heard the traditional shout of "All ashore that's going ashore!" even as the porters brought her luggage into the cabin. When they had gone she stepped onto the narrow deck, turning up her coat collar against the snow. She leaned against the rail and looked down. There was a sheer drop to the water, where a tugboat was already in position to ease the great liner out of the harbor into the sea. As she watched, the gangways were withdrawn one by one and the ropes cast off. The ship's foghorn sounded, a cheer went up from the crowd on the quay, and slowly, almost imperceptibly, the huge ship began to move.

Augusta returned to her cabin and closed the door. She undressed slowly and put on a silk nightgown and a matching robe. Then she summoned the steward and told him she would not require anything further tonight.

"Shall I wake you in the morning, my lady?"

"No, thank you. I'll ring."

"Very good, m'lady."

Augusta locked the door behind him.

Then she opened her trunk and let Micky out.

He staggered across the stateroom and fell on the bed. "Jesus save me, I thought I was going to die." He moaned.

"My poor darling, where does it hurt?"

"My legs." She rubbed his calves. The muscles were knotted with cramp. She massaged his calves with her fingertips, feeling the warmth of his skin through the cloth of his trousers. It was a long time since she had touched a man this way, and she felt a flush of heat rise at her throat.

She had often daydreamed about doing this, running away with Micky Miranda, both before and since the death of her husband. She had always been stopped by the thought of all she would lose—house, servants, dress allowance, social position, and family power. But the bank crash had taken all that away, and now she was free to give in to her desires.

"Water," said Micky feebly.

She poured a glass from the pitcher beside the bed. He turned over and sat up to take it, then drank it all.

"Some more . . . Micky?"

He shook his head.

She took the glass from him.

"You lost the snuffboxes," he said. "I heard the whole thing. That swine Hugh."

"But you've got plenty of money," she said. She pointed to the champagne in the ice bucket. "We should drink this. We're out of England. You escaped!"

He was staring at her bosom. She realized that her nipples were hard with excitement, and he could see them poking through the silk of her nightwear. She wanted to say *You can touch them if you like* but she hesitated. There was plenty of time: they had all night. They had the whole voyage. They had the rest of their lives. But suddenly she could wait no longer. She felt guilty and ashamed, but she longed to hold his naked body in her arms, and the longing was stronger than the shame. She sat on the edge of the bed. She took his hand, drew it to her lips, and kissed it; then she pressed it to her breast.

He looked at her curiously for a moment. Then he began to stroke her breast through the silk. His touch was gentle. His fingertips brushed the sensitive nipple and she gasped with pleasure. He changed his grip and held her breast in his palm, lifting and moving it. Then he grasped her nipple between finger and thumb and squeezed. She closed her eyes. He pinched harder, so that it hurt. Then, suddenly, he twisted her nipple so viciously that she screamed and pulled away from him, standing up.

"You dumb cunt," he sneered, getting off the bed.

"No!" she said. "No!"

"You really thought I would marry you!"

"Yes—"

"You've got no money and no influence anymore, the bank is bust, and you even lost the snuffboxes. What would I want with you?"

She felt a pain in her chest, like a knife in her heart. "You said you loved me. . . ."

"You're fifty-eight—my mother's age, for God's sake! You're old and wrinkled and mean and selfish, and I wouldn't fuck you if you were the last woman on earth!"

She felt faint. She tried not to cry but it was no good. Tears welled up in her eyes and she began to shake with sobs of despair. She was ruined. She had no home, no money and no friends, and the man she trusted had betrayed her. She turned away from him to hide her face: she did not want him to see her shame and grief. "Please, stop," she whispered.

"I'll stop," he spat out. "I've got a cabin reserved on this ship and that's where I'm going."

"But when we get to Cordova . . ."

"You're not going to Cordova. You can get off the ship at Lisbon and go back to England. I've no further use for you."

Every word was like a blow and she backed away from him, holding her hands up in front of her as if to ward off his curses. She bumped against the cabin door. Desperate to get away from him, she opened it and backed out.

The freezing night air cleared her head suddenly. She was behaving like a helpless girl, not a mature, capable woman. She had lost control of her life briefly, and it was time to seize it back again.

A man in evening dress walked past her, smoking a cigar. He stared at her nightclothes in astonishment but did not speak to her.

That gave her an idea.

She stepped back into the cabin and closed the door. Micky was straightening his tie in the mirror. "There's someone coming," she said urgently. "A policeman!"

Micky's demeanor changed in a flash. The sneer was wiped off his face and replaced by a look of panic. "Oh, my God," he said.

Augusta was thinking quickly. "We're still within British waters," she said. "You can be arrested and sent back on a coast guard cutter." She had no idea whether this was true.

"I'll have to hide." He climbed into the trunk. "Close the front, quickly," he said.

She shut him in the trunk.

Then she flipped the latch to lock it.

"That's better," she said.

She sat on the bed, staring at the trunk. In her mind she went over and over their conversation. She had made herself vulnerable and he had wounded her. She thought of how he had caressed her. Only two other men had touched her breasts: Strang and Joseph. She thought of how he had twisted her nipple then spurned her with obscene words. As the minutes went by her rage cooled and became a dark, vicious yearning for revenge.

Micky's voice, muffled, came from inside the trunk. "Augusta! What's happening?"

She made no reply.

He began to shout for help. She covered the trunk with blankets from the bed to deaden the sound.

After a while he stopped.

Thoughtfully, Augusta removed the luggage labels bearing her name from the trunk.

She heard cabin doors slam: passengers were heading for the dining room. The ship began to pitch slightly in the swell as it steamed out into the English Channel. The evening passed quickly for Augusta as she sat on the bed brooding.

Passengers trickled back in twos and threes between midnight and two o'clock. After that the band stopped playing and the ship became quiet but for the sounds of the engines and the sea.

Augusta stared obsessively at the trunk in which she had locked Micky. It had been carried up here on the back of a muscular porter. Augusta could not lift it, but she thought she could drag it. It had brass handles on the sides and leather straps top and bottom. She took hold of the leather strap on its top and pulled, tilting the trunk sideways. It tipped over and fell on its face. It made a loud bang. Micky began to shout again, and she covered the trunk with blankets once more. She waited to see if anyone would come to investigate the bang, but no one did. Micky stopped yelling.

She seized the strap again and pulled. It was very heavy, but she was able to move it a few inches at a time. After each tug she rested.

It took her ten minutes to drag the trunk to the cabin door. Then she put on her stockings, boots and fur coat, and opened the door.

There was no one around. The passengers were asleep, and if a crew member patrolled the decks she did not see him. The ship was lit by dim electric bulbs, and there were no stars.

She dragged the trunk through the cabin door and rested again.

After that it was a little easier, for the deck was slippery with snow. Ten minutes later she had the trunk up against the rail.

The next part was more difficult. Taking hold of the strap, she lifted one end of the trunk and tried to bring it upright. On her first try she dropped it. The sound it made when it hit the deck seemed very loud, but once again no one came to investigate: there were intermittent noises all the time on the ship, as its funnels belched smoke and its hull cleaved the waves.

The second time she made a more determined effort. She got down on one knee, seized the strap with both hands, and slowly heaved up. When she had the trunk tilted at a forty-five-degree angle Micky moved inside, his weight shifting to the bottom end, and suddenly it became easy to push the whole thing upright.

She tilted it again so that it was leaning on the rail.

The last part was the hardest of all. She bent down and took hold of the lower strap. She took a deep breath and lifted.

She was not taking the whole weight of the trunk, for the other end was resting on the rail; but still it took all her strength to lift the thing an inch off the deck, and then her cold fingers slipped and she let it fall back.

She was not going to be able to manage it.

She rested, feeling drained and numb. But she could not give up. She had struggled so hard to bring the trunk this far. She had to try again.

She bent down and seized the strap again.

Micky spoke again. "Augusta, what are you doing?"

She answered in a low, clear voice. "Remember how Peter Middleton died," she said.

She paused. There was no sound from inside the trunk.

"You're going to die the same way," she said.

"No, please, Augusta, my love," he said.

"The water will be colder, and it will taste salty as it fills your lungs; but you'll know the terror he knew as death closes its fist over your heart."

He began to shout. "Help! Help! Someone, save me!"

Augusta grabbed the strap and lifted with all her strength. The bottom of the trunk came up off the deck. As Micky realized what was happening his muffled shouts became louder and more terrified, sounding above the engines and the sea. Soon someone would come. Augusta gave another heave. She lifted the foot of the trunk to chest level and stopped, exhausted, feeling she could do no more. Frantic scrabbling sounds came from inside as Micky tried hopelessly to get out. She closed her eyes, clenched her jaw, and pushed. As she strained with all her might, she felt something give way in her back, and she cried out with pain, but she kept lifting. The bottom of the trunk was now higher than the top, and it slid forward on the rail several inches; but it stopped. Augusta's back was in agony. Any moment now a passenger would be roused from a half-drunk sleep by Micky's cries. She knew she could only lift one more time. This had to be final. She gathered her strength, closed her eyes, gritted her teeth against the pain in her back, and heaved.

The trunk slid slowly forward on the rail, then fell into space.

Micky screamed a long scream that died into the wind.

Augusta slumped forward, leaning on the rail to ease the agony in her back, and watched the big trunk fall slowly, tumbling end over end through the air with the snowflakes. It hit the water with a mighty splash and went under.

A moment later it surfaced. It would float for some time, Augusta thought. The pain in her back was excruciating, and she longed to lie down, but she stayed at the rail, watching the trunk bobbing on the swell. Then it disappeared from sight.

She heard a male voice beside her. "I thought I heard someone crying for help," it said worriedly.

Augusta composed herself rapidly and turned to see a polite young man in a silk dressing gown and a scarf. "It was me," she told him, forcing a smile. "I had a nightmare and woke myself up shouting. I came out here to clear my head."

"Ah. Are you sure you're all right?"

"Quite sure. You're very kind."

"Well. Good night, then."

"Good night."

He went back into his cabin.

Augusta looked down at the sea. In a moment she would stagger to her bed, but she wanted to look at the sea a little longer. The trunk would fill up slowly, she thought, as water squirted in through the narrow gaps. The level would rise up Micky's body inch by inch as he fought to open the trunk. When it covered his nose and mouth he would hold his breath for as long as he could. But in the end he would give a great involuntary gasp, and the cold salty sea would pour into his mouth and down his throat, filling his lungs. He would squirm and fight for a little longer, racked by pain and terror; and then his movements would become feeble and stop, everything would slowly turn black, and he would die.

6

HUGH WAS DESPERATELY WEARY when at last his train pulled into Chingford station and he got off. Although he was looking forward to his bed, he stopped on the bridge over the line, at the spot where Micky had shot Tonio that morning. He took off his hat and stood there for a minute, bareheaded in the snow, remembering his friend as a boy and a man. Then he walked on.

He wondered how all this would affect the Foreign Office and their attitude to Cordova. Micky had so far evaded the police. But whether Micky was caught or not, Hugh could exploit the fact that he had witnessed the killing. Newspapers would love to publish his moment-by-moment account. The public would be outraged by a foreign diplomat committing murder in broad daylight, and members of Parliament would probably demand some kind of rebuke. The fact that Micky was the murderer might well spoil Papa Miranda's chances of getting recognized by the British government. The Foreign Office might be persuaded to support the Silva family to punish the Mirandas—and to get compensation for British investors in the Santamaria Harbor Corporation.

The more he thought about it, the more optimistic he felt.

He hoped Nora would be asleep when he got home. He did not want to hear what a miserable day she had had, stuck in this remote village with no one to help her take care of three rowdy boys. He just wanted to slip between the sheets and close his eyes. Tomorrow he would think over the events of today and figure out where they left him and his bank.

He was disappointed to see a light on behind the curtains as he walked up the garden path. That meant she was still up. He let himself in with his key and went into the front room.

He was surprised to see the three boys, all in their pajamas, sitting in a row on the sofa looking at an illustrated book.

And he was astonished to see Maisie in the middle, reading to them.

All three boys jumped up and ran to him. He hugged and kissed them one by one: Sol, the youngest; then Samuel; then eleven-year-old Toby. The younger two were simply overjoyed to see him, but there was something else in Toby's face. "What is it, old man?" Hugh asked him. "Something happened? Where's your mama?"

"She went shopping," he said, and burst into tears.

Hugh put his arm around the boy and looked at Maisie.

"I got here around four o'clock," she said. "Nora must have gone out shortly after you."

"She left them alone?"

Maisie nodded.

Hugh felt hot anger rise up inside him. The children had been alone here most of the day. Anything could have happened. "How could she do that?" he said bitterly.

"There's a note." Maisie handed him an envelope.

He opened it and read the one-word message: *GOOD-BYE.*

Maisie said: "It wasn't sealed. Toby read it and showed it to me."

"It's hard to believe," Hugh said, but as soon as the words were out of his mouth he realized they were not true: it was all too easy to believe. Nora had always put her own wishes above everything else. Now she had abandoned her children. Hugh guessed she had gone to her father's pub.

And the note seemed to imply that she was not coming back.

He did not know what to feel.

His first duty was to the boys. It was important not to upset them any further. He set his own feelings aside for a moment. "You boys are up very late," he said. "Time for bed. Let's go!"

He ushered them up the stairs. Samuel and Sol shared a room but Toby had his own bedroom. Hugh tucked the little ones in then went in to the eldest. He bent over the bed to kiss him.

"Mrs. Greenbourne's a brick," Toby said.

"I know," Hugh said. "She used to be married to my best friend, Solly. Then he died."

"She's pretty, too."

"Do you think so?"

"Yes. Is Mama coming back?"

That was the question Hugh had been afraid of. "Of course she is," he said.

"Really?"

Hugh sighed. "To tell you the truth, old man, I don't know."

"If she doesn't, will Mrs. Greenbourne look after us?"

Trust a child to go right to the heart of the matter, Hugh thought. He evaded the question. "She runs a hospital," he said. "She's got dozens of patients to take care of. I don't suppose she has time to look after boys as well. Now, no more questions. Good night."

Toby looked unconvinced, but he let the matter drop. "Good night, Father."

Hugh blew out the candle and left the room, closing the door.

Maisie had made cocoa. "I'm sure you'd prefer a brandy, but there doesn't seem to be any in the house."

Hugh smiled. "We in the lower middle classes can't afford to drink spirits. Cocoa is fine."

Cups and a jug stood on a tray, but neither of them moved to it. They stood in the middle of the room looking at each other. Maisie said: "I read about the shooting in the afternoon paper, and came here to see if you were all right. I found the children on their own, and gave them supper. Then we waited for you." She smiled a resigned, accepting smile that said it was up to Hugh what happened next.

Suddenly he began to tremble. He leaned on the back of a chair for support. "It's been quite a day," he said shakily. "I'm feeling a little odd."

"Perhaps you ought to sit down."

Suddenly he was overwhelmed by love for her. Instead of sitting, he threw his arms around her. "Hug me hard," he pleaded.

She squeezed his waist.

"I love you, Maisie," he said. "I've always loved you."

"I know," she said.

He looked into her eyes. They were full of tears, and as he watched one tear overflowed and trickled down her face. He kissed it away.

"After all these years," he said. "After all these years."

"Make love to me tonight, Hugh," she said.

He nodded. "And every night, from now on."

Then he kissed her again.

EPILOGUE
1892

FROM *The Times:*

DEATHS
*On the 30th May, at his resi-
dence in Antibes, France, after
a long illness, the* EARL OF
WHITEHAVEN, *formerly Senior
Partner of Pilasters Bank.*

"Edward's dead," Hugh said, looking up from the newspaper.

Maisie sat beside him in the railway carriage, wearing a summer dress in deep yellow with red spots and a little hat with yellow taffeta ribbons. They were on their way to Windfield School for Speech Day.

"He was a rotten swine, but his mother will miss him," she said.

Augusta and Edward had been living together in the south of France for the past eighteen months. Despite what they had done, the syndicate paid them the same allowance as all the other Pilasters. They were both invalids: Edward had terminal syphilis and Augusta had suffered a slipped disc and spent most of her time in a wheelchair. Hugh had heard that despite her illness she had become the uncrowned queen of the English community in that part of the world:

matchmaker, arbitrator of disputes, organizer of social events and promulgator of social rules.

"He loved his mother," Hugh said.

She looked curiously at him. "Why do you say that?"

"It's the only good thing I can think of to say about him."

She smiled fondly and kissed his nose.

The train chugged into Windfield Station and they got out. It was the end of Toby's first year and Bertie's last year at the school. The day was warm and the sun was bright. Maisie opened her parasol—it was made of the same spotted silk as her dress—and they walked to the school.

It had changed a lot in the twenty-six years since Hugh had left. His old headmaster, Dr. Poleson, was long dead, and there was a statue of him in the quadrangle. The new head wielded the notorious cane they had always called the Striper, but he used it less frequently. The fourth-form dormitory was still in the old dairy by the stone chapel, but there was a new building with a school hall that could seat all the boys. The education was better, too: Toby and Bertie learned mathematics and geography as well as Latin and Greek.

They met Bertie outside the hall. He had been taller than Hugh for a year or two now. He was a solemn boy, hardworking and well behaved: he did not get into trouble at school the way Hugh had. He had a lot of Rabinowicz ancestry, and he reminded Hugh of Maisie's brother Dan.

He kissed his mother and shook Hugh's hand. "There's a bit of a ruckus," he said. "We haven't enough copies of the school song and the lower fourth are writing it out like billy-o. I must go and whip them faster. I'll meet you after the speeches." He hurried off. Hugh watched him fondly, thinking nostalgically how important school seemed until you left.

They met Toby next. The small boys no longer had to wear top hats and frock coats: Toby was dressed in a straw boater and a short jacket. "Bertie says I can have tea with you in his study after speeches, if you don't mind. Is it all right?"

"Of course." Hugh laughed.

"Thanks, Father!" Toby ran off again.

In the school hall they were surprised to meet Ben Greenbourne, looking older and rather frail. Maisie, blunt as ever, said: "Hello, what are you doing here?"

"My grandson is head boy," he replied gruffly. "I've come to hear his speech."

Hugh was startled. Bertie was not Greenbourne's grandson, and the old man knew it. Was he softening in his old age?

"Sit down by me," Greenbourne commanded. Hugh looked at Maisie. She shrugged and sat down, and Hugh followed suit.

"I hear you two are married," Greenbourne said.

"Last month," Hugh said. "My first wife didn't contest the divorce." Nora was living with a whisky salesman and it had taken Hugh's hired detective less than a week to get proof of adultery.

"I don't approve of divorce," Greenbourne said crisply. Then he sighed. "But I'm too old to tell people what to do. The century is almost over. The future belongs to you. I wish you the best."

Hugh took Maisie's hand and squeezed it.

Greenbourne addressed Maisie. "Will you send the boy to university?"

"I can't afford it," Maisie said. "It's been hard paying the school fees."

"I'd be glad to pay," Greenbourne said.

Maisie was surprised. "It's kind of you," she said.

"I should have been kinder years ago," he replied. "I always put you down as a fortune-hunter. It was one of my mistakes. If you were only after money you wouldn't have married young Pilaster here. I was wrong about you."

"You did me no harm," Maisie said.

"I was too harsh, all the same. I don't have many regrets, but that's one of them."

The schoolboys began to file into the hall, the youngest sitting on the floor at the front and the older boys on chairs.

Maisie said to Greenbourne: "Hugh has adopted Bertie legally now."

The old man turned his sharp eyes on Hugh. "I suppose you're the real father," he said bluntly.

Hugh nodded.

"I should have guessed a long time ago. It doesn't matter. The boy thinks I'm his grandfather, and that gives me a responsibility." He coughed in an embarrassed way and changed the subject. "I hear the syndicate is going to pay a dividend."

"That's right," Hugh said. He had finally disposed of all the assets of Pilasters Bank, and the syndicate that had rescued the bank had made a small profit. "All the members will get about five percent on their investment."

"Well done. I didn't think you'd manage it."

"The new government in Cordova did it. They handed over the assets of the Miranda family to the Santamaria Harbor Corporation, and that made the bonds worth something again."

"What happened to that chap Miranda? He was a bad lot."

"Micky? His body was found in a steamer trunk washed up on a beach on the Isle of Wight. No one ever found out how it got there or why he was inside it." Hugh had been concerned in the identification of the body: it had been important to establish that Micky was dead, so that Rachel could marry Dan Robinson at last.

A schoolboy came around handing out inky handwritten copies of the school song to all the parents and relatives.

"And you?" Greenbourne said to Hugh. "What will you do when the syndicate is wound up?"

"I was planning to ask your advice about that," Hugh said. "I'd like to start a new bank."

"How?"

"Float the shares on the stock market. Pilasters Limited. What do you think?"

"It's a bold idea, but then you always were original." Greenbourne looked thoughtful for a moment. "The funny thing is, the failure of your bank actually enhanced your reputation, in the end, because of the way you handled things. After all, who could be more reliable than a banker who manages to pay all his creditors even after he's crashed?"

"So . . . do you think it would work?"

"I'm sure of it. I might even put money into it myself."

Hugh nodded gratefully. It was important that Greenbourne liked the idea. Everyone in the City sought his opinion, and his approval was worth a lot. Hugh had thought his plan would work, but Greenbourne had put the seal on his confidence.

Everyone stood up as the headmaster came in, followed by the housemasters, the guest speaker—a Liberal member of Parliament—and Bertie, the head boy. They took their seats on the platform, then Bertie came to the lectern and said in a ringing voice: "Let us sing the school song."

Hugh caught Maisie's eye and she smiled proudly. The familiar notes of the introduction sounded on the piano, and then they all began to sing.

An hour later Hugh left them having tea in Bertie's study and slipped out through the squash court into Bishop's Wood.

It was hot, just like that day twenty-six years ago. The wood seemed the same, still and humid under the shade of the beeches and elms. He remembered the way to the swimming hole and found it without difficulty.

He did not climb down the side of the quarry—he was no longer agile enough. He sat on the rim and threw a stone into the pool. It broke the glassy stillness of the water and sent out ripples in perfect circles.

He was the only one left, except for Albert Cammel out in the Cape Colony. The others were all dead: Peter Middleton killed that day; Tonio shot by Micky two Christmases ago; Micky himself drowned in a steamer trunk; and now Edward, dead of syphilis and buried in a cemetery in France. It was almost as if something evil had come up out of the deep water that day in 1866 and entered their lives, bringing all the dark passions that had blighted their lives, hatred and greed and selfishness and cruelty; fomenting deceit, bankruptcy, disease and murder. But it was over now. The debts were paid. If there had been an evil spirit, it had returned to the bottom of the pond. And Hugh had survived.

He stood up. It was time to return to his family. He walked away, then took a last look back.

The ripples from the stone had disappeared, and the surface of the water was immaculately still once again.

For generous help in the writing of this book I thank the following friends, relations and colleagues:

Carole Baron

Joanna Bourke

Ben Braber

George Brennan

Jackie Farber

Barbara Follett

Emanuele Follett

Katya Follett

Michael Haskoll

Pam Mendez

M. J. Orbell

Richard Overy

Dan Starer

Kim Turner

Ann Ward

Jane Wood

Al Zuckerman

Ken Follett
16 March 1993